MESSIAH MAN

By

Dr. Russell L. Jaberg

ISBN - 1 - 882270 - 045
Library of Congress Catologing in Publication
93 - 83045

TABLE OF CONTENTS

For my dear Mother — who taught me about prayer and trusting God.

PAWLEY

The signs along Indiana Rte 37 read:

SPEED
LIMIT
45

The unidentifiable rattle in the dash which started when the car reached a speed of sixty miles per hour roused Dan. Without looking at the speedometer, he released the pressure on the accelerator. Instinctively, he looked in the rearview mirror, relaxing when he did not see a flashing blue light. That would have made the day for Bill Connolly! Since the night when Dan and Bill had clashed openly before the City Council, it seemed impossible to get any mention of Trinity Church in Bill's *NEWS-TRIBUNE*, but the Publisher of *PAWLEY NEWS-TRIBUNE* would have quit smoking long enough to write and position on the front page:

REV. DANIEL CLARK
TICKETED
FOR SPEEDING

. . . and to write and hide in an inside page:

REV. DANIEL CLARK
NAMED PASTOR
MESSIAH CHURCH

There was no reason to drive beyond the legal limit. After 88,794 miles, Dan's old Chevy was not straining to release hidden powers. Some weeks previously Mark had been looking out of the back window and saw a cloud of black smoke that had come from

1
Messiah Man

the tailpipe when his father stepped on the accelerator to pass another car. Since then, every ride in the car had called for a repeat performance, only now the smoke was produced following a countdown by Mark. Dan did not think he should shatter the illusion of "jet power" by explaining to an eight-year-old boy the cost of a ring job, or the economics of payments on a new car.

Dan was in no hurry to get back to Pawley, or to go home to face Mary. Again and again, he thought how quickly his world had changed. It was Sunday night – and that was only *last night!* – that Bishop Gossert called to say that he wanted to talk with Dan. Just three weeks ago this Wednesday the Bishop had been in Trinity Church for their annual meeting! At that time he had spoken enthusiastically of the work and program of Trinity Church, and of Dan personally. And after that meeting he had said he wanted to talk with Dan as the chairman of a newly established committee with the purpose of recruiting young people for Church vocations. Dan had assumed that the vocations committee was the purpose of today's appointment.

The Bishop addressed the topic as soon as Dan had seated himself. "Dan, for some weeks I have been consulting with the people of Messiah Church. We had a meeting after the service yesterday and they tell me that they are unanimous in their desire that you be named the Pastor of Messiah Church."

Dan sat in stunned silence as the Bishop continued. "That is why I asked you to come today . . . Messiah Church is asking for you." He leaned forward to place both hands on the top of his desk – palms down, fingers outspread. "I have been party to their considerations and I have concurred in their decision. So . . . we want to name you as my successor to the pastorate of this great Church."

For the moment, Dan could make no response. Apparently, the Bishop did not anticipate any discussion as he proceeded in more formal fashion and tone.

"As you know, you must indicate your willingness to accept this responsibility . . ."

Bishop Gossert's voice raised the question: 'Who would *not* accept the pastorate of Messiah Church?' The Messiah Church was known throughout the denomination as the congregation whose pastors had repeatedly been elevated to the bishopric. In his most ambitious imaginings Dan had never thought of himself as the Pastor of this well-known church.

On the other hand, there was Mary. But after all . . . what woman would not be delighted to have her husband become the Pastor of "The Church of the Bishops."

"Bishop Gossert, there are many other men . . . *capable* men . . ."

"That's right. There *are* other men . . . and g*ood* men, Dan. But Messiah Church is asking for *you*."

A semi roared around Dan only in time for him to meet another semi coming from the other direction. Dan's car was shaken in both passings sufficiently to remind him that he was on a public highway.

Even so, his mind quickly returned to the events of the day thus far. In the discussion with the Bishop and a luncheon meeting with several persons from Messiah Church, Dan now realized that he had agreed to accept the pastorate of Messiah Church. Putting the key in the ignition, Dan was much aware that the next item on his agenda for this fateful day would be for him to tell Mary . . . and Mark and Debbie. As he was driving now, he kept trying to formulate the most acceptable way that he could say that they were moving to Indianapolis. In previous conversations, Mary had acknowledged that they probably would not remain indefinitely in Pawley, *BUT* she said more plainly that she would be glad to continue to live there indefinitely. Certainly, Mary would be pleased at this great new opportunity for Dan in Messiah Church, BUT she frequently remarked that Dan's work was just beginning in Trinity Church. As Dan tried to anticipate the situation he would create, there was no doubt that there would be great distress regardless of what he said, or how he said it. The only reassurance he could manage as he drove was to say to himself: 'Well, a coward has no business going to Messiah Church.'

Amos Clark was comptroller of Redstone Construction Company, the only place he had ever worked. It was always assumed that Dan would study Engineering at the University and then come to Redstone; however, Dan went home for Thanksgiving after the last football game in his Senior year knowing that he must declare himself to his parents. On his first evening home, they were in the living room and his father said, "Al Beiswinger is retiring the end of the year. The President wants to hold that place open for you."

Dan seized the opening. "That is very flattering, Dad, but there is something that I want to say to you and Mother . . . I have come to the conclusion that I want to study to become a Christian minister."

After a reflective hush, his father's words were deliberate: "Dan, your Mother and I want you to do what *you* want to do. And most of all, we want you to do what *God* wants you to do."

A family decision was concluded, but that was not all. There was still Sally, for Dan and Sally had an understanding. At the earliest opportunity Dan and Sally had long but inconclusive talks which produced only a new strangeness. During the Christmas vacation, a note came from Sally.

> *Dear Dan,*
> *I must write what I cannot say. You know that I have cared for you deeply. I do respect your personal decision. I regret that I do not find it within me to share in your commitment.*
> > *Sally*

Back on the campus, Dan spoke to Sally in passing as he did to many others whose names were not known to him. Then too, Dan sensed that some of his long-time companions seemed uneasy in his presence, and his imagination would riot when he thought that they were avoiding him.

Stopping in the Campus Shoppe one day for a cup of coffee, he saw Mary Carter sitting alone in a booth. Dan had known her since second term Freshman days, when he sat next to her in a course on the History of Western Civilization; that was a course in which he needed a "B" to help his grade point average. A first glance at Mary now reminded Dan of what he had often heard about her:

"Mary Carter has the finest wardrobe of any girl on campus."

The place was luncheon-filled. He asked if he might join her and she nodded her assent. Dan sat in the booth across from her.

Mary frowned as the waitress served Dan. "Only coffee for lunch?"

"I'm in a hurry. I have to work on a bibliography at the library, and then I have a two o'clock class . . . American Literature I."

"How do you find the Lit class?"

The coffee was too hot to drink, so Dan unzipped his letterman jacket and leaned back. He tried to cross his legs, but the booth was too small.

"Oh, I guess I just haven't got the hang of it . . . How is that for a choice of words in discussing a literature class? But these fellows who are supposed to be the literati . . . I don't know . . . They seem to have acquired their reputations by using many words when ordinary people would need only a few . . ."

Dan realized that Mary was listening.

"This is the first English course I have taken since Freshman Composition. I had a couple of elective hours this term, and I thought I'd see if 'Brainy' Connors is everything I've heard about him."

Mentioning electives might lead to talk about his decision; Dan thought it might be better to be on his way, but Mary's interest encouraged him to speak further. "You see, I've changed my mind about what I want to do."

Mary nodded. "I won't pretend that I haven't heard talk about you."

Dan laughed. "Some of the stories going around are ridiculous, but I think I must try to do what I believe I *should do*."

Mary's voice was quiet. "God needs men. I think you will be a good minister of Jesus Christ."

The still waters in Mary ran deep, and Dan came to know which way they ran for the only child of Estelle and Blair Carter. People in Rockford had never figured Estelle and Blair for a match because she was twelve years older than he. Mary was born on their first wedding anniversary, and Estelle had a miscarriage fifteen months later. Much wanted, Mary was deeply cherished. The Carter inner family bonds were sustained with a passion such that to know Mary was to know the constancy of her family affection. She still telephoned her parents every Saturday night and wrote frequently. She would tell them in detail about the children, of a new piece of furniture or room arrangement, of new curtains for the kitchen, or what she had taken to a potluck dinner at the church.

To be in Mary's family, as Dan learned when they were married in the summer before his last year in Theological Seminary, was to know all-encompassing care. She made liveable and lovely the succession of rooms and apartments in which they lived during the seminary year, the ten months of an interim pastorate, and Dan's first year in the naval chaplaincy. When Mary learned that she was pregnant, she went back for Mark to be born in Rockford; she returned about two years later so that Debbie, too, was born in Rockford. With Dan's discharge they had come to Pawley, for what Mary called "our first home."

Dan found Mary's family commitment deepened with Mark and Debbie. There was no gush to Mary's love, but Mark and Debbie wanted for nothing which she might provide. There was the time, for example, when public opposition developed to a bond issue to provide funds for new elementary and junior high school buildings in Pawley. Mary was named chairman of the P.T.A. public relations committee. She was a woman with a cause, one that would benefit her children. Her satisfaction was obvious now when they would pass the building and she would point out which was Debbie's First Grade room and Mark's Third Grade room. She was ever occupied: making something for the children, trying a new recipe, washing windows, polishing silver or mirrors, and the like. Her reputation was that no one ever found her when she did not look as though she was ready to go out. Dan was pridefully conscious of a lovely wife, a well-managed home, and children that were almost too good to be real. So . . . as he said to himself . . . what if Mary did not seem as sensitive to his inner thoughts now as she had that day in the Campus Shoppe?

∝   ∝   ∝   ∝

There was a letter ready to be mailed from Pawley:

Monday Morning

Dearest Mother and Daddy,

I have time for only a note. I have just put a load of colored things in the washer.

The children loved the pictures from last summer, but they say they look like babies! I am keeping the prints a little longer as they want to see them again.

Dan is in Indianapolis this morning. He had a ten o'clock appointment with the Bishop, who called last night and asked Dan to come in. It is something about a new committee to recruit young people for church vocations. Dan is preparing to go to a number of High School Career Conferences.

Debbie is very proud to be printing. Mark says that that is not really <u>writing</u>. There is always some point to contend, if only to keep the conversations lively.

It seems so long since you have been here – or since I have been home. We cannot get away until vacation time, so I hope that you (And that's <u>you</u>, Daddy!) will pick up and drive over. The President of the Trustees spoke to me just yesterday, and he said they are going to do over our house. You <u>must</u> come to see our home <u>then</u>. From the way he talked, the workmen and the decorator will be coming the last of this week. He said that they decided they "simply must make this house a livable place."

I must go now. I only wanted to write to tell you that I think of you frequently because

I love you.

Mary

∝ ∝ ∝ ∝

Messiah Church was the largest church of the denomination in the Midwest. Dan, along with everyone else, had speculated on George Gossert's successor. Driving along, he could imagine what other ministers and many laymen would now be saying:

"Did you know that Dan Clark is going to Messiah Church?"

"Dan? He's only been in Pawley for six years."

"Has he served anywhere else?"

"Student pastorate and a year's interim some place."

"Right, and then four years in the Navy chaplaincy."

"Dan Clark to Messiah? I would have figured someone with a bigger name, or older."

"It's true! DanClark *is* going to Messiah . . ."

Dan glanced at the fuel gauge and was relieved that the car needed gasoline. As the wheels passed over a hose stretched across the drive of the filling station, a bell rang inside. A figure shadowed the window by the driver's seat.

"Howdy, Revner Dan."

"Hello, Tom. My car needs gas."

Tom cocked his head to one side. "From the way she sound, she need more than gas." He moved quickly to the front of the car and was fingering for the hood release. Over the sound of the engine, Dan heard: "Shut 'er off, Revner Dan."

In a few minutes the neighborhood heard the request for Dan to start the engine. Tom reached in to open the throttle and then release it; repeating the procedure brought a smile of approval. As Tom was running gas into the tank, Dan got out of the car and walked into the station.

Tom Davis was one of the few black people in Pawley. Dan's 6'2" and 195 pounds were dwarfed by the man now standing beside him as he signed the oil company invoice. For painting, tending any growing thing, waxing floors, fixing almost anything – the favored action was, "Call Tom." However, Tom had come into his own when he began to work at "SMITH'S GULF." He could somehow make new cars live up to advertising copy, and he could keep old cars – like Dan's – running. It was a matter of common knowledge in Pawley that Dan and Tom frequently had long talks. Again and again, Bill Connolly said to his wife, "Belle, how do those two find so much to talk about?"

As Dan picked up his credit card, Tom's eyes were on him.

"Somethin' botherin' you, Revner Dan?"

"Yes, Tom, I have much on my mind today."

"Nothin' but the best, I hope."

"That remains to be seen." Dan tried to quicken his voice. "Maybe we can talk about it sometime."

"You know, Revner Dan, I think about you yest'day. In my church last night, we sing about 'the touch of His hand.' I think when Revner Dan first come to Pawley . . . he say to me, 'Tom, you learn in Flippians: 'I can do all things th'ough Christ who st'engthens me.' And he do, Revner Dan."

Dan thrust out his hand abruptly. Tom rummaged about for a clean cloth, carefully wiped his hands and seized Dan's extended hand in an enveloping grasp.

"It always do me good to talk with you, Revner Dan."

"It was my turn today, Tom."

The garage was at the back of the lot, but Dan stopped in the driveway by the side entrance of the house. As he got out of the car, he saw Mark and Debbie in a group playing two houses away. Dan whistled. Mark started to run, then slowed up to grab his sister's hand and bring her in tow, laughing, to their father. Dan picked up Debbie and hugged her, and then swung Mark around before putting him down. Mark's light brown hair was uncovered with Debbie protesting that he wouldn't wear his cap and Mark saying it was too warm. The greeting with charges and countercharges finished, Dan let them return to their friends. Debbie was on her own as she skipped back to play. Watching Mark's headlong charge, Dan recalled that Mary had written that the obstetrician told her he had never delivered a baby with such broad shoulders. Watching the group for a few moments, Dan thought that one could tell three lots away which children belonged to Mary Clark. Taking off his topcoat, he entered the house. Dan paused in the kitchen and heard movement upstairs so he went to the stairway and called,

"Mary, I'm home. Please come down."

He went into the living room and sat in a straight chair. He had the uneasy feeling that he was trying to imitate his father in a formal family conference, and was doing the whole thing very badly. Mary came to the door, her hands full of children's clothing.

"Please come and sit down, Mary. We must talk."

Mary was not prepared to take time for comittee reports. "I am in the midst of cleaning Debbie's room. I have to go through her things when she is outside or she won't let me throw anything away . . . I must make salad to take tonight. I have to get dressed, and get the children cleaned and dressed. You haven't forgotten that we are going to a cook-out with Shackletons tonight?"

Mary did not come into the living room and now turned to leave to finish her announced program. Dan rose and spoke quickly. "Mary, we are not only going to Shackletons tonight. I have been asked to take Messiah Church. That is the reason the Bishop wanted to see me this morning."

Mary whirled to face Dan. Her voice and facial expression spoke unbelief. "But Dan, it's such a *big* church!" Afraid of the answer, she asked, "What did you say?"

"What could I say? Bishop Gossert and the people from the church were so positive that I said I would accept."

Mary stepped past him and began to circle the room slowly.

"But Dan, it's such a *big* church . . . And it's in the city . . . . and I – we – have never lived in a big city . . . . And you already said that you would accept? Wouldn't they give you some time to think about it . . . . or talk with me about it?"

Dan did not feel like a leader among leaders. "Yes, I said 'Yes.' Quite frankly, it seemed the only answer to make at the time. The more I think about it since, however, the more unsure I become."

Mary blazed as his champion. "You can be a good minister in Messiah Church, or *anywhere*." Just as quickly she lost her zeal. "It is just that . . . But where would we live? . . . And we just got new curtains for all of the bedrooms . . . and the workmen were to come this week to do over *the whole house* for us *here* . . . Where d*o*es the family of a minister live in Indianapolis? Oh dear, where would Mark and Debbie go to school? We have a new school here in Pawley now, and I worked so hard to get it . . . and the children have been so thrilled to be in a *new* school . . ." Her voice trailed off as she continued pacing about the room.

Dan found himself without satisfying answers, and he let himself fall on the sofa in a way which would have made his mother frown. Mary noticed for the first time that she was holding something in her hands, and she dropped Debbie's things into a chair in a disorderly pile. Her hands free, she came to stand in front of Dan to deliver her opinions with emphatic gestures.

"In addition . . . Everything is progressing here as never before in the history of Trinity Church. *You* know it, Dan. *The Bishop* knows it. *Everyone* knows it. *All* of the people are so happy with you here. *Why* should you not have the opportunity to *finish* the work you have begun here in Pawley? Mark and Debbie have so many friends *here*, We have talked and talked about their new school . . . We have enjoyed living here . . . This is *our first real home,* and I have begun to feel that we *have* a home, that we *are* at home, that we *are a home* . . . . . . Just last Friday, I agreed to be Vice President of the P. T. A. next year. And now, we must leave *our home* to go to the *city?*"

Mary gathered up the entire room in a frenzied glance as though to have one last look.

For his own self-persuasion, Dan tried to sound convincing. "I know, and I share all of what you are saying, Mary. But when the Bishop spoke this morning, this seemed a Christian challenge for *me* to take. *And I have said that I would accept.* This seemed to be the Lord's call for me, and I can not turn away from it"

Mary had paused only for breath. "But the school for Debbie and Mark? Did you see it? . . . . Do you know *anything* about it? . . . And *where* would we live? . . . OH, DAN! . . . Are you *sure?* . . . . . Can't you talk again with Bishop Gossert? Can't the Board here at Trinity refuse to release you . . . ?"

If Mary was more disturbed that he had anticipated, Dan found his responses less satisfying than he had hoped.

"Mary, Mary . . . There *must* be excellent schools in the city. Debbie and Mark will make new friends. Messiah Church *must* have an excellent residence for the minister and his family. George Gossert would not live in a hovel. We can, and we shall, drive over to see it . . ." Mary had not stopped walking about the room. "Mary!"

She stopped. "I am committed."

Mary shuddered and then moved quickly to pick up Debbie's things which she had dropped. She straightened up, looked at herself in a mirror, and touched her hair.

"We shall talk more about it later. Now I must put Debbie's room to rights, and fix the salad to take for dinner." As she abandoned the living room, she spoke to the hall: "You'll find two or three telephone calls there on the pad."

Fred Hudson observed that the lawn had been mowed. Bushes and trees were exploding green. He parked under the carriage porch, got out of the car, and made a professional appraisal of his property with the satisfactory feeling of being at home. Fred had been born in the back bedroom on the second floor, and had never lived in any other house. The rustic pool in the back yard with the flagstone paving was his wife's idea; the white iron furniture gave a touch of elegance even if it wasn't for sitting. The garage door was up, and he could see the top was down on Marge's convertible, and he approved from a distance the orderliness he could discern inside the garage, with tools hanging on the walls and lawn equipment aligned along one side. At the door he paused for a second review, but this time his field of vision included the house next door. These new neighbors weren't keeping the place as the Fredericks had done for so many years, or in the living-in-servants manner that Fred had regarded as proper and respectable. He turned to open his own door with a frown.

"Fred . . . I'm in the sunroom."

He walked through the rooms which were formal, polished and expensive-looking. Coming to the brightness of a room whose large panes of glass were a modern touch to an otherwise period dwelling, he kissed his wife lightly. She patted his arm. As he sat down she placed in front of him a glass of iced tea and a plate of wafers. She settled herself in her chair and watched him as he took a sip from the glass, started to place the glass on the coaster and then took another sip.

"Now! Tell me *all* about it. I have been waiting for *hours*. I thought you would call. When you didn't phone, I couldn't stand it any longer and I called your office; they said that you had not come back from lunch."

"Well, the simple word is: Dan is coming . . . About the first of June."

"But I want to know *all* about it. What did *George* say? What did *Dan* say? What did *you* say? Everything!"

Fred ate a cookie slowly, savoring the suspense in his role as news-bearer. "As you know, I made reservations at The Clarendon. We were to meet at Twelve Noon. Al, Ruth, Sam, Fred and myself. George said he would bring Dan over."

"Sam?"

"Sam Stockwell . . . you know, the druggist. I would rather have had someone else but Al thought it would be the politic thing to do. He said that if Dan was coming he would have to meet Sam sooner or later, and he might as well see us for what we are, all of us . . . Anyway, George and Dan came in right on the dot and we all had a good time. (A drink of iced tea was good for his throat and seemed to give him time to organize his story.) I couldn't help looking at George and then at Dan sitting beside him – kind of the old order and the new."

Fred was warming to his narration. He had a groomed audience to which he responded, and his tale gathered liveliness.

"Dan is even *better* than we thought. He's *big*. He's a *leader*. He's *good*. In driving home now I have been able to admit to myself some of the fears I have entertained for Messiah Church because I think we *now* have the *kind* of minister we need to get some real answers to our problems. We talked of many things. It was all so elevated that even Sam began to look and sound promising."

"What did Dan –" she laughed. "I guess I'll have to call him 'Reverend Clark,' at least for a while – anyway, what did Reverend Clark say about coming to Messiah?"

Fred frowned thoughtfully. "To tell you the truth, I don't re-member what he said about accepting this call, in just so many words. I assumed that George and he – I'll never get used to calling George 'Bishop' – I assumed that they had worked it out. Dan spoke with great reserve as though he didn't want to upstage George . . . But Marge, *he's got it*! I have seen enough men in my time to pick the winner out of a crowd, and Dan Clark is a *winner all the way!*"

"Did you talk about his wife and family?"

"I thought that that was your department. I was reasonably sure you would get all of the pertinent information at the earliest opportunity."

She smiled her acceptance of her role. "Now, Fred, that's not nice. You make me sound like a gossip, and I am only genuinely interested . . . Maybe I should telephone Mrs. Clark and give her a woman's word of welcome. By all means she should come and say what she wants done in the house."

Fred put down his glass and rose to his feet. "I'm going to change my clothes. I am certainly relieved to get this matter of a new minister settled. It takes away some of my anxiety about Messiah Church. Maybe now I can get back to the business of selling a little real estate."

YEAR ONE
AT
MESSIAH CHURCH

Messiah Church was an imposing limestone pile fronting on Columbia Avenue, three-fourths of a mile north of the center of the city; its mass and its copper roof expanse were visible landmarks. The church building complex was on the northwest corner of the intersection of Columbia Avenue and Church Street. The lot on the northeast corner had last been occupied by a used car dealer; there was still a platform for mounting an automobile identified by a fading sign as the "Car of the Day." In the center of the otherwise vacant lot was a house trailer of primitive design with "OFFICE" lettered on the side. At the rear of the lot were two cars now depreciated to $00.00. Cater-cornered from the church was a two-story yellow brick building. A sign spread between the first and second floors on both Columbia Avenue and Church Street sides identified the building as the home of "STOCKWELL DRUGS." On the fourth corner was a single-story structure which extended from Columbia along Church Street to an alley. An entrance to this building on Columbia Avenue was lettered as the office of "Gibson & Hill, Realtors." Display windows on either side of the entry contained pictures with prices of houses which Gibson & Hill had listed for sale. There were two shops in the building which fronted on Church Street: one with a barber pole outside and two barber chairs and one barber inside; the other with a sign offering the services of "FRENCH CLEANERS," currently featuring "2 Garments for the Price of 1."

Messiah Church was a Gothic structure of Indiana Limestone. When it was built some fifty years earlier it had created a "Messiah fad" which influenced local church building committees of all denominations. Widening Columbia Avenue for a third traffic lane in each direction had eliminated the parkway. The broad pyramid of steps ascending to two pairs of castle-like doors at the front entrance of the church now rose directly from the sidewalk along Columbia Avenue. The sanctuary extended back along Church Street where there was an entrance to the Church Office and Parish House. North of the sanctuary and in a parallel line, there was a smaller building of similar design and appearance to the sanctuary – The Chapel. These two buildings were connected at the rear by the Parish House – a structure with basement and two stories. The building complex as a whole formed a "U" which enclosed a garth.

Across the alley from the church with the address of "150 Church Street," was the residence for the Minister, built of limestone to match the church building. Dan came early to open the house for the movers; he parked on Church Street by the office entrance. There was no moving van in sight; to walk seemed better to Dan than to stand and wait.

At each corner of the sanctuary on Columbia Avenue, there was a bulletin board which was set with letters large enough to be read from cars moving on Columbia. Dan would have admitted to some indescribable feeling when he saw at the bottom of each bulletin board: "Daniel Witt Clark, Pastor." He walked past the steps leading to the front doors of the sanctuary, and then turned to take the walk leading through the garth to the main entrance of the parish house. The walk went around a planter (untended) in the center of which was a fountain (dry). The entrance to the parish house was locked, so he came back to go up the few steps to the Chapel entrance. The door, with gold leaf lettering "Open for Rest, Meditation and Prayer," was locked. Dan retraced his steps to their home.

Still no van!

Dan entered the door on Church Street marked "Church Office," and went up several steps to the main floor. To the left side was the office area. To the right, a door opened upon a side aisle of the sanctuary. In a recess directly ahead, a smaller door gave access to the chancel; Dan had used it once when he had a part in a district meeting. He would have to become familiar with this particular door, and he opened it now in a conscious effort to feel at home. Although he had been in the sanctuary on a number of occasions, it appeared different today. Stepping up into the pulpit, his sense of responsibility mounted as his gaze swept back over rows and rows of pews, then up to the balcony – seating for twelve hundred, or *more*! Trinity Church in Pawley had a closeness about it. This was much, much different – and much, much *larger* than he had remembered.

Dan walked down to sit in a front pew, where he faced the famous medallion windows high above the chancel; he followed the windows from section to section, beginning at the bottom which depicted the Birth of Jesus, then to the Transfiguration, and upward to the Crucifixion and Resurrection. With the chancel in carved antique oak, the ceiling arches reaching skyward, and windows on both sides rich in color . . . this was indeed a place for worship where he – Dan Clark – was the Minister. He walked the center aisle to the rear of the sanctuary. In the narthex he found some bulletins from the previous Sunday which contained a paragraph about his installation as Pastor. From the narthex he went up into the balcony and tried to picture the sanctuary filled with people worshiping God. Dan found himself impressed by the whole situation. It was rich in imagery, and it was big. It was beautiful, and it was big. It was impressive, and it was big. Dan forgot for the moment a sermon which he had preached very recently. He had used a passage from I Corinthians:

> "Because the foolishness of God is wiser than
> men; and the weakness of God is stronger than
> men . . . But God hath chosen the foolish things of
> the world to confound the wise; and God hath
> chosen the weak things of the world to confound
> the things which are mighty; and base things of
> the world, and things which are despised, hath
> God chosen, yea, and things which are not, to
> bring to nought things that are: That no flesh
> should glory in his presence."

Going down the curving steps to the narthex, Dan was brought out of his reverie by water marks on the walls. As he walked up the center aisle, he noticed that the carpeting was badly worn. Bishop Gossert had said to him, "We spent sixteen happy years at Messiah. You will find it a fine church. There are some few things that need to be done, but the Official Board thought it would be better to wait and have the input of the new Pastor."

Dan remembered the planter, the fountain, the broken walk in the garth. The doors at the office entry needed to be refinished, and the latch did not work properly. He glanced down a corridor . . . but enough of that now. At first opportunity he would walk about and through the building to make up a list of maintenance needs. He looked at his watch. 9:45. He went outside but there was no van in sight. Dan turned to go into the office and call the movers.

The church office had a grill-covered window opening into the corridor. There was no one at the desk behind the window, so Dan tried a door a few steps away to let himself into the office. Here he found a room with a high ceiling, woodwork stained dark, and walls of an indifferent color. The furnishings were "early miscellaneous"; a new typewriter at the desk by the "ticket window" was a bright spot in a room full of clutter.

The telephone rang . . . and rang . . . and rang . . . Dan picked up a phone to say, "Messiah Church." He tried to sound casual.

"This is Frances Horton speaking. I am calling for Bishop Gossert's telephone number."

Her diction was so precise that Dan thought that he must sound carelessly midwestern by comparison. "He can be reached at 952-0832."

"Thank you. And who is this speaking?"

"This is Daniel Clark." Better start using "Daniel" rather than the Pawley "Dan."

There was an awkward silence. "I'm sorry to have bothered you with something so insignificant. I know you must be very busy getting settled and preparing for the big service on Sunday."

As Dan replaced the receiver, he was aware of another person in the room. He turned to see a woman standing as though in obedience to the command: "*Achtung!*" Her appearance was without style. Any guess at her age would need to be give-or-take five years, at least. Dan pictured her working at a high clerk's desk, wearing an eyeshade and black sleeve protectors.

"I am Hazel Croft." She let that announcement sink in. "I am very sorry that you had to answer the telephone." Dan wondered how words could come from lips so tightly pressed together.

"How do you do. I am Daniel Clark. Answering the telephone was nothing, and I could hope that all of my tasks here would be so simple." Dan laughed, but Hazel Croft stood unrelaxed and unsmiling. "We have come to the city only last evening, and I dropped in to call Mary, that is, Mrs. Clark."

Still at *"Achtung!"* "Yes, but Messiah Church does not expect its Minister to answer the telephone."

Hazel Croft was an institution, or on other occasions referred to as "a character." She came with Messiah Church as the Pastor's Secretary. It was customary for a Minister to say publicly that he "did not know how he would get along without Miss Hazel." For his wife's hearing only, he would confess that he would not be unhappy with some other arrangement.

Miss Hazel assumed her accustomed role by taking command. "Mrs. Johnson stepped out for a few minutes; she needed something done to her car. Mr. Frenell has not come in as yet."

Miss Hazel did not miss Dan's eyes turning to a clock on the wall – 10:05. She added quickly, "Mr. Frenell's hours are from 8:30 to 11:00. Some emergency must have arisen this morning."

Dan reached for the telephone. "That's all right, Miss Croft. I had better call Mrs. Clark now . . ."

He was stopped in word and movement by a scowl.

"If you don't mind, sir, I have always been called 'Miss Hazel.' It has been so for all the pastors; I should be unfamiliar with any other form of address, Mr. Clark."

"That will be fine with me, Miss Hazel." He had the feeling that she had some difficulty in saying "Mister" rather than "Doctor."

Turning again to the phone, Dan dialed the hotel. "Hi, Mary . . . I'm at the church . . . No, the movers have not come yet . . . The Coffee Shop? . . . Good! Did they enjoy it? . . . I had a roll and a cup of coffee there on my way out . . . Yes, I'm calling the movers as soon as we hang up . . . That's a good idea. Get them something to remember the day . . . Yes . . . Yes . . . I'll call you at twelve straight up

. . . Then we'll have lunch and go to the zoo . . . Right . . . Bye now."

Miss Hazel had remained where she was, as she was. Looking at her, Dan had a shuddering recollection of big tackles who just would not be moved.

"Pardon me, Mr. Clark. I did not mean to listen, but you will not be in the office this afternoon?"

"No, as soon as I can get the movers underway, we are all going out for a family lark."

Miss Hazel gave him his revised schedule. "Miss Longaker of the JOURNAL called, and I made an appointment with her for 2:00 this afternoon – for a story and pictures."

"I'm sorry that I did not know sooner, but that is impossible."

"I have always made appointments for the pastors, and I assumed that you would want me to do the same for you."

In moments of exasperation, Dan was wont to describe the role of a minister as "trying to keep everybody happy."

"Oh, I do, but today I dare not disappoint my children, Mark and Debbie. We have built up our first day in the city and I know they are counting on it."

Twirling a sharpened pencil. "I suppose I could call Miss Longaker back, but you know how those newspaper people are . . ."

Dan had the impression that she was suggesting that he didn't know – She should try to deal with Bill Conolly! . . . But on with the concessions.

"We have much to do in getting settled, but you work out any other time and place and I'll be there. Today, I must keep faith with Debbie and Mark . . . and Mary."

Miss Hazel spun about and disappeared. Dan shook his head as he left the office to check again on the movers.

The van was in front of the house. Dan unlocked the front door, a side door, and raised the garage door. With notes Mary had given to him, he tried to direct the men to where various pieces were to be placed . . . Just to get things in! . . . Mary would arrange and rearrange everything several times anyway. To make the house seem more alive, Dan picked up a clock, wound it and set it on the mantle; to set the hands he looked at his watch. Already after twelve!

Hurrying back to the church, he barely missed bumping into a woman coming out of the office door. Dan made his apology.

"That's all right. You are Mr. Clark? I wanted to speak with Mr. Frenell, but apparently he is not in today. Would you be so kind as to give him a message for me?"

She removed a piece of paper from her purse on which she scribbled a note and handed it to Dan. He went into the office to telephone the hotel.

"Just a minute, Operator." Mary put the receiver on the bed and walked across the room to close the door to shut out the sound of a running shower. She sat down again on the side of the bed. "That's right, Operator. Rockford . . . Blair Carter in Rockford."

As she waited, she looked over the lights of the city. "Hello. Hello, Daddy . . . I'm calling from the hotel . . . Hello, Mummy . . . Oh, we're all fine, And tired . . . Yes, the church made a reservation for us, and we feel like visiting royalty with a two-bedroom suite . . . I am wearing my new robe – it's brown with a colored collar and belt. And I have new scuffs and a new nightie. The children have new pajamas . . . They're asleep; they almost went to sleep in the tub . . . They were just wonderful in the Coffee Shop this morning. The waitress was so cheery with them, and Mark asked her for some apple butter to put on his toast . . . a very nice lady stopped at our table and spoke to me; she said that they were so well-mannered that she couldn't take her eyes off them. I didn't say that she ought to see them most of the time! . . . We went to Mason's, and each was to make one choice to remember the day. Debbie picked out a pair of white gloves, and Mark got shoulder pads . . . *football* shoulder pads . . . No, we don't want you to send the money for them. The church gave us a purse and we'll include these things as part of our purchase of new clothes for everyone . . . Just a minute . . . Dan, do you want to say 'Hi' to my folks?"

Dan took the receiver. "Hello . . . That's right. Nothing but the best. We can look out over the city, which seems to spread endlessly; it is a lovely view. Yes . . . Yes . . . You are coming on Saturday? . . . Good . . . here's Mary."

"Mercy, I am afraid to think what the bill will be for this call . . . At noon Dan picked us up in front of the hotel. He said that he was proud of us, all in new garb, including a young lady with white gloves. While we were waiting, Mark was identifying the makes of most of the cars going by. I think he was a little ashamed of ours; at least he told Dan that our car didn't look very 'shiny' . . . Oh, yes. They had a wonderful time at the zoo. Three times through the Lion House . . . Then for a special dinner Dan was going to take us to The Steak House; it's famous for its atmosphere. Anyway, as we were driving we came upon a place with a sign in three-colored neon . . . How did you know that, Daddy? . . . Right! *Foot-Long Hot Dogs!* Mark read the sign and that was it! What is a steak if you can have a foot-long hot dog? So that was our dinner. The children loved it, and as Dan said, 'It was cheaper' . . . Mark and Debbie couldn't have been happier and I am glad for that . . . We're looking for you on Saturday . . . No, we won't. You will have to take us as you find us . . . Thank you . . . Bye, bye."

Putting the telephone back on the nightstand, Mary looked over at Dan lying on his back with both hands under his head. "Thank you for insisting that I call. That was good."

Mary went to check on the children.

Breakfast in the Coffee Shop was complete with apple butter, which was provided by Mark's new friend, the waitress. They drove to park on the street in front of their new home.

The residence of the Minister of Messiah Church had a limestone exterior to couple it with the church buildings. There were stone steps leading to a large front porch with a cement floor. From the front door, one entered a vestibule with a second door opening into a central hallway. Immediately to the right was an entrance to a den for the minister. Mark discovered the sliding door and was proud to be asked to push the door back so they could all go in to see the dark oak paneling, recessed bookcases, and a fireplace equipped with a gas log. Debbie climbed into a huge leather chair by the fireplace – she liked the feeling of being able to hide in the chair. Mark was soon spinning around in the high-backed swivel chair at the desk, all the while shouting for his sister to look at him. The sofa had matching leather upholstery. A small bronze plate fastened to the paneling about the fireplace noted that the room had been furnished as a memorial.

Out of the den and across the hallway was the living room with a large window at the front. The fireplace was framed with fruitwood paneling – with the clock sounding busy on the mantel. The appearance of their furniture in the room caused Mary and Dan to look quizzically at one another. Double french doors opened into the dining room where a small bronze plate indicated that the furniture in that room was a memorial. Debbie and Mark were finding the disarray, with assorted cartons and barrels, to possess great possibilities for running, hiding and shouting. Mary looked approvingly at the newly painted walls, the clean windows and the drapes which she had selected.

"Dan, come and see how well this paper has worked out in the breakfast nook."

Looking out on the back yard, Mark said, "It's not as big as ours."

They all peered through the door leading to the garage and the assorted clutter which filled it. Through a small door they were out of the kitchen and back into the center hallway where everyone inspected the powder room. An open stairway mounted easily to a landing and then turned to reach the second floor. Mark and Debbie were in and out of one room after another.

"Look at all of these bedrooms!" Mary stopped them in the pellmell rush down the hall. "We want each of you to pick the room you would like for your own . . ." Happily neither chose the same room nor the master bedroom, and Dan carried some boxes of their things into each of the rooms they had selected.

The doorbell rang. Dan answered it to find two women and one man standing at the door.

"We've come to help you get settled."

"Thank you, but we did not . . ."

"But we want to . . . we need to . . . we've already been paid by Mrs. Hudson to come and help you set your house to rights."

"Very well, come on in. This is a job that needs many hands."

One more night at the hotel. One more breakfast in the Coffee Shop with the nice waitress and apple butter. By Thursday afternoon, linens and clothes were in chests and closets. Dishes, glassware, kitchen utensils were washed and in cupboards with new shelf paper that Mary had brought from Pawley. The dining room had been re-arranged to give it what Dan called, "the Mary look." Boxes and barrels were gone. A dinner celebration was in order, which brought chorused demands for foot-long hot dogs. They slept in their own beds in their new home.

Saturday morning Mary's parents arrived. Mark and Debbie tried to outdo one another in showing their grandparents through the house, especially their own rooms . . . and the guest room, furnished with an antique chest and twin spool beds. For the first time since their marriage, Mary could have her parents stay overnight without sleeping plans that included the sofa in the living room, plus an involved bathroom schedule. The children saved the best for the last: the Saturday paper with a story by Miss Longaker, featuring pictures of them with their mother, and pictures of their father – one of which included Miss Hazel. Grandfather Carter took them out immediately to buy more copies of Saturday's *JOURNAL*.

Then, finally, it was *the* Sunday morning.

There was breakfast for those who wanted it. After getting the children on their way to Sunday School with Grandfather Carter, Mary and her mother were upstairs dressing. Dan went to the study, threw his coat on the desk and sat down with the copy of his sermon, which by now, as he told Mary, had 'all the tang of warmed-over meatloaf.' He would write between lines furiously, only to erase even more vigorously.

Dan answered the doorbell to open the door to his father and mother, who acted as though they were seeing him for a first, or more likely a last, time. They were already so moved that Dan wondered how they – and everyone else – would make it through the morning. Eventually, Dan and Mary gathered with their parents in the living room, everyone encouraging everyone else. They stood in a circle holding hands for a word of prayer, and Dan was on his way.

The Bishop was already very much there in the narthex at the center of a homecoming celebration, speaking with half a dozen persons at once. As Dan approached, the Bishop turned to him. "Be with you in a minute, Dan."

From somewhere the Bishop had a baby in his arms. "Lucy, this is *your* baby?"

In one motion the baby was returned and he had his arm about the shoulder of a young man. "Hello, Art, How is your mother? Be sure to give her our love . . ."

And a couple, the man taking one of the Bishop's hands and the woman seizing the other: "Fern! Charles! Did you get the tickets for the symphony? Ada asked me just yesterday about them."

The Bishop and Dan excused themselves to go to the Pastor's Study and don their robes for the service. When they returned to the narthex the organ prelude had begun and the choir was assembling. Dan thought that there were surely as many of these robed people as there were in the congregations at Pawley on Sunday mornings. To "Coronation," the choir started up the center aisle, four abreast in triumphal procession. The Bishop and Dan and Philip Frenell followed, walking in easy cadence.

Taking his place in the chancel, Dan looked over the large con-gregation which would be his responsibility to serve; in spite of the number present, Dan found himself surprised at the number of unoccupied pews in the sanctuary. He looked for Mary and found her near the front, wearing a hat purchased for the occasion, and with Mark and Debbie on either side of her. Directly behind Mary were her parents and Dan's parents. To Dan they all seemed glad to be there and full of anticipation. All of the problems of recent weeks appeared to have been resolved. Dan said, "It's all right, Lord. I am so thankful."

Mr. Frenell led in the worship service. The Bishop conducted the formal service of installation, and now Dan mounted the steps to the pulpit.

"In the Name of the Father, and of the Son, and of the Holy Spirit. Amen.

". . . The Church of Christ is given unusual opportunity in the contemporary American city. Change is an integral part of the life of man and certainly of our culture; nowhere is this more evident than in the city. A charge is placed upon the Christian Church to lay hold upon this state of flux and to make and mold it into a life and a community which acknowledge and exem-plify the Kingdom of our Lord and Saviour Jesus Christ. An open door of opportunity and responsibility devolves upon Messiah Church. No one might know what the challenges will be, or how or when they will come. For now, we can only dedicate ourselves to the end that we will together by God's grace, seize the day and wrest from it a victory to His glory. Amen."

The organ introduced the melody, and the choir raised the song as they went back down the aisle.

"Lead on, O King Eternal, The day of march has come;
Henceforth in fields of conquest Thy tents shall be our home;
Thro' days of preparation Thy grace has made us strong,
And now, O King Eternal, We lift our Battle song.

Lead on O King Eternal: We follow, not with fears,
For gladness breaks like morning wher'er Thy face appears;
Thy cross is lifted o'er us; We journey in its light:
The crown awaits the conquest: Lead on, O God of might."

Dan stood in the narthex with Bishop Gossert greeting the members of *his* parish as they went out. Seemingly all were gone when an elderly woman came from the sanctuary. She walked carefully, shadowed by a companion.

The Bishop exclaimed, "Cora! Cora Schuster!"

From the unsteady and frail appearing frame came a deep-toned and strong voice. "George, this is a good man and I want to meet him."

The Bishop put his hand on Dan's shoulder. "Dan, here is one of the finest people you will ever meet anywhere – Mrs. Cora Schuster."

Dan bent over to offer his hand to the stooped figure, more to catch her if she collapsed than to shake her hand.

"How do you do, Mrs. Schuster."

"Dan, I don't do so well anymore. But I am glad that I was able to be here this morning to learn for myself that *you do* exceedingly well. Come and see me."

Before Dan could reply she was on her way. As she went out of the door and down the steps, her companion was holding her firmly.

The Bishop spoke for Dan's hearing. "She has more money than any member of the church. You won't have any trouble finding her home – the property occupies an entire city block."

The discussion was ended by the arrival of Dan's family. Dan's mother kissed him, her eyes glistening. Mary's mother kissed him on the other cheek. Mary was standing by with one arm about Mark and the other about Debbie, so all three of them were kissed, too.

The Bishop protested that he was being overlooked. Dan presented each of them to the Bishop, who confided to Dan's parents and the Carters, "Everyone is expecting *great* things to happen in Messiah Church with Dan as the Pastor."

Dan suggested that they all keep their dinner engagement with the Hudsons.

Mark and Debbie had gone back into the sanctuary. As they returned, Mark was saying, *"Boy!* It sure is a *big* church!"

Dan's parents left following the dinner on Sunday. Monday morning found Mark and Debbie wanting to take Grandfather Carter to the Zoo, and especially to the Lion House; the whole idea acquired a "let's-get-going zest" when he suggested that the three of them "might look for a place to have lunch." Mary and her mother were going to check over the cupboards and closets and then go shopping. As for Dan, to be Pastor of Messiah Church was to have a big job in a big church in a big city, and he would have to start some time. And that time had arrived.

Dan walked to the church and into the Pastor's Study, where he stood in the middle of the room and looked about. The top of the large desk was clear, There was a badly worn oriental rug on the floor. The other furniture looked expensive and uncomfortable. There were two oil paintings in ornate frames; the brightest spot on each of them was a small brass donor plate. Although logs were in the fireplace basket, the firebrick was uncharred. Stained-glass windows made for a subdued atmosphere.

Dan thought to do something to make the Study belong to him. With the help of Bill Kuist, the Caretaker, they moved the furniture about and rolled up the oriental rug. They had paused to get their breath when there was a knock on the door which led from Miss Hazel's office into the Study. Bill Kuist smiled and closed one eye knowingly as he looked at Dan. The door opened to Miss Hazel who just stood in the doorway – looking.

"How do you like it?" Dan and Bill chorused the question.

"It's different."

Miss Hazel turned and closed the door. Bill was smiling as he left to get a vacuum cleaner.

Dan sat at the desk and looked around the room. The walls needed paint, and the floor covering was shabby; he had noticed that the office area needed attention. One of the elders had told Dan that the church had been setting money aside in a renovation fund. Dan thought that this was as good a time as any to familiarize himself with the physical plant of Messiah Church. He put some paper in a clipboard and started on his inspection tour. He had filled several sheets with notes when he returned to the entrance to Miss Hazel's office. The room was not large, and – as Dan told Mary later – it could belong to no one but Miss Hazel. Several bulging filing cabinets made the space even smaller.

"What is in these, Miss Hazel?"

She moved quickly to stand in front of them before speaking. "These are Dr. – I mean, Bishop – Gossert's personal files, covering the years he was Pastor of Messiah Church. Since he did not know if there would be room in his office downtown, he confided in me that he hoped there would be no objection to keeping these files here at Messiah. I told him I was certain that no one would object."

Dan went back to his desk and began to organize his notes and ideas.

Dan was at the church early on Tuesday to prepare for a staff meeting; he went to the chapel to pray about the meeting and those working with him. The bulletin from the Sunday service had listed the names of the Staff.

Rev. Daniel Witt Clark   Pastor
Rev. Philip Frenell   Assistant Pastor

Gerhard Hoffmeyer	Director of Music
	Director of Education
Miss Hazel Croft	Pastor's Secretary
Mrs. Charles Johnson	Church Secretary
Walter Bowman	Business Manager
William Kuist	Caretaker

Dan opened the staff meeting with prayer. He looked about the room. "This meeting is a beginning for us. We shall come to know one another much better in the days ahead as we work together."

He paused to check his notes. Mr. Frenell entered and slipped into a vacant chair.

"Can we settle on a time that would be most convenient for everyone for a weekly staff meeting?"

There was a pause, and Mr. Hoffmeyer spoke up: "This time for me would be good. Tuesday at the Conservatory is fairly free."

Dan waited. "Very well. Let's try this hour, for the present anyway . . . Now let me say that I want each of us to feel free to speak his or her mind on any subject."

They worked through Dan's agenda in good order. At the conclusion of the meeting, Bill Kuist expressed his appreciation on being included.

"Most people never ask a caretaker for his opinion. They only speak to him when they want extra work done, or when they want to complain about something."

"Well, Bill, we want you here with us every Tuesday. Mr. Hoffmeyer, may I see you for a few minutes?"

Dan watched the tall, disciplined figure walk into the Study, his height accentuated by a shock of white, white hair. There was a vigor about him which suggested mountain climbing or wood chopping. He was all robustness except for his hands, which had the look of delicate instruments.

"The music in the service on Sunday was a wonderful contribution to the worship." Mr. Hoffmeyer smiled in acknowledgment. "Please tell me about yourself. My parents asked so many questions which I promised to answer after I had a chance to talk with you."

"I am born in the old country. I always remember the organ in our parish church. Herr Kleinhanz was a master. My parents come to America when I am nine years old. It was fulfillment of my boyhood dream to go to Heidelberg where Herr Kleinhanz had studied. I am at the Conservatory for nearly twenty years now, and at Messiah Church I commenced about the same time."

"We certainly . . ."

"If I may say one thing more, please. You are the Pastor. If you should want to make other arrangements for the music, please feel free to speak to me frankly."

Dan almost rose to his feet. "No . . . No . . . No."

"But I insist, sir. I am chosen by another Pastor for this position. I have been a long time here. One can become uncreative. New leadership can give new direction."

Dan looked at Mr. Hoffmeyer, liking what he saw. "I remember your recital at the University when I was an undergraduate." (Mr. Hoffmeyer nodded.) "And too, one time I attended an interseminary conference here in the city. One evening a group of us came to Messiah Church for 'The St. Matthew Passion.' (Mr. Hoffmeyer nodded vigorously in recollection.) . . . Mr. Hoffmeyer, *I want you.*"

"Thank you, Pastor Clark." He rose to leave, but he was stopped by Dan's request that he prepare his recommendations for work on the organ.

Bishop Gossert had spoken highly of Philip, but as Dan walked into the restaurant to have lunch with Philip he was conscious of how little he knew of his Associate. When they had given their orders, Dan opened the conversation: "Tell me about yourself, Philip."

"There isn't much, really. Kansas State and United Seminary. Nancy and I have three children." He stopped.

"How long have you been now in Messiah Church?"

"Five years."

Have you enjoyed your work in Messiah?"

Without looking at Dan, animation entered his voice. "There's only one Dr. Gossert!"

"Agreed. What were your parish responsibilities with Dr. Gossert?"

"I was his assistant. I tried to help when and where I was asked."

Dan was grateful for the interruption by the waitress in bringing their orders. They ate quietly for a few minutes.

"Tell me, Philip. Is there some area of parish life in which you wish to concentrate your efforts?"

"You are the pastor, Mr. Clark."

Dan placed his fork on the plate and wiped his fingers on his napkin. "Yes, Philip, and I think we should make some division of the work load."

Dan waited, but Philip continued to eat without looking up.

"What has been your preaching schedule?"

"I have taken a service only as Dr. Gossert requested."

"I plan to be away at the end of the summer. Let us plan for you to take the last two Sundays of August and the first Sunday of September."

Philip *could* be definite. "I'd rather not. I don't know that I could prepare three sermons in as many weeks."

"Very well. But as to our organization, let us say that you will be responsible for the education program of Messiah Church."

There was no acceptance in Philip's reply. "That is a big order."

"Yes, it is. Assuming the concurrence of the Official Board, let us agree that as of now this is your area in the total program of Messiah Church."

Philip stirred. "Before this is presented to the Official Board, I should like to think about it."

"All right . . . You have been at Messiah Church for a time. Tell me how you see the church and what you think is needed in its life and program."

"I have no special suggestions. I was satisfied that Dr. Gossert offered a distinctive ministry to the city."

Dan felt that the conversation had never been in hand – maybe another day. "Let's get together again soon, Philip."

Philip pushed back his chair.

Dan did not move. Before he had time to choose his words, he said, "Philip . . . Do you *resent* me being the pastor of Messiah Church?"

Philip *could* speak. Philip *could* look at Dan.

"I was very happy to be associated with Dr. Gossert for five years. After his election as bishop, I spoke with the committee of Messiah — *at their request*. I told them that I thought Dr. Richard Cogswell could best continue the kind of city leadership that everyone expects at Messiah Church. I called Dr. Cogswell and had his permission to submit his name in making my recommendation. I was not aware that you were being considered; the decision of the committee came as a complete surprise to me. From what I have been able to learn, the committee did *not* take my word seriously. To answer your question, I am *still* of the opinion that Dr. Cogswell would have been the proper man for Messiah Church."

Philip now leaned back and waited for Dan's response, which came with deliberateness.

"Thank you for being frank with me. I do not know what were the determining factors in my being chosen to serve Messiah Church. Two things I do know: One, *I am here*; Two, *you are here*. Whether we would choose one another is beside the point. But you and I *must* work together for the good of Messiah Church . . . If we can't, then one, or both, of us will have to leave. Let us have no personal problem which would interfere with our best efforts as good soldiers of Jesus Christ."

Both men were anxious to conclude the discussion. At the door, each went his own way.

Memorial Hospital was on Dan's way back to the church. Miss Hazel had typed on a card the names of parishoners who were patients at Memorial, so Dan stopped to make a call on each of them.

Dan returned to the church and had barely seated himself at his desk when Miss Hazel tapped on the door, stepped into the room and waited.

"Come on in, Miss Hazel."

Miss Hazel took two steps forward and waited as Dan closed a drawer in the desk. "I have several items for you. One, Fred Hudson phoned and asked that you return his call. Two, the Council of Churches is asking you to preach for the union service in Wentworth Park on the first Sunday of August. I said you would let them know. Three, the Y. M. C. A. asked you to give the invocation a week from today at a luncheon meeting of the membership drive committee. I accepted that for you and put it in your book."

She handed Dan a piece of paper with notes and numbers, and stepped back to her place Dan thought he would look for an "X" on the floor where she was standing. Miss Hazel spoke faintly, "Is there anything else?"

"Not now, thank you . . . unless, of course you have something more."

"I thought you might want . . . You see. I realize you have been talking with some of the staff . . ." She tried but could not continue speaking. Her lips were quivering, and each of her shaking hands tried to hold the other. Tears filled her eyes. Dan went to her and led her to a chair.

"Miss Hazel . . . Are you ill?"

She took a handkerchief from her pocket and wiped the palm of each hand. "Well, Mr. Clark . . . naturally, with a new pastor . . . people have been saying there would be changes . . . . I just didn't know what . . . You talked with Mr. Hoffmeyer . . . . today . . . . and with Mr. Frenell . . . . you have not spoken with *me* . . . about my working . . . Mr. Clark, *do you want me to stay?*"

She was not an office autocrat. Dan saw a woman not young, not certain of herself . . . a woman afraid. Thinking about it later, he scolded himself: 'Why did I not take her into my confidence at once?'

"Miss Hazel. Please . . . Just sit back in that chair and talk with me now . . . So that we may understand one another, *I want you to continue.* I know how former pastors of Messiah Church have relied on you. I need all of the help they received, plus a lot more." Dan was surprised at his own sincerity.

Miss Hazel bowed her head and pressed her lips as she sought to take command of herself. She removed her glasses to wipe them; replacing them, she rose abruptly to stand stiffly on the spot where Dan thought to look for an "X". She was again the "Miss Hazel" that everyone thought he knew. Dan promised to talk further with her first thing in the morning; whereupon she did an "About Face!" and marched out, apparently as formidable as always.

From the slip of paper Miss Hazel had given to him, Dan dialed a number on the telephone.

"Fred? Dan Clark."

"Yes, Dan. I'm trying to put together a church foursome for

Thursday morning. I thought we all might talk over a few things while you try out our course."

Dan accepted the outdoor preaching engagement. He sat back thinking about his day. Then he leaned forward to look at his calendar for the next two weeks. It was only his first week at Messiah, and Trinity Church in Pawley had never looked so good!

∝　　∝　　∝　　∝

Friday

Dear Mummy and Daddy,

It hardly seems possible that a month has passed since you were here.

I finished the curtains for the master bedroom on Wednesday. I am glad we decided to make this change. But then the furniture needed to be rearranged. Dan was going to help but he was called out – two members of the church passed away. But Mr. Kuist – the caretaker – came over to help me. The room has a whole new look. Then Dan came in late. Not knowing I had changed things about, he knocked over a chair before I could get a light turned on.

Thank you again for the play equipment for the back yard. It is a big help since Mark and Debbie have not found any other children with whom to play. Somehow everything seems to be going over the fence.

The people in the church are so enthusiastic about Dan. I am so thankful. He hardly seems to be the same person. I always thought he was a good preacher, but in these few Sundays I can hardly believe I'm seeing and hearing the same "Dan." If you think this is a biased opinion, I can only say that everyone else is even more complimentary. No one can believe that the congregations could be so large – and growing – in June.

Dan is very busy. He wants every thing done at once. The officers tell him to take it a little slower, but he wants a major renovation job in the church to be done as quickly as possible. I never knew there could be so many people in hospitals, and Dan thinks that he must call on all of them. Then, too, there is something about Mr. Frenell; I don't know what it is and Dan is not talking.

To help pass the time, we have a reading period every morning. First I read. Then Mark reads. Debbie feels that she should read as well. Best of all, Mark tries to be the big brother helper.

Daddy, I am glad that the Osteopath is helping your shoulder. As much as you drive the car, you had to get some relief. I hope that the pain will soon be gone entirely.

I'll call tomorrow night. I have the children resting for a while now, and this was a good time to write.

With my love,
Mary

∝   ∝   ∝   ∝

Dan walked past the iron gates which closed the drive and turned through an opening in the stone wall. At this entrance there was a shining brass plate with a button beneath the engraved word: "RING." Dan pressed the button. To have turned away from the traffic of Columbia Avenue into grounds of summer color and odor was to enter another world with a single step. Approaching the castle-like house, Dan would not have been surprised to find it surrounded by a moat with access only across a drawbridge. The front door opened as Dan came to it, and Dan was ushered directly into the library. The voice of Cora Schuster came with throaty forthrightness out of the recesses of a barrel-back chair.

"Come in and sit down across from me, young man."

Dan sat in an arm chair. "It is good to see you again." He gathered the room up in a quick sweeping glance. "This house! Forgive me, but I have never seen anything like it."

"Pretty big for just one old lady . . . But I have several things to discuss with you. First of all, Dan, don't let any of the talk about me and the money I am supposed to have bother you. I hope you never cheapen the Gospel by adapting it to money – mine or anyone else's. My father was a section hand on the railroad. He had seven of us children to feed. Keeping alive seemed to take all of our effort; yet we had a wonderful life. No money, but an abundance of love, family loyalty and trust in Almighty God."

She seemed to have used up her strength in talking. Dan rose as if to help in some way, but she held up her hand. After a time she continued as vigorously as before.

"Kurt – Mr. Schuster – was a farm boy. He had to quit school when he was big enough to handle a team and a plow. He was working as a blacksmith when we were married. Kurt was smart. He went from the shop to the Iron Works and into the steel company as though he was born to it all. *You* would have liked him! He was a sorghum molasses farm boy who always wanted his white shirts boiled. But, Dan – you won't mind if I call you 'Dan'? – there was never anything in his company, or in the mayor's office, which gave him the personal satisfaction which he received from serving his Lord and the Church. When some loose talkers accused him of trying to run Messiah Church with his checkbook, he resigned as an officer. It nearly broke his heart – and mine, too! That was one of the few occasions when I ever saw tears in my Kurt's eyes."

They waited in a hushed room. No sound from the street could be heard. Cora Schuster continued. "I don't know how I got into family history. Some of us think, I suppose, that the only important events are in the past . . . Oh, yes! I said I hope you won't be persuaded by money . . . I don't want to turn your first call into some kind of confession, but you know that Kurt and I have had a great disappointment in David."

"David?"

Cora Schuster leaned forward as though to assess the honesty of Dan's one-word question. Apparently satisfied, she settled back into the recesses of her chair.

"If you haven't heard about David already, maybe people have finally quit talking . . . David is our son . . . Kurt and I always said that we wanted to spare David some of the hard things that had come to us as children. He was our only child, and there is no disputing that we tragically failed him. He is a superbly educated and most charming alcoholic. Kurt tried to use him in the business, but being the son of the President was not enough to hold his job for him."

This subject seemed to be more exhausting. Dan was apprehensive that she might have lapsed into unconsciousness. Abruptly she continued. "I understand that you have played golf with some men of the church. You would not have encountered David on the course, for he never gets much beyond the bar. David and his wife are not divorced, but they have not lived together for years. Nan left to take the children to a private school in New England. I don't blame Nan at all. I love her as my own daughter. David has been a heartache to all of us. Kurt used to say: 'What's success when your son is a fool?'"

"Is there something for me to do?"

"I am only telling you about David; I am not asking you to do anything. I spoke to George many times, but he was always so very busy in church matters . . . . Forgive an old lady, but I went to your installation for selfish reasons. I came away with a prayerful hope that you might be the one who would at least try to bring our David to Jesus Christ . . . Messiah is a big church, and I know that you will be very busy. I don't know how many more there are who are like my David, who need someone to help them find the Way, but there must be many. Please, Dan, don't become so occupied that you have no time for the Davids . . . . . . I don't want to put you in a difficult position by what I am going to say, but I am afraid that that is just what I shall do . . . Even so, I must say it . . . . I feel somehow that you – *you, Dan* – are my *last human hope* for David's restoration."

Dan felt himself moved. "Mrs. Schuster, I will do everything I can, with God's help."

"Now then, Dan. If there is ever some need for which there is not money available, please come and see me. I do not want any good work for Christ in Messiah Church to be left undone because there is no money. That is how Kurt would have it."

Dan had never experienced such an offer, and he did not know what kind of reply to make. "I am most appreciative of your willingness to help." (Mark would have done better than that ! ! !) "I'll not come unless there is genuine need."

"Now I am going to take an old lady's prerogative. I daresay you haven't made much money, and I don't know what salary you receive at Messiah. As I said, I know what it means to be without money . . . If you ever have need for yourself or your family . . . if there are bills for which you simply don't have the money . . . you are to come to me. I want you to keep working at your job without financial harrassment."

"What can I say but . . . 'Thank you'."

"Don't say anything except what you want in your tea. Come, Mildred, bring in the tea." The maid appeared immediately with a tray in her hands. "You may want one of those fluffy, sweet things. I get more plain as I become older; I take bread and butter."

Fred Hudson parked his car, glad to have found a place where it would be in the shade. He stepped away from the car to enjoy the green expanse of the country club; he frequently told Marge that he wanted to move his office next to the Pro Shop. Traffic had been lighter, and he was early for the meeting of the real estate board, of which he was the president. His moving vision caught sight of a familiar figure in a chair by the pool, and he went to him. The greetings were warm.

"Dave! How are you?"

"Hello, Fred. What are you doing here at this hour? And how is Marge?"

"Real estate board meeting, and she is fine. I'm early for a change . . . . Gosh, it's been a long time since I've seen you."

Dave had risen and they walked down a path toward a bench under a tree facing the practice green; the asphalt under their feet was spike-pitted.

Fred continued as they seated themselves. "I hear you have

moved."

"For some reason, not known to me, I stayed on in the house. Now the place needs a complete renovation, and I'm not interested in that project. I felt that the house was communicating a dirty dreariness to me; so I locked it up and moved to City Manor . . . Do you have a buyer for a good house that needs a lot of work?"

"Finding buyers is my business. City Manor? . . . Marge claims she would like to live there."

"It's a bed and shelter."

"When I tell Marge that you are living in City Manor, she'll ask a . . . Dave, why don't you come and have dinner with us and tell her yourself?"

Dave's reply was open and easy. "Now, Fred, you know I'd love to come. We've been friends since Fifth Grade. But if this is to be a let-Dave-have-a-home-cooked-meal evening, let's not bother Marge."

Fred's voice was pleading. "No, Dave. No strings. No pitch. Just come, and bring a brochure that shows floor plans of different apartments."

"I'm sorry. I don't mean to be unappreciative. If somebody isn't trying to pity me, then Mother is enlisting some unsuspecting spirit to be my Good Samaritan . . . I am waiting for her to set the new Messiah preacher on my trail."

Fred laughed in the freedom of an old friendship. "She . . . and you . . . could do worse. He's been in our foursome a couple of times."

"I saw a young fellow with you once and I wondered if he was the new minister . . ."

"Young , and *good*! He said he was only having beginner's luck."

They acknowledged greetings from new arrivals at the practice green.

"He swings as though he knows what the clubs are for."

"Yes, he means business – on the course and in the church."

"I wouldn't know about that. The church and I are not very close."

In silence they followed rolling balls on the green.

"Dave, you really ought to come to a service of Dan's at least once . . . Say, I'd better get in for my meeting. By the way, what do you hear from Nan?"

"Not much. Kurt will be a senior this fall, and Peggy will be a sophomore."

"Hardly seems possible . . . ."

"It's a coincidence that you should ask. Today is Nan's birthday."

"I'm sorry that I'm committed this noon. But you come for dinner. Marge will be calling you."

They rose from the bench.

"And Dave, I do wish you would come and hear our new minister. It wouldn't do you any harm."

"Nothing much can do me any harm."

Fred turned at the door of the clubhouse and saw the figure of his friend sitting on the bench – alone now. Fred shook his head in regretful agreement with Dave's self-evaluation.

Sitting at her desk, Nan's thoughts raced: 'This is only my first week. I didn't realize there are so many hours in a day and so many days in a week . . .

'It was difficult at first at the School of Commerce. Goodness! All the students there seemed as young as Peggy and Kurt . . . (The girl who just brought this correspondence . . . I'm old enough to be her mother.) . . . But the two trial courses were not formidable, so maybe my job will become easier . . .

'Of course, it would be my luck to get a typewriter with proportional spacing. Now, now, take it easy! No mistakes! . . .

'I really should like to quit now, if I could do so decently. But Peggy and Kurt were so proud of me when I got this job and I dare not let them down . . .

'The Office Manager said he anticipated that it would require a bit of time for me to feel confident with all of the details of this position. (The phone. It's ringing!) . . .

'It isn't as though we need the money. There . . . That letter is done and it looks professional with the "n's" there at the bottom . . . Coffee break? . . .'

Nan sat in the employees' lounge and toyed with a cup of coffee.

'I wonder if I shall ever develop self-confidence. The summer I had the job in the pattern shop, and Dave came into the office . . . I was more scared than anything when he asked me for a date. Mercy! He had everything – clothes, education, money, personality. I was positive that he was ashamed to be seen with such a bump-kin. (I'm glad I took Peggy's suggestion to have my hair done differently, and Peggy will be thrilled to go shopping with me on Saturday for some new clothes – if I am not fired by Friday!) . . .

'How well do I remember when Dave took me to meet his par-ents. Sunday afternoon in the parlor, it was. But the contrast! Dave and his clothes on one side of the room, and the plain garb of his parents on the other . . . but they were such wonderful people! . . .

'I tried to be so very proper. Maybe if I had been a little less in love I'd have seen more clearly . . .

"Poor Dave! He couldn't succeed or fail on his own. If he did well, it was only what one would expect of Kurt Schuster's boy. If he was found wanting, he would be reminded that something better was expected from Kurt Schuster's son . . .

'Maybe if I had tried harder, but I insisted that he see somebody or anybody. He refused. Perhaps we should have moved away . . .

'I couldn't help him, hold him or steady him. Then the de-pression, and then the drinking. I had to leave for the childrens' sake . . .

'What must Dave be like now? . . .

'Grandmother Schuster can be proud of Kurt, a mature camp counselor. She will love Peggy. Grandmother seems to have lived in a man's world, and she will have a special delight in Peggy as a young lady . . . (Ugh! this coffee is cold.) . . .

'Five minutes more and back on the job. Maybe people have been so helpful because they feel sorry for a person of my age . . .

'I didn't know I could get so tired, but it is good to have a schedule, a place to be on time, a reason to get tired . . . But right now . . .

'I know people are wondering about me – "Mrs. Schuster" but no wedding ring. Now I can't remember when or why I took it off and left it off . . .

'Dear Peggy! In our last woman-to-woman she suggested that I might be too old to remember when I did have feelings. (Ooh, look at the smooth skin and willowy figure of that girl who is in the secretarial pool.) How could I tell Peggy of my own surprise at the stirrings within me? She thinks she shocks me! Maybe I should tell her. Mercy, No! *She* would be shocked beyond recovery if I told her of waking at night wanting to be touched, longing to hold and be held, aching to possess and be possessed. At least this job is making me so tired that the nights are for sleeping . . .

'It would really shake Peggy if I told her that the personnel interviewer approved of me . . . as a *woman*. They never considered anyone else for receptionist, who is supposed to exude the prestige of the company . . .

'Well, one more sip and it's back to work . . . I really ought to make a decision about my marriage. If I am to do a good job here, I need some greater peace of mind . . . I will see a lawyer . . . And I will talk it out with a minister . . .'

Dan put the car in the garage and let himself into the kitchen. He went to the refrigerator to pour a glass of orange juice which he took with him to the den. He managed to get the light turned on with the glass in one hand and a sheaf of papers in the other. He sank into the desk chair to sip the orange juice from time to time as he thought about the events of the day, and especially the issues of the long committee meeting from which he had just come. He suddenly realized he was still holding the papers, and placed them on the desk. With a spurt of energy he finished the juice and arose to turn out the light, leaving the glass on the desk.

Dan made his way up the stairs quietly and was surprised to find Mary sitting in bed, reading by the light of a lamp on the bedside table. He kissed her lightly and went off to the dressing area to remove his clothes. Mary put down her book and listened to the sound of the shower.

"I've been waiting for you, my dear."

"I'm sorry to be so late, but the meeting ran out longer than any of us expected. Even so, we managed to conclude the whole business."

"I've been waiting to hear you tell me that you still love me."

"Of course I love you. What would I do and be without you?"

"I need to hear you say it, and to hold me and show me that you love me. Today, I have not seen you since breakfast. When the children seemed to tire of playing in the back, we went to a mall and walked about for a while. Then we went to a movie that has been highly recommended for children. Mark and Debbie loved it and wanted to stay through a second showing. We had dinner and came home. We had our reading time and watched a program on television. Then it was time for prayers and bed . . ."

Mary stopped to look at Dan, only to find him asleep. With a deep sigh, she arranged the pillows and turned off the light.

In the morning Dan was making his apologies, after Mark and Debbie left the breakfast table. Mary interrupted: "Dan, would you have any objection if I took the children to Rockford, for a visit with Mother and Daddy?"

"I have no objection, but I certainly would miss you."

"You are so very busy all the time, and I am at the end of my string with the children in a new home, with no playmates of their own ages, and all that. I need a break in my child care routine."

"I am sorry that I have not been of more help. If a visit in Rockford would help you right now, then call your parents and set it up . . . But know that I shall miss you."

Dan left for an appointment with Miss Hazel. He had asked her to prepare a summary of the statistics of Messiah Church for recent years. He needed to know if there were any definable trends that he might make a more accurate appraisal of the present situation in the church, and plan more realistically for the future.

"Come, let's sit here at this table so we can lay things out."

Even though she had never done such a thing, Miss hazel acceded to Dan's request and they sat down in chairs that Dan pulled alongside each other in the church library.

"Where would you want to begin?"

"Let's begin with church membership."

Miss Hazel selected one sheet with columns of figures. She placed it before Dan who read it over.

"You will notice, sir, that the church membership peaked at a figure of 3,078, and that was twelve years ago . . . The membership hovered at that figure for two years, and then there has been a steady decline. The membership now is at 2006."

"Whew! Those losses have been serious, and we shall certainly need to do everything we can to stop the decline . . . Of course, two thousand is a lot of people. Well, please, let's go on and try to get a total picture."

The decline in Sunday School registrations is even more of a problem. Twelve years ago, the figure stood at 1,500. As of now the best figure I can get is 345."

"Oh, my . . . I knew that there had been some loss, but I had no idea that it was that great. But go on. Tell me about the church attendance."

"The attendance had dropped to about 800. Since you have come, the attendance in the morning worship is nearly one thousand. Surely you must know that everyone is tremendously encouraged."

"What else have you discovered by your review of the church statistics?"

"The total of the contributions has declined, but not as much as one might expect from the losses in membership."

"Have we acquired some unpaid obligations?"

"The church has no debt. The officers have managed in a number of ways. Staff people who have left for one reason or another have not been replaced. We have done only the bare minimum of maintenance work. We have sought to cut expenses as much as possible. Even so, the Official Board has had to supplement the income of the church with some additional funds."

"Miss Hazel, you have done an excellent job in putting this together. I knew that Messiah Church would be a big challenge, but until now I did not realize how big . . ."

"Mr. Clark, excuse me, but there is something else. As you know, I maintain the church roll and mailing list. I do not have any statistics, but I am aware of the increasing number of changes of address for the members of the church. I have one distinct impression, and that is the numbers of families who are moving out of this area, indeed out of the city and into the new suburban developments that are springing up all over."

"And we have not seen the end of that . . . Miss Hazel, I am grateful for the report you have prepared. Please let me keep it to study it at greater length. We obviously have much work to do. The Lord knows all of this, and we shall have to look increasingly to Him for guidance and strength."

"I feel as though I have been the bearer of bad news."

"No, no. The truth is necessary, and we must face things as they really are."

"Hello . . . Mother . . . Mother? . . . No. There is no tragedy. Before Dan left this morning he suggested that I call you. Yes, they are fine; I'm watching them in the yard as I talk with you . . . Yes, I'm all right . . . I have things organized now so that I can find what I want . . . Just a minute, I don't see them now . . . . Hello, Mummy. They had gone into the garage for some of their things . . ."

"But that is not why I have called. What would you think if the children and I were to come down now to be with you for a while? . . . *Now!* . . . This week . . . Would it upset Daddy's schedule? . . . I told Dan that the children are so restless, and they say that they have no friends to play with. That disturbs Dan not a little . . . Well, we have visited the Zoo till both the keepers and the animals know us by name. We've ridden on the bus till we should own part of the franchise . . . Staying in the back yard is too confining . . ."

"Well, I talked with Dan about it and I thought – if it is all right with you and Daddy – that we might come down to Rockford now, and be there until Dan has his vacation . . . Well, Friday of this week? . . . We shall have to come on the train because Dan cannot get away to drive us . . . Oh, he's fine, but we don't see much of him. He is out for lunch every day, and he is working long hours to get the renovation project started immediately . . . I keep telling him that . . . No, I think he will be glad to get the children out from under foot. Recently, if he comes home late and tired, all he needs is to have Mark and Debbie say that they want to go back to Pawley! ! ! . . . I had better not run up the bill any more; we can talk when I get there . . . Yes, I'll tell Dan . . . And we'll be on the train on Friday, unless I call you. Bye."

Friday morning brought excitement. There would be a train ride. The car was filled with chatter on the way to the station. The conductor looked like Grandfather Clark. Mary became involved with him in shepherding the children safely on the train and getting their luggage on board with other people about. The train started and she had not kissed Dan, nor said "Good-bye" to him. She tried to get to a window to wave, but the train had already left the platform.

The car seemed empty and quiet when Dan got in, and he sat for a moment with a feeling that a significant door had been closed. He shook his head, remembered that he had a 10:00 o'clock appointment with Philip, and put the key in the ignition. It was not a long drive to the church, and he had some time . . . he stopped at a coffee shop to have a cup of coffee and a doughnut; and to collect his thoughts for the coming conference with Philip. By the time he had returned to put his car in the garage, it was Rev. Daniel Clark, Pastor of Messiah Church, who walked through the office and into the Pastor's Study.

There was a knock on the door. Miss Hazel opened the door and Philip walked in. Dan looked at his watch; it read 10:09. Dan motioned Philip to one of the arm chairs, and he took the other. Dan wasted no time in getting the meeting under way.

"Philip, I have heard nothing from you concerning your decision on assuming responsibility for the education program of Messiah Church."

"Well, sir, I think that this is a big responsibility in an area which would not be my first choice."

"All right. What area would be your first choice?"

"The field is so broad that I hardly know . . ."

"I have been going over statistics on Messiah Church in recent years. We have sustained serious loss in membership. We must undertake a program of outreach to rebuild the membership, and we must begin this effort without any delay whatsoever. Will you assume the task of setting up a program of evangelism and recruiting and training lay people to share in the effort?"

"I think I would be quite out of character in that. I am not an evangelist in nature or by training . . ."

"Very well, Miss Hazel is making up lists of the church membership according to geographical areas. We must make every effort to hold the membership that we now have in Messiah Church. To that end, I want that we shall make a personal call at the home of every communicant member of Messiah Church. I shall take half of the names, and I want you to take the other half. Let us see how quickly we can make the rounds of the church members; I am persuaded that such effort is vitally important at this time."

"That is a tremendous undertaking, and, frankly, I don't know what is to be accomplished . . ."

"Philip, the value of these calls depends upon us. They will derive their worth from what we make of them."

"I don't think I want to commit myself . . ."

Dan made no effort to mask his impatience. "Philip, I have made several suggestions for your meaningful participation in the life and work of this church. You have rejected all of them, and you offer nothing in return . . . I must tell you that this situation is totally unacceptable to me. If you are going to be on the staff of this parish, then there must be some area of the program of this church for which you sustain a personal responsibility."

"When I was selected and engaged by Dr. Gossert, he did not make any such stipulation regarding my place in Messiah Church. I must take exception to the terms of my call to this church being changed . . ."

Dan leaned forward. He looked directly into Philip's eyes. "Dr. Gossert is not the Pastor of Messiah Church. *I* am the Pastor of Messiah Church. You may resent my presence in this position, but *I* carry a responsibility for this parish before Almighty God and the people of this church . . . Now then, let me be quite clear. Either you assume the leadership for some major program area in this church, or I want you to see Bishop Gossert about a transfer to some other appointment."

"The Official Board must vote . . ."

"Philip, I do not need instruction in church policy . . . Nor do I need anyone to tell me that I think that we have arrived at a time for decision. Let me be clear. As of now, I am willing to try to work with you, but I must tell you that anyone on the payroll of Messiah Church is going to earn his keep. I am making September 10 the time for decision." Dan paused. Philip was looking about the room, and Dan was not certain that he was listening. "Hear me well. If by that date – September 10 – you are not committed to an identifiable work load in this church, I shall ask the Official Board in its meeting on September 11 for a formal vote on your discharge from the staff of Messiah Church."

Dan waited, and Philip said nothing.

Dan stood up to conclude the conference. Without a word of response and without a look at Dan, Philip strode from the room.

Whenever he found himself dealing with professionalism in the clergy, Dan came away with a sense of defeat and disgust. He needed to get back to his roots as a servant of human beings in the Name and by the grace of Jesus Christ. He went out into the corridor only to see Philip leaving the building. He turned into Miss Hazel's office. "Miss Hazel, may I please have a couple of those geographical area lists on which you are working. I shall be out making calls the rest of the day."

If the children were bubbling upon arrival and continued cheerily busy, Mary was quiet. Estelle Carter anticipated that Mary would be full of news about their new home, Messiah Church, all of the new things they had been doing, and their plans for the future. Mary, however, answered only to direct questions. Her mother knew that Mary would talk when she was ready. On their third day in Rockford, Grandfather Carter stated that he had some calls to make in the country, and he wondered if anyone would like to go with him in his pickup truck. The announcement enlisted two companions for the trip and the promised luncheon. Mary said that she needed to get everyone's clothes in order.

Estelle Carter was at the door of the linen closet when Mary called from her room, "Mother, when you have finished whatever you are doing, would you please come and talk with me?"

She finished putting sheets on a shelf, closed the door and went to Mary's room. Mary was standing and looking out of the window which opened to the front of the house. She was fingering the curtain.

"My dear, what would you like to talk about?"

"Almost everything, I suppose."

The tone of her voice quickened her mother's steps across the room. "What is wrong? Has something happened?"

"What has happened is that Dan – and the rest of us – have gone to Messiah Church . . . and to the city."

"Mary, whatever do you mean by that? It is such a wonderful place for Dan."

Mary left the window to move some things about on top of the dressing table. "It may *seem* to be that . . . . Oh, Mother! I don't know . . . Perhaps I am just thinking of myself, or taking a short view . . . I don't like changes. I always wanted my room to stay the same. Remember?"

Her mother nodded. "I remember well enough. Have you talked with Dan?"

"I have tried *several* times to talk with him . . . But, Mummy, it's no good. He is either tired, or in a hurry, or just plain gone somewhere on business."

"I don't know how I can help . . . But come and sit here on the bed. Tell me what is so disturbing in your new home."

Seated on the bed with her mother, Mary was ready to "open up." "My first concern is for Mark and Debbie. It is because of them that we have come here earlier than we had planned. They don't know what to do with themselves, and I have reached the point where *I* don't know what to do with them. There are no children in the neighborhood. Many houses are occupied by older people. Many, many places have been made over into apartments that have old people, single persons, or couples with no children. I guess when a couple have a child, they move from the neighborhood."

"You have a nice enclosed yard."

"That was familiar ground all too quickly, and I cannot turn the children loose. The traffic is so heavy on Columbia Avenue, and trucks use Church Street as an east-west short cut . . ."

"Mary, you are here for a few weeks. Let's all enjoy this time together. When you return, Mark and Debbie will be going to school . . ."

"The *school!* That's another matter! *You know* how the children loved their new school in Pawley. I looked up the school in our district, and it is old, and I do mean *OLD!* I have checked, and they will ride a bus to the school, but when I think of them and all that traffic. Columbia Avenue! You have seen it. Six traffic lanes! And the way they drive! Well, I just go cold thinking about it."

Mary's voice was rising in pitch. Her mother touched her as though to turn something off or down. "Mary, Mary, Mary. We must never borrow trouble. There must be special officers for protection of children.Why, we even have that here in Rockford. I am sure that the authorities must be as responsible in Indianapolis . . ."

"And you ought to see that old school . . ."

Mary's mother continued as though to remind her to listen when *her mother* was speaking. "You ought to know as well as/or better than anyone, that education begins with teachers and not buildings. Frequently, the cities have a pay scale and professional advantages that enable them to attract the best; only last week I heard that two of the finest teachers in Rockford are leaving to teach in the Chicago area because they will receive a much better salary. Wait and see. Wait and see. Mark and Debbie may well have opportunities in a city school system that would not have been possible in a small community like Rockford, or Pawley – even with new buildings."

Mother and daughter sat for a time holding hands.

"But there is *more.*" She waited for her mother to sense the ominous. "One day I had the car. My iron was not working and I wanted to take it to an appliance shop. I thought there was one in our area, but I made a mistake on the address. Anyway . . . I drove around looking for the shop. Do you know that within three blocks of the school that the neighborhood is totally black? On our side of Columbia – that's the west side – the neighborhood is black almost to Broad Street, and that's only eight blocks or so from Messiah Church."

Estelle Carter crossed her legs to make for time. She tugged and flat-handed the bedspread to remove some wrinkles. "I don't know. I always thought of Messiah as being a city church, not a neighborhood church."

"Mummy, I know that black people must live somewhere, but when they take over an area . . . Well, I just read an article in a magazine about inner city areas in other communities, and I showed it to Dan. We have not talked about it, but Mummy, I am appalled at the thought of living in such an area. To think of raising Debbie and Mark there . . . the thought terrifies me!"

"When Dan gets settled a little more . . ." Mary's mother brightened with an idea. "When Dan gets a little more settled in his work, it may be that the church would purchase a new house in some suburb. Mr. Hudson was speaking with Daddy about a development of his – 'Cedar Knoll' is what he called it."

Mary found the prospect to be pleasing. "Cedar Knoll is one of the finest new developments. We have driven through it, and Dan says that a number of members of Messiah are moving in there."

"For now, you should put more trust in the Lord . . . and you could place a little more confidence in your husband, too."

"I'll try, Mother. And thanks for listening. It helps to get things out in the open."

Mrs. Carter came back from the hall to stand in the doorway and voice a final word to Mary, who was still sitting on the bed. "I think you ought to talk this over with Dan."

The start of Dan's vacation was put off about ten days by reason of delays in working out details in the plans and the financing of the building renovation. Dan would still be in the pulpit for the first of the three Sundays he had initially planned to be away. Bishop Gossert was taking the service for the last Sunday of August, and a missionary on furlough would have the first Sunday of September. Philip had excused himself from taking any of the services. The Official Board held a special meeting on Wednesday evening to hear the report of the Building and Grounds Committee, and to give formal approval to the project in detail and in its entirety. The contractor had already begun moving equipment and supplies to the church property. On Wednesday evening, everything was in order.

Dan had a feeling of satisfaction as he folded his coat and placed it on the front seat and then climbed in behind the steering wheel. He would now go directly to Belvoir, where he had agreed to preach in his home church on the last Sunday of the month. When Dan wrote in reply to the invitation, he said to himself, 'They never asked me before.'

Then he would go to Rockford, to pick up Mary and Mark and Debbie. They had reservations for a time at Swan Lake. Back to Rockford, and perhaps he and Mary could get away for a short trip. He hoped that somewhere and sometime he might hit a few golf balls.

Dan looked around inside the car. Boy! Mary would be surprised! Mark would be ecstatic with a Buick! It all happened so fast that he could hardly accept the fact that this new car, their first *new* car, was really theirs – or would be after a number of "easy" payments. One night he went to the home of Al Hirter, who was Chairman of the special Renovation Committee. It was nearly midnight when Dan went to his car and couldn't get it started. When they finally had it running, Al suggested, "This car needs some work. Bring it in tomorrow morning, and we'll have our Service Manager go over it."

The next morning, 'the American inevitable' occurred. Al said that he had one car on which he could make a "special deal."

Mary would like the power steering of the white hardtop. Mark would go absolutely crazy over the new instrument panel! When he arrived at Rockford, he would park it in the drive. When one of them noticed it, he would say with practiced nonchalance: "Oh, yes, that's *our* car. I guess I forgot to tell you."

Mary would be pleased, and she would ask him privately if they could really afford a car like this. He would tell her that Al took their car in trade; he would have his shop work it over and then he was giving it back to them for a second car.

The *BELVOIR REPUBLICAN* had the story on Friday:

DANIEL W. CLARK

The last Sunday of August was also a homecoming in Indianapolis, as Bishop Gossert conducted the services in Messiah
Church. Seated at a table in the Pine Room where they had gone
for dinner, the Bishop said, "It was like coming home, Ada . . . Like
coming home."

"It *was* a fine service, George. It did me so much good to see and
hear you again in the Messiah pulpit."

The Bishop picked up a knife and turned it slowly. He was
shaking his head. "I enjoyed it so much that I have been wishing I
had not left . . ."

"Don't say that! We are not going through the pros and cons of
that decision again." As the Bishop sipped some ice water, his wife
looked at him intently. "No, George. There is something else. What
is it?"

The Bishop glanced about quickly as though to make sure that
no one could hear him. "Very well. If you *must* know, it's Messiah
Church."

"Messiah Church! What is wrong with Messiah Church? I
thought Dan Clark was most impressive and I like his wife, too."

"It is not that there is something *wrong*. Of course, some of the
people were talking with me today, and I am just a bit uneasy."

Ada Gossert was not to be satisfied with an observation, so her
husband welcomed the interruption of the waitress bringing their
soup which gave him time to collect his thoughts. He continued in a
subdued voice. "For one thing, I hardly recognized my office this

morning. It was all changed . . ."

"*Your* office! George, that is *not* your office any longer."

"Yes, I suppose so, but I only mentioned that in passing. Last week the Official Board accepted a program of building renovation, and some of the work has already commenced."

His wife relaxed – just a little. "Al Hirter has claimed that such work is needed for as long as I can remember. Why does this bother you? Does Dan want to do the sanctuary in lavendar and old lace?"

"Oh, don't be ridiculous, Ada. You know that Dan has an engineering degree. Corey said that Dan's presentation was a model on how to do your homework. Apparently, everyone was impressed."

Ada Gossert leaned back. "That all sounds *good* to *me*. The church property has needed attention for years."

The Bishop frowned. "Some of the men are disturbed because Dan insisted that the work be done in spite of the fact that it will put the church in debt . . . and Messiah Church has *never* been in debt."

"As I recall, there has always been a lot of to-do about a building fund. How much does Dan want to spend?"

"We have been accumulating a building fund. The figure was . . . well, someone gave Dan the figure of fifty-two thousand dollars. He and Al's committee came in with projects for that amount."

The waitress brought their dinners. Ada Gossert broke off a piece of biscuit to taste it. The Bishop tried his coffee. "It's a long story so let's eat our dinner now."

"Very well, I'll eat, but I want to hear the rest of the story. You seem to have had your ears open for all the gossip . . ."

The Bishop paused, holding his fork with a bite of meat. "I was *not gossiping*! I have something more than passing interest in Messiah Church." He took the bite and chewed reflectively. "The Official Board accepted the program and agreed to go into debt to do it."

"But I thought you said that there was money in the Building Fund."

The Bishop ate as though wanting strength before continuing with what obviously would have to be a complete account.

"There was a figure of more that fifty-two thousand dollars in the Building Fund. You know as well as I do that in the operation of a church, there are some years when there is an overage in the general fund, and there are years when there is a deficit. For two or three years there have been some deficits, and the Official Board decided to make up these deficits by borrowing from the Building Fund. They opted to borrow from themselves, rather than to cut the budget, or go to the congregation for extra monies, or borrow from a bank and incur interest charges."

"I don't know . . ."

"Everyone knew about this – that is, everyone on the Offical Board. We simply expected to replace this money from overages in another year . . . . . Ada, I feel awkward about this . . . . . Of course, I know that Dan did not intend anything personal, but I understand that he spoke rather positively of how we had used some of the Building Fund money. Some of the people wanted to limit the work to the amount presently in the Building Fund. Several said that he was adamant that *all* of the work be done now, even if this meant borrowing. He proposes that they make the effort to raise the money in the November canvass."

Ada Gossert was interested but showed no concern when she asked, "How much money is involved?"

"They will be borrowing about forty thousand dollars . . ."

"FORTY THOUSAND DOLLARS ! ! ! ! ! Whew . . . . ."

The Bishop wanted to lay what he would rather not have raised in the first place. "Oh, Ada, don't carry on so! . . . And please keep your voice down. Don't look and act and sound as though there is a case of embezzlement or fraud . . . Dan was absolutely firm – so Sam Stockwell told me. Sam said that the board is not happy about going into debt, but they finally agreed to proceed with the whole project recommended by the committee."

"Good for Dan! It looks as though he'll get things done."

The Bishop continued his recital. "Miss Hazel telephoned me the other day about my files. She was very apologetic, but she said that Dan wanted them moved. I had hoped to speak with him before he went on his vacation . . ."

"What files of yours?"

"The files from my years at Messiah. One might think that these records and papers would be of historical importance and interest to the church. Sixteen years! Frankly, my first reaction to

Miss Hazel's call was that this did not display much appreciation."

Ada's tone of voice displayed unbelief. "George, this doesn't sound like you. Where are those files now?"

"In Miss Hazel's office. She never made any complaint about them."

"Miss Hazel's office is an oversized closet at best. From the way you are sounding, I assume you think the church ought to have them mounted beside the communion table."

"Oh, Ada . . . If it will help your digestion, I am having them picked up on Tuesday."

Ada was dead serious. "Good . . . But don't you let such a thing color your attitude toward that young man."

Several persons stopped at their table to speak with them. The table was cleared and their dessert served. The Bishop tried to sound casual.

"Philip spoke with me. He said that Dan had talked quite roughly to him."

"Nothing he didn't deserve, I'll bet."

"But think of it, Ada. All of this in the first few months."

"*I* was never sure what Philip was doing."

"He was my assistant. You *do* remember t*hat?* Philip said he feels that Dan dislikes him and wants him transferred from Messiah. But we were interrupted and didn't get to finish our conversation."

Ada Gossert sipped her coffee; the saucer clinked as she replaced the cup. "I think you talked too much already."

The dinner had been good. George Gossert laughed. "There *was* something else. Carol Robertson and her mother asked me if I would marry Carol in November . . . You remember Carol. She said she wouldn't feel married if I didn't peform the ceremony."

Ada Gossert had not finished her cake. "I hope you said 'No'."

"As a matter of fact, I said 'Yes'."

"George, you know better than that. When Dr. Fairfax showed up for a wedding . . . now I am going to quote George Gossert, 'The Pastor should conduct the weddings in Messiah Church.' I think that is a verbatim quote. Now you call Laura Robertson when we get home. "

"All right. From the way you have been talking, I think that I should never have gone to Messiah today."

"You may be the Bishop, but you installed Daniel Clark as the Pastor of Messiah Church. You must give him a chance."

"Well, I *thought* I was the Bishop until now." He pushed back his chair and picked up the check. "Anyway, I hope you enjoyed the dinner. Do you want to stop at Larry's?"

"Were they in the service? I didn't see them."

The Bishop was behind his wife's chair. "Larry was there and he spoke with me. I didn't see Gwendolyn."

"Let's take a little ride."

"Good. We'll drive out and see some of the new developments where we are considering the establishment of new churches. I have asked Fred Hudson to speak to a diocesan committee about this."

Monday morning, Dan went with his father to the Redstone Executive Office Building. Even though he knew most of the individuals, his father insisted on taking him about to introduce him to everyone. Having completed the round, he spent time with his father in the privacy of his office. He went home to sit down with his mother, who said that she had been on the telephone all morning listening to people who had called to talk with her about her son and the service in Third Avenue Church on Sunday.

After a sandwich, Dan left about noon to drive to Rockford, where he arrived in late afternoon. Dan was quite sure that Mark was more thrilled to see the *new Buick* than he was to see his father. The first item of business was a series of rides around the block: first, Mark and Debbie; then Mary with the children in the back seat; then, with Mary to drive with Dan beside her; then, Mary driving alone (! ! !); then Mary taking the children; and finally, Mr. and Mrs. Carter, Mary, Mark and Debbie – *everybody* at once. Dan thought he would need to make a trip to the filling station if the schedule was to continue indefinitely. The driving finally ended with Mark and Debbie taking turns sitting on a pillow behind the steering wheel.

At the dinner table, Mark was unimpressed with the word that they would have *two* automobiles, and he expressed his firm purpose to ride "only in the Buick." The evening passed quickly and the house became quiet.

Dan emerged from the shower to find Mary sitting upright in bed in the light of the bedside lamps. As Dan climbed into the bed and reached out to put his hand on Mary, she said, "Dan, we must talk."

"All right, we'll have lots of time in the next couple weeks . . ."

"No. I mean that we must talk now. I have been thinking of our living situation in the city . . . . . . I have had a chance to see the free and happy existence the children have enjoyed here in Rockford . . ."

"Mary, it has been a long day. I have been working long hours. Come now . . . . I have missed you so much . . ."

Mary was not to be turned from her purpose. "I think that first we must live and I have come to the conclusion that Church Street does not offer us a good basis for living and raising children. Frankly, Dan, if the church can not, or will not, provide some other living accommodation for us, I think you should go to the Bishop and ask to be transferred immediately."

"I am not prepared to discuss your conclusion here and now. I am going to try to get some sleep."

Dan rolled over and was asleep almost immediately. For some time, Mary sat unmoved with the lights burning.

When Dan awakened the next morning, Mary was dressed and sitting in a chair beside a window. She was a woman with a purpose and her purpose was to effect a change in their living circumstances in the city, and this change should be carried out in time for school registration. She was persuaded that they should make any sacrifice – including Dan's transfer to another parish – for the sake of their children. She was talking as Dan left the room to go downstairs to get a cup of coffee.

When Mary came downstairs, Dan was on the telephone. He announced that some important matters had arisen in the church and that he would be leaving immediately.

"What about our reservations at Swan Lake?"

"I don't know. I shall have to see how things work out for me."

Mary could see that Dan was angry, and it seemed best to let him drive away. Her explanation to the children and to her parents was that Dan 'was called back on some emergency.' Her mother was not to be put off, and she questioned Mary closely on what had transpired.

After a long and detailed narration, Mary said, "I only tried to do what you suggested. I tried to talk with him."

Estelle Carter stared at her daughter. "I don't think I am hearing what I am hearing. I can't believe that I raised a daughter who would be so insensitive . . . so *stupid!*"

She wheeled about and went to another part of the house, as far removed from her daughter as she could manage.

The church office telephone was ringing and ringing. Miss Hazel stepped into the office, emptied of its old furniture and partially refinished. Mrs. Johnson was not seated at the folding table which held both the telephone and her typewriter. Miss Hazel picked up the receiver to say: "Messiah Church." There was no answer and the connection was broken. In puzzlement, she stepped out of the office and saw Mrs. Johnson down the corridor, leaning against the wall. She went to her.

"Is something wrong, Mrs. Johnson? Are you ill?"

"Miss Hazel, I have worked here for four years and no one ever complained about my work, did they?" Miss Hazel was not given time for reply. "Just a little while ago Mr. Clark spoke to me so sharply. I am shocked that a Minister could be so unfeeling, and I thought he was on vacation." She wiped her eyes and her nose.

"Mrs. Johnson, the Pastor is a very sympathetic man. I am afraid I do not understand . . ."

Lucille sniffed. "Well, my Charlie's girl was to have medical appointments for a couple of days. And Charlie is in the midst of a special drive right now, and Charlie thought – I thought – it would be all right to have his calls switched here where I could take them for a couple days. When Mr. Clark had some difficulty with the telephone – and like I say, I thought he was on vacation – he spoke to me about it. I explained to him what I was doing. I didn't try to hide it, or anything; I simply told him as quietly and plainly as I could. Well! He said to me, 'Mrs. Johnson, this telephone is for *church* business.' I tried to say that it would only be for a couple days till Charlie's girl gets back, and I said that Charlie pays his own office expenses and can't afford to hire another girl . . . Do you know what he said to me? He said, 'That would seem to be Charlie's problem. This use of the church's telephone must stop immediately . . .'"

"Mrs. Johnson, you – or your husband – should have spoken to Mr. Clark, or maybe to me, before he arranged this . . ."

"And that's not all. I tried to be honest with him. But do you know what he said to me? He said that he had received too many complaints about me not being on the job. Now you know that's not so. And I told him that *no one* ever complained before. He said that I am always doing personal errands on the church's time, and leaving my place empty. And then he didn't exactly threaten me, but he said that he would expect me to be here and on time for the scheduled office hours. I started to answer, but I couldn't take any more, so I left and came out to the Ladies Room . . ."

"Now, now, Mrs. Johnson. Let's both get back to work. I'm sure we can straighten all of this out."

Dan had encountered the difficulty with Mrs. Johnson almost immediately upon entering the church. When she had run out of the office he had stood still, feeling embarrassed. 'If I would have stayed in Rockford, this would not have happened.' He thought it might help to go outside and get some fresh air. Then he said to himself, 'I should return and apologize to Mrs. Johnson and tell her that the telephone arrangements could stand – for this time only.' The traffic light changed and Dan walked across the street. 'There are times when one must be firm.'

Walking, thinking, talking to himself, Dan looked up to find himzelf near Memorial Hospital. He pulled from his pocket Miss Hazel's typed lists of church members in the hospitals. 'Heavens! The hospitals must be half-filled with people from Messiah Church!' 'Will there be enough healthy members to have a service next Sunday?'

Dan tapped on a door and entered the room of a man whose name he had not recognized. He found another visitor already in the room. Dan introduced himself, and was in turn introduced to the other visitor, David Schuster. After a few minutes, Dan said, "I hope that your recovery will be complete and soon accomplished. May I pray about it?"

"Uhhh . . . Yes, that'd be fine."

Dan stepped beside the bed.

"Almighty God. We bless Thee because Thou dost forgive all our iniquities and heal all our diseases. Strengthen all who attend this man. Grant unto him the work of Thy Spirit that he may be sustained and re-stored whole. Through Jesus Christ, our Savior and our Lord. Amen."

Dan walked from the room to continue his hospital calls.

"That was nice of him. Makes a fellow feel better somehow. How did that verse go that he quoted: 'Fear thou not; for I am with you.'?"

David Schuster was in his own world. "So *that* is the new Minister of Messiah Church."

"Said he is. I hadn't seen him before. I haven't been to church much lately. I wonder how he knew I was here . . . I'll tell you this David. The first Sunday I am out of here, I am going to get my wife in the car and we are going to church."

David laughed. "I am disappointed in him."

"Why? You never met him before, did you?"

"No, that is why I am disappointed. If I know my mother, she has tried to set him after me – and I *do* know my mother. But he has *not* been looking for me to convert me."

"He's probably heard enough about you from others besides your mother; so he must think you're hopeless and he's ignoring you. At least, he hasn't given up on me."

Dan sat in the den with his thoughts that evening. The house was totally without sound. He thought that perhaps he should call

Mary and try to patch up things with her. 'I should have been patient and listened to her, and talked with her.' Then too, there was no point in taking out his personal frustration on Lucille Johnson. He looked at his watch, and it was too late to telephone Mary . . . Tomorrow . . . And tomorrow he would try to get a better relationship with Lucille; he should have taken time to get to know her from the beginning and to win her as a friend and a colleague. Of course, he had finally met David Schuster face to face . . . Already there seemed to be workmen everywhere throughout the church, and there seemed to be disorder wherever he went in the building.

He was disappointed in himself. The day was marked with personal failure. He had forgotten that the experiences of human life are a mixture which can catch us unawares at any moment. Joys and satisfactions come mixed with frustrations and disappointments and even defeats, and much of the time they come to us without forewarning. If he would live an exemplary Christian life, he must be prepared to take what came to him in living moment to moment, and day by day. He needed now to look to his own spiritual resources that he might face successfully whatever the next turn of the corner might bring. He reached for his Bible.

With new resolve, Dan went to the office the next morning. Before he had opportunity to set things right with Lucille, she had come into his office, quit as of that moment, and walked out.

'O, Lord, I will remember: Trust in the Lord with all thy heart, and lean not to thine own understanding.'

Miss Hazel tapped on his door and entered with a sheet of paper in her hand.

"I am very sorry about Mrs. Johnson. I shall work in the front office to handle things there."

"Thank you, Miss Hazel. I do appreciate your help in this."

When Miss Hazel had gone, Dan looked at the typewritten sheet she had placed on his desk. It was from Philip, who said that he would be leaving Messiah Church as of October 31. He would take October as his vacation month, so he would be terminating his active service in Messiah Church as of September 30. Philip had left the sheet with Miss Hazel and left the building. Dan would speak with Philip later . . . His resolve of the night before was being challenged: 'Had he failed Philip in some way? Certainly, he wanted them to part as Christian friends.'

Lucille gone . . . Philip leaving . . . He had an unresolved situation in Rockford. The church building was all torn up. 'I, Dan Clark, have become a one-man wrecking crew.' He needed to get out before he did any more damage. He had several errands. He telephoned and went to see Cora Schuster to tell her that he had finally met David. He stopped somewhere to get a cup of coffee and eat part of a sandwich. All the while, he continued to ask God to help him get his situation in hand.

Dan returned to the church in early afternoon to find Carol waiting to see him. Miss Hazel had suggested that she wait. Dan invited her into the Study and introduced himself when they were seated.

"I am Dan Clark. I am Pastor of Messiah Church. Miss Hazel said that you wanted to see me, and here I am. How can I serve you?"

"How do you do. My name is Carol King. Thank you for seeing me now. I hope that I am not interrupting your schedule." Dan shook his head and waited. "I was walking by the church, and somehow I felt led to come in . . . but let me go back a bit. I have been in graduate school in Texas, but I developed a health problem that required surgery, and I had to drop out of school. My parents had moved here, and I came to be with them for a time of recuperation. I have been feeling more like myself, and I have been thinking that I might do well to get to work – have something to do that puts me on a schedule and makes me feel that I am living again. I have prayed much about it, and I have felt led to do this – if a Psychology major may speak that way. Today I was walking, and as I came to the church, I felt an urge to come in and say that I am looking for a job . . ."

Dan spoke up. "I don't know that we should have anything presently in your field . . ."

"Excuse me. At this point I am only looking for something that will keep me busy and make me feel that I am functioning as a person again."

"We are in need of a church secretary and receptionist, but I would not want to offer that to a person with your qualifications. As you noticed, we are in the midst of a renovation of our facilities, including the church office. We anticipate the installation of new furnishings and equipment for the office. But for now . . ."

"Please, Mr. Clark, that sounds wonderful to me and for me. What must I do to make formal application?"

Dan told her what the compensation would be for the Church Secretary. He explained something of the duties and role of this position and introduced her to Miss Hazel. As a matter of form he asked for some references. He showed her about the office complex and took her into the sanctuary. Before she left, Dan had offered her the position and she had accepted it, beginning next Monday morning.

Dan telephoned Mary that evening. He apologized for his want of patience that he might hear her out in her concerns for the children. He said that he knew she only wanted the best for Mark and Debbie, and that he shared in that desire. He told her that the Secretary of the Official Board had stopped to express the opinion of the Board members that Dan should add a week for his vacation inasmuch he had lost more than a week at the beginning. For now, Dan would return to Rockford on Friday, and they would leave for Swan Lake on Saturday . . . And would she see if she could extend the time from one week to two weeks?

"I have really called, Mary, to tell you that I love you, and that I need you."

"My darling, I miss you terribly, and the children miss you. I want you to know that I love you, and I am with you wherever you believe God has called you to serve. I am going to spend the next two weeks making sure you know how much I really love you."

It was with lighter heart that Dan began the next morning. He was grateful for the talk with Mary. He was encouraged with the prospect of Carol King on the staff. He did not know that he could rightfully make any further requests of the Lord. And yet, he had to believe that God knew the needs for the work of Messiah Church.

Marjorie Porter – President of Messiah Women – came to the office on the chance that she might find Dan. She wanted to discuss the women's program emphases for the coming year. When they had finished with the specific purpose of her visit, she added, "'Three of our children have just returned from the summer youth conference. They had gone with some reluctance but they returned in high spirits."

She went on to explain that there was a new Director of the program and that the whole week had been a wonderful experience for their kids, and apparently this was the general reaction of all the young people who were there. Her enthusiasm made Dan listen to the extent that he reached for the Directory of the church officials, and he dialed a number.

"Ken, this is Dan Clark . . . Right . . . Well, some of us don't have the privilege of an office looking out on a wooded lake . . . I'll tell you why I called. Some of our young people have just returned from the youth conference and they found it to be a thrilling experience . . . Yes, I heard of her and that is the reason I am calling. Her name is Kathryn? Kathryn McDonough . . . Who is she, Ken? I haven't heard her name before . . . Just graduated? . . . With whom has she been talking? . . . Ken, we need a Director of Education here at Messiah. From what I heard and from what you have just told me about her, I would like to talk with her if she would be interested . . .I'd appreciate that . . . Tell her to call me collect . . . Thank you, Ken. Thank you. You are doing a great piece of work for our young people and the Lord . . . Some time as you jog down a wooded lane, think kindly of those of us who have only cement and asphalt . . . I'll be waiting for her call . . . I'm going on vacation on Friday. I'll see you at the district meeting, if not before. Bye now."

Dan had lunch with Al Hirter and the Church Treasurer. Everything was working out in the financing of the renovation program. The Church Treasurer had received a call from First Fidelity, and they had offered the best package on the necessary borrowing. Vince, the Treasurer, said, "I am amazed at the special gifts we have received without any sort of campaign. The people agree that work is needed and they want to help get it done."

When Dan returned from the lunch and a call at the emergency room of a hospital on the north side of the city, he thought he would step into the sanctuary to see what work was being done there. There were no workmen, but there was a young couple walking slowly about and stopping to look out of each of the windows.'

Dan went to them and introduced himself. The young man responded, "We are happy to meet you, Pastor Clark. My name is Fred Anderson, and this is my wife Charlotte."

"I am sorry that you find us with so much dust and disorder generally. I just came in now to see if any of the work had been started here in the sanctuary."

"You wouldn't know me, and I should tell you that I, too, am a Minister. I am serving the church in Millston."

Dan walked them about the sanctuary and invited them to come into his study. After he had secured a Coca Cola for each of them, they sat down to get acquainted. They had come to bring their daughter to the University Medical Center. She was suffering from a life-threatening illness and their doctor had referred them to that facility. In the morning she had undergone a series of tests, and the people at the hospital had encouraged them to go and let her rest. They would serve better when she came out from under the heavy sedation which she had received.

When Dan returned home that evening the telephone was ringing as he entered the house. It was Rev. Fred Anderson, who asked if he could make an appointment to see Dan as soon as possible. "Andy" was waiting as Dan came into the office on the following morning. Andy was quick to tell him that their worst suspicions about their daughter's illness had been confirmed. Lynn was a very sick little girl; she would need to be hospitalized immediately for additional tests and treatment. In addition, she would need to be under the supervision of the Medical Center Staff and to receive continuing treatment if there was to be any hope for her survival. Andy needed someone who could be sympathetic and objective – who would listen. He said that he and Charlotte had talked through much of the night trying to figure out how they might manage this care for their Lynn.

Dan straightened up. He could hardly believe that a possibility opened out before them. Without second thought, words rushed from his lips. "Andy, I want to say two things: First, I am going to be away for an additional Sunday, and I do not yet have anyone to take the service for me. Will you take the 11:00 o'clock service here at Messiah a week from Sunday?"

"Oh, my goodness! I don't know. I am hesitant to try to stand in the place of some of the greatest preachers of our church . . ."

"I need someone. You are here. I think that the Lord is opening a door for both of us. We can make a pulpit robe available for you."

Andy smiled broadly. "I'll do my best . . ."

Dan interrupted and rushed on. "Second. We need an Associate Pastor here at Messiah. I would like to invite you to come and be my Associate here at Messiah Church. I need help, and I need help NOW. There are some of the formalities to be worked through, but I would be pleased to have you here on our Staff as soon as possible.

After a time of prayer together, Andy hurried back to the motel "to talk with Charlotte." Dan called the Bishop and was told to "come in as soon as possible." He walked directly into the Bishop's office and sat down at the Bishop's invitation.

"Bishop Gossert, I shall come directly to the point."

"Please do." There was an edge in the Bishop's voice.

"Philip Frenell has resigned as of October 31. He is leaving the end of this month to take October as his vacation month . . ."

"Yes, Philip has come to see me. I must say that I am very sorry that it has not worked out for you and Philip to be together in Messiah Church. It had seemed to me that Philip might offer some continuity in the ministry of that great church."

He stopped with his eyes intent upon Dan, as though waiting for an explanation – or maybe even, Dan thought, an apology of sorts.

"I am sorry, but it was not working out. It was increasingly evident to both Philip and me that it was not going to be a working situation for either of us. I think it is better for us to admit this up front and to get on with the work of the Church."

"Well, of course, you are the Pastor and you have the right to establish the personnel of your Staff . . ." Dan thought the Bishop seemed reluctant to confirm this principle in this instance.

"It is in that connection that I have come today. I am leaving tomorrow for some vacation, but I want to get something before you."

Dan told the Bishop about Rev. Frederick Anderson. He said that he had personally invited Rev. Mr. Anderson to come as his Associate. He noted that Andy would be taking the service in a couple of weeks; after that service he could meet with the Official Board who could then vote to support the invitation and the terms of the proposed contract. Dan said that Andy would be calling the Bishop to come and meet the Bishop, who did not know him personally. The Bishop agreed to give the whole matter his personal attention.

The meeting with the Bishop took somewhat longer than he had planned, and Dan was a few minutes late for a lunch meeting with Fred Hudson and three other officers that Miss Hazel had arranged for them to meet Rev. Frederick Anderson. The lunch went well, and all of the officers liked Andy upon first meeting. Fred Hudson would chair a meeting of the Official Board following the service a week from Sunday. The question arose concerning a residence for the Anderson family, and Andy said that Charlotte had inquired and they could get a two-bedroom apartment in a building adjacent to, and part of, the Medical Center.

It was a beautiful Friday as Dan was driving to Rockford. The trees along the road and across the countryside were beginning to acquire a bit of color. He was looking forward to seeing Mary and the children again. He found himself humming. The world was looking ever so much brighter today.

As he thought about it, Dan could scarcely believe the changes that had transpired in a matter of only a few days. Carol King would be starting on Monday. Philip was gone, and everything seemed to be in place for Rev. Fred Anderson to begin as the Associate Pastor some time in October. Kathryn McDonough had telephoned and she was interested; she had some necessary chores to wrap up her summer assignment at the camp, and she would be coming to see Dan upon his return from his vacation. Their telephone conversations – they had talked three times – had gone well. Dan had tried to describe their situation and spell out the job responsibilities. They had agreed on everything, including the financial terms of her possible employment. Kathryn would attend the service on the final Sunday of September, and she would be talking with Dan on Monday. She was ready to go to work as of October 1. The Messiah Staff was in place, or at least it gave every promise of being complete. Miss Hazel, Mr. Hudson and Bill Kuist would continue.

Dan marveled at how his life had been turned around in less than a week. In his most roseate moments he never would have imagined that he could have effected all of the changes in the Staff over a period of months . . . but this had been accomplished in *less than a week! A matter of days!* The church officers could not believe that so much could have happened in so short a time! They had all been most enthusiastic in complimenting Dan! . . . . . Dan looked for a place where he could drive off the road and park.

Turning off the ignition, Dan leaned forward in the driver's seat until his head touched the steering wheel. He voiced aloud his words of prayer:

"Oh, my God! Forgive me . . . Forgive me that I have not seen, nor acknowledged Thy gracious hand of blessing and working in these days. I know that I could not have done it. It would be stupid of me to say that it all just happened. I gratefully acknowledge Thee as the One Who has moved in ways beyond my powers and beyond my own reckoning. I am thankful for Carol, for Andy, and for Kathryn. I am thankful for Miss Hazel, Bill, Mr. Hudson and Mr. Hoffmeyer. Most of all, I am grateful to acknowledge Thy hand in Messiah Church. With all my heart I thank Thee. Please, Lord, grant Thy power and blessing in all of our efforts to serve our Lord Jesus Christ in Messiah Church. In His Name. Amen.

The vacation at Swan Lake was more than they could have hoped for, and they now returned to life in the city: Dan back at work and the children in school for the first time. As they came to the garage, Dan asked Debbie to push the button on the genie, only to have the garage door open before them. More than this . . . there was a *new* car already in the garage. At least it looked new! It was their old car with a new coat of paint. Al Hirter said that he thought they might as well add a paint job to the mechanical work they were doing on the old car. It would work out that the new Buick would be Mary's car and Dan would be back behind the wheel of the old Chevy, which he found not only looked but ran like a new car.

Much had been accomplished in the church. The office complex was completed, and Carol was the finish to the transformation of this reception and work area. Miss Hazel "looked" happier, and she was obviously pleased to have more room in her office. Dan couldn't have been more satisfied with the person he found in Kathryn Mc-Donough, who was there to meet him on his first day back in the office. She was prepared to begin as soon as she found a place to live. She even had some books in her car which she moved into her redecorated office; Bill Kuist and Dan moved furniture about to set up her office and working quarters.

Dan worked with Miss Hazel to make reply to accumulated correspondence, and to prepare the church calendar for the month ahead. Fred Anderson called to say that the Millston Church had been most sympathetic with their personal situation and that all of the formalities would be completed for them to move and for him to report for work by October 20. The Bishop telephoned to confirm Philip's release from his commitment at Messiah, and Frederick Anderson's appointment as of October 20.

Dan wanted to go to the hospital, but he thought he would look in at home before taking off in "his car." He opened the front door and entered only to hear animated chatter and laughter from upstairs. He went through the house. As he reached the door leading into the kitchen there was a "thump" upstairs, followed by a burst of laughter. 'Wherever she is, that sort of thing will bring Mary on the run.'

He opened the door to see Mary and a young woman sitting at

the breakfast table.

"Dan! You're home early. Lois, I want you to meet my husband. Dan, this is Lois Luke."

Lois nodded with a brush of a smile.

"Will you sit with us and have a glass of iced tea? Lois' children – Bob and Ruth – came over after school to play with Debbie and Mark. They are all having a wonderful time upstairs, in case you didn't notice as you came through the house."

Lois pushed back her chair. "Oh, my . . . Look at the time! The baby will be awake and I must get my dinner on."

The Official Board met in a redecorated Board Room for its October meeting. There were smiles all about the room as Al Hirter reported for the Renovation Committee.

"We have made some progress. The exterior work is done. The landscape people have given the property a new setting; the garth especially is green and alive. The exterior doors have been refinished and the hardware has all been cleaned and repaired. Overall, we now present a clean face."

Sam Stockwell spoke up. "Al, I appreciate the work of your committee, but it seems to me a waste of money to fix that old fountain that has not run for years."

"'Fix the fountain' as you call it, Sam, consisted in cleaning the debris from the pool and opening a valve in the basement."

Corey Williams wanted to be heard. "Al, I know I speak for lots of people in the church when I say that we don't know how you managed to get so much done so quickly."

"Thank you, Corey. The general contractor promised to get in, do the work, and get out. Some of the members of our committee have stayed on the telephone to collect some favors owed by many of the subs. The main office complex is finished. Corridors and classrooms have been redone; we are about halfway through with the installation of new lighting. New equipment for the social hall will be delivered as soon as the new floor is laid."

Sam broke in again. "You have certainly done a lot of work, Al, but I fail to understand why we did nothing in Mr. Frenell's office . . ."

"Sorry to interrupt, Sam, but let me set the record straight. We did not go into Mr. Frenell's office because he was most emphatic that he did not want the room touched. He said he did not approve of us spending all of this money on ourselves. He called it 'an idolatry of plaster and paint.' As soon as he clears out his personal things, we shall do this room over for Mr. Anderson."

"We have done necessary things in the sanctuary. The organ is being overhauled completely. We discovered that one manual, which is approximately one-fourth of the organ, was not working at all."

Sam looked at a sheet of paper he was holding. "Al, how much is all of this going to cost? It seems to me that we have to draw the line somewhere,"

"Good point Sam. We are far enough along that we can project our costs. Using the money in the Building Fund, the Board authorized borrowing up to forty thousand dollars. We have received unsolicited monies to the extent that we shall need to borrow ten thousand dollars, at the most. And we have taken the approach that anything that needs painting, paint it, and anything that needs fixing, fix it."

∝   ∝   ∝   ∝

October 20

Dearest Mother and Daddy,

I don't know when I have gone so long without writing. Since you were out last Saturday night, I couldn't call you.

Mummy, you were right about the school. Mark and Debbie love their teachers. Lincoln School is old and dark on the outside, but they have done lots of work to make the interior like a new building.

Last Friday night we had a Staff dinner. There were nine, counting Dan and myself. I decided on a buffet. Wow! My food budget for this month is ruined, but Dan said that we shouldn't count this. I had both baked ham and chicken a la king, biscuits, some of the strawberry preserves we made. I used the last of the apples we brought back to make apple pie. Everybody raved about the dinner. Mr. Hoffmeyer played and we all sang. Dan thought the evening went very well.

Miss Hazel insisted on helping me clean up a bit. One time when we happened to be alone in the kitchen, she asked me if I would help her. I had no idea what she might have in mind. Then she said she wants to get some new clothes and to have her hair fixed differently. I am not to say a word to anyone here. We are going shopping this Saturday as a start.

Dan puts in terribly long hours. I know that he has many problems, but he doesn't talk about them. The church really looks different; people talk about it being transformed.

I had a telephone call from Bishop Gossert's daughter-in-law. She wanted me to get donors and sell season tickets for a Civic Music series. She wasn't very gracious when I said I couldn't do it now. I was reminded – not very subtly – that her husband's father is the Bishop! She expressed unbelief that our children do not attend Stone School. Dan says that Larry works like a dog to support her and the girls. Larry quit teaching a class in Sunday School, but he still attends the services. "Gwen" – she said I was to call her that – and the girls rarely come.

Debbie and Mark have some nice playmates. Their parents are a young couple who moved into the neighborhood; they also have a baby. Lois is a good person, and she is careful with her children. She holds preachers in great awe! Dan came in one day when she was here and I thought Lois would faint!

I must stop now, but I'll call you on Saturday. Debbie and Mark want to stay up so they too can talk with you.

I love you both,
Mary

∝   ∝   ∝   ∝

Bishop Gossert replaced the pen in its holder and pushed back from his desk. He looked up to face Fred Hudson.

"There. I am glad to get this purchase finalized. I do appreciate your help, Fred. This will make Thanksgiving for me."

"I'm glad to get this settled, George. Cedar Knoll has received an acceptance beyond our wildest hopes, and I have been under considerable pressure to sell off some of the seven acres that I promised to hold for the church."

"We were ready to move long ago, but we have had delay after delay in the local comity committee."

"I'd better get these papers to our attorney . . ."

"Don't go yet. Talk to me a bit before you go. Tell me how things are at the church."

Fred relaxed with a happy subject. "Great! Just great! We have finished the restoration work without having to borrow any money. Finances are in shape for next year. The congregations are tremendous . . . and growing."

The Bishop sat for a moment trying to phrase his question: "I take it, Fred, that you're satisfied with Dan Clark, from what you've seen thus far."

"He has more than exceeded our most optimistic expectations." Fred stopped as though he was hearing the Bishop's question anew. "George, is there something back of your query?"

"Oh . . . I heard that Mrs. Johnson had left . . ."

"George, at least two years ago, *I know* I told you that she wouldn't last one pay period in my organization. I can't afford help like that. And too, there is a marvelous young woman in the office now."

The Bishop shrugged his shoulders. "I have had to transfer Philip Frenell, and I suppose I was wondering if Dan was having personnel problems."

Fred leaned forward. "There have been personnel problems, and I can speak with some knowledge because Dan talked with me."

The Bishop waved his hand to say, 'Carry on.'

"Philip was irked when we did not take his recommendation. I tried to talk with him. Dan tried to win him, but Philip let his resentment fall on Dan. He avoided Dan and communicated with him only by leaving little notes on Dan's desk . . . Frankly, if you had not transferred Philip, I would have been here with Dan *to demand* his transfer *immediately.*"

"All right. All right. Don't get excited. Dr. Cogswell needed an assistant and it was a good move for Philip."

"If it has not come to your desk, the Official Board has worked out a Lease/Purchase agreement for the property across the street that used to be a used car lot. We need more parking space for the people coming to the church."

'That is interesting. But, speaking of real estate, Fred, you know more about this city than any other one man. Think about it and tell me where you think would be some strategic areas for the establishment of new churches."

"Hello, Daddy . . . I'm fine . . . They are both well and busy. How are you and Mother? . . . Hello, I was just asking about you . . . We hope to come for a visit between Christmas and the time that school begins . . . They are doing exceedingly well . . . It has helped to have some friends, and they *are* nice children. I see Lois – their mother – almost every week day. We both walk our children to the corner and wait for the bus, even though there is a regular po-liceman on duty. Sometimes she stops in for a cup of coffee; she went with me to the last P. T. A. meeting . . . She really is a lovely person and she takes wonderful care of her children . . . She said the other day that I am the first college woman she has ever had for a friend . . . She has told me about herself and her family only bit by bit because she is shy and does not readily talk about herself. Her husband's name is Matt; I have not met him. They went to school together from the First Grade; she said that they always assumed they would be married . . . From some small town in Tennessee . . . Matt quit school to work in a small factory in the county seat; when that place closed, Matt could only work at odd jobs. He had an un-cle who lived here in Indianapolis, and that was a big reason for coming to this particular city . . . But his uncle was transferred to Cleveland, a week after they arrived and they have been very much alone. Matt did get a job at General Machine . . . No, I haven't seen

75
Messiah Man

their place because I haven't been invited. Lois said they took it because they have debts from moving, and medical bills for the baby. They are living in this apartment while they try to get on their feet financially . . . Well, that's the kind of housing that we have in the area about us . . . Thank you . . . I'll tell them . . . Oh, that sounds wonderful! You could be here for the Christmas Eve Service, and Christmas Day . . . and then we could ride back with you. Yes, yes . . . I'll tell Dan . . ."

Dan was toying with a dish of cereal and looking at the newspaper when Mary returned from walking the children to the corner.

"Oh, Dan! The best news! Lois just told me that she is going to send Bob and Ruth to Sunday School this Sunday. She mentioned casually that the children have new clothing. I knew it! I'm glad that I didn't say anything more than to invite them. Several times I almost offered to help, and I know that I would have offended because they are very proud people . . . Anyway, they are coming Sunday. Bob and Ruth were telling Mark and Debbie, and it was good seeing them all so happy."

"Good! I hope Lois will come too – and Matt."

"I wouldn't count on Matt. You look as though you should have stayed in bed longer. I tried to keep the children quiet."

"Mary. Look here." He pulled an appointment book from his pocket and opened its pages before Mary, who had seated herself across the table from him. "Look at all of these places where I am supposed to go and do one thing or another. And I am not the preacher I was a year ago because I don't have the preparation time that I used to have."

"I know someone who thinks it is all too much."

"Who?"

"Mark! Last night he said, 'Doesn't Daddy eat here any more?'"

"I'm sorry. I took on too much before I realized what I was doing. Miss Hazel always handles my appointment calendar with a deep frown."

Mary reached out to put her hand on Dan's. "Let me go on record now by saying that I miss you. I always thought you were a good preacher; I guess I should not say that I am surprised but you have become a *great* preacher . . . and I am so proud of you. Even so, I am feeling as though I am losing a husband to the Church. You come in late and you leave early; you are always busy. I am not complaining, but I worry about you becoming so tired. Now that I am started . . . . Dan, I miss the times of loving closeness with you . . ."

"Forgive me. Please, just let me get through Christmas. Help me to get through Christmas, and I'll try to make it up to Mark and Debbie – and especially to you. That's a promise."

Mary noted that he left most of the cereal in the bowl as he rose from the table. She walked with him to the door and assured him that she would hold him to that promise. With a sudden impulse she put her arms about Dan's neck and kissed him longingly.

Dan effected a hoarseness in his voice. "Just hold that thought till I get back." But it would be late, late in the evening before he would return.

All things pass. Dan slumped wearily in a chair in the Study without bothering to remove his robe following the Midnight Christmas Eve Service. Mary and her parents had taken the children home to get them in bed. For a preacher of good news about joy in the world, it did not seem right that he should have a feeling of jaded exhaustion.

Fred and Marge came excitedly into the Study. Fred's words burst from him. "Dan, do you know who was here tonight?" Waiting for no one to answer. *"Dave! Dave Schuster* was in the service tonight!"

Marge began to speak before Fred was finished. "When I looked around at the end of the service, I *thought* I saw Dave."

"And Marge said, 'Isn't that Dave Schuster?' I thought she was really carried away . . . By the way, that *was* a *great* service, Dan. I looked, and it *was* Dave."

"We tried to get to him to let him know we were glad that he had come, but we missed him."

"I am very thankful . . ."

"Well, Dan, as you said tonight, 'Emmanuel.'"

Fred and Marge were still buoyant about Dave when they met the Bishop and his wife at a dinner party a few days later. The Bishop's reply was tempered with the words, "You know that Larry and Gwen transferred to St. John's Church."

His wife spoke as though she had said the words before, "George, the church is in their neighborhood. Maybe Gwen will now go to church with Larry, and maybe they will have the girls in Sunday School, in a choir, or a youth group."

"I know, Ada, but I wish they would have stayed within our denomination."

The Bishop read and reread the annual report of Messiah Church. He frowned at one item:

"Removed by action of the Offical Board . . . 250."

There was a note from Miss Hazel, saying that she had personally checked every one of these names, and that the people were gone . . . moved without leaving any forwarding addresses. The Bishop thought, 'If Miss Hazel checked them, they were double-checked.'

Even though the number of new members was the greatest in years, the membership of the church showed a net loss.

Finances were in excellent condition. There had been a major renovation of the church property, and there was no indebtedness. The church was purchasing the site across the street for parking. Attendance had increased and they would begin a second Sunday morning worship service in Lent.

Rev. Frederick Anderson was the Associate Pastor. When the Bishop checked on Rev. Mr. Anderson, one reference said: "He is so good that I cannot believe he would be coming as an *Associate*. If you can get him in any way, you are very fortunate." Ada said that he was being "nosy" when he made some inquiries about Kathryn McDonough, so he told her that he had heard only the finest things about Kathryn. Dan Clark *was* doing a good job in Messiah Church.

With much to encourage, Dan found life and work at Messiah was not an unmixed blessing.

Philip Frenell's resignation had produced words about "poor Philip" that had run through the congregation.

"He's been with us for six years."

"I never saw him do anything so wrong that he should be fired."

"Fired?"

"And I heard without any notice!"

"Why, there was a Women's Luncheon once when the devotional leader didn't come. Mr. Frenell was so very good to read some Scripture and lead in prayer."

"How could Mr. Clark accept his resignation?"

"Someone on the Official Board said that Mr. Clark practically demanded Mr. Frenell's removal."

Dan met David Schuster one day on the sidewalk in front of the church. They had only exchanged greetings when Dan heard himself addressed. With only a nod toward Dave, Sam Stockwell launched into the matter of Philip's leaving.

"*I* have known Philip since the first day he came to Messiah. As a matter of fact, I was a member of the committee that selected Philip. I find it hard to believe some of the things I heard you say in the Board meeting. Beside's that, I think that Ministers of the Church ought to set an example."

Dan was worried about the smile on Dave's face.

"I have missed many of the services lately. Haven't you missed me? . . . Well, I didn't come because I didn't think I'd get very much out of the service, what with feeling as I do now."

Sam repeated himself once and yet again. Without waiting for Dan to make reply, he stalked away, red-faced and positive.

Dan was worried about Dave's laugh. "My, the saints are restless today."

Dan learned – again from Fred and Marge Hudson – that Dave attended an Easter Sunday service. David made no secret of his coming, for on both occasions he had gone to see his mother – who called Dan each time. Dan thought he should try to speak with Dave, and after several futile attempts encountered Dave one day outside the Pro Shop at the Country Club. Over lunch, Dan found Dave to be gracious and most pleasant company. With very little probing, Dave gave a most articulate expression of purpose-lessness. Dan thought his efforts to respond were fumbling at best, and he found himself without reply when Dave referred to Sam Stockwell and said, "If that is what Christianity can do for a man . . ."

It was an early spring afternoon when Mary met Dan at the door and asked him to look for Mark and bring him home. Debbie said that Mark had gone to Bob Luke's for something. Dan walked down Church Street to the corner, turned north and came to a large house in the middle of a long block. Going up on the porch, Dan saw four buttons and pushed the button beneath a mailbox with the name "M. M. Luke". He did not sense any ring inside the building, so he tried the front door, which opened into a large central hall. He went to a door with an aluminum numeral "1"; in the old days it had opened into the parlor. Loud, angry voices inside stopped suddenly with his knock. The door was opened by a young man, barefoot and wearing a soiled T-shirt. Dan introduced himself and held out his hand. Matt Luke looked around for a place to set the bottle he was holding, and finally took it in his left hand to shake the hand which Dan offered.

'Yes, Mark had been there. He had picked up a ball and left for home, probably by a short cut through the alley. It was good to meet the minister. Excuse my appearance, but I have just come home from work. Yes, he and Lois had talked about coming to church, and they knew that they should. Yes, they would try to come next Sunday.'

Dan told Mary that maybe university and seminary training made a person like him less capable of speaking meaningfully with people like Matt.

Dan was invited to State University to be a panel member of a Student Activities program on "Religion in the Modern World." He was the Vesper Preacher for a Pastors' Pre-Lenten Retreat. He reported to Mary, "A year ago most of them did not know or much care that I existed, but now they are making notes on what I say." Then he was at Huron College for Religious Emphasis Week; there was a return invitation to speak at the baccalaureate service, and the college awarded him a "Doctor of Divinity" degree in the commencement exercises.

The first evening at home, Dan suggested to Mary, "Perhaps you would feel more at ease if you addressed me as 'Dr. Clark' in our personal conversations."

"Sorry, but I knew you when. I am certain that Miss Hazel will find it much easier to refer to the Pastor as 'Dr. Clark,' as I am also reasonably sure that your presence will be even more formidable to Lois."

Dan acknowledged that it might be all right to be "*Dr.* Daniel Witt Clark," but he wished the title would do something to help him reach Dave and Matt for Jesus Christ.

YEAR TWO
at
MESSIAH CHURCH

September came with a common feeling of a new spirit in Messiah Church. There was now an 8:30 Service of Worship that was well attended, and the sanctuary was filled for the 11:00 Service. The former used car lot across the street had been purchased and a contract had been awarded to have it paved. The morale of the Staff was high. They had learned to know and to trust one another; to a considerable extent their programs were in place. Church organizations possessed enthusiastic leadership. Some additional renovation and restoration work had been done so that the building and property were a gleaming spot on Columbia.

In comparing notes, Dan and Andy had observed a significant number of housing units in the area that had been abandoned, with some of them having already been razed. On Columbia Avenue there seemed to be more business places standing empty with "FOR SALE / RENT" signs in dirty front windows.

Several stories had appeared in the newspapers about "The Bishop's Fund." The Bishop had been going about and speaking to churches and individuals about the Fund, which was for the purpose of buying property, erecting buildings, making loans, paying salaries – whatever was necessary for the establishment of new churches in the new and growing suburban developments. His enthusiasm was unbounded. The Bishop was not displeased with stories about the fund that referred to him as "a modern St. Paul."

One of the sites already purchased was in Cedar Knoll. A

team of seminary students had been working during the summer to make a religious census of this area, in addition to several other real estate developments. The Bishop's Fund had reached a level of usefulness. The time had arrived to begin the program of founding new churches. The Bishop telephoned Dan.

Dan sat in an arm chair in the Bishop's office, the place where he had been eighteen months before.

"Dan, I hear so many good things about Messiah Church."

"Thank you. We are grateful for encouragements."

"And how is Mary?" Dan replied that she was fine. "And Debbie and Mark?" Dan made the same reply. "You have a wonderful family." Dan nodded in agreement, but it was all too obvious that the Bishop had not invited him for a conference to discuss his family . . . He would have let Ada do that.

The Bishop picked up a letter opener and examined it minutely. He mused, "You know, of course, of the proposed new church development program."

"Yes. Messiah Church has made a contribution to The Bishop's Fund."

"Yes, a very generous response indeed." He moved about in his chair; he didn't want to talk about money now. "This whole program is the reason why I wanted to see you today."

Dan was alerted. "Oh?"

"Yes, I want you to let Messiah Church see that there is a way to new life and spirit."

Dan suppressed a response to say that Messiah Church did have new life and spirit. He waited.

"We have the results of a religious census which was done in Cedar Knoll. There are some of our people living there, including some from Messiah Church."

"I suppose that Fred and his people have done their usual good selling job." They both smiled at the thought of a friend.

"Yes, Fred has been a prime mover in this area . . . We have title to a site in Cedar Knoll, and we want to establish a new church there . . . It has occurred to me that there would be a new spirit of adventure and challenge if you would take the lead in urging members of Messiah Church to colonize this new church."

Dan sat up straight. *Now* he had the message. "You mean you want *me* to *urge* people to le*ave* Messiah Church?" . . . .

The Bishop cleared his throat. Perhaps he had not stated the matter as well as he had hoped to do. "Not just you, Dan . . . I am thinking of Messiah Church as a whole . . . as a church reaching out to meet the challenge of Twentieth Century urban life and growth."

"I know that we have some people who have built new homes in Cedar Knoll . . ."

The Bishop picked up a folder from his desk and opened it to look through sheets of paper which were enclosed.

"Here is a list of Messiah Church members which we made up from the census done this past summer." He handed a sheaf of papers to Dan.

The only sound in the room was the crackling of paper as Dan turned the pages. From sheet to sheet, Dan was shaking his head without realizing it.

"These are all fine people. In this list there must be a fourth – at least – of the present officers of Messiah Church."

"Yes, I know many of them well. They represent fine leadership for the solid grounding of a new church."

"And the destruction of an old church!" Dan's words rushed out. As he placed the sheets back on the Bishop's desk, he tried to speak slowly, picking his words. "I should be less than honest if I did not say that we should definitely miss leadership of the number and caliber represented among the people on that list . . . To lose them would be little short of an outright disaster!"

The Bishop rose. This wasn't going as he had intended. Dan was not catching his vision! He walked about the room, speaking all the while with great animation.

"Dan, let's look on this as a *new seizing* upon the Kingdom of God . . . . I should hope that Messiah Church would give up three hundred of her people . . . and by this sacrifice . . . for it would be a sacrifice . . . find an *exciting, living spirit* within herself . . . a spirit to develop *new leadership* . . . a new commitment to *evangelism* to replace each of these persons with *two* souls brought into the fellowship of the church . . .

Dan, I have every confidence in *your* ability to make the *most* of this *opportunity* . . . *You know* that I do not want to *take from* Messiah Church, which is *close to my heart* . . . I'd like to feel that I was *giving* something to Messiah . . . giving an opportunity to accept a challenge . . . an opportunity for the Kingdom . . . an *opportunity* to become a *stronger* church."

After a time the Bishop resumed his place behind the desk. Dan reached out to take up the folder enclosing the list of Messiah people living in Cedar Knoll. Both Dan and the Bishop rose to acknowledge that the meeting was ended. Dan leaned forward to face the Bishop directly. He spoke softly: "I shall go now. I shall present this matter to the Official Board . . . I must tell you now that *I* regard this as a deliberate and unconscionable attack upon Messiah Church."

Cedar Knoll and the Bishop's proposal was the subject for long and serious discussion in two special meetings of the Official Board. They finally decided – with at least half of the Board abstaining in the formal vote – that they would encourage members of Messiah Church living in Cedar Knoll to colonize the Cedar Knoll Community Church.

The Bishop "asked" that there be a special service on a Sunday morning in which the people would be formally commissioned to go out and establish a new church. The Bishop took over preparation for the service until Dan felt himself to be little more than an observer in his own church. Newspapers carried accounts of the event with what for Dan was a maddening repetition of the phrase "Mother Church."

On the second Sunday of November, the Bishop pushed his oratorical limits in extolling Messiah Church for its "vision" and "sacrifice" and "response to the challenge of the modern city."

The members who were to colonize the Cedar Knoll Church were seated together in the sanctuary; Dan looked upon this group and tried to picture the church in coming weeks without these people. He had difficulty, indeed he found it impossible to "enter into the great inspiration of this present hour in the life and work of Messiah Church."

In the weeks that followed, Dan and the Staff worked under considerable pressure to rebuild a working parish organization. Kathryn Mac sought help from Dan and Andy for suggestions to make replacements in the staff of the educational program,. The counselors for the Senior High Fellowship had gone to Cedar Knoll – and as Kathryn said, "They were *good!*" The Official Board combined committees and adjusted responsibilities until there could be an election to replace Board members now gone. The new Chairman of the Finance Committee, who had replaced Al Hirter, said that they would make the current year's budget, but that it would be necessary to revise the budget for the coming year.

Al Hirter had come to see Dan to say how sorry he was to be leaving Messiah Church.

"For years I have campaigned to do the renovation work, and now that we are finally getting it accomplished . . . here I am leaving it all. I want you to know, Dan, that I wouldn't be doing this if George had not come to me personally to insist that I was the key to the financial success of this new venture."

"I didn't know that Bishop Gossert had entered personally into what I thought were individual decisions . . ."

"Betty and I have promised each other that we will come back to Messiah when we are starved for some good preaching . . . Then, too, let me say that I'll be glad to take good care of you any time you have car problems."

As Al left the Study, Dan was thinking that it was much easier to make car payments than it was to get a man of ability to dedicate his personal gifts to the church – a man such as Al Hirter.

Dan and Andy took personal responsibility and gave leadership to redoubled efforts to build the membership of the church. They did so, knowing that their best efforts would not stand off the inevitable: Messiah Church would show a decline in membership for the year.

Dave Schuster found a subdued Dan when they had lunch

together two or three weeks after the "day of opportunity" in Messiah Church.

"You seem preoccupied today, Dan."

"I'm sorry, Dave. I'm not very good company, I suppose. We have not a few problems to work out."

"I was in the 'Cedar Knoll service,' if that is what is involved. Maybe I shouldn't tell you, but Mother is disgusted with George. She is threatening to call 'St. Paul' and ask for the return of her gift to The Bishop's Fund . . . I can imagine that this has created difficulties for you."

Dave seemed to be very understanding. Dan spoke to him: "Yes, Dave, we have the problem of recruiting and training a group of new leaders in the church . . ."

Dan was looking at him too directly, so Dave changed the subject.

In the first week of December an ebullient Bishop called Dan.

"Dan, I wanted you to know that Cedar Knoll has been self-supporting from the very first Sunday."

Dan made no response.

The new Finance Committee prepared a revised budget, and was asking for a supplementary fund drive. The Nominating Committee was working on nominations for new officers and they had asked Dan for suggestions. He was working in his den when Carol called to say that Mrs. Larry Gossert wanted to see him if he would come to the office.

"Hello, Gwen." Dan motioned her to a seat and pulled up a chair for himself. "How are you, and Larry, and the girls?"

Gwen touched her eyes with a handkerchief. "Excuse me. That's being terribly feminine."

"That's all right. Come now. Talk to me."

Gwen clasped and unclasped her hands. She pulled her handkerchief from her purse to have something to hold.

" I came to see you about Larry. He has left."

"Left? Left for where? And why?"

"He moved out. He won't take my calls at his office . . . I have come to see if you would talk with him."

Dan was wishing he had told Carol to say that he was "out."

"I don't want to seem indifferent, but you have a pastor. Really, Gwen, you should talk with him."

Gwen's words were impatient. "It wouldn't do any good to talk with Mr. Williamson. Larry doesn't care for him, and he has not attended church for weeks and weeks." Gwen paused; her words now were more measured. "Dr. Clark, Larry was always very fond of you. He admired you so very much. If you would speak with him, I am sure that you could get this cleared up."

"Does the Bishop . . . do his father and mother know of this situation?"

Gwen was clearly startled. "Oh, my. No! I . . . we . . . don't want them to know."

"Gwen, I shoud be glad to help in any way I could, but I think you should first talk with your own Minister."

A perturbed Gwen left abruptly. When Larry would not answer her calls to his office, she did go to see Mr. Williamson, the Minister of St. John's. He told her that marital counseling was not his forte and that he would be pleased to have her confer with Dr. Clark. Mr. Williamson spoke to Bishop Gossert following a Rotary luncheon.

"I'm sorry that I could not help Larry and Gwen, but I know you would be glad for my suggestion they see Dr. Clark."

At Dan's invitation, Larry came and talked freely. He said that Gwen was always out somewhere on some "good cause." He told Dan he felt that he was little more than a source of money for Gwen and her ambitions for herself and their girls. He noted that she had buried him "up to here in debt." Gwen returned to say to Dan that she assumed Larry, being the son of the Bishop, would want his family to "be somebody." She was trying to do her best for their girls, and she thought Larry would be, and should be, proud of her roles in community affairs. Then, the three of them met in the Study. Finally, Larry and Gwen agreed to try again, to talk out their problems with each other, and to go to church together. Larry said he would like to bring his family to Messiah Church, but Gwen reminded him that the girls had so many of their friends at St. John's. In it all Dan tried to strike a spark in Larry; he wished Larry would become stirred up sufficiently to shout a little, or pound his fist on the table. Larry displayed only the deadness of defeat.

After Larry and Gwen left, Dan was thinking about them. His thoughts of Larry turned back upon himself.

"Why! I, Dan Clark, have let the problems created by the Cedar Knoll transfers become so big as to defeat me!'

The sight of a whipped man had excited his pity. The picture of Dan Clark as a whipped man . . . Well, that was too much! He shook himself. He prayed. He talked to himself. He was determined that he would not be a whipped loser. The Cause of Christ demanded something better. Almost daily his routine involved seeing people who had been bludgeoned by circumstances in their lives: job loss, career disappointment, family misunderstanding, breakup of a relationship, financial crisis and / or failure, death of a loved one, the demise of good hope, boredom in a lack of purpose for living, and on and on. He had confidently referred individuals – and congregations – to the resources in Christ for living. He recognized that he himself now stood in personal need of this help which he had too easily commended to others . . . By the grace of God, somehow he would manage to win.

Plans for Christmas celebration were called into question, but with extra effort by those remaining and many new recruits, everything was carried through with triumphal spirit. There was a feeling throughout the congregation as one Board member put it, "Messiah Church is still Messiah Church."

∝   ∝   ∝   ∝

January 6

Dear Mother and Daddy,

Since you left only two days ago, I don't know that I have enough news to warrant a postage stamp.

We were so glad to have you with us for Christmas and New Year's Day. Mark and Debbie feel so grown up since they were allowed to stay up on New Year's Eve. It was _good_ for all of us to be together around the fire in the fireplace.

The children are in school today. There was a story in the paper that the Principal of Lincoln School had received an appointment to some post in the school administration center. The Vice Principal is the Acting Principal. He is a black man. I have talked with him two or three times; he spoke in a P.T.A. meeting. He uses beautiful English — much better than two or three members of the School Board whom I have heard on TV. A decision on the new principal will be made at the next School Board Meeting.

This morning Lois told me _again_ how much she had enjoyed helping me make angel costumes for pre-schoolers in the Christmas program. As you know, the whole program at Christmas was so well received, and people continue to talk about it. Dan has been much encouraged by it. This has helped in some measure to balance the disappointment which he felt with the loss of membership in the church last year. He and Andy continue to work tirelessly, but it is especially good to have Dan in better spirit.

Since the last paragraph Dan came over to tell me about some plans for this summer. I think there had been some correspondence, but this morning he received a telephone call inviting him to be the Preacher for August at Glen Rock. And he had accepted! He said Glen Rock is an exclusive resort community in northern Michigan; they have a delightful chapel in the compound where they have services from June through August. They invite three ministers for one month each. They told Dan that they have a log house as a residence for the Minister and his family. It is completely furnished, *with dishes, linens and the daily services of a maid! Mark will be excited with the news that there are two boats – a sailboat and a motorboat of some type.*

Thanks for letting us know that you were home safely.

The telephone is ringing . . .

Love,

Mary

∝   ∝   ∝   ∝

Andy followed Dan into the Study at the conclusion of the weekly staff meeting and sat in a chair beside the desk.

"Dan, I had a letter at home last evening from Dr. Ted Martin. He could come for a Lenten series."

"As I told you, I think that such a series depends almost totally upon the leader. I know you mentioned his name, and I would trust your judgment. But tell me more about this man."

"He was a couple of years ahead of me in college, where we worked together at the student center. He went on to medical school, and then he became a medical missionary in Korea. He is now back in the States on a furlough, and he is doing a residency in pediatrics. Even so, his schedule permits him to have some time available once in a while for meetings or programs of this kind."

"What would he be doing? What might we hope to accomplish with him?"

"My plan would be to have Dr. Ted for a Sunday and three or four days following. He has pictures and artifacts for both children and young people. He could meet with men's and women's groups. We should allow time in the afternoons for personal conferences . . ."

"That would be . . ."

"One thing more. He believes in divine healing. Our Lynn seems to be holding her own, but Charlotte and I would cherish the opportunity for Dr. Ted to put his hand upon her and pray for her healing. So I guess that sometime in the schedule I would hope that we might have a service of divine healing."

Before Dan could reply, there was a knock on the door from Miss Hazel's office. The door opened and Mary looked in.

"Oh, I'm sorry. Hello, Andy. Miss Hazel thought that you were alone, Dan, but I'll see you later."

"I was just leaving, Mary. I'll write to Dr. Ted and make some suggestions for a schedule and the like . . . It's good seeing you, Mary."

Mary held the door open. "I feel as though I am interrupting."

Dan waved to Mary to come in. "Andy, why don't you phone Dr. Martin? You can clear up the details easier and faster."

Dan's words stopped Andy, who nodded and then went out. "You never interrupt anything for me, Mary. And besides, I'd rather talk to you because you're prettier than Andy."

Mary unbuttoned her coat and seated herself on the edge of the sofa. She spoke impulsively. "Dan, I came because this is serious. I have come now directly from a long time with Lois."

"What's the trouble today? More of the same?"

"That and more. This morning I asked Lois why she had quit coming to church and bringing the children to Sunday School. That did it! . . . She really opened up! Matt has lost his job! He had missed so many days, and he had showed up unfit for work so many times . . . Even the union wouldn't try to save his job. He has now been working at whatever jobs he could find. They simply have no money, but lots and lots of debts. Lois was really desperate, or I know she would not have spoken so freely. They had practically no food. They are six months behind in their rent. She said they quit coming to church and Sunday School because they didn't have money for the 'collection' – as she called it."

"That wouldn't make any difference . . ."

"Maybe not to you, but it makes a difference to Lois. Anyway, let me tell you what I did . . . First, I took Lois to the market; they *needed everything* . . . Dan, I feel guilty that someone so close to us should have been in such great need. Then, while we were in the car, I went around by Block & Co. – Lois objected strongly – and I gave Block's a check for two months' rent. I dropped Lois off at home and helped her carry things into the house and then came right over to tell you. It's all right, isn't it? I mean, we *can* afford that much till something can be worked out for them . . ."

"Yes, we can. And even if we couldn't, we should do that much and more, if necessary."

"Dan, Matt needs a job."

"Let me see what I can do, Mary. Bill Kuist said this morning in staff meeting . . . You sit right there for a minute."

Dan found Bill in the sanctuary. A few brief words and Dan was back.

"Bill says that he can use Matt for a couple weeks; he has a lot of things to pack up and store until next Christmas . . . But Bill also said, 'He'll have to show up sober.' And Matt can start today . . . right now."

Mary kissed Dan on the cheek. "Thank you, my dear. That's wonderful. Now I must go and tell Lois that it was all right for me to have spent the money without asking you first. She was worried . . . Miss Hazel wants to show me a couple things on the way out."

After Dr. Theodore Martin spoke in the morning services, so many people came in the evening without having made reservations that supper plans practically collapsed, but no one seemed to mind. Indeed, everyone was delighted as the crowd grew and grew until it was necessary to go from the social hall to the sanctuary for the evening meeting. Dr. Ted had a contagion for living which enthralled all who came into contact with him – including Dan. Andy had arranged a full schedule, with a service each night from Monday through Thursday. Small groups met in the morning. There was a men's luncheon on Monday, and a women's luncheon on Wednesday. There was a high school youth meeting and supper on Tuesday. Afternoons were set aside for personal conferences for anyone who might want to talk with Dr. Ted. The Wednesday evening service was set aside as a service of divine healing. Single young adults had a supper meeting with Dr. Ted which could last up until the time for the final service in the sanctuary to begin.

Dan stopped in the office on Wednesday afternoon, and Miss Hazel said he was wanted in the chapel. He went over to find Matt with Dr. Ted.

"Dr. Clark. Matt has something he wants to tell you."

"Dr. Dan. I've been saved."

"Tell me that again, Matt."

"I've been saved . . . converted . . . Right here . . . this afternoon."

"Yes, Dr. Clark. Matt came to see me this afternoon. We talked and we prayed. A little while ago Matt committed his life to Jesus Christ."

Matt was finding his tongue. "You know, Dr. Dan, that I've been havin' my share of trouble. I been thinkin' I wasn't right with the Lord. When I heard about these meetings, they kinda seemed like a revival to me. (Dr. Ted smiled.) So I came. Then it came to me that I'd kind of like to talk with Dr. Martin. I didn't tell Lois. Like he says, we talked, and he prayed, and I gave my life to Jesus. I even said a prayer myself."

"Matt, I'm more thankful than I can say."

Matt rose to his feet. "If you all will 'scuse me now, I think Lois'd like to know."

He started to turn to leave. "Things will be different now. You'll see."

The next morning in some free time, Dr. Ted was in the Study telling Dan of the people, the hospital, the program in Korea. Dan asked Dr. Ted, "Don't you get discouraged by the ignorance, the lack of adequate equipment and supplies, the loneliness, and all the rest?"

"Oh, Dan, there are always circumstances to discourage us if we look for them. There are always people to dishearten, if we allow them . . . But we Christians may live in the strength and by the promises of God. That changes our present outlook, and makes the future as bright as the assurances of God."

"Matt and Lois were in the meeting last night; I'm sure that they came to you. I don't know which was the happier."

Ted nodded and smiled. "I like to think how fortunate I am to be Christian. Now then, what did I do? Not very much. really. But I had the privilege of seeing the work of God. As I see it, a farmer ploughs, sows, cultivates, and God gives the increase which he reaps. Or, in my work, I probe, I prescribe drugs, I perform surgery . . . and it is God who heals. In something of the same way, we teach the Word, we bear our witness, but it is God Who works and by Whom alone men are born anew."

Dan was sober. "Goodness knows, I tried to help Matt . . ."

"Best of all, Dan, is that whether I am in Korea, or here in Indianapolis, or wherever – I may live in a personal relationship with my Lord."

Andy burst into the room. "Dr. Ted, I've got to tell you. You know that we brought Lynn last evening. This morning both Charlotte and I thought she seemed different somehow. We decided that we had to know. I called the doctor, and then took them to the medical center. The doctor has agreed to run some tests on Lynn starting this morning."

There were many and significant changes in Messiah Church in the days and weeks following the visit of Dr. Ted. Dan found himself recalling again and again the inner strength and the sense of Presence which Dr. Ted possessed. He read and reread the portions of the Scriptures to which Dr. Ted had made reference. He tried to tell Mary of his efforts to get a new hold upon his life and work in Messiah Church. He talked with Matt on several opportunities, and questioned him closely. Andy and Charlotte repeated again and yet again the results of the latest series of tests on Lynn, for there was no trace of the life-threatening illness; however, they were to keep in close touch with the Medical Center and bring Lynn back for routine testing. They told everyone how they looked forward to bringing her to Sunday School for the first time; they spoke to each other of their hope that maybe they might have another child. Members of the congregation compared notes with one another to mark some words which they thought Dan was now using more frequently: "redemption," "Saviour," "transformation," "new birth," "the Holy Spirit."

David Schuster sat across the table from Dan to have lunch. He listened to Dan for a time and then spoke lightly, "Dan, my friend, if you are going to talk like this, you should really mount a neon sign in front of the church. The sign should read: 'Messiah Gospel Tabernacle.'"

Dan smiled. "Maybe so, Dave. What I really want is for you to give the living Christ a chance to come into your mind and heart. I don't want public displays of any kind; my great desire is for you to let Jesus Christ control your life. He can do what you cannot do for yourself, and what no one else can do for you. I pray for His working, and not words – in neon or otherwise."

"I'm sorry, Dan. You *are* in dead earnest about this, aren't you? All of this is something concerning which I have no knowledge whatsoever. It is another language to me."

The word was out, somehow, and Holy Week in Messiah exceeded anything in recent memory. On Palm Sunday the sanctuary was "beginning to look full." Andy asked and was given permission to have a "Healing Service" on Wednesday night. Maundy Thursday Communion services started at 12 noon, and continued on a two-hour schedule. Easter Sunday there was a large congregation at 8:30 and the sanctuary was filled at 11:00. Andy conducted additional services in the chapel at 8:30 and 11:00. The newspaper on Monday featured a picture of a large crowd on the sidewalk and the steps to the main entrance.

Two weeks after Easter the Staff and the officers of Messiah Church were still exuberant. Bishop Gossert called and asked Dan and Andy to come to his office for a conference.

The Bishop began without any formalities to question Dan closely about Messiah Church and the Lenten program. With only an occasional recognition of Andy, the Bishop changed the thrust of his questions. The atmosphere in the room became more and more charged as Dan made response to the Bishop's inquiries which became increasingly personal.

Dan held up his hand to stop the Bishop in mid-sentence. "Bishop Gossert, you obviously have something in mind, and I think we might as well get to the substance of the matter. Why don't you just state the problem as you see it?"

The Bishop paused to collect his thoughts and choose his words. "Well, Dan, word has come to me several times over about you becoming *radical*."

Andy had been apart from the conversation, but he now called for attention. "To all the gossips who have been trying to hang labels on Dan and Messiah Church, I would volunteer one very personal word . . . Tell them to come and read the test results and diagnosis on my Lynn, before and after . . . before and after the work of God in her body . . . Bishop Gossert! My child is a living, growing, happy miracle! Just to see her now . . . Well, I think that anyone would go about saying, 'Praise the Lord!'"

Andy was surprised at himself, and he settled back after this outburst. The point was not lost on the Bishop who wanted to change the subject and seemed sorry that he had ever brought up the whole matter. He straightened up in his chair and started again to speak in formal fashion.

"We have been diverted from the reason that I asked you both to come in today . . . As you know our program to establish new churches in the housing developments about the city is underway. It received a most auspicious beginning in the colonization of the Cedar Knoll Church. This church is doing very well, and the congregation is in the first stage of a building program already . . ."

He paused for some response but Dan and Andy sat quietly.

" . . . We have a group meeting in Lewiston, which is on the very edge of our jurisdiction. There is good reason for us to give immediate attention to an area known as Brookmede. I have here the results of our survey, if you would like to to see it . . ."

"Andy and I know the Messiah people in that area."

"The reason that I called you is that I thought that the commissioning service which we had for Cedar Knoll was a great event and provided high inspiration for the new church . . . and for Messiah Church, and I was thinking that . . ."

"Bishop Gossert, if you are talking about another service in Messiah Church to signal the raiding of the Messiah Church membership, let's understand each other. The answer is 'No.'"

The Bishop was clearly stunned by Dan's bluntness. "Dan, I don't understand. I thought everything went so well. I told you that Cedar Knoll has been self-supporting from the first Sunday. And I must take exception to your use of the word 'raiding.' We are only trying to meet the needs of an expanding metropolitan area. Brookmede has grown to the point that it possesses both numbers and character."

"Unless I am mistaken you are talking about something more than two hundred Messiah members in Brookmede, and another two hundred in Glen Valley. If not now, very soon you will be back regarding another one hundred and eighty-five in Coventry . . ."

"What, or how do you know about . . . The Bishop's Fund committee has been working in strict confidence . . ."

"As you said, Bishop Gossert, people talk . . ."

There was no disguising that the Bishop was taken aback. So Dan continued. "The loss of the Cedar Knoll people was a staggering blow. Andy and I have worked and worked to rebuild the leadership and the organization of Messiah Church which is facing an increasing challenge by the shifting urban patterns of life and work. And now, three more blocks of members to be deleted. That's about one thousand members pulled out of Messiah Church! And to be quite frank, I do not see this kind of load being placed upon other city churches. Why is it that Messiah almost singly gets this load? No. This program simply represents the elimination of Messiah Church. I would rather that we just took one Sunday and carved up the membership of

Messiah and dispersed all of it's members to close the church down. That would be simpler and more gracious than its calculated destruction over a period of time."

Dan's passion filled the room. Andy had never seen Dan let himself go in such abandon. The Bishop was backed away from all thought of the moment, as well as the program which presumably this occasion was to forward.

Suddenly, Dan heard himself and caught himself. Regardless of how he felt, what he may have thought, the weariness of mind and body which seemed at times to drain him of everything but sheer existence . . . he knew that he never had the right, or privilege, of losing control of himself to this extent. He was surprised and ashamed at this display of inner weakness . . .

"I am sorry. I speak out of turn. I must be and I can be better than this." He stood up and faced the Bishop. "My apologies, sir. When you start these churches, we shall issue letters of transfer for the individuals involved. I repeat, however, that I cannot accept such diminution of our strength and celebrate it as a triumph for the Cause of Christ in this city."

Andy caught the signals and rose to follow Dan from the room. They drove back to the church without speaking.

YEAR THREE
AT
MESSIAH CHURCH

September 8

Dear Mother and Daddy,

I just wanted to let you know that we are home and getting settled. Especially, I want to thank you for letting me come with the children at the end of the school term and be with you there in Rockford, until time for us all to go to Glen Rock. I can appreciate that we upset your routine, but it was especially good for the children to be out of the city.

I was sorry to be away from Dan for these summer weeks. I told him that I did not like leaving him here by himself for all of this time, but that I thought it was best for the children.

I know I have already said it, but I must repeat that Glen Rock was lovely. There is a beautiful rustic chapel. I know that they were more than pleased to have Dan as the minister for a month. They have already invited us back for next summer.

Dan is in staff meeting this morning. I know that Dan is concerned about the church; while we were away, his conversations kept coming back to the church. Last year some three hundred members left to establish the Cedar Knoll Church — you know, the suburb I showed you. The Bishop has started two more churches, with a third just announced. Two or three industries have closed down; quite a number of our people were transferred or laid off.

The house looks pretty good after being away for three

months. We are having a staff dinner in a couple weeks, and I shall get some help to clean and prepare.

We stopped in Fairfield on the way home. When we arrived, Dan left us at the motel, saying that he had an appointment. Later he told me that some men had come to see him at Glen Rock; he has been invited to become the Pastor of the University Church in Fairfield. I hope he will accept it.

When I went to pick up Mark and Debbie at school yesterday, it seemed to me that Lincoln School was much more black than last spring. I have heard that some black families are now living on this side of Broad. There are many, many "For Sale" signs all over the area around us.

Debbie is happy to have school begin again. Mark is too — but he won't admit it.

Thank you again, with love,

Mary

∝ ∝ ∝ ∝

Dan admitted to himself that he was swimming against the current when he had declined the invitation to go to University Church. He had so many friends and acquaintances on the State campus that it would have been a virtual homecoming. Mark and Debbie would have attended the University Laboratory School with many educational advantages. Mary would have delighted in the circle of acquaintances and the round of activities which Fairfield offered. Dan would have had a ministry to the university community, and it could not be denied that this would be a position of untold influence.

But Dan said "No."

When he finally told Mary of his decision she said to him, "Dan, I used to think that no disappointment would exceed my experience when you accepted the call to Messiah Church, but I find myself even more disappointed that you have not accepted this invitation to University Church. This represented for me a bright and promising future for all of us. I will never understand your decision – or the reasons for it. I do know that I feel as though light, and promise, and hope have been eliminated from our future."

It was late, and they were alone in the living room.

"I am truly sorry to disappoint you, Mary. I can tell you truthfully that I should like to be in University Church for many reasons. However, it would be a piety which I do not possess for me to say that I did not have 'the call' to University Church. I have been here in Messiah for . . . what? . . . for two and one half years. Much of this time has been rough, and frankly, I think it is getting worse . . . With the apprehension of trying to sound noble or pious, I think I have a responsibility to Messiah Church to stay here until the church has regained her stride . . . until we have established a new program that is going and growing. Then, and only then, I would feel free to leave. If it were left to me, and if I was to be honest . . . I'd like to leave yesterday."

Mary was not to be persuaded. Moving to Fairfield became her cause. Any conversation with Dan was quickly turned to a renewal of the consideration to move now. Dan thought that he knew his own mind, but his inability to convince Mary to look at the situation from his point of view became increasingly frustrating. Their discussions became arguments. There was no new ground to be covered. Mark and Debbie became subdued with the realization that their home was dominated by a strained relationship between their parents.

For want of some new perspective, Dan simply told Mary that he was going to be away for two or three days; he went to Belvoir, to talk at length with his father and mother who listened to Dan's recital of his situation. His mother spoke only once.

Dan said, "I am having to take a whole new look at my marriage. In our discussions, I have learned where I stand with Mary. As I have come to see it, Mary has a set of priorities in her love: First, of course, come Mark and Debbie; then there are her Mother and Father in that order; then Mary's own view of herself as a person in society; then there are cultural and social activities; and I guess that I appear somewhere down the list, if at all."

His mother was quick in her defense of Mary. "Dan, I think that I know Mary and her values. I think you are being unfair in such a picture of her. You are *my* son and I don't know of any woman to whose care I could commit my son with greater confidence than Mary. Whatever you may decide to do about your work is one thing, but don't let this color nor compromise your appreciation of what you have in Mary as your wife."

Dan mumbled his apologies and said something about letting things get out of hand in this issue.

Dan didn't know what to expect of his father, but when he had said everything two or three times, he just stopped and waited for his father to say his first word. After a long silence, during which Dan wondered if his father was going to say anything at all, his father's words came out deliberately.

"Dan, I cannot adequately judge your potential for service in one parish over against the other . . . If you are going to serve the Lord Jesus Christ usefully, I think that you must have an absolute integrity of person. I wouldn't presume to tell you what to do in this instance. I can say that I hope your decision will leave you with the feeling that you are a whole person, that you have not compromised yourself before God nor man."

Dan's mother kissed him before he got into his car. Dan's father embraced him, and stepped back, smiling, to say, "Dan, I don't want to complicate your situation further, but Redstone needs an engineer with executive leadership."

Dan returned to say to Mary that his reply to University Church would still be "No."

Mary did not say a word. They were in the den and she rose and walked from the room, The children knew at dinner that there was a family problem, making specific note that their mother and father did not speak to each other during the meal. Dan rose from the table to go out. The house was dark and quiet when he returned late. Mary was not in their bedroom, but he found her in one of the twin beds in the guest room. The next day, somehow – Dan never knew how it was accomplished – she exchanged the bed in the master bedroom for the twin beds in the guest room. University

Church in Fairfield was a closed issue; it was never again a subject of conversation in the residence of the Minister.

The only officer or lay person in Messiah Church with whom Dan spoke about the invitation from University Church was Fred Hudson. Fred left no doubt as to his opinion.

"I must say, Dan, that I think it would be devastating to Messiah Church if you were to leave now. The people know you, and like you, and trust you. We were really beginning to make progress until 'St. Paul' got started on his program. I don't know why, but there is no question that he has laid the chief burden of this whole program on Messiah Church – on you and Andy. There is no question of the utter devastation that this has wrought in Messiah Church, and the end is not yet. I don't like to lay this burden with you, but if you were to leave at this particular time, I do not think that Messiah Church would survive."

Whatever his role as Pastor of Messiah Church might involve, Dan told an uninterested Mary that there was always something different to keep his life from getting into a rut.

It was a pleasant autumn day, and Dan decided to go to two hospitals which were within walking distance. He was roused from a preoccupation with his thoughts concerning the church by a glad shout.

"Revner Dan!"

Dan swung about to this familiar address.

"Tom! Tom Davis!" He put out his hand to see it disappear in a two-handed grasp. "What on earth are you doing here?"

"I move here, Revner Dan." He continued to hold and to pump Dan's hand. "My, O my! It's good to see you!"

"Doggone it! It's good to see *you*, Tom. Where are you going?" Tom let go with one hand to point. "Good. I'm headed that way. Come. Walk with me. I'm going to a hospital."

"I'll walk with you, Revner Dan." He fell into step beside Dan. "You know I don' hold much for hospitals . . . but I'd go about any place with you."

Seated in the hospital coffee shop, Dan learned that Tom had come to Indianapolis only the day before with the intent to buy and operate a Gulf service station on Broad Street.

"Revner Dan, you always tell me I ought to have my own place."

"That's right, Tom. You have the touch, and you have *one* regular customer already."

"Thanks, Revner Dan. You always say to me, 'Tom, you ought to have your own place.' I work for other people since I was a little boy, and everybody like my work . . . But you the only one who ever say to me, 'Tom Davis, you ought to have *your own place.*' I think about it. And I think about it. I talk to Rose about it. I pray about it. Finally, I say to myself, 'Tom Davis, if Revner Dan say you ought to have your own place, then you get out and get your own place.'"

"Where is this service station?"

"Broad and Fifth. Mista Brownlee, a white man own it. Down in Pawley, I hear from the gas truck driver that Mista Brownlee wanta sell. So I come. And I have my own place next Monday."

Listening to Tom, Dan became uneasy. He said, "Tom, I want to make a suggestion. I think you ought to have this whole deal, checked by a lawyer. Just sit there a minute."

Dan went to a telephone and called Jerry Whitman; he told Jerry the story and asked for his help. he returned to the table to write Jerry's address on the back of one of his calling cards. They walked outside the main entrance of the hospital, and Dan gave Tom directions on how to find Jerry's office.

A depressed Tom was waiting for Dan at the church when he returned. Dan got him into a chair in the Study and asked Tom to tell him what happened.

"Revner Dan, Mr. Whitman don' like my deal. He call Mr. Brownlee, and Mr. Brownlee get mad because I see a lawyer. Now Mr. Brownlee want more money for the contract Mr. Whitman say I need. I don' have more money, Revner Dan. I'm 'fraid I lose my whole deal for a place of my own."

"Tom, Jerry knows what he is doing. Now, trust him." Dan called Jerry, who had been talking with an acquaintance in the regional sales office of the oil company. "Tom, Jerry says for you to come to his office tomorrow at 3:30. They hope to have the deal in proper shape for you by then."

Jerry was overly optimistic. It had become obvious that an up-to-date inventory and audit were needed. With some difficulty, Dan was persuading Tom every day to be patient. When the whole deal was set, Tom had been delayed one week in taking over operation of his own place. It would cost him one-third less, and he had an option from the oil company to purchase the whole site of which the station occupied only a part.

"Mista Whitman, how much do I owe you?"

Jerry reached out first to shake Dan's hand. "Tom, if Dan will preach an extra good sermon next Sunday, you and I are even. Of course, if I can do some legal work for you some time in the future, I'll get my money *from you* then." Now Jerry was shaking Tom's hand.

It was the third week of October when the Official Board met to discuss the budget for the coming year. It was another occasion to make Dan regret his decision to remain at Messiah Church. At one point the meeting lost all semblance of an orderly conduct of business. Everyone seemed to have something to say:

"I think we are doing fairly well financially, considering . . ."

"Yes, considering all the people we have lost . . ."

"Last Easter was the high point . . ."

"Yes, but since then the succession of blows . . ."

"And how? Three hundred to Cedar Knoll originally . . . then two hundred or more to Brookmede . . . another two hundred to Glen Valley . . . most recently one hundred and eighty-five, or more to Coventry . . ."

"And that's not the end of it from what I hear . . ."

"The Bishop says that the Church must act to meet the challenge of the modern city . . ."

"Fine, but why does George Gossert want to wreck Messiah Church?"

"He says that he is giving Messiah Church an opportunity to grow in meeting the challenge of the contemporary . . ."

"Nah . . . I think Gossert is carried away with this St. Paul image bit . . ."

"We lost a lot of good people when Master Appliances shut down. . ."

"And a lot of members moved just to get out of this area . . ."

"Some black people have started to come to the 11:00 o'clock service . . ."

"The children from three or four black families started this month to come to Sunday School . . ."

"My wife said they were scrubbed and wearing new clothes."

"Kathryn Mac told me they were accepted simply as new children . . ."

"I think our people deserve a lot of credit . . ."

"It isn't that we have just lost numbers. We've lost a lot of heavy givers . . ."

"Yes, but there are more new members than any time I can remember – thanks to the work of Dr. Clark and Mr. Anderson . . ."

"Don't these new people contribute?"

"Some of them just don't have it to give . . ."

"Right! Take an example. I don't like to mention names, but Matt Luke can't afford to give what Al Hirter used to give."

"What we really need is more people with money . . ."

"Dr. Clark, could we concentrate our new member efforts for a while on people of substance . . . ?"

All faces turned to Dan and Andy, and the room became quiet.

"We cannot seek to win men and women for Christ on the basis of their financial position. It is the task of the Christian Church to declare that the offer of God's redeeming grace in Jesus Christ is for all persons. I think that we must sustain our witness to all people, regardless . . ."

"But we need money," came from every part of the room. They were not voices of opposition. They were voices of concern and uncertainty . . . even desperation.

Dan tried again. "I know we have financial problems. If Messiah Church is to function, we must have the money to pay our bills. We are called to seek first the kingdom of God, and to trust that in God our needs will be met." Dan paused to look about the room, and then he continued with a wry smile. "I guess maybe you would find fifteen or twenty sizeable new gifts to be helpful in believing that word. So we understand one another, a dozen such contributions would be encouraging to me, too."

The schedule between Christmas and New Year's day was light. Miss Hazel had gone to visit a married sister in Chicago, and Dan insisted that Kathryn Mac and Andy get away. Volunteers were substituting for Carol for this period. Mary and the children had left for Rockford about noon on Christmas day. Her mother had undergone surgery the day after Thanksgiving, and she could not yet travel. Mr. Hudson, however, was busy preparing the annual financial statement, and setting up the books for the coming year. There was no sound of telephone, typewriter, or organ.

Matt Luke – who was now the Caretaker – was removing holiday decorations and putting the whole building to rights. Dan went into the sanctuary to seat himself in a pew about halfway down the center aisle. The sanctuary decorations were lovely, and they would keep them through the following Sunday. Dan thought about Messiah Church. 'Things could be worse.'

1. Membership would be down seriously for the year. In addition to other normal losses, they had transferred about six hundred persons to the new church developments.

2. Attendance in the services, the Sunday School, and the parish groups had declined.

3. By the second week of December there were funds in hand to pay all bills for the year.

4. He still had a staff of loyal and capable co-workers. Individually and together, there was no better leadership available.

5. He had the companionship and the power of One greater than all things earthly and human.

Finally, Dan stirred from his lost sense of time. Returning to the office door, he saw a woman coming slowly down the corridor, looking about as though to gather it all in. Dan walked to her and introduced himself.

"I am pleased to meet you, Dr. Clark. I am Anna Schuster."

Dan groped desperately for a moment. He regularly visited Mrs. Schuster, who was now confined to her bed. He never told her of long talks with David, who spoke freely, asked many questions, and was always willing to get together another time. Of course, he would not tell of such encounters with Dave as he experienced the week before Christmas.

Dan was not sure what he might have said or done. It had seemed the thing for him to say, "Dave, it says in John 1:12, 'As many as received Him . . .'"

Dave had flared up and backed away in unexpected fashion. "Oh, come off it, Dan. Don't try your evangelist pitch on me – 'Come to Jesus, and everything will be all right.' Keep that soul-saving routine for fellows like your *caretaker*. Tell me, Dan, how much of a bounty has my mother offered you for my poor sinner's scalp?"

But, Dave had come to the Christmas Eve Service.

Dave's wife! Anna . . . Nan! Of course! There was a picture of her with two small children on Cora Schuster's bedside table. This was *Nan*! Of course! Dan tried to speak in a quiet voice.

"It's good to meet you. I've heard so much about you that I should have recognized you . . . Please . . . would you care to come into the Study?"

"Thank you. It's good to meet you; I've heard much about you. We were in the Christmas Eve Service . . . I have been walking about through the church. It is now a long time since I have been here." She stopped to look into the church office, and then back down the corridor. "Everything looks much as I remembered – only better."

Dan led the way into the Study.

"I think I was in this room only once in my life."

Dan didn't know what he had expected Nan to be, but for some reason he was unprepared for the beautiful woman he was now seeing. The best he could manage was, "We are delighted to have you in Messiah Church again."

After seating herself Nan spoke. "We heard that Mother Schuster is not at all well. It seemed to work out for the children to spend Christmas here with her."

"From all she has said, I *know* what joy she must have in seeing her grandchildren . . . And I hope that you will all enjoy your time here."

"We were happy that our schedule permitted us to be in the Christmas Eve Service. Peggy and Kurt and I enjoyed it very much. Mother Schuster was thrilled to hear them say that they want to come again on Sunday before we leave."

Dan was groping for words. "I probably should not ask, but I shall . . ."

Nan smiled. "You want to ask whether we have seen Dave." Dan nodded. "The answer is that we have not seen him. This was a trip to see Mother Schuster." Nan put one glove in her lap, then laid the other exactly on top and smoothed them "There would be no point . . . in seeing Dave . . . I noticed that the house is closed and looks run-down . . . I don't know . . . where he is living . . . Mother Schuster has not mentioned Dave to me . . . And to tell the truth, it really is a matter of not thinking of him any more . . ." She looked up quickly. "Have you seen Dave?"

The subject was opened. "Oh, yes. I know Dave quite well. I see him from time to time, and he comes to service occasionally. Indeed, he was in the Christmas Eve Service."

"May I ask you something?" Nan was still wearing her coat and plastic boots.

Certainly, but wouldn't you be more comfortable if you took off your coat and removed your boots?"

Nan stood up and Dan went over to take her coat. As he was hanging the coat in a closet, Nan seated herself to slip off her boots. Dan set them in the closet and returned to his chair.

Nan glanced about the Study. She crossed her legs.

"Where shall I begin? I wanted to get away to do some thinking about myself." She tried to smile. "To tell you the truth, I am glad to find *you* here in your office; I did want to talk with someone."

Dan turned his hands, palms upward. "If I can help at all . . ."

"But I wouldn't want to take your time. After all, I am not a member of Messiah Church any longer."

"You are *not* . . . *taking* my time. Please."

"You know that Dave and I are not divorced. I am working . . . I think I should do something about my marital status . . . I am most happy in a good position . . . To continue to be married to Dave is rather pointless, really." She stopped and looked at Dan as though waiting for an answer.

"All right. I'll begin by saying what a Minister is expected to say. Marriage vows are taken for life."

"I know, and I daresay this may be a subconscious reason why I have never done anything. My family are plain people (Dan thought that she certainly did not look 'plain.'), and divorce is completely unknown to them . . . But now Peggy and Kurt are in college, and I have found . . . ."

Dan supplied words. "Another interest?"

"If you mean 'someone else,' the answer is 'Yes.'"

"Tell me about him."

"I am an executive secretary in an insurance company. My immediate supervisor was asked to head up a community project, and he requested that I attend committee meetings and take notes. One of the members of the committee was especially nice. He is a bachelor. He is a doctor, who works as a medical officer for another insurance company . . . The children are away. I live by myself. To be honest – and I have come to the place where I *must* be honest – I was lonely. Lee – that's his name – is a wonderful person. Peggy and Kurt are very fond of him . . . Anyway, I was lonely, and he was lonely. We found that we have much in common. We like football . . . and we go to every musical event within reasonable distance."

Dan tried to remember a recent book on pastoral counseling which he had been reading. "Does this doctor – Lee have any interest in you other than as a social companion?" Dan thought that his question sounded stupid, but a light came to Nan's face.

"Oh, my goodness, yes! He has asked me *many, many* times to marry him. Of course, he knows that I am married . . . I tried to talk with Kurt and Peggy, but they have their own lives now . . . I think I am entitled to think about myself."

"Then why have you not filed for divorce?"

Nan shook her head. "I really don't know. That is partly why I made this trip. I guess I wanted to see if there is anything which holds me to the past."

"Does Lee (Dan felt awkward in calling him by name.) . . . does Lee know of this trip of decision, if I may call it that?"

"Indeed he does. He said that he was for anything that might work toward our getting married."

Dan worked on the adhesive of a bandage on his left thumb.

"And your relationship with this man? . . ."

Nan smoothed her gloves again. "He is a wonderful person . . . Lee is a gentleman, and a very gentle man. He is an officer in his church, which we attend regularly. He never married because he was an only son, and he cared for his mother until she died two or three years ago. Lee and I are about the same age."

"Well then, what is your problem as you see it?"

"I don't know." Nan opened her purse to rummage through it; taking nothing out, she closed her purse. Dan waited

"I should be going. I have taken too much of your time already." But she did not stand up.

"If he asked you to marry him, what have you said?"

"I told him that I couldn't, inasmuch as I am presently married."

Dan still fussed with the bandage in a most unprofessional manner.

"Have you got yourself involved with him?"

"Yes . . . I guess . . ."

"How much involved?"

Nan hesitated. She took a deep, audible breath. "All the way, I suppose one could say."

The room became frighteningly attentive.

"Do you want to talk about that?"

Nan uncrossed her legs and moved forward in her chair. She spoke more to plead than to discuss. "You must understand that there is nothing sordid about our relationship. It is a wonderful . . ." Her words came faster. "It was this way. One day we went to the beach. It was a beautiful day, and we had a great time. It was late when we finished our dinner at a most atmospheric shore restaurant. The next day neither of us had to be at work, or had to be anywhere for anybody. We were the only people who wanted us. So we stayed in a seaside hotel."

Nan stopped to sense Dan's reaction. His voice was non-committal. "Has your relationship continued on this basis?"

"Yes . . . And it has been wonderful." As Dan listened, she sounded warmly womanly.

"Do you think it is *right*, however wonderful it may be?"

Nan's voice leaped to the defense. "I have had no husband for *years*! I have taken care – and *good care* – of my children! I think I am deserving of *some* companionship and love!"

Dan spoke gently. "Do you think that this is right . . . before God?"

Nan colored. She lost her composure. "That is unfair!"

"It is never 'unfair' to inquire what the Lord might think of us and our actions."

Her irritation subsided in an apologetic voice. "It isn't really 'unfair.' I suppose that that is probably the question I came to discuss . . ." She asked to be excused. Dan secured her coat and boots; without putting them on, she walked rapidly from the Study and from the church.

Nan and Peggy and Kurt were in the service on Sunday morning. She asked Dan if she might see him at 4:00 o'clock in the afternoon, as they were to leave that night. Seated in the same chair as before, she picked up the discussion where they had left off earlier, and then waited for Dan to comment.

"He said, "There is a word in the Bible for this."

Her voice grated with annoyance. "That is not kind, Dr. Clark."

"Have you tried reading the Scriptures for yourself?"

"Yes, I have." Her voice begged for help. "I don't understand. I keep finding passages which make me feel that something which is so wonderful is really wrong somehow . . ."

"Then what do you *do* about it?"

"*I don't know*. I have come out on this trip hoping to receive help for making a decision. I'm sorry, but I seem to be going back with more confusion than before."

Dan tried to tell himself that he had said and done what was right, but he was uneasy in the persuasion that his best had been a fumbling effort. This seemed to be as good a time as any to talk with Dave again. Dan met him for lunch at the Country Club."

"Yes, I saw Nan and Kurt and Peggy at the Christmas Eve Service."

Dan looked at him closely. "Dave, you are in no condition to think or talk seriously about anything."

"Well then, Dan boy, why don't you preach to me? You're thinking that I need some religion."

"No, Dave. We'll talk another time. I'm going now."

"Come, come. Work the big miracle on one of us sinners . . ."

"Dave, I don't work anything. What I want is for you to let Jesus Christ work His work of redemption and renewal in your life."

"Oh, that's good. You must remember to tell Mother you said that . . ."

Dan pushed his chair back. He leaned over, and with his face close to Dave's he threw his words at Dave.

"Enough . . . I was a sanctimonious piece when I tried to hold Nan to a vow that would bind her to what you are. Any consideration of decency, or common sense, would tell her to get a divorce and find a new life. Looking at you and listening to you now, I wish I had told her to get free from you as fast as the most liberal state law would permit."

Without another look at Dave, Dan rose and strode from the room. The waiter arrived with a luncheon plate in each hand; Dave waved him away as he watched Dan disappear through the door at the far end of the room.

Mary and her mother set out to make a round of the After Christmas Sales. Grandfather Carter had left with Mark and Debbie ". . . to run some errands . . . maybe do a little shopping . . . and have a bite of lunch – if they could find a place."

At the second store where Mary purposefully sought out the bedding department, her mother asked if she was looking for anything in particular.

"Yes, I'm looking for some bedspreads for our twin beds."

"Did something happen to the ones you had? I thought they were lovely, and the colors fitted the decor of the room."

"Yes, they did, but we now have the twin beds in the master bedroom, and the colors clash with the drapes. The rug, too, would call for something different."

When they arrived home, the busy business trio had not yet returned. Mary and her mother sat down in the breakfast nook with some coffee. Estelle tried to sound casual.

"How long have you had the twin beds in the master bedroom?"

"Since September, as I recall." Mary sipped her coffee.

"Was there any particular reason for the change? I thought the

114
Messiah Man

queen-size fitted your room beautifully."

"Well, since Dan is out so much and comes in at all hours, I thought he might rest better."

Mary did not sound very convincing. Both Mary and her mother drank from their cups to pass by the awkwardness.

"Mary, I know you too well not to be getting bad vibrations. Is there something wrong between you and Dan?"

It was an opportunity that Mary wanted. She poured out her story about the call to University Church, all of the advantages for them and especially for Mark and Debbie, and of Dan's turning down the call to stay at Messiah. She told of the decline in Messiah Church and the changes in the neighborhood and the school. She told how hard – and futilely – she had tried to persuade Dan to accept the call to Fairfield.

Her mother nodded. "I suppose that every wife has tried to persuade her husband about his work – including me – but there is something we must accept. If a man is going to spend his strength and working days and years to support his home and family, he is entitled to choose what he does and where he does it. I learned that early with your father . . . But that doesn't explain the change of the beds."

Mary tried to put the best face on her decision and action.

Her mother interrupted. "Mary, your words are not very convincing. What you are not saying is that you changed the beds because you were piqued with Dan."

"Well, I didn't think he showed much consideration . . ."

"*Stop it Mary.*" Mary had not heard this tone in her mother's voice since her childhood. "I am going to ask you a question which you may very well say is none of my business . . . So you have twin beds instead of the queen-size . . . all right! . . . But how long is it since you and Dan have been in the *same* bed whatever its size?"

"Mother! I am surprised at you . . ."

"*How long?* Mary . . ."

"I don't know. That isn't something . . ."

"*How long*, Mary?"

"Mother, I am surprised at you . . ."

"If what I suspect is the truth, you had better hope that your father never finds out. He would leave me here to drive over to change the beds back all by himself, and then he would sit you down and explain to you what he would call: 'the facts of life.' How long, Mary?"

"All right. All right. I still think it is my personal business . . . Not since we returned from Glen Rock . . . Not since I changed the beds . . . But Dan hasn't said anything to me about it."

"Good heavens, Mary! You ought to get down on your knees and thank Almighty God that you still have a husband. *Your father* would not – would not NOW – tolerate such a state of affairs." She paused but obviously had more to say.

"I have always said that you are welcome here, but not this way. I know you were planning to be here until the weekend, but not with this. I want you to pack and go back home the first thing tomorrow morning. And the first thing you do when you get there is to change those beds back again."

"Mother, that's like throwing me out."

"You're damned right! I want to know that tomorrow night you are together with your husband in bed, and by 'together' I mean *together*."

The discussion was ended for Estelle Carter, and the only thing left for Mary to do was get up and leave the room in awkwardness, to go and start packing things for her return home.

Dan had been in the den for some time, reading and working on his sermon. He found his thoughts wandering.

'I'll have to apologize to Dave for losing my patience. I think that I'll tell him that I don't understand him, because I don't. Golly! To turn away from a warm. lovely woman like Nan . . . Dave has got to be out of his mind . . .'

'Several more black youngsters have started coming to the Sunday School . . . and their parents, too. And they come to the morning service. There will surely be talk . . . and what will Mary say? Perhaps I should go again to see the Bishop about another parish . . . if he will still talk with me after our last encounter! One thing is for certain. We dare not let the matter of race merely drift . . . We might as well take it up, and have at it . . .'

He was roused from his meditation by the sound of voices. Mary and the children were coming in from the garage. Mary offered no explanation for their return earlier than planned. Dan offered to take them all out for dinner to celebrate their return. The next day the furniture in the master bedroom was changed without comment.

Maybe it was coincidence. Dan could hardly accept that. He believed and he taught that God is the Lord, and that the affairs of men are directed by His gracious purpose. Dan said to himself on occasion the he wished the Lord did not love him so much that He wanted to show Dan His power and love. At the first meeting of the New Year, Dan had suggested to the Official Board that there be a formal Messiah statement of policy on matters racial. And the next day, when Dan stopped for gas, Tom had come to him, saying that he was bringing his family from Pawley, and that they would be living in the area.

In an after-dinner conversation, Dan said, "I stopped at Tom's station. I was complimenting him on the appearance of his station. I told him that it is the brightest corner anywhere in this part of the city, and that I could only hope that other establishments would follow his lead . . . Oh, yes. He said that his wife and boys have arrived and they are living on Fourth Street."

Holding her cup in her hand, Mary said, "Where will they be going to church?"

"I don't know."

"What do you mean, you 'don't know'? Messiah Church is as close as any other church to a Fourth Street address . . . Aren't you going to invite them?"

When Dan could not sleep later that evening, he went down to the den to read, to think, to pray, and just to sit quietly. After a long time he returned to the bedroom, and a voice came out of the darkness, "What's the matter . . . Tom?"

"Yes. I'm sorry to have wakened you."

"I've been waiting."

"I don't know. It seems so easy to say what is and ought to be Christian practice. After the reaction to my proposal on a formal statement on race, I have begun to think of myself as a martyr of sorts. And my martyrdom was beginning to sit well. And now, to find myself confronted personally, it somehow seems to be a new issue."

Dan did not know what he expected when he set out the next day to call on Tom and Rose Davis. The house on Fourth Street – Sam Stockwell's house – needed paint, and two basement windows on one side were broken. But the shabbiness ended upstairs at Rose's door. There was the odor of new paint, and the curtains had a just-hung look about them. As a part of the family reception, Rose brought out their boys – dressed for Sunday School.

Dan was pleased to find that the conversation turned easily to their faith in Jesus, and Dan heard himself saying, "I want to invite you to come to the church which I serve."

Tom answered, "That's a big church for white folks."

Dan's reply was directed word by word alternately to Tom and Rose. "We want it to be a church for Christians."

Although they had been coming to the services and Sunday School in increasing numbers, most of the black people seemed to come and go rather unobtrusively. There was nothing unobtrusive about a man the size of Tom, when he and Rose came to the 11:00 o'clock service the following Sunday. Seeing Tom in the congregation, it struck Dan forcefully that this was the first service which he conducted in which Tom – his "friend" – was a member of the congregation. As he was preaching, Dan was immediately aware that the Christian convictions of Tom and Rose were following him word by word. Dan's apprehension concerning how these friends might have been received by others disappeared when several persons spoke to him.

"Those two have beautiful voices. They ought to be in our choir."

Mark and Debbie were back in Lincoln School for the second semester. When Mary had broached the idea of their attending Stone School, Mark's reaction was instant and definite. He said that he didn't want to go to "another school." Mary had taken the children to Stone School to look about, and Debbie was enthused with the possibility of going there until she asked, "Would Ruth go there with me?" Mary's plans could not be salvaged for now, and she agreed that the children would go back to Lincoln for *"one more* term."

There was one thing to be said for Mary. She was unyielding in her pursuit of her goals for her children. Two days after the start of the second semester, she was suggesting that the church get a new residence for the Pastor. She had been talking with Fred Hudson, who suggested the possibility of a home in HILL & DALE, a new community he was developing which he said was "the loveliest yet."

The January meeting of the Official Board promised to be significant.

1. Despite the best efforts by Dan and Andy, as well as the laymen's outreach efforts, the church membership had declined to ca. 1100. They had been unable to sustain accessions to the membership in sufficient number to replace the numbers lost in the colonization of new churches by The Bishop's Fund program, plus the normal losses of members which a church regularly sustained. At about 1100, the church was now at a financial breakpoint. In addition, there were yet major problems to be resolved in positive fashion if the church was to survive.

2. Dan was not surprised that Fred Hudson asked for the floor at the outset of the meeting. He *was* surprised at the subject which Fred introduced.

"Messiah Church is not just any church; it has always been a church which stands at the forefront of the Christian cause in the capitol city. We have already done extensive work to restore the physical presence of the church as it stands so prominently here on Columbia Avenue. I would like to think that I know a *little* about real estate, but it doesn't take an expert to recognize that there have been drastic changes in the area surrounding the church property. I have been talking with the Pastor's wife, and she would agree with me that it is in order for this Official Board to consider another place as the residence for the Minister of Messiah Church. We have done some work on the present house, but it is still an *old* house. It would seem to me that a *new* home in HILL & DALE – which I happen to know something about – or in some prestigious community, would more properly serve as a home for the Pastor of Messiah Church . . ."

Fred's words elicited comments from about the room:

"Fair enough, but how would we pay for it . . .?"

"Where will we get the money?"

"My wife said that she and Mrs. Clark have talked about the house, and she wouldn't want Mrs. Clark's job of keeping up that place."

Dan suggested that a committee be appointed to study the matter and report back to the Board when they had a recommendation. When the Official Board accepted this course of action, Dan felt that he had probably been spending too much time too close to the Bishop.

3. Dan now directed the Board's attention to a major item for consideration. He began by urging everyone to feel free to speak his/her mind on the subject.

"Messiah Church has been shaken by people leaving the church in large groups to establish new churches in the burgeoning suburbs. In addition, Messiah Church is being affected by many new people who are coming to the church in increasing numbers. The problem is that the new people are 'different.' It is true that the new people are human beings. It is true that the new people are confessing Christians. But they are different in that they are black!"

Dan reminded the Board that the subject of black people in Messiah Church had been hinted and skirted in previous meetings. The whole issue had come sharply to the fore when Thomas and Rose Davis united with Messiah Church. He stated that he thought the Official Board should now establish and declare "the position of Messiah Church on race."

Then Dan opened the meeting for discussion.

Some said that they would prefer to have no blacks in the church, and they wanted to say as much in plain language. Other Board members declared with spirit that the doors of the church, and membership in the church, must be open to all people. "Where would we be if St. Paul had not gone to the Gentiles?"

Everyone had read stories and articles in newspapers and magazines, as well as church publications. They had seen pictures of racial strife. While the Board members were informed in varying degrees, they all had opinions. No one, however, seemed to have been forced to formulate a course of action which he could, and would, have to face personally. Several talk-filled hours failed to develop a consensus.

Dan pointed to his watch. He said he did not want the Board to be pressured into a decision, and suggested that everyone think and pray about this matter. They would hold a special meeting in two weeks. When everyone felt prepared to make a personal commitment and vote to establish a public policy for Messiah Church, they would do so. Dan was asked to prepare a statement to give them something on which to focus their attention.

Later that evening, the Secretary of the Board telephoned Dan to say that he left the meeting only to find the wheel covers missing from his new car. He said he had already notified the police.

The first Sunday of Lent was wintry. With gusty, cold wind, the streets and sidewalks were icy. A snowfall which commenced on Saturday continued through Sunday morning. There was only an occasional car on usually busy Columbia Avenue. Matt worked continuously to keep the front steps cleared. Dan was certain that the service and the sermon left much to be desired. Later at home, he told Mary that all *he* could remember from the sermon was the text:

"If any man be in Christ, he is a new creature."
II Corinthians 5:17.

When the schedule for the first Sunday of Lent was completed, it was time for a family night. Mary and Dan and the children were seated around a folding table in front of the fireplace to play a game. Furniture in the room was moved to accommodate the table and chairs before the fireplace, with a small table beside each chair to hold a plate and cup.

Mark said, "This is the only time Mother lets us eat in here."

Debbie responded, "And we must not spill anything or drop any crumbs on the carpet."

The world with its weather and its problems was shut out; for a while they would play as a family. The spirit was high. Markers on the game board indicated that Debbie and Mark were leading; Dan's lot in the game had left him far behind to the great delight of the children, but he kept promising that he would come through with a final rush to win. From time to time, Mary interrupted her part in the game to fill cups or serve empty plates. Later, they would have family devotion, in which Debbie always wanted to read. For now, they asked only that there be no intrusion, especially a call that might take Dan away.

The doorbell rang. Mark ran to answer, and returned. "Daddy, there is a man to see you."

Dan groaned inwardly, 'Please. Not tonight, Lord."

He went into the hallway to see David Schuster standing in the vestibule.

Dave was apologetic. "This is no hour to be bothering you, Dan. I won't take much of your time."

'Not take much of your time!' Dan thought of the long and futile hours he had spent with Dave. "Come on in, Dave."

Dan made as though to return to the living room, but Dave held back with a suggestion that they go into the den. Dan turned on a light, and Dave entered to sit on the edge of a chair, holding his hat and without opening his coat.

"*I had to come NOW*. Dan, I had to come to tell you that HE has won!"

"What is that again?"

"HE has won, Dan. CHRIST! I had to tell you first of all."

Dave was now sitting erect. "I was in the service this morning, and frankly, it seemed like most other services. But . . . after I left I found the words of your text coming to my mind with an insistence and a persistence which I could not understand, nor put aside. 'Therefore if any man be in Christ, he is a new creature: old things are passed away; behold all things are become new.'"

Dan wanted only to listen.

"I have so long been dissatisfied with myself. I have really wanted to be something and somebody wholly different, because the David Schuster I have known was hopeless. I needed a whole new existence somehow, but this has been impossible and I could see no better prospect for the future. You have talked not a few times (a trace of a smile) about Jesus Christ . . . Then as I was walking today, it all came clear to me."

"*Walking? Today?*"

"For some reason I had to walk. I am aware that this is hardly the day for a stroll in the park, but I walked and walked . . . Then at last it all came to me! What I wanted and what I hoped to be, I could have in Jesus Christ . . . This is probably not good theology, and I can't command the right words . . . But, Dan, as best as I knew how, I told Jesus Christ that I would be His for whatever He could do with me and whatever He could make of me. Just like that!" Dave slapped the arm of the chair. ". . . I felt myself changed somehow . . . changed basically in some fashion. I didn't know what to do, Dan, so I thanked Him."

Dan could not move lest the moment be lost forever.

In later years, Dan would look back on his pastorate in Messiah Church, and he would realize that Dave's conversion was the event which marked the time when the Lord turned about the fortunes of Messiah Church.

"I realized that I was cold; so I went back to my place. I tried to thank God again. Then it came to me that I should tell someone, and here I am . . ."

Dan could not speak his thoughts. 'He *does* work! It's *all really true*! God does work!'

Dave now unbuttoned his topcoat. "I am reasonably sure that you have felt you were wasting your time with me. I can only hope that you will feel that way no longer."

Dan felt momentary embarrassment that he had revealed his impatience. "Do you mind if I tell Mary? . . . Better yet . . . Would *you* tell Mary what you have just told me?"

"Of course. I shall tell everybody I know."

They went into the living room, and Dave spoke in simple language of himself and what he believed was the work of the Saviour.

When he had finished, Mary said, "You just said that you don't know where you go from here. Well, I'll tell you. You will make yourself comfortable here by the fire . . . Mark, put another log on the fire . . . You will have something to eat with us here and now."

After a time, they invited Dave to stay for the night. He asked if they did not trust him, and quickly apologized to accept the invitation.

At the breakfast table the next morning, Dave said that he wanted first of all to go and talk with his mother.

In succeeding days, Dan seemed to be on the telephone continuously as man after man, and woman after woman, called to talk about Dave, for Dave was telling his story to anyone who would listen. So very many of those who called were persons who had been members of Messiah Church, but who had dropped out or transferred their membership to other churches. Al Hirter's words were typical.

"You're doing a great work there at Messiah, Dan. There will never be another church but Messiah as far as I am concerned. I want you to know that I am with you in spirit. Keep up the great work, Dan"

Dan fought back the words, 'If Messiah is such a great church, then why did you leave it?' That was unworthy. What he really wanted to say was, 'There won't be a Messiah Church at all, if things continue as they have been going.'

Some of those who called attempted lamely to make excuses:

"You know, Dan I never really wanted to leave Messiah Church. But my wife – or son, or daughter – has good friends in the neighborhood where we live . . ."

As Dan listened to such words, he felt that he was being asked the question, "What indeed is the Christian Church?" Is it an institution in society, one among many? To ask the question was to receive an answer for what Messiah Church should be.

No one knew better than the Rev. Daniel Witt Clark that questions concerning the nature of the Christian Church, or questions concerning the character and role of Messiah Church, did not originate with Mary's dissatisfaction, nor with Dave's conversion. After nearly three years, Dan found himself surrounded – if not overwhelmed – by the never-ending demand that an answer be found for the problem: 'What place, if any, does Messiah Church have in the Cause of Christ in this city?"

Everything had commenced with such great promise, but the first hint of success had been scrubbed by successive blows. It was true that the Bishop had stripped the church both of numbers and leadership, but it was too easy to blame this program as the source of all the problems in Messiah Church. There was the force of urban change which spread inexorably and omitted nothing from its devastating touch. Residential blocks, businesses and industry deteriorated and died, leaving empty hulks of buildings. Mansions of another era were converted into multiple dwellings; indifference by lessor and lessee had reduced these structures to hazardous piles, now roped off and unsightly, awaiting the wrecking crew. There seemed to be some insatiable cancer at work which would not stop till all evidence of man and human civilization had been erased.

It was not an unexpected call which came to Dan asking him to schedule a Memorial Service for Cora Schuster. She had been in failing health for a long while and confined to her bed in recent weeks.

Her physician said, "Something more than modern medicine and good nursing care is keeping her alive."

One morning – the first Monday of Lent – she had awakened more alert than she had been in weeks. It was commonly observed that it was a "sheer coincidence" for her son David to have come to see her on that very day to tell her of a new life which had come to him in Jesus Christ. She responded by insisting that she get up and sit in a chair to talk at length with her son. She sent for Dan, and questioned him closely to ascertain to her own satisfaction the genuineness of what David had said in several long talks with her.

For more than a week she surprised everyone with her renewed vigor. And apparently, when she was satisfied with the answers to her questions, she had returned to bed and her physical condition deteriorated rapidly. It seemed as though she had waited for God to do the one thing closest to her heart; and now that the Lord had brought it to pass, her vigil was ended.

Dan returned the telephone to its cradle and set out immediately to find Dave, with a concern for what his mother's passing might do to him. Finding Dave, Dan quickly confessed that he was ashamed of his own faithlessness. Dave thought that Nan should be informed, but he was reticent to communicate with her. Dan volunteered and telephoned Nan. She thanked him but said she did not know if she would be able to come for the memorial service.

Dave Schuster seated himself in the second pew – it had been the family pew for years – for the Memorial Service to be conducted for his mother in celebration of the Ressurection. He sensed movement and turned to see Nan with Kurt and Peggy being ushered into the pew with him.

No word was spoken among the Schusters until they were riding back from the cemetery. Dave turned to Nan. "It was good of all of you to come for this service for Mother."

Kurt and Peggy nodded their agreement with their Mother's words. "We all wanted to come and we felt we should do so."

"Let me reimburse you for your expenses."

Nan was definite. "No, thank you. That is not necessary."

Conversation among them was obviously a struggle. "Do you have return reservations?"

Nan looked straight ahead. "Yes. Tomorrow at 9:00 . . . TWA, Flight 451."

The car stopped in a line of traffic. They moved ahead only a few car lengths and stopped again. The second stop seemed to present an opening for Dave.

"Tell me. Would you all have dinner with me this evening?"

Nan looked at her son. "What do you think, Kurt?" He smiled. She turned her head slightly. "Peggy?" There was the briefest hesitation, and Peggy nodded. Nan faced Dave for the first time. "Well, all right."

"I'll make reservations and plan to pick you all up at 6:30. Where can we take you now?"

"The LaSalle."

Dave spoke to the driver of the limousine. "Sandy, you can drop me off anywhere as we go through town. Then will you please drive to the LaSalle Hotel?"

Whenever Nan remembered a history of personal and public embarrassments with Dave, she would resolve to cancel the dinner plans. Then she would be stopped with the thought, 'We *agreed* to go. But I'll caution Kurt and Peggy, just in case . . .'

She did not do so, and at 6:30 they came out of the elevator to see Dave in the lobby. He looked different than she remembered or expected. Then it came to her. 'He is different. He is *on time!*'

Nan was uneasy when Dave announced that they were going to the Country Club. There was bewilderment for her when the waitress asked if they wanted cocktails and Dave had answered immediately for all of them, "NO." Their dinners were served and Nan began to relax when they seemed to be making it without any awkwardness. It was interesting to see Kurt and Peggy warm up to a father whom they scarcely knew.

Dave stopped in front of the hotel. To everyone's surprise – her own, most of all – Peggy leaned forward and impulsively kissed her father, and then quickly jumped out of the car. Kurt thrust out his hand and grasped his father's hand to pump it vigorously. Dave asked Nan if he might talk with her for a minute; she agreed hesitantly as she watched her children enter the hotel lobby.

Dave told her of his new life in Christ. Nan listened and recalled that Dave could be most persuasive when and if he had some ulterior motive. Even so, she felt she was hearing a Dave *she* could not identify with anyone she had known.

"Please believe me when I say that only now have I come to a realization and accepted the responsibility for the many injustices I have done to you, and to Peggy and Kurt. I *must* ask you to forgive me – if you can."

"It's all right, Dave. I hold nothing against you. It's been *so long* now."

"Yes, it has." Dave ran a finger around the steering wheel. "Has it been too long?"

"Too long?"

"Has it been too long . . . would it be no longer possible for you and me . . . for us?" He squirmed about in the seat. "Nan, do you think it is at all possible that we could pick up our marriage again after all these years?"

Nan struggled against the panic which was overwhelming her, lest she be the one who made a scene.

"Oh, Dave . . . So much has happened . . . I don't see how . . . It has been *so long* . . . It would be almost like strangers . . ."

"Not *total strangers*, Nan. We did have some good times, and I

127
Messiah Man

know that the best is yet to come for my life."

"Dave. The weeks . . . the months . . . the years . . . the times I have waited and wanted . . ." She shrugged her shoulders.

"I'm genuinely sorry. You know of course, that you are the only girl I ever loved. Whatever else I may have been, or may have done, I have never changed in my love for you."

"Dave, there have been many lonely years . . . Raising the children *all by myself* . . ."

"And you have done so most wonderfully!"

Nan felt that she had herself in hand. She knew that she must and that now she could speak honestly to Dave.

"I have been alone. There was so much loneliness. I have needed someone . . . And *now* there *is* someone who was a friend when I needed a friend, who has been good for me . . . He says that he loves me very much, and I think that I love him."

Dave was uncomplicated. "Nan, I know I could not reasonably expect you to wait forever. Frankly, I should never have had the courage to come to you, but seeing you today I *had* to try."

Nan paused inside the door. 'Why didn't he try harder? . . . Did I expect him to beg? . . . But, there is Lee, dear Lee . . . The warmth of his love . . . The thrill of his touch . . . The confidence of his presence . . . Dave said he has a new life. Well, I, too, shall have a new life.' She straightened her shoulders and walked purposefully through the lobby to the elevator.

The Official Board met again in special session. Dan opened the meeting with prayer. The Secretary announced the loss of his wheel covers during the previous meeting, although everyone seemed to know about this already. In some effort to move ahead, Dan submitted the text of a resolution for the Board's consideration and possible adoption.

Sam Stockwell stood up to speak.

"Now I think I have something to say on this whole matter. As some of you may know, I happen to have a business just across the street. I know what is happening to my store and my business. I saw what happened to our house and our street until we finally had to move. I have tried to sell that property, and I can't get anything for it now. I'm renting it, and it is nothing but trouble. If we vote a resolution like the one which Dr. Clark has suggested, a lot of people will leave the church. We're having enough trouble now in meeting our bills. I predict that the publication of a statement such as this will cause a stampede of folks leaving and transferring to other churches. I have lost my home. My business is being ruined. I hate to have my church taken away from me as well. I shall vote 'Nay.'"

Sam sat down to a room hushed by his passion. The Secretary was the first to speak.

"Maybe we should all think and pray about this some more before taking formal action."

Dan spoke meditatively. "Mr. Secretary, and members of the Official Board. This is not a new subject. We have already had several weeks and months with this issue before us. We have talked about it in one way or another in about every meeting of this Official Board. We all know that in this life there come again and again those times when we must make a decision. The question here is not one of strategy, or convenience, or finance. I suggest the question is one of right and wrong – what is *right* for *Christians*. Our Lord Jesus said: 'Go ye therefore, and teach all nations . . .'; and St. Paul said: '. . . for you are all one in Jesus Christ.' I think it is time for *Messiah Church* to take *its stand* in this present world on this issue. The day is far spent . . . As your Minister, I would ask that you vote your Christian conscience, and that you do it *now*."

Fred Hudson was in no hurry to go home following the meeting. He needed time to think. He needed an opportunity to formulate what he would say to Marge. At long last he turned into his street and then drove ever so slowly, taking in every neighborhood detail with a lifetime of familiarity. From a distance he could see that the Hudson home glowed. Marge said, as had Fred's mother before her, that she liked "to have the lights on as though somebody lives here." The driveway was flooded with light as Fred put his car in the garage. Walking to the house, he heard the garage door come down. When the garage door control was installed, Marge said that it was a luxury gift to herself . . . and Fred.

"Fred. You're late." Marge kissed him at the door. They started for the library, and Fred turned in the hall to go into the living room.

When he had seated himself, he sat quietly and shook his head before speaking. "I couldn't take many days like today . . ."

"Can I get you something to drink – hot or cold?"

"Neither, thank you. Let's talk a bit."

When Marge had seated herself to face him, he began. "We voted . . . if that is what you want to know. Dan had rewritten the resolution. He asked again if anybody wanted to speak; so we all had our turn, and Marge, a tape of any of the other meetings would have been a script for the discussion tonight. Dan keeps talking about a 'Christian' position; of course, each of us thinks that that is what he is voicing."

"Well, I guess we shall have to wait and see what happens."

"We won't have to wait long. The statement is to appear in the bulletin this Sunday."

Fred's head dropped as he sat quietly. Marge knew that this was a time to wait. With some energy, he straightened up in his chair and spoke briskly. "I have more news. I want to talk with you about our house. We have a chance to sell it."

Marge was unbelieving. "Sell *our* house?"

"Let me continue. You know that this is the only house I have ever lived in. I love every feature of it, and I have always relished being at home in this place. But things are not the same. As we have said times without number, 'The neighborhood is changing.' We have our third set of neighbors to the north of us, and each crowd seems to take less pride of home than the one before. Furthermore, this house is so big for just *two people* . . . And it means a lot of work for you . . ."

"Who wants to buy it? When and how does this come about?"

"There is a corporation interested in it for a retirement home . . . They say that they are especially interested in the setting with the grounds and gardens about."

"Oh, dear! Do you think they would be putting hospital beds and such in this lovely room?"

"Marge, I don't like to think of what they would do with a place which means as much to me as this house does. However, they have made an offer which is a lot better than we could get on the open market, because there isn't any sale for houses like this any more . . . especially here in the city. *That I know.*"

"But what would we do?"

"Do you remember when we drove through HILL & DALE a couple of weeks ago?" She nodded. "Was there any spot which you liked more than any other?"

"Yes, I remember distinctly one place with many big, old trees. You said that a stream runs across the back of the property."

Fred smiled. "Good! I took several of those lots off the market . . . just in case we might ever want to make use of them." He paused for effect. "Marge. I propose that we sell this place and build a new home on that site which you like."

"Oh, my goodness! I hate to think of leaving our home here . . . but you know best about such things."

"I also propose that you come down to the offices of our architect. I will ask Ned to work with you in planning a new house."

Marge rose to cross over and kiss Fred on the cheek. "I hate the thought of leaving here . . . But it *would* be nice to have everything new and modern . . . Mercy! As you said, this *is* some day!"

The Sunday Service Bulletin of Messiah Church contained a notice which was enclosed in a box.

OFFICIAL POLICY STATEMENT

In its Stated Meeting of March 20, the Official Board adopted the following resolution in the establishment of a policy for MESSIAH CHURCH.

"The Official Board of Messiah Church declares that inasmuch as the Gospel is to be preached to all people, and inasmuch as the Christian Church is a fellowship in Jesus Christ for all persons, membership and the program in Messiah Church are open to all persons regardless of race or color. Amen."

City newspapers on Monday publicized the action of the Official Board, with photographic reproduction of the Sunday bulletin. Comments of various Board members were included in the stories. Dan was quoted. Bishop Gossert was interviewed, and he had spoken of "the challenge of contemporary urban life." Tuesday editions editorialized on the policy statement of the Official Board. Commentators spoke of Messiah Church:

". . . blazing a way of Christian witness . . ."

". . . a meaningful testimony to Christian fellowship . . ."

". . . a modern church facing the modern world . . ."

One writer described Dan as ". . . having donned the mantle of a prophet."

Jerry Whitman, a member of the Board, telephoned his reactions. "If nothing else, Dan, we are making copy for the papers."

"Yes, Jerry, but I'd trade some of the publicity for a few substantial contributions to the church. Even so, it is gratifying that we have had very few requests for letters of transfer because of the policy statement. Indeed, about the only ones who have left are some of the very people on the Board who voted for this resolution in the meeting."

Somehow, by the grace of God, Messiah Church seemed to be straightening out. There was much publicity as a result of the policy resolution. Unpublicized was the word of mouth attention to the church which began with David Schuster. He missed no opportunity to tell of his new life among his wide, wide circle of acquaintances – he always added a word of invitation to visit Messiah Church. If nothing else, curiosity about Dave and the ministry which everyone acknowledged had turned Dave's life for good . . . this curiosity was bringing people to Messiah Church for a first time. And many continued to come.

There was no present project of The Bishop's Fund to lay claim to a large group of the members. If one were to offer an observation on the whole area about the church, one might have said, "Nothing much is happening. At least it isn't any worse."

There was a growing sense of stability about the current membership and program of Messiah Church. Given such feeling and circumstances, the attendance in all aspects of church life was increasing. Not much. BUT . . . it was a vast difference from the two years when the life and strength of the church seemed to be draining from open wounds.

Dan was saying to himself, and to any whose ear he might catch, "We can, and we shall build anew from here."

Kathryn Mac called Dan to say that she wanted him to meet some people. She came into the Study to introduce Helen Benson, who had spoken to Kathryn on Sunday, and now had come to volunteer her help with the pre-school nursery — because she "loved children." With them was her husband, who was introduced as the Rev. Willard Benson. He had recently retired from the parish ministry, and they had come to live in Indianapolis, because it was central to the places where their children and their families were now living.

Kathryn told Dan later that Mrs. Benson had confided to her some concerns about her husband. "She says that her husband probably would not admit it, but he is not adapting well to retirement. He needs to be doing something that, as she put it, *he* believes is worthwhile. They are attending here, but he will not volunteer because in all of his life he only served two small churches."

Two days later, Rev. Mr. Benson was telling Dan that visitation was the part of the work of a parish minister which he had always enjoyed the most. Further conversation led to an agreement, by which Rev. Mr. Benson would do visitation as a part-time member of the staff. Dan noted that there were the formalities of approval and appointment by the Bishop, as well as a vote by the Official Board; even so, Dan suggested "today" could be a starting date, because he liked what he was seeing and hearing with Rev. Mr. Benson. Dan said later he had a sense of leading about Mr. Benson; he brushed aside Mr. Benson's words that he didn't want any compensation, and said he would talk with the Finance Committee and they would work out something suitable for doing the work of the Lord.

Dan took the first opportunity after Easter to make an

appointment with the Bishop. He asked for formal approval of Rev. Mr. Benson as a part-time Assistant. He also made note to the Bishop that he had been in Messiah Church for three years. He had seen the church through a series of crippling and discouraging blows. There was reason to think that the church had now turned the corner, and it might be in order for Messiah Church to have new pastoral leadership. The Bishop listened, and the Bishop asked questions. Dan was keenly aware during this conference, and upon later recalling this time to Mary, that the Bishop had made no commitment to him.

∝   ∝   ∝   ∝

May 15

Dearest Mother and Daddy,

I have been talking with Dan about our plans for the summer. We are now agreed on a schedule.

On June 2, Mark and Debbie and I will be coming to be with you. The last two weeks of July, the children and I will be going to Belvoir. Dan will pick us up there to go to Glen Rock, where he has been invited for August and the first week of September. The Board has urged him to accept this invitation.

The church was in a state of turmoil following the policy statement on "race." The officers of the church have let the criticism fall on Dan, and some people went to see the Bishop. I know that Dan was upset about that because he thought that the Bishop should have stood back of him, and apparently the Bishop did not do so.

Mark and Debbie are doing very well in school. You know, of course, how unhappy I can get about the school. But . . . they do have wonderful teachers. Mark will be in the Sixth Grade, and he says that he wants to begin learning French. Even so, I have talked with Dan about schools, and he has agreed to talk with the people at Stone School.

Fred Hudson has spoken with me – and to the Board – about a new home for the Minister. Dan thinks it would not be appropriate for us to move, or even talk of moving, at this juncture.

When we mention going to Rockford, Mark talks of going with you (Daddy) to the farm. He thinks he will be big enough to do some real work this summer. He pictures himself coming back all tanned and muscular, ready to compete in the sports of his choosing – and right now, that's all of them.

I forgot to mention that Dan was persuaded of our summer schedule when he learned that Lois is taking their children to be with her parents for two months this summer. Her father just had major surgery and her mother is unwell; she says that they need help and she is all they have.

It is wonderful to think of the days we shall have with you.

Because I love both of you,

Mary

YEAR FOUR AT MESSIAH CHURCH

Dan's vacation at Glen Rock was interrupted by a not wholly unexpected turn. Rev. Frederick Anderson and his wife, Charlotte, together with their daughter Lynn arrived for a brief visit, after a telephone call to schedule their appearance. Andy and Charlotte were visibly ill at ease, and Andy asked almost at once if he might speak with Dan. They went outside to sit on the porch overlooking Lake Michigan.

An unhappy Andy spoke up immediately. "Dan, I have received an invitation to become Pastor of a parish, and I think that it is time for me to get into a parish of my own . . . Dan, I'd rather take a beating than to be saying this to you . . . It is a fine parish with great potential for the Lord . . . I have told them that I must talk with you before I give an answer . . ."

"Andy, we both know that you must say 'Yes' to the Lord. If you believe that this is a call of the Lord for you, then there is only one answer you can give."

Andy pulled his chair a bit closer to Dan. "It's been just great working with you. I happen to think that the relationship between a Pastor and an Associate is in many ways more delicate and demanding than the relationship between a man and a woman in marriage. So far as I am concerned, working with you has been a great Christian experience."

"Thank you, Andy. You know what I think of you. I have many, many selfish reasons for wanting you to stay . . ."

"Both Charlotte and I feel that we have an unpayable obligation to Messiah Church and to you. You were there for us in the most crucial time of our marriage – and of our lives – when Lynn's life was in question. Just look at her now! She must still have a periodic check, but the wonderful word is that she is a perfectly healthy and beautiful young girl . . . Our whole life is different . . . Indeed, Charlotte has just learned that she is pregnant again."

"Andy, I am only thankful for any and every evidence of the blessing of God in your life . . ."

"Excuse me, but I must say one thing more. I don't want you, or anyone else, to think that I am leaving because working in Messiah Church has become too tough. You and I have talked and prayed together so many times about the problems of Messiah Church. My biggest problem in accepting this invitation is the feeling that I am backing away from a hard fight."

Dan raised his hand. "No, Andy, you don't have to justify your decision to me. Go freely to accept this call of God, and we shall pray for God's most gracious blessings upon you, your family and your contributions to the Cause of Christ in this day . . . Messiah Church will miss you, and I shall miss the feel of your shoulder next to mine in the work of Messiah Church

∝   ∝   ∝   ∝

September 16

Dearest Mother and Daddy

We are back. I say that more out of shock than anything else. I don't know whether I have come with the standards of Glen Rock in my mind, or whether I had forgotten . . . but I could scarcely believe the appearance of the neighborhood which we presently call "home."

The Hudsons have sold that beautiful mansion in which they lived, and they are building a new house in one of the suburbs which he is developing – HILL & DALE. On our first day back, Mr. Hudson came to see me and to talk about the church establishing the residence of the Minister in HILL& DALE. I told him that he doesn't have to persuade me. He knows, and so do I, that Dan thinks it would not be advisable for us to be moving at this time . . .

Dan received an inquiry from Eastminster Church in Spring-

field, Illinois. He completed a questionnaire for them. There were three people from the church in the congregation on a Sunday in July. Dan went to see Bishop Gossert to say that he would certainly be interested in Eastminster Church. There has been no word from anyone since.

Mark and Debbie are back in Lincoln School. They are not happy with their teachers this year. However, Debbie is having a course in "Dance." She says that they are to learn some of the traditional dances, and spend some time on ballroom dancing. If there is time, the instructor wants to introduce the class to ballet. Mark has started with French. There are not too many in the class, and there is a question whether they will be able to continue because of the small enrollment. He hopes this won't happen, because he is very proud of the bit of conversational French that he has learned in two weeks.

We want to thank you for the wonderful time we spent with you. I think Mother and Father Clark are perplexed about our being with you for <u>six</u> weeks. They were "on the ropes" after only two weeks of ACTIVITY.

Rev. Fred Anderson is leaving the end of this month. Dan says Andy has been a wonderful Associate, and Dan doesn't know how he can get along without Andy. But I must say that Dan seems to be riding on top of it all.

Thank You Again!

Mary

∝   ∝   ∝   ∝

The spirit of the first Staff meeting began with a sense of loss without Andy's presence. This was accentuated when Mr. Hudson announced at the outset of the meeting – he had not spoken to Dan previously – that he wanted to retire as of December 1. Responding to a question from Dan, he said that he would go as far as possible in the preparation of a budget for the coming year.

Dan invited Rev. Mr. Benson into the Study following the meeting. Responding to Dan's questions, he said that he was enjoying his work and association in Messiah Church. His eyes sparkled in an unwrinkled visage as he told Dan that he had had a complete medical checkup after which the physician said that the only thing that qualified him for retirement was his birthdate. Dan had received only enthusiastic reports on Mr. Benson's service; the two words which Dan heard most frequently to describe Mr. Benson's ministry were: *warm* and *personal*. They readily agreed that Rev. Willard Benson would become the Associate Pastor of Messiah Church. This, of course, was subject to approval from his "superior" – Mrs. Benson.

A few days later, Mr. Benson came to tell Dan that he had received official and formal approval. He added, "I don't want to presume. I don't know what you and the Official Board are planning. Please do not think me to be presumptuous, but I would like to mention something to you . . ."

Dan nodded for him to go ahead. "I want you to know that I am appreciative of the opportunity for serving the Lord Jesus Christ which you have extended to me here in Messiah Church. All of the years of my ministry, I have served in small churches, and I know that I was regarded by all and sundry as 'a small church minister.' Finding myself in Messiah Church, I have felt that I have something professional to prove. It has been a new working life for me . . . Now then, I hope you won't think I am being officious, but I want to suggest a name to you – Rev. Charles Padgett. Charlie and I were classmates in theological school. Our situations parallel at this point in time, for he retired and came here to live for much the same reason that I did. We hadn't seen each other in years until he and his wife attended a service while you were on vacation. Of course, when I saw his name on the Guest Register, I called and went to see him immediately. This story is too long. Dr. Dan, Charlie is in the same position that I was, and if you need some additional visitation effort, he is available for part-time service."

Dan needed only a few moments with Mr. Padgett to recognize that this man was cut from the same cloth to the same pattern as the Rev. Willard Benson. As Dan said to the Official Board, "The only thing better for Messiah Church than *one* benson, is *two* bensons. With Charles Padgett we double the kind of ministry and witness and loving concern that we have presently with Willard Benson."

The Board voted to engage Mr. Charles Padgett as a part-time Assistant Pastor without anyone asking where the money was in the budget to pay him. Mr. Benson and Mr. Padgett asked if they might share the office formerly used by Rev. Mr. Anderson. They asked for approval to recruit, organize and train a group of lay people to engage in evangelistic visitation.

∞ ∞ ∞ ∞

September 28

Dearest Mother and Daddy

I'm sorry. I know you will have a scandalous bill from my call last night.

Things are really at low ebb in 150 Church Street. And after all of my complaining and carrying on, I am scarcely the one to be sincere in offering encouraging words for Dan to continue as the Pastor of Messiah Church.

Dan is bitterly disappointed. He is trying not to show it, but I don't know that I have ever seen him so "down." (We really make a great couple at this point!) The Bishop stopped at the church yesterday to tell Dan – and Dan says he did it "as a kind of afterthought" – that Eastminster Church had decided to call a man who is now in Cincinnati. If the Bishop would have stopped there, it would not have been so rough on Dan. But Bishop Gossert went on to say that Eastminster is in a growing area, and they were looking for a minister to lead in building up the church. He said that they liked everything about Dan personally but they did not think they should consider a man whose church had declined in membership. Dan said that the committee never mentioned anything like this to him. The Bishop said something to the effect: "You know it is a matter of common procedure for committees to consider seriously the statistics of the parish which the minister is presently serving."

In response to a word from Dan, the Bishop said he told the people from Eastminster that "there were some mitigating circumstances about Dan's situation." Dan assumes that he has probably alienated the Bishop forever. He said he confronted the Bishop with a question: "Did you say <u>anything positive</u> in support of me?" Dan says that this door has been closed and that probably any future door will remain shut.

Dan went with me to Stone School this afternoon. We had agreed to enroll Debbie, beginning with the Second Semester. Lincoln School had changed, and is changing by the week. Mark will go to Middle School next year, and I can't see Debbie continuing at Lincoln by herself.

Thank you for letting me run on and on last night.

I love you very much,

Mary

∝   ∝   ∝   ∝

Dan was disappointed in the Eastminster decision, but he did not have time to wallow in self-pity. Messiah Church was alive and moving. Almost too quickly the assistance of Rev. Mr. Benson and Rev. Mr. Padgett was beginning to appear in the attendance figures, and in the number of persons who were making decisions to become Christian and to unite with the church. With Mr. Hoffmeyer the music of the church had never been more glorious. Kathryn Mac's face and spirit reflected weekly gains in all aspects of the education program. Plans were being made for the annual Christmas celebration. Dan had not encountered Bishop Gossert lately. Dan felt that the situation returned to normal when everything in Messiah Church was thrown into turmoil by a sudden turn of events.

It all started when Dan was invited to come to the offices of the senior partner of Halford, Lehman and Brumman, to learn about the will of Cora Schuster. Dan asked Dave to go with him. It was assumed that Mrs. Schuster would remember Messiah Church in her will, and just about everyone had played a guessing game. In the office of her attorney, Dan learned what Dave already knew from his mother. Mrs. Schuster had bequeathed the property on Columbia Avenue to Messiah Church. Some items in the house were objects of special note – the china and silver, for example, were to go to Peggy. However, other than specific gifts of personal items, the furnishings went with the house.

In addition, Messiah Church was to receive a sum of $500,000.00. In her will, Mrs. Schuster said that it was her hope that the church could make use of the property; however, the Official Board was to be free to sell it and use the proceeds of the sale, together with the cash bequest, in any manner which the Board felt would be to the greater glory of God.

Dave stopped Dan in the reception room of the office.

"Dan, Mother told me what she planned, but she made me promise to keep it to myself. In case you have any question, I want you to know that I concur most heartily in what she has done. I told her so, and I want you to be assured of that fact."

Waiting for an elevator, Dan finally found his voice, "Well, Dave, this will call for another special meeting of the Official Board. We seem to have nothing but special meetings as we go from crisis to crisis, but goodness knows that we can use a new subject for discussion"

Dan called a Special Meeting of the Official Board. Cora Schuster's attorney who had drawn up her will was present. Every member of the Board was present, including David Schuster, who had been installed following a recent election. The attorney read the portion of Mrs. Schuster's will which related to Messiah Church. He remained to answer questions from members of the Board; when he had responded to their many questions, he asked to be excused. Dan declared a fifteen-minute recess for some cake and coffee. When they returned, it seemed that everyone had questions and comments. After a time, Fred Hudson asked for the floor.

"I should like to offer a possibility for your consideration. We all know that the neighborhood here has changed and is changing. Every meeting of this Board calls attention to two problems: membership and money. As for my suggestion, it would make sense to me for us to sell out completely. By that I mean, let's sell the Schuster property. Let's sell this church property, including the house for the Minister. Let's put together the total of what we would realize from these sales and add that to the cash bequest; that would come to a considerable amount. I know of a choice fifteen-acre site in Indian River Heights. We could use the money to build a beautiful new church – a church worthy of being called 'Messiah Church.' My firm will handle the real estate end without charging any sales commission, and I will be glad to contribute all that I can if we must put on a building fund drive."

He sat down to smiles and nodding heads all around the room. In calling this meeting, Dan thought they would merely engage in some preliminary discussion. When Fred had finished, Dan looked at the Board members, and he realized that they would have voted then and there to sell and move.

Dan spoke. "It is proper to enter into our discussion the words of Mrs. Cora Schuster, who made it clear to me that she hoped Messiah Church would sustain its ministry on Columbia. That may, of course, be only a hope of a generation now gone."

Dan found little response to this word, and he asked for their agreement that he discuss the whole matter with Bishop Gossert. Fred Hudson made a motion to this effect.

The following week Dan found the Bishop waiting cheerily to talk with him. As they entered his private office, the Bishop asked, "Would you like a cup of coffee? Anne may have some Danish."

Dan declined. Before he could take a seat, the Bishop invited him into "The Conference Room." The room seemed to be dominated by an enlarged map of the metropolitan area, enlarged so that it covered most of one wall in the room. The Bishop walked directly to this map and began speaking. He pointed with his finger from time to time to illustrate his words.

"Now, Dan. The red pins on this map indicate existing churches . . . You can see Messiah Church there. (Pointing) . . . The yellow pins mark the new churches that have been established by The Bishop's Fund. And, finally, the green pins identify the areas which are yet to be established according to our master plan . . . You will notice a shading here . . . That is the area known, or to be known, as Indian River Heights. Of *all* the metropolitan developments, this is in every way the most ambitious and prestigious; as such it would appear to offer the greatest growth prospects for a new church . . ."

When they returned to the Bishop's office and seated themselves, the Bishop inquired about Messiah Church, which he said ". . . is closest to my heart."

Before Dan could make reply, the Bishop brought up the matter of the Cora Schuster bequest. His questions were only a matter of form, inasmuch as he obviously possessed all of the information that was available. The only thing he wanted to talk about was Indian River Heights, and it was quite evident that he and Fred Hudson had already talked about this at length. As he now listened to the Bishop, Dan thought he was hearing Fred's presentation to the Official Board the week before.

Dan fought the temptation to voice his resentment, as it became quite evident that the Bishop and Fred Hudson had already reached an agreement about Messiah Church, and now he – Daniel Clark, the Pastor – was being pressured merely to rubber-stamp a decision that had been made behind his back. Dan struggled for some way to enter the discussion meaningfully without negating anything he said by some display now of ill temper. For the Bishop, the decision was a past event, and they should now discuss only the proper steps to bring it to a reality. Then the Bishop made an unguarded comment.

"And Dan, this would offer to you an opportunity to build a church of almost unlimited measure . . ."

Something inside of Dan snapped – Bishop or no Bishop!

"If you think that I am one who can lead in building a church, then *why did you NOT support me for Eastminster?*"

The Bishop was stunned. The whole meeting had gone awry. He did not expect to be called on the carpet by one of his clergy. There was an awkwardness in the whole present situation which rendered impossible any further discussion of the Indian River Heights project. The Bishop discovered that an aroused Dan could be downright formidable. Dan and the Bishop both quickly recovered their professional demeanor and volunteered apologies. Even so, this conference was at an end, and Dan left with an understanding that they would talk later.

The Bishop telephoned Fred Hudson to say that the meeting had not gone as well as they might have hoped, and that Dan might very well be a problem in pursuit of their plan.

With Peggy home from school, and Kurt and his wife who had come the week before Christmas, Nan's apartment was full. Together with Lee, they went out for dinner and attended a midnight Christmas Eve Service. The young people left in the afternoon of Christmas Day, and a short time later, Lee knocked at Nan's door. He kissed her gently.

"Merry Christmas, Nan."

"Thank you. A merry Christmas to you."

Lee laid his topcoat over a chair. "How merry it is will depend upon you."

Nan sat down on the sofa and patted the cushion beside her. "Come. Sit down. Talk with me."

"That is one of my chiefest joys." Lee pointed to his watch. "The train leaves at 5:30."

"I know. And you have no idea how I have been looking forward to this week in Vermont . . . But, Lee, . . . my mind is not clear."

"Is it the same thing as we discussed the other night?"

"I'm afraid so. I'm sorry, my dear . . . Please be patient with me." She was looking at her hands in her lap.

With one finger. Lee guided her to raise her head and to look at him. "You don't have to ask that."

"It disturbs me that I cannot keep my mind made up. Take today . . . I assumed that Peggy was going to visit a girl she knows in school, and then at the airport, she said she was going to spend a few days with her father."

"And *that* upset you?" Lee's relief was in his voice. "I think it is good for Peggy and Kurt to have acquired a feeling for their father."

Nan rose and looked down at Lee. "It *did* upset me. She could have said something." She sat down again. "But I wondered – forgive me, Lee my dear – but I wondered if I, too, should be going *that* way . . ."

"Nan, if you are asking *me*, you should put on your hat and lock the door and come with me to Vermont."

"If I ask myself what I *want* . . . *that* is what I want. If I ask myself if that is *right* . . . then I am not so sure."

Lee put his arms on the back of the seat to move closer.

"My dearest, dearest Nan. This is one of the reasons I have been saying for so long now, that you should get yourself free. I am quite certain we'll both feel better if someone asks, 'Who is that lovely person?' and I can say, 'That is my wife.'"

"I'm sorry, Lee. I seem to be spoiling our trip before we start." She made no effort to move.

"You never spoil anything." His voice now became firm. "Here is what we shall do. We shall spend the week to take up everything and anything that is bothering you. We'll get it all worked out. I can tell you right now what you can count on from me . . . I love you, Nan. I want you to be my wife."

"Why is it. Lee, that there are some times when I am so very sure? The other day, I almost walked out of the office to come to you. I could picture myself brushing by a very startled Mrs. Hopkins to go into your office. I could have begged – with the door standing open for everyone to hear – for you to marry me . . . And then when the thought came to me that you might have changed your mind, I nearly panicked." She stopped. "And now . . . here . . . I ask you . . . and I don't know. Oh, Lee, you must think me a silly fool."

Lee laughed easily. "No, no, no, no. To me, you are what you have been since that first committee meeting – the Nan whom I want for my wife."

Nan sat unmoving. From somewhere – in the building, or from the outside – they could hear Christmas music.

Nan jumped up. "Don't move from there." In a moment she was back, wearing her coat and hat and carrying her bag.

∝   ∝   ∝   ∝

January 5

Dear Mother and Daddy,

We were so happy that you could be with us again for Christmas. It seemed like a family reunion with Dan's parents here for the Christmas services. Dan was especially grateful that the Christmas programs and services seemed to fulfill what he calls the "Messiah standard." It was not easy. We have lost so many, many people, as well as many individuals who have taken big roles in the leadership of the church and in special events as well.

Anyway Christmas Day was really a time to remember with all of our family together.

As you know, Debbie was to begin at Stone School for the second semester. We have finally worked out the transportation problem, and it is worth it. She already loves it, and I like to think that I can see a difference in her already. I want to thank you, Daddy, for your very generous check which I used to help pay her tuition. I have not yet told Dan, but I shall.

I really wanted to write to tell you about a "date" which Dan and I had today. He said that he ought to be better informed about the Schuster mansion, if he is going to think what to do with the property. We had a date to meet David Schuster at the house at 11:00 o'clock this morning. I must say that going through the gate on Columbia was to enter a totally different world.

Entering the house, David said that he had some things to do and that we should wander about at will — and make sure the door locked when we left. On the first floor there is a formal parlor with windows from ceiling to floor, a music room, a library with a fireplace and books lining all of the walls, what I would call a state dining room, a breakfast room with French doors opening out on a sculptured garden. The kitchen was huge, and to my sur-

prise, completely modern; there was a very large pantry and another room which Dan said they called "the scullery." Then there was a family room which looked comfortable even though it was very large. On the second floor there were suites instead of bedrooms: each suite with a bedroom, bath, dressing room, and walk-in closet. There is a third floor; you can walk up, but there is also an elevator, as we discovered. There are quarters for servants, but mostly it is one huge room, a ballroom.

Try to picture this. In the front hall, there is a stair which leads to a landing, and this landing runs across the full width of the hall, which is really a big room. I said I could imagine a young man waiting for his lady who would come down the steps and walk across this balcony in royal splendor. Dan insisted that I show him what I meant . . . Then he said he hadn't realized till that moment how lucky he is. So I said, "Do these look like the hands of a grand lady?"

The furnishings are out of the book; they are genuinely beautiful.

The grounds have been kept with care; Dan says that the property is a riot of color in the summer. And a swimming pool! It hasn't been used for a while, but Dan said that Mrs. Schuster insisted that everything be kept in perfect condition.

The carriage house is built of stone — just like the main house. It has a delightful second floor apartment. It is the kind of place I've always dreamed of for Dan and myself when the children are grown. Is that ever running ahead!

The big question is now: what to do with this? Dan said that someone suggested it be the residence for the Pastor. Seriously though, it is a big problem, and there is very serious difference of opinion on this. We seem to go from one crisis to another.

It was past one o'clock when we finally came out. So we went

out for lunch. So long as we were in the car, Dan took me to HILL
& DALE – among other places – and he pointed out the house
that Marge and Fred Hudson are building. Coming down to earth,
I told Dan that I would like to have one of that kind.

With all my love,

Mary

∝   ∝   ∝   ∝

Dan sensed and stated repeatedly that there was a reasonable question as to what might be the first order of business of the Church. It seemed that stated meetings of the church as well as chance conversations sooner or later turned to the decision regarding the Schuster property. "Is Messiah Church an agency of the Gospel of Jesus Christ, or is Messiah Church primarily a real estate and financial institution?"

Two suggested solutions continued to be offered, even though they had never needed formal action to reject them:

a. The property would serve as the residence for the Pastor of Messiah Church.

b. The church would simply decline to accept the bequest.

Eventually alternatives seemed to be worked down to two in number:

a. The property and all contents would be sold. The funds realized from the sale would be combined with the cash bequest to establish a church endowment fund. The income from such a fund would be used to help sustain the operating budget of Messiah Church. It was common knowledge that maintaining the budget of the church at an adequate level was more and more of a problem.

b. Adopt the Bishop's (and Fred Hudson's) program to sell *both* the Schuster property and the Messiah Church property, and to use the total amount to rebuild Messiah Church in Indian River Heights.

It was an open secret that both the Bishop and Fred Hudson were actively engaged in trying to "sell" their program to officers and members of Messiah Church. They were careful not to mention Dan in any of their conversations. The whole matter reached the place where Dan felt that he had to get everything in the open. With great reluctance he made an appointment to see Fred in his office.

"Fred, I think it is long since time that we put the game on top of the table."

"What on earth do you mean by that? I think that I don't like the suggestiveness of your words."

"From my first day in Messiah Church I have shared everything with you, other than personal confidences. I am at a loss to understand why you would go behind my back to work out a deal with Bishop Gossert."

"Now, Dan, I have not gone 'behind your back' to make or engineer any kind of deal with George. It just so happens that George and I agree on the course for Messiah Church at this juncture."

"I won't quibble about terms. I do know that you and the Bishop formulated this whole program and launched a selling program without ever once talking with me. And I am aware that both of you – individually or together – have been campaigning with individual conversations with small groups for lunch or breakfast. I have had telephone calls from most of the people in the church who might be regarded as leaders . . . *But not one word with me.* I would frankly admit that I do not trust ecclesiastical bureaucrats. But, you . . . Fred . . . I am not angry, but I must say to you that I am deeply hurt."

Ignoring the issue at hand, Dan and Fred tried to repair their bonds of friendship. With mutual reassurances, they shook hands, and Dan left.

Dan made an appointment with Bishop Gossert and went to his office. He continually reminded himself that he had promised Mary that he would not again lose his cool. Even so, Dan took charge of the conversation immediately, as he made it quite clear to the Bishop that he did not appreciate the fact that the Bishop and Fred had formulated a course of action for Messiah Church of such consequence without ever consulting with him. He said that the Bishop should request a meeting with the Official Board if he wanted to make any presentation, but that buttonholing of individual officers and members would have to come to a halt immediately. Dan reminded the Bishop that under their church law, the Bishop had no authority to enter the affairs of a parish over the head of the pastor; and he added – or threatened – that he, Dan, was prepared to press this matter at the next district meeting.

The next day Bishop Gossert and Fred Hudson met to agree that Dan Clark was indeed "the problem" in working out their proposed move of Messiah Church to Indian River Heights. They were both encouraged by reason of the fact that Dan did not have some alternative program to which he was committed. Fred suggested to the Bishop that he could remove "the problem" with Dan's transfer to another parish.

"Well, Mary, it makes life interesting, if nothing else."

It was a bedtime discussion on a day in which Dan had been visited by three members of a committee from a parish seeking a new pastor. He told Mary that later in the same day he had received a telephone call from a man who identified himself as chairman of the committee seeking to name a minister for another parish.

"How many such invitations have you received now . . . and are you, or could you be, interested in any of these?"

"The two today brings the number to six. Isn't it something, Mary, how all at once I am receiving these calls? And to answer your question, Pawley would be a step up from any of the six churches that have approached me."

The discussions on what to do with the Schuster bequest continued with no progress toward a consensus. The worst thing about it all for Dan was that he realized that he as the Pastor, the presumed leader of Messiah Church, was not offering any distinctive leadership. He readily admitted that he had reservations about the existing alternatives, and he was equally honest in saying that he had no better suggestion. After a time, even Dan thought that it sounded lame at best for him to say that they should all "pray about it and ask for the guidance of the Spirit of God."

YEAR FIVE
AT
MESSIAH CHURCH

On the same day, Dan received a telephone call and a letter from one of the officials at Glen Rock; the man said that they wanted very much for Dan to be their chapel preacher in August again. He said that their committee was unanimous in supporting the invitation to Dan, and he did hope that they would soon have a positive reply. Dan went home to have a cup of tea and a sandwich for lunch with Mary.

"Mary, we have been invited back to Glen Rock for the month of August."

"That's good. The children always have a wonderful time there."

"I know, but I want to try out another possibility with you . . ."

"I'll listen, but I have my own reasons for wanting to go to Glen Rock . . . I can adjust very quickly to having the services of a maid; by the end of the month I am thoroughly persuaded that I was born to be waited upon . . . But there is something much more important. You are not out working, and we have time to be together; I have a chance to learn again to know the man I love. Marriage and life and love are renewed for me, and it is all wonderful."

"Oh, boy! I can't say anything to top that!"

"No. please. Tell me what you were thinking."

"The push for a decision on the Schuster property goes on and on; at Glen Rock we are within telephone and even driving

152
Messiah Man

distance, and I think that we would have a running discussion with some one or another unceasingly throughout the month . . . If nothing else, I need to be far enough away to see this in some different perspective."

"I'm sorry, my dear. You know that it's all right with me if you want to accept one of these churches that have been in touch with you. Maybe that is what you should do. Just leave the whole mess. Let Fred and the Bishop go ahead with their big ideas."

"I know I want to get away, if only for a while. And it has occurred to me that we might take a trip. I have been thinking that we might go eastward. The children are old enough to appreciate historical sites and a visit to Washington D.C. Something of the sort, is what I'm suggesting."

"Oh, Dan. That would be wonderful! We've never done anything like that, and as you say, the children are old enough to be good travelers and to appreciate the things they would be seeing."

"I was thinking that you could take Mark and Debbie to spend some time with my parents and then with your parents. We could leave on our trip when my vacation time comes up."

"Good. Let's talk with the children tonight and get their reaction. As of now, I know they have been thinking of Glen Rock."

Dan declined the invitation from Glen Rock on the basis of "other commitments." As he and Mary and the children were looking at maps to plot the course of their trip, it was obvious that they would be going through other cities. It occurred to Dan that as a minister, he might still be "Pawley-minded." Perhaps he could and should arrange to talk with some ministers who were serving in city churches in other metropolitan areas. From somewhere he remembered a minister who was serving in a center city and was quoted somewhat to the effect that he hoped the time would never come "when the Lord couldn't afford to own a corner lot in the city." He needed to talk with someone like that, as well as other clergymen who were waging the fight in the city.

The Clark family discovered that they adapted well to travel. Mark and Debbie each had a notebook in which they wrote every night all that they had seen and done during the day. Mark did not need any prompting to make note of the fact that he had been "swimming in the Atlantic Ocean."

Mary and Debbie spent time "for women only" on Fifth Avenue in New York City. Dan managed to have conversations with no less than six ministers who were serving in center-of-the-city churches. The first night when the children were back in their own beds, Mary and Dan talked into early morning, and they agreed that it had been a wonderful family experience.

Dan vowed that he would not let his time be consumed in talk about the Schuster bequest; they would work that out somehow and in some way and at some time. He and Rev. Mr. Benson and Rev. Mr. Padgett were spending uncounted hours in personal visitation and contacts. Dan was holding small group luncheons with the understanding that the only topic of conversation during the hour would be on things of their faith: an experience in bearing witness to Jesus Christ, a passage of the Scriptures that one had discovered to be helpful, issues before the church, God's answer to prayer, and the like. The Bensons and the Padgetts were involved in small dinner groups with the same purpose and spirit. A growing number of members were meeting weekly for prayer and instruction and assignment; they had committed themselves to make a minimum of two personal calls per week in the Name of Christ and His Church.

Messiah Church was becoming increasingly personal as it was growing almost weekly in number. The transfer of one hundred and twenty-five members to colonize the Birney Community Church was only a pause in the growth of the church. Indeed, Miss Hazel prepared a memorandum for Dan to call his attention to that fact that so far, in the current calendar year, one hundred and seventy-eight persons who had been transferred to colonize new churches had returned their membership to Messiah Church. The current year promised to show the greatest numerical gain in the history of Messiah Church.

However, Dan's vacation conversations with other city pastors had persuaded him that he had been too easily receptive of urban changes. In some positive fashion, Messiah Church should be more actively engaged. He was persuaded that the church – that he – was letting the urban change go on without some positive effort to guide or to lead in making it a change for the better. Dan had returned with the purpose of gathering together a group of concerned persons. He put together a list and began telephoning and calling personally. His list included:

1. Two district councilmen.

2. The Mayor, or someone from his staff.

3. The Principals of two schools.

4. Ministers of churches located within some geographical boundaries which he established arbitrarily.

5. A representative group from the businessmen of the district.

6. At least two persons representing each of the professions: medicine, law, and dentistry.

7. Two or three persons from as many financial institutions.

8. _____

9. _____

He said later that his calls to other clergymen should have been a clue to the possible success of this approach.

The first person he called replied, "Dr. Clark, I share your concern; however, I have received another appointment. Naturally I cannot speak for my successor . . . Perhaps I should say that a successor has not yet been named because our Superintendent is thinking seriously of discontinuing the work here."

A second clergyman said, "Frankly, Dan, I don't think there is much which can be done, but I'll come to the meeting if I don't have a conflict in my schedule."

Dan stopped to see the Minister of Zion Church, who listened impassively and then responded, "Dr. Clark. We are planning to put our church property up for sale. The people of Zion Church are not at all happy in being forced to move. To be quite honest, Dr. Clark, the people of Zion Church do not understand why Christian Ministers take it upon themselves to encourage black people to move into an area where white people are living, and have always lived."

Dan was not sure that he was hearing correctly.

"Are you suggesting that *I* am personally responsible for the demographic changes in this part of the city?"

The Zion Church Pastor pursed his lips as he contemplated his reply. "These things do not just happen. *Someone* takes the lead. A direct answer to your question is 'Yes!' Many of the responsible people in Zion Church feel that *you* must bear *your* share of the responsibility for the movement which is forcing us from our homes, taking away our church, and imposing many burdens upon us."

"You can't be serious! We . . . I . . . How on earth? . . . Do you honestly think that *I* could have brought this change to pass?"

Dan left after futile efforts toward understanding with his "Christian brother."

Businessmen, when approached, had little disposition to be of assistance; most of them admitted that they were trying to establish themselves elsewhere in the city. Sam Stockwell was holding a "Going-Out-Of-Business Sale." Professional people said they were finding it advantageous for many reasons to move to other sections of the city. The Principal of Lincoln School said he was being transferred to the post of Assistant Superintendent of Elementary Curriculum Development, with an office in the central Board of Education building.

Mary was in the kitchen one late afternoon when Dan

arrived home. She stirred something in a saucepan, clapped the lid down, took off the lid to stir again, slapped the lid down and threw the spoon across the room into the sink. Dan went to her.

"What's the matter, my dear?"

"Ask Mark." Mary spoke to the window.

"All right. I'll ask him. Where is he?"

"Upstairs in the bathroom . . . where I sent him." The lid came down again like a cymbal crash.

Dan went to the foot of the stairs. "Mark."

"Yes, Daddy." At least Mark could still speak.

"Will you please come downstairs for a minute?"

As the Seventh Grader from Forest Middle School came down the steps, Dan could see torn slacks and a ripped shirt pocket. There were scratches on his face and a bruise on his right forearm

"Mark! What happened to you?"

Mary appeared, talking. "The coach said there were three of them."

Dan turned to lead the way into the den.

"All right, Mark. Start from the beginning and tell me what happened."

"Well, Daddy, it started in the hall, and then we had a little trouble in the locker room."

Mark obviously was ill at ease with everyone staring at him.

Debbie had come into the room and needed only an opening.

"Some boys told Mark that his father is a 'nigger lover.'"

"So, that's it?"

Mark muttered something about a "little sister with a big mouth."

Mary returned to the subject. "From what I learned, it must have been awful . . . Shouting and fighting. Some furniture overturned and broken, locker doors pushed in . . . Really, a kind of riot . . ."

"Mark, were the boys black or white?"

"White."

Mary used a pause to say, "The Principal called and he wants us to come with Mark to his office tomorrow morning."

Dan confined his attention to Mark. "Mark, we believe that Jesus Christ died for all persons. We must love those whom God loves, and forgive those whom God forgives."

"Oh, it's all right, Daddy . . . but I won't let *anyone* call you names."

Dan went over to throw his arms around Mark in a bear hug. When Mark squirmed in his grasp, Dan assumed that the family name had probably been defended rather well.

"Thank you, Mark. But in the future, supposing you let me fight my own battles."

Later in the evening, Mary came downstairs from checking on their children. She sat down in the den

"Now really, Dan . . . where is it going to end?" No answer. "You know as well as I that this sort of thing will probably get worse instead of better."

Dan couldn't think of a reply that Mary would accept.

"*I* want our children to respect all people, but the way things are going *here*, they will grow up with a distorted view . . ."

"Mary. Boys will have their differences. I had mine. If it isn't one thing, it will be another . . ."

Mary interrupted with passion. "Dan Clark, *this* is *different* and *you know it*! What kind of school days are these for Mark to remember? How is he going to learn in this kind of atmosphere? At least I have Debbie removed from much of this."

The next morning, Dan and Mary and Mark were in the office of the Principal, with three other boys and their parents. There were explanations, apologies, handshakings, forced smiles all around, and the Principal ushered them to the door.

Behind the closed door, the Principal sank into a chair. He spoke aloud to a calendar on the wall. "If I can only get by this year without any more outbreaks, I'll be out of this mess and in the Administration's Finance Office . . ."

Dan called a meeting of his projected Citizen's Committee of Concern. Attending as a representative of the business community was Thomas J. Davis, whose service station had grown to an extent that he was now seeking a franchise – with the assistance and guidance of Jerry Whitman. Tom waited about after the meeting to speak with Dan.

"Revner Dan. Nobody ain't gonna do nothin'."

Dan thought that Tom pretty well summarized the meeting, even without help from Rose' daily tutoring in English.

"Yes, Tom, I think that we write off this approach to our problems. But come sit down for a minute. I have another difficulty with which you can be helpful in finding an answer."

When they were seated, Dan continued. "There are many black people in the morning congregations."

Tom nodded.

"The same is true for the Sunday School classes."

Tom nodded.

"We have tried – I have tried to make *everyone* feel that this is the house of God for *all* people."

Tom continued to nod his head.

"Many, many persons are joining the church."

Nodding continued.

"But Tom, the *black people* are *not joining the church*."

Tom stopped nodding.

"Many, many black people come regularly, and I have every reason to believe that they confess Jesus Christ as their Saviour and their Lord."

Tom was nodding again.

"But, Tom, they don't *join* the church!"

"Revner Dan, they're waiting to be asked . . ."

Dan voiced frustration and impatience. "Waiting to be asked? ? ? I . . . I have asked them! I have personally invited many of them! And some of them *several* times!"

"They want to be asked in a meeting." The final "g" was clear.

Dan leaned forward to touch a forearm that stretched the sleeve of the coat. "Do you mean that they want to be invited in a service? To come down the aisle? . . . Like an evangelistic service?"

"Some do, Revner Dan."

"But we don't do *that* in *our* services." Dan was shocked to hear himself sounding so stuffy. "At least . . . we have never done that. You know that we have classes . . . but an invitation to come down the aisle? . . ."

Dan talked with Mr. Benson and Mr. Padgett. They agreed that an evangelistic service – perhaps on Sunday evening – would open another door by which people could be brought to the Lord and into the church. Mr. Benson said that he would "just love" to lead and preach in that kind of a service. The Official Board authorized an "Evangelistic Service" to be held at 6:30 p.m. every Sunday night. They would try this for a period of months to see if the attendance merited the continuance of such a service.

With some hesitation Dan approached Mr. Hoffmeyer, only to be surprised at Mr. Hoffmeyer's happy response. Indeed, he could and would arrange for the music. The service would be held initially in the chapel, but they would need piano accompaniment for the hymns in addition to the organ. And Mr. Hoffmeyer said he would recruit students for "special music," both vocal and instrumental.

The first service found the chapel filled. To everyone's surprise, a student played the organ and Mr. Hoffmeyer played the grand piano. And how he played! Later, Dan told a beaming organ teacher, "I never knew that piano had so many notes, and chords, and runs, and arpeggios in it! And that male quartet was magnificent."

Tom had been correct. With the invitation, it was difficult to find Mr. Benson among the many persons who went forward "down the aisle." Mr. Hoffmeyer – who confessed that years before he had been the pianist for a traveling evangelist – had the congregation singing "Just As I Am" with a fervor Dan would not have believed "if I hadn't been there myself."

From the first night, the Evangelistic Service at 6:30 became a regular feature of the Messiah Church program.

A final disposition of the Schuster estate was imminent. Messiah Church had talked and talked and talked – without coming to a final decision. Weeks and months had added nothing new to the alternatives before the Official Board. There was now to be one new element in the situation: Dan had come to a conclusion on what he thought the church should do. He called a Special Meeting of the Official Board in the first week of October. When the Board assembled, Dan asked to speak.

"As you know we have discussed repeatedly the possible use of the Cora Schuster bequest. We have been weighing the merits of two alternatives, with which we are all familiar. At the risk of complicating the situation, I want now to present another alternative course of action which I believe has merit.

"It is no secret that this section of the city has changed, and is changing. Fine dwellings are being reduced to slum housing, and then destroyed. Much of what is offered for housing is disgraceful. The figures on vandalism and crime in this district are shocking. There has been an exodus from this area by families, businesses, professional offices, churches and light industry. As you know, one proposal before the Official Board would utilize the Schuster bequest to help finance the relocation of Messiah Church in Indian River Heights.

"I have come to believe that the Christian Church should be a leader in the modern city – not a victim. In one effort to grapple with some of the problems in our own geographical parish, I sought to organize a Citizen's Committee of Concern – so-called. I invited ministers, business people, professional men and women, politicians, school officials, and some select individuals. We held *one* meeting. The response and the spirit of a select group was luke-warm . . . and that description is an exaggeration. Tom Davis would confirm this appraisal. (Tom was nodding his head.) Ours is a wounded area, and there are too many who find it easier to pass by on the other side.

"So then to my suggestion: In a dedicated effort to meet the problems of the community and problems of people in the community, I suggest that we use the Schuster property as a community center. It would provide accommodation, as well as an imposing front, for a broad program of community assistance and interest. Properly exploited, it might be a means to give residents of this area a sense of community and encourage a feeling of community pride.

"It would work in cooperation with governmental and other social agencies. It could be a front to enlist commercial and cultural and financial interests for what they might contribute, not just to maintain what has been, but to lead in rebuilding a new way of living that would contribute to the development of the city as a model for urban living in our time.

"Let me suggest some services which might be sponsored:

1. Nursery and child care for working mothers.
2. A free medical clinic for children.
3. An employment service.
4. An office for legal aid.
5. Classes in English, in civic affairs, in personal and household finance.
6. Marriage counseling.
7. Programs of education and recreation for youth.
8. Housing information and referrals.
9. Senior citizen activities – perhaps including luncheon on weekdays.
10. Musical and cultural activities.
11. Courses to teach people how to maintain and furnish

their properties.

"In general, the program would be devoted to meeting needs to improve the quality of life in this district.

"No one knows better than I that we have problems with our church budget; so this would have to operate on its own. A sale of the furnishings plus the cash bequest might be put into an endowment fund to provide for utilities and maintenance. The bulk of the work would have to be done by volunteers under the guidance of a minimal paid staff. This is all quite sketchy, but I want to know if you think that such a center would serve community needs and – as I said – serve to improve the quality of life about us. I would see the whole operation under the leadership of a board, or a committee, which would be named in its entirety by the Official Board of Messiah Church.

"Before opening the subject for discussion, I want to admit that the possibility of such a center and a successful program would depend almost entirely on the kind of leadership we might be able to recruit to get it started."

Marge was eagerly awaiting Fred's return from the meeting.

"Did the Board vote tonight?"

"No, the Board did not vote . . . More than that, Dan came in unexpectedly with a whole new proposal which has put a new look on the whole situation."

"Here, come and sit down. Tell me all about the meeting."

When they were seated with a cup of coffee and a piece of cake for each of them, Fred gave Marge an account of the Board meeting.

"Do you agree with this proposal of Dan's?"

"Of course not, Marge. But it was obvious that he was making sense with many on the Board. As I listened to Dan, I must admit that he was almost persuading *me*. It's difficult to disagree with the assertion that the Christian Church must serve people."

"What do you think that the church should do?"

Fred was pacing up and down. "I think Dan is being too much of an idealist. I think he is seeing possibilities of great good, where they simply do not exist. In my judgment, there is realism to the proposal that we sell and move . . . We would *still* be serving people."

"Fred, please sit down. You're making me nervous walking about the room . . . Did you speak your thoughts at the meeting?"

Fred stopped to lean against a door frame. "Yes, I spoke, but not in those words . . . Anyway, there are two important factors in this whole situation. I know George wants to use the assets of Messiah Church for the establishment of a church in Indian River Heights. And secondly, Dan himself admitted that his community center idea will be able to get off the ground only if the right leadership is available."

"Does Dan have anyone in mind?"

Fred sounded almost cheerful. "I'm sure he doesn't, or he would have said as much tonight. However, to keep this whole thing in hand, I should probably see George tomorrow."

When Fred called, he learned that the Bishop had just gone as a delegate to a meeting in London; from there he would be going to another meeting in Geneva. He and his wife were then planning to go to the Holy Land, and they would be returning for a vacation trip in Canada. The date for his return to his office had not been fixed as yet.

It was Indian Summer, and Dan was unable to settle down to his work. He sat idly at his desk. He looked outside for a time and picked up the telephone to call Dave. "These days are too good, and they will come to an end too soon . . ." They met in the parking lot of the Country Club.

"This is good timing, Dan." They shook hands. "You know, I was thinking of calling you when the phone rang." They started to walk to the club house. "How much time do you have? Would you mind if a friend of mine joined us?"

"All afternoon . . . and 'No'"

"Good. We'll have lunch first. John Phillips will meet us at the first tee at one."

They went through the pro shop and into a dining room. "John Phillips. Do I know him?"

"He has been in church with me a couple of times. I have wanted to get the two of you together. John and I had talked of playing today, and then you called. God has a way of fitting pieces together."

"Should I know anything about him?" They were seated at a table.

"John and I are friends of long standing. He is Midwest Director for Massachusetts Mutual. For years I have heard him say that the church is nice, but innocuous. Lately, I have been telling him what Christ has done with me."

Their food was served and they ate in silence for a time. As Dave looked for the waitress to get more coffee, he spoke casually. "What is happening to your suggestion for a community center?"

"We keep coming to the question, 'Who will head up the program?'"

Dave toyed with his cup, which was now full. "Feel free to stop me, Dan, at any point that I don't make sense. I have been working at my job, and things are going quite well. From Father and now from Mother's estate, I have more than enough. I can't see myself working just for money. Kurt will be married when he graduates, and he will go into the military or graduate school . . . The truth is . . . I'd like to do something for personal satisfaction . . . Well, I don't understand fully what is required for the proposed center . . . I've been thinking that I might try to help . . ."

"Dave, are you saying what I think you are saying?"

"I'm not saying it very well, Dan. But what would be the reaction if I volunteered my services for this project?" The offer did not sound ridiculous, hearing him say it out loud. The expression on Dan's face was encouragement to continue.

"You have said that much service would be needed by volunteers. I do know a lot of people around town, and not a few of them owe me favors, and most of the people I know would be better off if they would give something of themselves for others . . . and for the Lord."

Dan's response was really in his face and voice. "I'd like to call a Board meeting for this afternoon. Finish your sandwich, because I'll be a tiger on the course today."

Dan called a special meeting of the Official Board. He presented Dave – not that it was necessary – to the Board and asked him to speak.

"I have been thinking about the proposal to establish a community center and program. I would like to do something about it. If the Official Board approves of the project itself, I am willing to assume the responsibility of an effort to formulate and manage a meaningful program. To clear the air, I would do this for personal compensation of one hundred dollars per year, and the right to live in the apartment in the carriage house."

There was an immediate motion to go ahead with the community center with David Schuster as the Director. No dissenting opinion was registered in the vote.

Dave spoke again. "Thank you for your confidence. Let us understand that ultimate control should rest with the Official Board of Messiah Church. I suggest that immediate supervision be exercised by a Board of Directors elected by and responsible to this Official Board.

The Official Board unanimously adopted an enabling resolution which Dave submitted.

"I have presumed to take the liberty of approaching some individuals in this regard. I will now read a list of twelve names, all of whom have agreed to serve, if elected by you."

The Official Board approved unanimously a proposal by Dan that they have a ceremony in a Sunday service to launch

"Schuster Center" formally, and to commission its Board of Directors.

The next day Fred Hudson altered his daily schedule to return home at noon. He sat down with his wife in their new family room.

"Marge, I talked with George this morning. He gave me the old line about this being his first week back in his office. So I said, 'Stop it, George! What about Dan?'"

"I daresay I already know the answer."

"He fiddle-faddled around and finally said he had done nothing before he left. So I asked, 'What about NOW?'"

And he said that there really isn't any opening which would be a decent alternative for Dan."

"Does he know about the Official Board meeting?"

"Yes, he knew *all* about it. His only comment was that the people Dave recruited would come close to being a Who's Who of the city."

"So then, what are you going to do?"

"What we decided."

At 1:30 p.m. Fred walked into the Study and seated himself at Dan's invitation. "Let me come directly to the point."

"Please do."

Fred looked at a point over Dan's head. "Dan, Marge and I want a transfer of our church membership to Hilldale Methodist Church."

Dan could not speak. From his first day in Messiah, Fred Hudson had been his personal friend, his advisor, his confidant; the Schuster bequest had been their only serious difference of opinion.

"I *am* sorry, Dan. Believe me . . . Marge and I have been talking about this for some time."

Every word hurt as Dan spoke. "Fred . . . you have never even hinted . . ."

"I didn't see any reason for bringing it up unless Marge and

I were sure in our own minds." He paused, not liking his own words. "You know, of course, that most of our friends have left Messiah . . . Dan, it isn't this race business. Of course, while you were on vacation there was the incident when a boy tried to grab Marge's purse as she was walking to the door of the church while I parked the car."

"As I said to both of you, I am sorry about that."

Fred waved a hand. "Oh, don't think I hold *you* personally responsible . . . Dan, I have never attended any other church than Messiah . . . You know well that I am very fond of you personally. Way back, I told Marge that I intended to stay with Messiah as long as you remained the pastor here."

"Fred, *I* am not the church."

Fred looked at his watch. "No, you're not, but I have thought so many times in recent months that your abilities are being wasted here . . . Frankly, Dan, it seemed to me that Cora Schuster's bequest was a real chance to gather up what remains and build a *new* Messiah Church. I wanted so much to see *you* in an enterprise like *that* . . . But when the Official Board rejected that course and decided to try for your community center idea, Marge and I talked it over and we have decided that this is what we should do . . . . Now Dan, don't think I'm angry because the Board didn't do as I wanted."

"Fred, what can I say?" Dan threw up his hands in a hopeless gesture.

"Oh, I certainly am not indispensable. There will probably be a dozen men who can be of much more help than I ever was . . ."

Fred heard the lameness of his words, and so he stood up. "I must be going. This is one of the hardest things I have ever had to do." The whole business had gone badly; he didn't like the way he was sounding and appearing; he would like to salvage something. "I want you to know that Marge and I will always be 'Messiah people' at heart. If there is ever anything which I can do to help, feel free to call on me . . . And I hope we can have lunch together from time to time – I'd miss those personal contacts with you."

For all the responses that rushed to Dan's mind, the only words to which he could give voice were, "I'll ask Miss Hazel to send the letter of transfer."

Fred made his way from the room with an unaccustomed lack of self-possession. Dan told Mary later, "I didn't know I could so easily be a little boy again. It would have helped if I could have gone crying to my mother."

In the dark cloud of the following days, Gwen Gossert called Dan and wanted to make an appointment to come and see him.

Dan asked, "What do you want, Gwen?"

"As you know, Larry and I are divorced. Even so, I want to talk with you about seeing Larry and maybe straightening him out again so that we might possibly re-establish our marriage."

Dan was never very proud of himself for this moment.

"Gwen, you are a member of St. John's Church and you have a pastor. If you want the help of a minister, I suggest that you call Mr. Williamson. If you had wanted me to serve as your minister, then you should have remained a member of Messiah Church."

Over the line, Dan heard a gasp. "I never thought I'd hear a minister of the Gospel talk like this! *I'm very sorry to have bothered you, and I most certainly will not do so again!*"

Dan said good by to a dead phone.

Dan stopped by the general offices of the power company. Larry suggested they go into a conference room where they would not be disturbed.

"Dan, I think I know why you're here. I don't want to take your time to no purpose. Let me say that everything is the way it was before . . . only more so . . . Dan, I've had it! I appreciate your willingness to help, and I truly wish there were some other options. I would not have moved out if I thought there was another course; however, there is nothing to be done now, but the obvious."

There was much publicity given to the establishment of "Schuster Center." A Sunday edition of one newspaper did one feature story on the Schuster family, and another on Messiah Church as the "mother church" of many new suburban churches and now of this service center. Fred Hudson read the columns and threw down the paper." Marge, listen to this! 'Bishop Gossert has commended the vision of the Minister and the Official Board and the members of Messiah Church.' Oh, Marge! Why doesn't George be honest and say what he really wanted to do with the Schuster money and Messiah Church?"

The Bishop participated in the service which officially founded "The Schuster Center.' In the Study before the service he said to Dan, "Dan, I hope that Fred will continue to be helpful in The Bishop's Fund program, even though he is now a member of a Methodist Church."

Later at home, the Bishop said to his wife, "Ada, in answer to my question, Miss Hazel told me this morning that the membership of Messiah Church is now over sixteen hundred. That's almost unbelievable!"

"The church was overflowing at 11:00 o'clock. Someone said there was a large congregation at 8:80. But, George, I went to speak to Mr. Hoffmeyer and Miss Hazel; I seemed to know so few people in the congregation. What's happened?"

"I knew Charlie Padgett years ago, but I think today is the first time I had a chance to talk a bit with Willard Benson . . ."

"I was talking with Grace Morgan – one of the few people I recognized. I said something about Messiah Church, and her face lighted up. She started talking and I had to be almost rude to get away from her."

"What did she have to say that took so long?"

"She wanted to tell about Larry. She said that he is Superintendent, or something, of the Youth Department. That's both Junior Hi and Senior Hi. She said that Larry has recruited some college boys and girls to help him, and that there have never been so many young people in the church. They want to buy the property across Church Street for a Youth Center. Grace said they have all sorts of musical groups: choral and instrumental; best of all, she said, is to see their faces when they talk about Jesus . . . Just think. Our Larry is in the thick of that, indeed the leader of that!"

"I know. A sales contract for that property went through our office . . . But, Ada, I'm concerned about Larry . . ."

"For goodness sake . . . Why?"

"Well, he has followed Dan into a theological position and a practical expression that leans far, far to the right. It is a fundamentalism that can go to extremes. And it can mean trouble. The Chair-person of our Christian Education Committee spoke to Larry about the publication materials which they are using with their young people. Larry was quite blunt with her. He said that our church materials don't teach nor believe in the Bible; he said he had gone through publications for the year ahead and they did not mention salvation – or as he said – young people putting Jesus first."

"George, what's wrong with that? I'm surprised at you, that you would fault Larry . . . and Dan . . . for something like that. You will have to admit one thing. Whatever they believe and do . . . it's certainly working."

"I don't want to talk about that now."

"There is something that somebody ought to talk about. Did you take a good look at Dan Clark this morning? He looks *awful*! If I were his wife, or his mother . . . or his Bishop . . . I would be terribly concerned. Dan Clark is a good man and a *great preacher*. The Church can't afford to lose even one of his kind."

"I know, Ada . . . Wow! I don't know what Dan said to Gwen, but she was hopping mad when she called me. She said Dan ought to be thrown out of the ministry."

Ada Gossert was grim. "I guess I feel even more sorry for Mary Clark, having to live and bring up her children in that neighborhood with what has happened to it and all."

The Gossert's son had not told them of a conversation with Dan Clark. He had stopped at the church one day after work to make some preparations for the Youth Department for the coming Sunday. He encountered Dan as he was leaving, and they went into the church office to talk; all of the office staff had left for the day.

"Dan, I'm glad for this encounter. I've been wanting to talk to you about a couple of things."

"First of all, let me say what a wonderful work you are doing with the youth program. There is no question that you are enjoying the Lord's blessing."

"That leads into what I wanted to discuss. You see, I find myself being asked questions again and again, and I am embarrassed to be without answers. These are questions about the Bible, about Christian Faith. I am getting my work schedule arranged so that I can take a class at Midwest Seminary in the second semester."

"That is splendid. I hope that it's feasible for you."

"It was not all that difficult. The thing is that my contacts with the seminary to set this up have started me to thinking on another track. Dan, I am thinking about studying for a seminary degree to become a minister . . ."

Larry stopped and waited for Dan's response.

"Yes. And what's the problem?"

"Come now, Dan. I am older than you. I am divorced. I have two daughters who are young ladies, so I have financial commitments. My father is the Bishop, and right now that's more negative than positive . . ."

"Larry, we must do what we believe the Lord would have us to do. Everything else is incidental. Whatever we may regard as difficulties, are simply problems to be worked out along the way."

"This was a passing thought at first. It has become more and more insistent. Wherever I read in the Scriptures, this rises before me in one way or another. I have needed to get it out and hear how it sounds when I speak it aloud. I'm sorry to burden you, but meeting you here today struck me as the time to declare myself to someone. What can I do? Should I sit down with Dad . . . and Mother?"

"I may change my mind tonight, but I'll give you an off-the-cuff reply. Continue to read the Word and to pray for guidance. Take this one course. See how it goes. Don't make any commitment, and *don't* feel *pressured* to make any decision until you have done this one course."

Larry sat for a moment thinking about Dan's words.

"Thank you, Dan. That seems clear and positive and straightforward . . . And now, if I may, I have another question for you. Since before my divorce, I have had no personal social life. Goodness knows, I spend hours with these kids, but there are times when I feel as though I need to have a private life. Would you understand that?"

Dan nodded.

"Very well. I want to know if you have any objection, personal or professional or Christian, if I asked Carol King to have dinner with me some evening?"

"Larry, I am opposed to anything which might take Carol away from her place in the life and work of this parish. If you can offer me any guarantee on that, I think you both are adults and Christians, and you are privileged to make your own decisions."

∝   ∝   ∝   ∝

November 15

Dear Mother and Daddy

I am sorry I have not written, but it is hard to let you know something of the tumult in which we live at the moment.

This past week was my turn on the car pool to get Debbie to school. It is a real burden, but as I keep saying – I think it is worth it for what I can see happening in Debbie's life and development.

Mark has made the basketball team. He is a substitute, but he is a member of the first team and he is thrilled. It is rare for a Seventh Grader to make the first team, and Mark is aware that he is the only Seventh Grader on the team. As you know, Dan put a backboard and hoop on the garage. Well, I don't have to wonder where Mark is; I have the sound of a bouncing ball as a familiar part of my background. If at all possible, Dan goes to their games, and it is a great time for both of them if Mark gets some playing time. He seems so tall because he already towers over me.

Last Sunday there was a big ado in the 11:00 o'clock service with the Bishop here to institute formally The Schuster Center. The newspapers have played this up tremendously. Dan says that Dave is responsible for this, even as he has enlisted the support of a blue ribbon panel for the Board of Directors. Apparently everyone is surprised to see the leadership ability which Dave has displayed; Dan says that Dave will take every opportunity to give credit to the Lord Jesus Christ.

As I told you on the phone, it was a real blow to have Fred and Marge Hudson leave the church. He was very angry that Dan and the Official Board did <u>not do what he wanted</u>, which was to use the Schuster money to move and rebuild Messiah Church. What can I say? I thought it was a wonderful idea, and I told Dan as much. Fred left in a huff, and now he doesn't like that image of himself. He has called Dan several times to invite Dan to have lunch with him. I think that Dan is to have lunch with him and the Bishop some day next week.

All of us are working now to prepare for the celebration of Christmas. Lois and I are working over some old costumes to make them usable; Dan says we can't spend the money for new ones.

We are looking forward to a happy Christmas time. We have already made reservations at The Hoosier for Father and

Mother Clark.

With all my love,
Mary

∝   ∝   ∝   ∝

Activities would commence at The Schuster Center as of January 1, and Dan anticipated his own involvement in some of the work to get this program launched. However, his plans somehow simply disappeared. His mother was aghast at seeing him; she talked of nothing else to his father when they were alone.

"He looks awful!!! I hardly recognize him as my son!!! Something must be done, and done now . . ."

She talked with Mary. She talked with Mary's mother, who voiced her concerns to Mary.

"Mary, what is wrong with Dan? He looks more dead than alive . . . Can't you see?"

Mary confessed to her mother that Dan seemed more tired, but the Christmas season was demanding and she thought he would be much better with all of the extra load behind him now.

Her mother was not to be put aside. "Mary, you always write and talk about the children and the things which you are doing in your care of them. Anyone can see the beautiful job which you are doing with Debbie and Mark; but a husband like Dan needs attention, too. He is totally committed to the Church to a point that I doubt that he gives a second thought to himself and his own needs. Whether you like it or not, you have a responsibility to Dan and for Dan."

The Clarks and the Carters met in the Clarks' hotel room. They sought to arrive at what help they might offer to the four people who were dearest to them. They came to agreement at several points. As a matter of habit, Amos Clark made note of these points on a piece of the hotel guest stationary.

1. Dan and Mary should both have complete examinations.

175
Messiah Man

2. Dan should be away from his work for at least three or four weeks. (Speak to Bishop Gossert about pulpit supplies.)
3. They (Clarks and Carters) would split the cost of this time away.
4. Mark and Debbie should be enabled to go about their lives with as little change in schedule as possible.
The Carters had some commitments. The Clarks could and would stay, move in, and take over to look after the children and run the house. Carters could come in two weeks and stay indefinitely.

Three days later the Clarks moved in. Reservations were made for four weeks in a winter resort lodge. Medical tests had been made. Rev. Mr. Benson was completely taken aback when he was asked to take the Sunday services for three weeks, but he agreed and vowed to do his very best. The Bishop would take a fourth Sunday. Mrs. Clark – and later, Mrs. Carter – would share in the pool to get Debbie to school. Mark thought it would be great if his grandfathers could come to some basketball games. Dan and Mary were on their way, wondering to each other how this could be happening to them.

When Dan and Mary arrived at the lodge, he was too weary to engage in any of the winter sports activities. If he was not eating or napping, he was content to sit by the huge stone fireplace and let his thoughts and prayers wander over his life and work. It was obvious that Messiah Church had turned about. The membership of the church at the end of the year, the number who had participated and attended the Christmas programs and services, it was all most encouraging – "like the old days" was voiced again and again.

Dan asked himself repeatedly, 'What had they done, and were doing that had served to effect this upturn in the church's program and ministry?' There were several answers that stood out:

1. The thrust of the church's ministry and witness was unashamedly based on the acceptance and teaching of the Bible as in fact "the Word of God."

2. The spirit and conduct of the ministry was evangelical and evangelistic. The healing ministry had become an essential factor in the life of the congregation.

3. There was a changed and changing spirit in the people of Messiah Church. For a center-of-the-city church, he could look from this perspective and see that the whole atmosphere of the church had become personal. In the impersonal atmosphere of a modern metropolitan community, men, and women, and young people were recovering and living in a sense of individual importance.

Andy had been a splendid Associate, and Dan was not a little disheartened to lose him. Now, in reflection, Dan reproached himself for his failure to realize that God had some new work to be accomplished. There were two – better, four – people who were chiefly responsible for effecting this change: Rev. and Mrs. Willard Benson, and Rev. and Mrs. Charles Padgett.

Willard and Charlie had quickly become bright lights in the life of Messiah Church. Both of them had spent their lives and ministry in small churches in small communities; this was their first living and working experience in a city. Dan confessed to himself and the Lord that he had no inkling of a persuasion that these ministers would be making a major and significant contribution to the renewal of Messiah Church. As the picture of the church became clearer to him, he was ashamed of his shortsightedness. He had written off both of these men as temporary assistants while the church looked for an Associate "worthy" of that role in both secular and sacred eyes. These two men – and their wives – had something to offer which was beyond the pale for Andy . . . and for Dan himself.

Willard Benson and Charles Padgett were gifted with "a Pastor's heart." They dearly loved to call on people, as they said "in the Name of Jesus," and sit down with them, and let them talk. They always seemed to have "all the time in the world," and parishioners found it easy to confide in either of them. Neither of them made appointments to call, and not a few persons confessed their consternation at hearing the doorbell and looking out to see "the Minister" at the door. No one ever expressed regret for admitting them with a word about "taking me as I am today." One lady spread throughout the congregation her story about Mr. Benson calling and discovering that she and her husband were both feeling unwell; upon learning that they had been unable to get out for several days, he demanded a shopping list and went to the market for them.

Something happened in the congregation when the story went around about Mr. Padgett and his wife calling at a home, only to find the lady alone and quite ill. He telephoned her physician, and they took her at once to the doctor's office. (Mrs. Padgett had helped her get dressed). He picked up some prescriptions on the way back. Returning to her home, they looked about. After getting her in bed, they had picked up and straightened up her house, emptied trash, and run the vacuum cleaner. They had cleaned her kitchen, putting dishes and kitchenware in the dishwasher. Charlie telephoned a sister who lived in another part of the city; she quickly agreed to come and stay until her sister was recovered, and they waited till she arrived.

Nobody could remember exactly how it started, but Mr. Benson, or Mr. Padgett, had called on one elderly shut-in. In some group, or some occasion, a word had been spoken about the squalor in which this woman was forced to live. One young couple had followed up with a call on this lady, and they left saying that they wanted to do something to help her. Other people were recruited. Two or three couples went back to find out what was needed, *and what she would like*, to renew her home. They all chipped in to buy paint, curtain material and the like. On an appointed Saturday, a crowd showed up to work. When they left, her home was painted and papered, with new curtains. There was a new, bright-patterned spread on her bed, and a cracked mirror had been re-placed on the dresser in her bedroom. It took a little longer before her kitchen was attractive and everything worked. Plumbing and electrical facilities were modernized. She was overwhelmed and wanted to pay for the work. They asked her to thank God, and on the final day they all stood about in a circle holding hands, to pray for her, for each other, and for their church.

The lady was telling her grateful account to everyone. One renewed place called for another. It never was really organized. No one kept any statistics. There were many answers, plus the fact that this was still going on. Older people were helped. Young couples found assistance in establishing a place worthy of being called "a home." Homes with children were of special concern. This was going on apace. It was not a program of the church or a social agency. It was more of a movement than a program, but there was never any doubt in anyone's mind that this was something which had arisen out of Christian concern.

No one would contend that either Willard Benson or Charles Padgett was a great preacher. And yet, when Dan was away they had taken the services to the spiritual satisfaction of the congregation. Admittedly, they were different. Mr. Benson was Christian love personified, and there was a universal acceptance of him. When he preached, he was helpful and people said that he made for great good "when he simply talked to them."

Mr. Padgett was to be associated with a well-worn Bible; he knew the Scriptures at first hand. When he was the preacher, the words of The Book became "in fact the Word of God" for each person as he or she seemed to need at that moment. The man himself was an engaging message.

Dan believed that it was indeed the specific working of the Lord that two individuals should have come out of nowhere to bring to the life and ministry of Messiah Church a Christian answer for people living in a metropolitan community where individuals could be lost and lose themselves, where personal values and the value of "person" could disappear in the crowd, with the loss of human values and human beings.

Dan returned to the city and to his work a chastened and thankful person, who was thoroughly persuaded of the present working of Almighty God in Messiah Church.

Dan and Mary returned to find The Schuster Center bustling with activity. The carriage house apartment had been redone, and Dave had decorated it with items which he selected from the house. He had already moved in. He was currently engaged in a private offering of the furnishings, for which he was asking a full market price "plus a little for the cause." The music room would be kept intact and roped off as a memorial to Kurt and Cora Schuster. The third floor had been sealed off for the time being. Work was going forward to prepare space for some service activities which welcomed the use of cost-free facilities. In ten days, there would be a much-publicized auction to dispose of all unwanted furnishings and equipment. Contractors seemed to enjoy being persuaded to reduce their bills through the blandishments of Dave and one of the members of the Board – Thomas J. Davis.

The multitude who were attracted to the auction created traffic problems in the area, but by mid-afternoon everything was sold, leaving the directors with what Dave called "lovely cash." There was an "Open House" for the formal opening of The Center, with Directors and their wives or husbands ready to tell of the program and their hopes for the usefulness of The Schuster Center. Dave reported to Dan that during the hours of the Open House, he had received job offers from three local companies. Dan also heard that at the same time, Dave took every opportunity to tell of his personal satisfaction in this endeavor as his way of serving His Lord and Saviour.

Kurt Schuster received his bachelor's degree from the university in the December graduation. A week later, he and

Katherine Oldham were married and left on a wedding trip, which included a visit to his father. When they arrived, they were surprised to find Peggy, who was just leaving to return to work in Washington, after having spent a few days after Christmas with Dave. They returned from their trip in time for Kurt to enroll in Wharton for the second term, and they quickly invited Nan to come to Philadelphia, to see their new apartment and their wedding pictures. Peggy came up from Washington to join them for the day.

At one time when there was a break in the conversation Peggy blurted out, "You should have seen Dad! He is the most wonderful person . . . I never realized . . . he is so . . . so . . . wonderful, is all I can say!"

Later, when Peggy had opportunity to speak privately with her mother she said, "I'm sorry, Mother, if I said the wrong thing. I feel as though somehow I might have embarrassed you."

"No. Peggy. You said nothing wrong. If it would help you to feel better, tell me right now about your visit with your father."

The program at The Schuster Center seemed to be something that had been waiting to happen. Carol King would participate in a counseling program; she had worked out with her Chairman an area in which she could work that would provide a basis and data for her doctoral dissertation. Tom Davis brought Lou Street to Dave. Lou Street's name was legendary in high school athletics; he had gone to the university and achieved national recognition. In his first year of professional football, he had been injured and would never play a contact sport again. Back home and casting about for something to do, he had met Tom, who took him to Dave, who hired him as Youth Director. Legal and medical professionals readily gave of themselves and their talents. Rose Davis was teaching a large class in a course of "remedial English."

It was true that black people had moved into the district. That was not the whole story, and everyone was surprised when Dave brought two Korean men to see Dan. A group of Korean immigrants also had settled in the area; they missed their Christian Church. An arrangement was worked out for the Korean community to have a service of worship in the chapel of Messiah Church every Sunday at 3:30 p.m. Until they mastered English sufficiently to participate meaningfully in the worship of the church, one of the Ministers of Messiah Church would preach for them as frequently as possible, with the aid of an interpreter.

There were various types of community gatherings under the auspices of The Center. But whatever the purpose, there was always some discussion of the neighborhood and what they could *do* to make the physical setting of their existence more livable. It became obvious that there was need of improved public services. The City Commissioner from District One was repeatedly invited to come to community meetings; he always accepted the invitation with a word about how much he wanted to attend, but somehow something wholly unexpected always happened the day of the meeting to make it utterly impossible for him to be present. Dave used his role as Director of The Schuster Center to campaign publicly for an improvement of city services. It was known that the Commissioner claimed an apartment in the district as his place of residence; however, a series of events disclosed that he and his family had long since moved to a country club community.

The word was out that the district needed representation on the City Commission. There would be an election in November, and the only name that anyone ever entertained seriously was "David Schuster."

After Easter, Dan reviewed the program and status of the Church with both the Staff and the Official Board. Each Sunday of Lent, new members had been received into membership of Messiah Church. Mr. Benson and Mr. Padgett had requested that this continue as a regular part of the 8:30 and 11:00 services, at least until the summer months. Miss Hazel supplied statistics and added a word that the church membership was now approaching "the figure that it was when Dr. Clark had come as the Pastor." Tentative vacation plans were made for members of the Staff. The Official Board discussed the addition of another minister to the Staff, and, in addition, a person to direct the adult program of the parish. It was noticed that another full-time caretaker was needed to service the activities using the church facilities.

The children were asleep when Dan came home from the Official Board meeting. He sat in the kitchen with a glass of iced tea to talk with Mary.

"We might look ahead to the summer. The Chairman of the Glen Rock Board called me, and said that everyone wants us to come back this year. In addition, he said that both July and August are open in the event that we want to be there for July instead of August. He also said that they would be gratified if we could come for both months.

"You know, I am sure, that Mark has been saying he wants to be here in August, because he wants to go out for football. Their practice is to begin August 16."

"Yes, I know. He has been after me to show him how to throw and to catch a football . . ."

"Dan, I become terrified at the thought of my boy being run into, knocked down, and at the bottom of a pile of bodies on a football field. I read an article only recently by a physician who recommends strongly that boys not play football until their bodies have matured. He also said that if he had his way, no boy would ever risk damage to himself on a football field."

"Mark said that you had told him you don't want him playing football."

Mary sounded as though she had surrendered to the inevitable. "He will be in the Eighth Grade. He says that the other boys are no bigger than he is; the coach met with them to say they should work to be in the best physical condition, because this is the best protection against injury. And as I understand it, much of what they will do is to work on body building so they know what to do in the years ahead if they do decide to play football."

"It's no secret, and Mark knows that I played football at his age. Mary, he is a big boy, or at least he feels that he is a big boy. I think we go along with him for the time being at least."

They settled on a schedule by which Mary would take Mark and Debbie to Belvoir when school was dismissed in June. Dan would pick them up to go to Glen Rock for the month of July. When Dan returned to work the first of August, she and the children would go to be with her parents for a couple weeks, and return before August 16.

∝   ∝   ∝   ∝

May 22

Dear Mother and Father Clark,

The time gets away so swiftly that I think I should write to apprise you of our plans for this summer.

We have been invited again to Glen Rock – however, we are going for the month of July this year. This change works out better for everyone.

As of now, I shall be driving – with Debbie and Mark – to Belvoir on June 12. I don't know what day of the week that is, and I can't find a calendar. We should arrive at your place by the middle of the afternoon at the latest. That is our schedule as of now.

Dan can get away here on the 27th or the 28th, and he will come to Belvoir. We shall all leave the next day for Glen Rock. The arrangement is that the children and I will be with my parents for the first two weeks in August. Then we must return.

Mark will be in the Eighth Grade. This makes him eligible for Junior Hi football. Please get ready Father Clark. Dan has been trying to teach Mark how to hold and throw a football, and they are throwing it to each other whenever they can get some time. Now then. Dan told Mark that all he knows about handling and throwing a football, is what "My Father taught me." Mark is *coming with the expectation of learning from the <u>Master Teacher</u>.*

Mother Clark, some time – if we can – we must let Debbie prepare and serve tea. This is a <u>warning!</u> This is something which she has learned at school. She must make everything from scratch. She must serve. (Please don't be insulted if she insists on washing the teapot and the creamer!) And finally she <u>must pour</u> the tea. She must have some Japanese blood in her, as she takes the whole thing very seriously.

I don't need to tell you that Dan is busy all the time. I tell him that I have to go to the church services to see him. Dan says that there are encouraging signs and movements in the church.

With all our love,

Mary

∝   ∝   ∝   ∝

Two days after Mary and the children were off to Belvoir, Matt came to tell Dan that he wanted to resign.

"I have a chance to get on as a machinist in the new aircraft plant. It'll mean more money, and we're going to need it because Lois is going to have a baby. It is costing more for the children . . . well, I don't need to tell you how Bob can clean out the refrigerator with between-meal snacks."

"Goodness, Matt, we shall miss you. We have come to depend on you for just about everything."

"Lois and I want to buy a house with a yard, and we think we will be able to do this . . . Dr. Dan, I'm sorry, but I feel I've got to do this for my family . . ."

Dan looked at the unhappy figure of Matt. "Of course, I know you must do what you think is best for your family. I also know that Mary will miss Lois. And Mark and Debbie will be lost without Bob and Ruth."

"I know, I know. Lois couldn't bring herself to say Good-bye to Mrs. Clark, and she made me wait till Mrs. Clark left before speaking to you."

Dan nodded and shook his hand.

"Now, Dr. Dan . . . the reason we are movin' . . . well, it's not what you might think . . . I'll admit . . . where I come from, we don't make company with black folks. For most of my life, I wouldn't spit in the same street with 'em, let alone clean a toilet one of 'em used . . ."

"You never said anything . . ."

"*But that isn't it*. Things seem different . . . Now, you take that Tom Davis. Dr. Dan, there is a Christian gentleman if I ever saw one." Matt stood for a moment in the recognition of his personal discovery. Tears commenced to run down his cheeks.

"We'll never forget you and Mrs. Clark. You all helped to bring us to Jesus . . . This job was a life saver for us . . . And you have always treated me like I was as important as you . . . But I have to try to get ahead, to do the best I can for my family. And the baby will make six of us." He seized Dan's hand and bolted from the room.

Mary read Dan's letter as far as the news about Matt and Lois Luke, and she went to Dan's mother.

"Lois was the best friend I had . . . At times she was the *only* friend I had. And now she is moving away. Mother Clark, *I feel trapped*! There is no money for another house for us. The Bishop can't, or won't, do anything about another parish for Dan . . . Tuition at Stone School for Debbie is going up this fall, and Dan has taken several cuts in his salary . . . Now this! Matt Luke, a church janitor, can pick up his family and move out! There is nothing wrong with being a church janitor, but even a janitor who is a country high school drop-out can get his family out of that jungle . . . Mother Clark, I have to do something . . . It isn't for myself. And yet I have seen so much beat-up and broken-down housing that I even find myself accepting slum conditions as *my* neighborhood . . ."

Mary did not wait for reply. She spun about to go upstairs to her room and close the door; she did not come out until Debbie called her for dinner. That night she called Dan. In the days that followed she asked to be excused from trips and outings to spend her time writing a continuing series of long letters to Dan.

Arriving for his vacation, Dan took them all out for dinner at a place which Mark and Debbie had chosen. Mary stated her views on their situation at the dinner table as everyone tried to eat in an awkward silence.

"The shower felt good." Coming into their bedroom, Dan went to Mary to put his arm about her. "It's wonderful to see all of you again."

Mary wriggled free to go to the bed and begin removing the spread. "I must turn down the bed."

Dan helped her fold the spread and sat down on the side of the bed. "I've missed you, Mary. I've needed you. Come."

Mary walked over to stand in front of Dan. "What are we going to do about school this fall for Debbie and Mark?"

Dan took a deep breath. Without looking up he said, "I assume that we shall try to continue what we . . ."

"Has Bishop Gossert said or done anything about another parish for you?"

Dan's voice was tired patience. "Only what I have already told you several times over. He said there were two or three places in which I might be interested. That was it. He wants to talk about Schuster money. Now, go on. Take your bath and hurry back."

Mary turned out the lamp by the bed. She asked Dan to raise his head and she put another pillow in place for him.

"I'll have my bath and look in on the children. I must do some packing for them and for myself if we are going to drive on to Glen Rock tomorrow. She kissed Dan lightly on the forehead and hurried out.

Dan lay for a moment and suddenly jerked the pillow out from under his head and hurled it across the room into a corner. "Damn!"

Arriving at Glen Rock, Mark and Debbie quickly found old friends and made new ones with whom to swim, play tennis, or go riding. Dan admitted that he was not up to being the director of vacation activities; he was tired and for now he was content to lounge and look at the water, even if he did have work to do in preparation for the next Sunday.

Mary wanted to talk. "Dan, you are out and away so much that we don't seem to have time to discuss important matters relating to the children and our life. I know that money is limited. I know that the tuition will be higher for Debbie at Stone School, and we must keep her there. Your mother commented several times about how Debbie is becoming a young lady with good manners and a gracious air. As you know, the Principal of Forest Middle School retired at the end of the school year; he said that it had all become too much and that he wanted to get out while he could still enjoy life. You know that I think we should get Mark out as well. If I spoke to him I know Daddy would give me some money for Mark's tuition at Stone School . . ."

"No!"

"All right . . . All right . . . I knew that is what you probably would say. But it is something to keep in mind . . . It has occurred to me that we might do something else . . . and you must know, Dan, that I have been concerned about this for a long time, and we are always postponing any decision or positive action for doing something for our children . . . There are times that I feel desperate inside thinking that these years are going by and we shall have failed our children in most critical aspects of their development, and we shall have let them go out into the world without the kind of preparation that would enable them to be successful adults and well-adjusted human beings . . . Anyway, I have talked with my parents, and I know it may seem somewhat far-reaching . . . But I have thought of the possibility of enrolling them in the schools in Rockford. We could stay with Mother and Daddy, and drive back to the city for the weekends . . ."

"Now, *really*, Mary . . ."

"Then I think that I have come upon an answer. Since it is a money problem which prohibits enrolling both of them in Stone School, unless or until you should take another parish somewhere out of the city . . . As I said, since it is a money problem, and you won't let Daddy help . . . then I'll get a job. I have made some enquiries and two of the department stores said that they would be delighted to have me and that they would work out a time schedule that would enable me to get the children to and from school . . ."

"Oh, Mary . . ."

"They didn't say how much I could earn, but it would, of course, depend upon the hours I could put in. Then too, one day I stopped in to have my car checked . . . it didn't seem to be running as smoothly as it did . . . Anyway, while I was waiting, I saw Al Hirter, and one thing after another came up, and I found that he needs someone in his office, and he said that the job was mine if I wanted it . . ."

"You didn't really ask Al for a job?"

"It wasn't so crude as that. Our conversation sort of came around to . . ."

Dan rose from his chair. "I'm going for a walk."

The second week of their vacation, Miss Hazel called to tell Dan of the death of a parishioner. She said that Mr. Benson would do the memorial service, but Dan said that he would do it. He hung up the phone to call the commuter airline, and he left that afternoon to return to Indianapolis. There was work to be done, so he called Mary to say that he would return on Saturday.

The following week there was another death in the parish,

and the family called to tell Dan. He returned to the city again to take the service and to do some work. This time Kathryn Mac spoke with him.

"Dr. Dan, I am submitting my resignation as of September 30. There is this boy whom I have known since high school. We dated a good bit, but somehow we had lost touch in recent years. He went into the military service and was stationed overseas in one tour of duty. While I was home on vacation he was back in town on leave, and we met quite by accident. We saw a lot of each other, and we have been talking long distance every other day since. To get to the point, we have decided to get married. He will be discharged on October 22, and we are planning for a wedding on November 1, in our home church. I am so very, very sorry to be leaving. I almost feel as though I am deserting you and the Lord in doing this."

At the end of July, as planned, Mary and the children went to Rockford to spend a couple weeks with her parents. Mary's conversations were singular in theme. The evening of the second day, her father said to her mother, "I'm worried about Mary. Has she flipped her lid?"

Two days later when she broached with her mother the possibility of enrolling Mark and Debbie in Rockford schools, her mother lost her patience.

"Mary. I think you have said enough on this subject. You have talked constantly since you arrived, and you have dwelt on one subject only, and repeated yourself *ad nauseam*. Haven't you noticed that your father is avoiding you? He says that Dan must be a saint, if you are like this in your own home. We might as well get it out on the table. Your father is a fair, but not a patient man. I ought to know him, and I think I do. I can tell you that if you keep this up, he will ask you to leave, and he will tell you that you are not welcome here till you get another string on your violin . . . And to talk of putting the children in Rockford schools as though this were heaven, you simply show that you don't know what you are talking about. Apparently it did not make the news in the capitol, but the school authorities in Rockford have revealed that there is a major alcohol and drug problem in the high school here . . . and they say that some *junior high* students are involved."

Mary left the room without a word. For several days she kept to herself and spoke only when a question was addressed to her directly. They were in the second and final week of their stay when Mary's mother spoke to her after breakfast and invited her to bring a cup of coffee and sit down in the family room. "Gramps" and the children were on a "business trip" for the day. When they were seated, her mother spoke directly.

"Last night, your father was telling me something that you may or may not know. He and Mark were together yesterday. Did you know that when you were in Belvoir, that Mark went to the Library to look at old high school yearbooks. He was looking for pictures and information on his father. He went to the newspaper and asked to see microfilm of the paper on some dates which he had. I think it was in the newspaper file that he found stories about Dan when he was playing football at the university. He said to me, 'Did you know that Dad was offered a contract by the Chicago Bears, and he turned it down to go on to school to be a minister?'"

Mary was about to respond when her mother held up her hand to continue.

"There's more. He said that he believes in Jesus, just like his Dad does and preaches. He told your father that he knows that his Dad has had a real tough job, and he is very proud of him, because he says his dad is 'a tough fighter.'"

Mary acknowledged her surprise at Mark's actions and words. Her mother's voice was kind, but insistent.

"Maybe you should be listening more, Mary."

YEAR SIX
AT
MESSIAH CHURCH

The new caretaker was James White. There were a few words to the effect, "Maybe we'll have a black minister next." But James White was a gracious man. The property was clean. All went well for two weeks, until Dan went to the church earlier than usual on Sunday morning to check on some arrangements for the Sunday School.

Kathryn Mac had worked until the end of August and had taken the month of September for vacation. She was sorely missed the first week.

The church was still locked, so Dan went about opening doors and turning on lights. Jim White did not appear at all on Sunday, or the next day, or the next. Friday morning he came in and acknowledged that he had been celebrating his first – and now his last – paycheck.

The House Committee Chairman had already hired Will Brown, after questioning him specifically if he was a drinking man. He had received the solemn assurance, "I never touch the stuff."

After a women's meeting during Will's second week, some of the ladies spoke to Miss Hazel to say that they thought they smelled liquor about the caretaker. Will reassured Dan, "I'm not a drinkin' man." Then he remembered. "I have trouble with my gums, and the dentist gave me some mouthwash to use two or three times a day for the trouble with my gums."

Dan repeated the word about the mouthwash to some of the people who had spoken about the new caretaker. Within the week, the House Committee Chairman stopped by the church one night to check on some reported needs, only to be greeted by a very lushy

Will Brown – who promptly offered him a drink. When the word of this went around, Dan received numerous requests – Dan said, "Every one who spoke to me, by my tally" – for the name of the dentist who prescribed "that wonderful mouthwash."

Dave and Tom were not only unsympathetic with the caretaker difficulty, but even reproachful. Dave said to Dan and the House Committee Chairman, "Both of you should have remembered that we have an employment service at The Center. Now, maybe you will give us a chance to give a proper person a chance."

The Annual Bishop's School would be the third week of October. Dan did not see how he could be away for the better part of a week since losing Kathryn Mac, but Mary insisted that he attend the School.

"I think you should go just to get away, and to get away from me. I know that I was a nag from the first day of your vacation. Before we left Rockford to come home, Daddy scolded me and said, 'I would have played more golf than Dan did.'"

And, too, Dan would not miss one of the Junior High football games; Mark was the back-up quarterback. Dan said to Mary, "It would not be difficult to choose between a session of The Bishop's School and one of Forest's football games."

The Annual Bishop's School was held at Wildwood Park, a state conservation preserve with a lodge, a golf course and hiking trails. Dan managed eighteen holes of golf the day he arrived. And too, there were friends and acquaintances with time to talk. The hymns, and Scripture, and prayers of the vesper service – all seemed to give Dan a better vantage point for consideration of the status of Messiah Church. He telephoned Mary to thank her for insisting that he come.

The lecturer at the 10:30 series on "CONTEMPORARY ISSUES" was Professor Maynard of Midwest Seminary. He said, in part:

"The church should recognize the changing social patterns as an opportunity rather than as a tragedy. With community life in a state of flux and transition, the church is challenged to seek to effect a structure of society which is patterned after the claims of the Kingdom. To grapple realistically with the situation, customary programs and groups, old forms, time-honored hours and patterns of worship – none could be regarded as sacrosanct. There must be a recovering of the sense of mission which was one of the characteristics of the New Testament Church."

A question period followed. At one point Dan rose to ask for some specific suggestions as to program and message; the speaker referred him to two publications of the denominational Committee on Society – of which he was a member. There was a pause, with no one else raising a question, so Dan inquired about financing in a period of transition.

Professor Maynard replied, "It is a part of Christian tradition that great works have usually been accomplished by great sacrifice."

He paused and stepped back to await another question. Then he stepped forward to the microphone to speak to Dan.

"The Church too, must walk by faith."

Someone in the group made a perfunctory observation. There was a long pause . . . Maybe the meeting was over . . . .

Dan rose again to ask Professor Maynard if he would cite some examples of church programs which were standing up to the contemporary urban challenge. Professor Maynard replied, "I have been speaking in terms of ideals. I am afraid that I should have to say that no work would satisfy the ideal criteria of adequacy. I myself have not served in this situation."

As Dan stood up again, the moderator said, "The meeting is . . ." He was interrupted by Rev. Theodore Caldwell of Brookmede Community Church, who said, "Mr. Moderator, for my part, I want to express my appreciation to Professor Maynard, who has come to us as a *teacher* of Christian Faith with words for us working Christian pastors. There are many of us who are grateful for the presence of a Christian scholar in our midst, and we want to assure him of the spirit in which we receive his exposition."

"Thank you, Mr. Caldwell. The meeting stands adjourned."

Dan went immediately to Caldwell. "Ted, I have the impression that you think I was not being very gracious with Maynard."

"Well, Dan, some of us thought you were getting rough with Professor Maynard. We are sympathetic with your problems at Messiah, but I just didn't think you ought to take it out on Maynard."

Some of the other men stopped in mid-sentence to listen. Others close by turned to look at Dan and Ted.

"Look, Ted, I was not trying to 'take out' – as you say – anything on anybody. I *liked* what he said, and I was hoping we might come up with something helpful if we pursued a few points."

A few more had gathered about the two of them.

"But Dan, every situation is different. You couldn't expect him – or anyone else – to have detailed answers for you and Messiah Church."

Professor Maynard joined the group just as Dan said, "Of course not. But as it developed, I think he was presuming to offer himself as an authority in some areas with which he has no personal experience nor expertise."

A couple of men moved to permit Maynard to push in closer. "Dr. Clark, I am a teacher. That is *my* job. One person cannot be and do everything."

Thinking about the scene later, Dan admitted to himself, 'I should have dropped the whole thing . . . *right there*!' But that was hindsight, for Dan was up for the encounter.

"Tell me, Sir. What church do you and your family attend?"

"I daresay, Dr. Clark, that you know that we attend Covenant Church."

"Isn't Ballew Avenue Church closer to the seminary where you live?"

There was an obvious stirring in the group which had grown in number. "Well, yes. We both know that."

"How many black people are there in Covenant Church?"

To a room suddenly quiet, Maynard spoke. "None that I know of. However, Covenant Church sustains . . ."

Dan's voice cut in sharply. "Do your children attend the public school in your neighborhood?"

"No, we send them to Classic School. On the basis of tests, it was determined that they need an enriched curriculum to challenge them." Maynard was unsmiling.

Dan turned at the sound of Ted Caldwell's voice.

"Dan, I don't know what you're trying to prove. This doesn't sound like you. You're letting your experience at Messiah make you bitter."

"I'm not bitter, Ted. But at Messiah we have problems that do not yield to pat answers nor academic theories."

Many eyes turned to see the flush on Professor Maynard's face.

"Dan, every church has its problems . . ."

"Of course, Ted, but I'm talking about problems which are greater than one church, or one minister . . . problems which ought to be the concern of the whole church, and yet we are left to work them out by ourselves. Not only are we alone, humanly speaking, but the membership of Messiah Church has been raided by every . . ."

Ted bristled with the support of murmuring throughout the group. "Dan, 'raided' is a strong word . . ."

Dan acknowledged Ted's interruption by emphasis. "The membership of Messiah Church has been *raided* by every suburban church in the city. We have been repeatedly *stripped* of leadership when our situation would seem to demand the best talent the church can muster."

"'Raided is a *harsh* word. It is an *unfair* word. You well know, and so do I, that there are families in Brookmede who came from Messiah. It is all part of the changing pattern of the city. But for you to use a word like 'raided' makes you sound bitter – and jealous."

As he spoke, Ted began waving his arms about so that men near him moved back to give him room.

Dan stepped squarely in front of Caldwell as though to block Ted's exit until he had finished speaking. "Not bitter, Ted . . . Not jealous, Ted . . . Disappointed? Well, yes. Disappointed in *you,* for example." The "you" was rammed home.

Men who left the room had now returned. Chairs were pushed back to form a small arena in which Dan and Ted had squared off, surrounded by their fellow ministers. In the many discussions which followed, not a few observed that an aroused Dan was an awesome animal force.

Ted sought to quiet the storm. "Dan, I don't understand why

you insist on making personal what should be a theoretical discussion."

Hands on hips. "Very well, Ted . . . Didn't you call on Walter Meyers and his family and say to them that 'Messiah Church would soon be only a mission for black people'?" Dan waited for an answer that did not come. "What were you suggesting to Forrest Andrews when you said you 'never understood why Philip Frenell left Messiah so soon after I became the Minister'?" Again Dan waited for a reply. "And then . . ."

"I don't understand . . ."

"*Walt* and *Andy* told me." Again Dan waited. There was a heavy stillness in the room. "And didn't you say to Nelson Courtney that I had gone 'to the right'? I think, however, that you used the word 'fundamentalist'."

"Look, Dan, I didn't mean to do any harm or . . ."

"And *you* raise the issue of being *personal?* Ted, I shall never understand ecclesiastical hypocrisy."

Ted held up a hand. "All right, Dan. All right.

He pushed his way through the group to leave the room. No one had noticed two men who had come to the door. Bishop Gossert stood, listening but not looking. Beside him was Philip Frenell, whom the Bishop was planning to introduce at the dinner hour, as his temporary new assistant.

Dan went back to his room. 'Did I come here to make a scene? . . . What is happening to me? . . . I sure made an utter fool of myself . . . I blew this one!'

He quickly threw his things into a bag and started for the parking lot.

He was stopped several times before getting into his car

"Thanks for speaking your mind . . ."

"Caldwell has been getting more high and mighty every time three more people join his church . . ."

"I'm with you, Dan."

"You're not leaving, are you? That's the first honesty we have had in a long while."

"You're right. If Maynard is a sample of what we have in the seminaries now . . ."

"Thanks, Dan! I wouldn't have missed that for a salary

increase."

Dan stopped at the church before going home. Rose and Tom Davis were practicing a duet with Mr. Hoffmeyer. Dan told Mary later that he had gone to The Annual Bishop's School for inspiration, and then had to come home for what he was seeking. He told Mary about his conduct at the first class. Mary nodded as he said he would write to Professor Maynard, and go to apologize to Ted.

Dan was always grateful that Larry Gossert had not been present for that day of The Bishop's School, or he might not have come to see Dan shortly before Thanksgiving.

"Dan, I want you to be the first to know of a decision which I have made. As you know, I have been doing some work at Midwest Seminary. I have now come to the conclusion that where the Lord wants me is in the Christian ministry, and I am already older than the average seminarian. I don't think that I want to drag this out interminably with one course a term. I still need a year and a half to complete the requirements – that is, if I carry a course overload for two terms."

"One course per term would stretch out . . ."

"Exactly, and I want to get where I belong. So, here is what I am trying to set up. Finances, of course, are a major problem. I have a retirement credit with the Power Company. If I leave the company, I have the option of cashing that in. The lawyer has negotiated a cash settlement with Gwen and for the girls' college education. I would have enough to finance three semesters at the seminary – if I am careful. That is what I have before me, and I want to know what you think of this course of action for me . . ."

"Larry, what can I say? If you feel led to do this. I could only say 'The Lord bless you.' Have you talked with your parents about this?"

"No, that will be my next stop. Let me say that I would hope to continue to work with the Youth Program here at Messiah, that is, if you all still want me.

"Larry, you are almost indispensable in that post. Now then, let *me* go on. As you know, Messiah Church contributes to all sorts of causes. Indeed, we make a special gift each year to a fund for theological education. I know the Official Board will think that we should put up money for your expenses. Then, too, you will be out of school for three months next summer. Supposing you come on staff here at full salary for that time . . . We always need more help than we have available."

"Dan, there is something else that I should say to you. Carol . . . Carol King . . . and I have been spending time together. As you know, she will be getting her degree very soon now. I suppose that I am here today because Carol and I were talking last night. We want to get on with our relationship. In a word, we want to get married, and we are asking you to marry us on the twenty-eighth of December. We both want *you* to conduct the service; we sense no responsibility to ask Dad. We want you because you are the one who has led us to Christ. We think it will be helpful for both of us to face the demands of the coming months if we have made a commitment to one another."

To do the right is sometimes only to do that which appears most obvious. On the other hand, if there is need of moral commitment and we find perplexity where we need certitude, then we may be helped by consideration of an ultimate goal or good. By whatever means we arrive at a decision, we are never more fully human than when we do the right just because it is right and nothing more – yet rarely do we find ourselves more desolate.

Nan had worked rather than to have the entire day to think about the meeting of the evening. She was wholly unready when the bell rang and she opened the door to Lee. He moved as though to sit down beside her.

"No, please sit there . . . in the chair beside the window. It may be easier for me to speak . . . . You know why I want to talk tonight . . . . I have asked for some vacation and today was my last day of work . . . I am going to see Dave . . . And if he will have me . . . ."

"Nan." Louder to get her attention. "*Nan*! Are you sure that this is what you want to do?"

"No. Lee. No . . . . I am not sure at all . . . I have had difficult things to do, but . . . . never . . . *never anything* as hard as this . . ."

"Then, why? . . . Please, Nan. WHY?"

It was even worse than she had anticipated. "Let me say what I *must* say . . . I didn't know that love could mean . . . what *you* mean to me . . . our love and companionship have . . . have been *so wonderful!* . . . it seemed to me that it *had* to be *right* . . . I have never wanted *anything* so much as to be *yours* . . . *really yours* . . . Right now I know that I want *nothing* more . . . I deeply resented Dr. Clark saying that there is a word in the Bible . . . more and more it seems that there are words which catch me up when I open the Bible . . . you know, Lee. We have talked . . . I . . . found I didn't want to read the Bible for this reason, and that isn't right . . ."

"Nan, my dear, it is painful to see you in such distress." Nan held up both hands to stop him from coming to her.

"Lee . . . . little by little I have come to believe that a marriage vow is a commitment . . . a commitment that admits of no reservation . . . That is what I want to offer you . . . But, I have a duty . . . not to Dave, but to Almighty God . . . I have always taught Kurt and Peggy that the way to happiness is to do one's duty . . . And now I know what I must do, yet I find only sadness . . . When I think that I shall not see you again . . . not hear your voice . . . not feel your arms about me . . . not hold you and have you . . . I really don't know how I can live . . ."

Nan broke down to sob uncontrollably. After a time she left the room. When she returned, she was in possession of herself. She walked to Lee and put a ring in his hand. Returning to seat herself, she said, "What I *must do*, I must *do*."

Lee knew Nan, and he realized that Nan had cast her lot.

"My dearest Nan. I love you . . . I shall always love you."

He struggled to his feet and stood, not knowing or caring how he wept. His arms dropped in resignation. He started for the door. He turned about to look at an unseeing Nan. "If you ever change your mind . . . If you ever have any need . . . If there is *ever anything* that I can do for you . . ."

Nan rose to follow him to the door. Lee tried to speak again but could not.

Nan said, "Good-bye, Lee."

Lee went out, and Nan closed the door.

As darkness claimed the room, Nan sat at the window, so badly wounded she did not think she could even move. She knew only a numbness within, for life and liveliness had departed from her. She thought she would make a cup of coffee, but she didn't. It was midnight when she stirred to look at her watch. She had to finish packing. Every motion was an effort. Like some dull mechanism, she went about putting things together for a trip to Indianapolis.

The plane from New York was air-borne. It was only when the "Fasten Seat Belt" sign was turned off that Nan seemed to realize the enormity of what she was doing. 'What if Dave won't have me? He knows about Lee, and he must know that . . .' She looked at the city falling away beneath. At the thought of Lee somewhere in that complex, she would gladly have run back to him – if she could. 'Well, I shall tell Dave . . . And when I do, what will he think? Dave and I are practically strangers . . . Dear, dear Peggy. Each time she has seen her father lately, she has talked and talked about him . . . But he has no idea that I am making this trip . . . The mirror in the women's room at the terminal . . . Ugh! I look like a hag! Mercy! What shall I do when I get there? Where shall I go? Maybe Dave is interested in someone else . . . I never thought of that . . . But I only asked for a part of my vacation now. I can always go back.' Nan stirred and felt lighter in spirit at the prospect of returning. 'Nothing will probably come of this. That's it! A vacation trip! I'll go to a hotel. Then when I feel like it, I'll call Dave. Nothing will come of it. Then I'll return . . .'

It was early afternoon when she tried to call Dave. No answer. She waited for a while and tried again. Still no answer. For want of any better idea she called Messiah Church and inquired for him.

"Have you tried The Schuster Center?"

The young lady who answered the phone at The Center said he

had left at noon and was not expected back. On second thought, Nan called back and asked the secretary to give Mr. Schuster a number if he did happen to return. She waited. She prayed. She lay down on the bed. Her mind raced. 'Perhaps this is all a mistake. Maybe this is a sign . . . Well, I'll get a reservation to return tomorrow . . . I could stop and see the children . . . A week's vacation might be the very thing that I need . . .'

The ringing of the telephone awakened her.

"This is David Schuster."

"Dave . . . This is Nan."

She stopped.

"Nan! What . . .? How . . .? What are you doing here?"

"It may not be proper, but can a lady ask to be taken out to dinner?"

"Oh . . . Indeed! Indeed! Wait, I have to be at the church at 7:30. Supposing I pick you up at 5:30 . . . How long will you be here? This is wonderful! Let's see . . . It is now 4:15 . . . Would you care to go to the service tonight? It is a Midweek Communion Service . . . in the chapel. But, look! I'll see you in a little while."

One hour and fifteen minutes! Nan showered. She worked on her hair. She tried on three dresses that she had brought with her. She didn't know how, but she was ready at 5:29 by her travel clock, when Dave called from the lobby. She went back twice to look at herself in the mirror.

Dave was waiting at the elevator. "I thought we might save time by going to the dining room here – if that is all right with you."

Everybody knew Dave, as they walked through the lobby. The hostess in the dining room brightened when she recognized him. The waitress acted as though she had won a prize in having Dave at one of her tables. Nan observed all of this and more. 'There *is* something about him . . . Peggy has mentioned this every time she spoke of her father.'

Dave had already ordered dinner. "If you don't like my choice for you, we can send it back . . . But tell me now. What are you doing in Indianapolis? How is Peggy, and have you seen Kurt and Katherine? How long will you be here? Is there anything I can do for you?"

Dave stopped and laughed when he realized he was giving her

no time to answer.

Nan thought she might as well get it out. "Dave, I don't know how to say it, but I have come back to Indianapolis . . ."

"That's great news! What can we do to make you feel welcome?"

The waitress served a salad. Nan did not touch her fork; she had to make her statement, at least . . . . before she could eat one bite.

"No, Dave, that's not quite it . . . I came back to try to talk with you about the possibility of picking up the pieces of our marriage . . . that is, if you want to talk about it . . ."

When Dave made no reply, Nan was almost overwhelmed with the awareness that she had given no notice to Dave . . . and had received no invitation from him.

'This is most presumptuous of me!' She wished she could run . . . NOW . . . FAST . . . BUT NOW. Her voice was unsteady.

"Dave, I *know* that *I* left. I know that I have not written nor even tried to discuss with you what I am now trying to say. If you would rather not talk or think about it . . . or, if there is someone else in your life . . . it's all right."

Dave leaned forward with his folded hands on the table in front of him. He was the picture of Father Schuster asking the blessing at the table.

"No, Nan. I find myself at a loss for words . . . You see, ever since I came to Christ and He brought me to myself, I have prayed for you to come back. To see you . . . and to hear you now . . . Well, it is an answer to a prayer which I had almost begun to regard as futile."

"Dave, it's been so long. We have both changed."

Dave had not moved. "I know, but I regard it as a miracle to come this far."

(How to say what must be said sooner or later? 'Just say it!')

"I told you once that there was a man who loved me and whom I had come to love . . ."

Dave was shaking his head. "How well I remember. I almost quit praying that night!"

('Say it. Don't go any further without being honest! Don't you dare to go to a Communion Service till it's all out!')

They needed a break and toyed with their salads.

"I must tell you, Dave, that we – this man and I – have been very good friends. I learned to love him. However that may be, I have come to believe that my place is *here* . . . *with you*. I would need your patience."

(It's his eyes. There is compassion in them!)

"Patience? Patience is a small price to pay . . ."

(He doesn't understand yet!!! He must know!!! There can be no uncertainty. *So, just say it!*)

"Dave . . . Lee and I . . . This is not easy . . . Well, I must ask for your forgiveness. Do you understand me?"

Dave did not take his eyes from her face as he nodded.

"I could not make a try at our marriage again unless you understood completely. As I said, I must ask your forgiveness, even as I have asked for God's forgiveness."

Dave did not move; he appeared to be praying. "There is so much for which I need to beg *your* forgiveness."

"I determined that I would tell you *everything* . . . up front."

"So now you have said it. Enough! What God forgives, we must forgive."

Dan had come to the chapel early in order to hear Mr. Hoffmeyer's prelude in its entirety. At a break in the music, Dan looked about only to see Dave and Nan Schuster coming down the center aisle. DAVE and NAN!!! They sat down in a pew side by side!!! He had seen Dave at three o'clock and Dave had said nothing about Nan.

In the foyer at the conclusion of the service, Dave said, "Dan, you remember my wife, Nan."

There was something about the way he said, "my wife."

Dave and Nan talked and talked. They went to a park to stroll about unaware of the passage of time. They *were* aware that they needed to get to know each other. For Dave, Nan was the person he had remembered. For Nan, Dave was not the same Dave, but a new Dave – everything that Peggy and Kurt and Katherine had been trying to describe, and more. They drove into the countryside to see fall coloring now in its fullness.

Nan continued to live in the hotel at Dave's insistence.

"You must have no sense of outside pressure to do this."

Nan said she would like to see Dave's apartment, but he resisted and found excuse to do other things.

They sat down with Dan for a long time, and decided they would like to continue this discussion. They came back the next day to talk for more than an hour. Nan tried to recall some of the problems she had anticipated, for it was all working out too easily to be real. Surely, there would need be some agonizing and suffering! If there were problems of the years to work out, the answer seemed to be in Dave himself. The children had said repeatedly, "There is *something* about Dad." Now she was seeing this for herself. Finally, Dave took Nan to The Center. As they walked about, he explained the program they were trying to offer to people in the area.

"For me, it must be something more than hand-to-mouth assistance. In it all, we are trying to find and provide substantial answers to basic human problems. This is our larger challenge, as though meeting human needs were not in itself a sufficient goal . . . I might as well tell you that I don't make much money at this job, but I have a personal satisfaction such as I have not known before in my life."

"Of course, the Music Room is all that looks familiar to me. Oh my, everything is just beautifully maintained, and if The Center is serving the causes you have described, I am certain that Mother and Father Schuster both would be pleased."

Sooner or later . . . Dave took a deep breath and said, "Would you like to see the carriage house apartment where I now live? I'm afraid you'll find it very masculine."

They walked through the apartment. Without saying a word, they went from room to room, very slowly. Nan broke the quiet.

"Dave, it's beautiful!"

"If you would like to try it here . . ."

"If this is where you live, then, of course . . ."

They were standing in the living room. Dave waved his hand in a circle. "You are free to do whatever you like, to make the place your own . . ."

Oh, Dave. It's lovely, just lovely."

"And you are welcome to move in whenever you feel you are ready to do so."

Nan stood with her hands at her side. She looked up into Dave's face. "My dear, dear Dave. I cannot comprehend, nor believe, the changes in my life that these last ten days have made. I came in such questioning and apprehension, only to find the old life simply transformed . . . Yes . . . I'm ready to move into my new home with my husband . . ."

Dave and Nan went to the hotel that afternoon for her to check out and to move her things into her home. As soon as possible they would go to New York, to close that chapter of her life. But right now! They must make two telephone calls: One to Peggy. One to Kurt and Katherine.

∝   ∝   ∝   ∝

November 4

Dearest Mother and Daddy

Thank you for sending me the check. I have not told Dan, because I know he would not want me to accept it. I used some of it for clothes for Debbie; and too, she needed a new school uniform. Then I bought a skirt, sweater and blouse for myself. They are very nice.

Whatever it costs, it is worth it to have Debbie in Stone School. She is doing well in her academic courses. This year she has a course in "Dance." They are doing ballroom dance now; I gather that most of the class think this is old-fashioned. Before they finish, they will have an introduction to ballet. Then too, she has a course in body fitness. They have played tennis and field hockey so far. They are to receive instruction in exercising. She has become very conscious of her posture and the way she carries herself.

Mark has French again this year. At the end of the term, he says he would like to go to Paris, to try out his French. In math he has commenced with Algebra; when he needs help in this, I am useless, and he goes to Dan. Classwork for Mark, however, is only a side issue to football. He started out as the back-up quarterback. The Coach found out that Mark was the best receiver when the other boy was the quarterback and that the other boy is the best receiver when Mark is the quarterback. Anyway, in one position or the other, Mark is on the <u>first team</u> in offense. He says that other boys are trying ever so hard to take his place; so at every opportunity he and Dan are throwing and catching a football. Then there was also something about "handling" the ball.

The church is doing very well; there are crowds for every service. I have told Dan that I think we have now given our share to a city ministry. I know that Dan has begun to insist with the Bishop that he be assigned another parish. He is not optimistic. He says that he thinks The Bishop's School — I told you about that — was a "disaster" for him, even though many, many men have been calling him to encourage him. Some people "in the know" have told Dan that the Bishop and the Council want Dan to stay here because of the way Messiah Church is now going. I say that this doesn't help our personal situation. Then too, Dan says that with Philip Frenell in the Bishop's office, there is little chance that anything decent will be offered to him. I think that is awful.

I do miss Lois so very much. I hear from her, and I am thankful to learn how well everything is going for them. She expects to have her baby in six weeks or so.

It is particularly hard to get along without Kathryn Mac. She was married on the first of the month; we wanted to go, but it was too much of a trip. Kathryn is particularly missed as preparations are under way for the Christmas programs.

We are sorry you cannot come for Thanksgiving. Mother and
Father Clark are planning to come the week before Christmas.

My love, as always,

Mary

∝   ∝   ∝   ∝

Dan admitted to himself and to the Lord that he had been un-
duly glib in the past to speak and to preach about faith and hope
and trust in the promises of God. As he lived and worked within the
inner city, he felt at times that the night was closing in about him
and The Cause which he treasured – he was very sure of it – more
than life itself. As some inexorable disease ate away the community
about Messiah Church, he confessed to himself – and the Lord –
that it was increasingly difficult to offer hope and speak a positive,
uplifting message. Then, unexpectedly, something would happen to
reassure him that by the grace of God, the word of faith and hope
was closer to reality. The world of faith in God was the real world.

The matter of the Christmas program was approached with
hesitancy. In recent years Kathryn Mac had taken a leading role in
the celebration of Christmas in Messiah Church. BUT, the time
was at hand and Kathryn Mac was not there and would not be
there. The brightest spot in the education program was the Youth
Department in the Sunday School; Larry Gossert was putting in
untold hours of time and effort, and displaying personal talents
and a leadership potential which no one – including his mother –
ever suspected that he possessed. Larry now came forward with
the support of dedicated young people to assume major responsibility. Then there was John Phillips. It was common knowledge
that John would accept any opportunity given to him to make
known what a difference Jesus Christ had effected in his life. Dave
had recruited him for responsibility at The Schuster Center. He
now came to Dan most hesitantly with a suggestion. It started with
the Korean community. John thought that the Korean people
would be helped with their faith and life in a new land if they could
have something that would have been a traditional Christmas cel-

ebration in their homeland. John pushed the idea to include other identifiable groups with whom they were in touch, either through the Church and/or The Center.

And there *were* other groups who had found themselves homesick at Christmas:

1. The black community.
2. A southern white bloc.
3. A sizable group of Mexican farm workers who had settled in the city . . . at least temporarily.
4. A small group of Vietnamese who had made their way to Indianapolis, in their trek looking for a new place to call home.
5. John's search discovered, as well, a sizable number of bohemian people.

It all came together in an authentic presentation of Christmas as experienced and expressed in a variety of cultures. John saw to it that the word was out, and this resulted in having to present the program for three nights to "standing room" crowds. There were extravagant media stories and reviews. Pictures and columnists were acclaiming Messiah Church as a "leader in the city portraying Christmas at its very best."

The Official Board noted a membership at the end of the year of 2,347. There was a couple in charge of the adult programming. A Director of Christian Education was needed desperately. Another minister was needed to share the pastoral load.

It was the beginning of a new year, and Dan thought that he should try to make this a time for a major turn in his own life. As he walked into the office, Miss Hazel said, "The Bishop is on the line."

Maybe this was a leading. The Bishop wanted to see him at 2:00 o'clock, if Dan would be free at that time. Perhaps this was the opening, for he had told Mary that he planned to make an appointment with the Bishop to press the matter of a new direction for his ministry in the immediate future.

On the agreed hour, Dan sat back in a chair in the Bishop's Conference Room. To open the exchange, Dan waited for the Bishop, who began as usual by inquiring about Mary and Debbie and Mark. And his parents. And Mary's parents. Dan always had the feeling that the Bishop's secretary had briefed him on names just before the appointment hour.

"And how are things in Messiah Church? (Without waiting for an answer.) The idea and the performance of the Christmas program was little short of brilliant; Ada and I managed to get seats on the third night . . . Oh, and incidentally, we ran into Fred and Marge Hudson there . . ."

The Bishop paused, and Dan thought that he might as well get on with *his* concerns.

"Thank you. It is a coincidence that you called this morning, as I was planning to seek an appointment with you . . ."

"Yes, Dan . . . there is a matter concerning which I wanted to confer with you . . . The work of this office has grown beyond me and I need some help if we are to stay on top of the challenge to the Church in this time. As you know, I have indicated that I would like to enlist the permanent assistance of Rev. Philip Frenell in the work here."

He waited and Dan nodded. "You know, of course, that the Bishop's Council must approve this appointment, and they will want the approval of the clergy of this district" . . . Again he waited, and Dan remained silent. "Now I know that things did not work out too well with you and Philip a few years ago in Messiah Church, and I suppose that I want to know whether you would be standing in opposition to this appointment for Philip."

The Bishop now was going to wait until Dan said something.

Dan straightened up in his chair. "Is Philip here . . . here in this office . . . now?"

The Bishop seemed reluctant to acknowledge that Philip was indeed available.

"If I am to say anything about Philip, then I must insist that he be present. He has a right to hear anything that I say, and to correct or to call into question anything which he might feel is wide of the truth."

The Bishop saw an adamant Dan, and picked up the phone to

invite Philip to his office. When Philip had seated himself, the Bishop explained the situation to him and the reason he had been invited into the conference. Philip merely nodded.

The Bishop looked at Dan. "Now let me hear from you, Dan."

"Let me say at the outset that if you want Philip here with you, I shall enter no objection. If you need help, then you are privileged to name the person, or persons, who can, in your judgment, provide the assistance you need. The matter ends there with me."

The Bishop seemed relieved. "Very well. I am pleased to be apprised of your support. So, if there is nothing more . . ."

The Bishop and Philip rose, but Dan remained seated.

"As I said to you, I have a matter to discuss with *you*."

The Bishop excused Philip, who left the room without any recognition of Dan. The Bishop resumed his seat behind his desk.

"Tell me now, Dan. What is on your mind?"

Dan leaned forward. "The subject is not a new one, sir; but it has become demanding upon me. I speak of my appointment to a new parish. I have been in Messiah Church for nearly six years. These have been traumatic years for the church, for my family and for me. I believe we have reached a place where the church is stabilized and growing in a wholly new situation. We have made positive moves toward a program for the changed world in which the church must now serve and live . . . Frankly, I think I have made my contribution . . . I have done my share. It is time for someone else with new vision and new strengths to take up the responsibility of this church. My personal family situation is in tatters. I am physically exhausted. For the sake of Messiah Church, and for my own personal situation, I need to be in another parish. Not today. Not tomorrow . . . but yesterday."

"I hear you, Dan. I am sympathetic with your personal situation. You and I may have differed on some few items, but I want you to know that I think you have done a sturdy job. To be quite honest, I don't know *anyone* – including myself – who could have done what you have accomplished in Messiah Church in these last six years. Even now, if I ask myself for someone to replace you, I honestly don't come up with a single name. That, of course, is not answering your personal problems."

"No, sir. It is not the word I need. If this is the only role to which the church will assign me, I have reached the place where I feel that I must turn for employment outside the church. I have made inquiries. It is necessary for me to return to the university for post-graduate work to prepare myself for either of two positions which I have been offered in industry."

The Bishop was visibly stirred. "No, no, no, Dan! *The Church needs you*! Now don't do anything rash!"

'RASH!!!! HOW MANY TIMES???? FOR HOW LONG???? Have I been asking, pushing, almost begging for a change?'

Dan took himself in hand to reply calmly, "Very well, Let us agree on some kind of time frame. Four to five months? The summer term begins the first of June, and I would hope to return to the university at that time, if the Church has no other use for me and my services."

"Dan, you know how these things do or do not work in the church. We cannot pick a date and say, 'This is it.'"

"Sir, in recent years the church has been able to say repeatedly, 'These particular people . . . on this date . . . and this amount of money.' And so wreak havoc in the leadership, membership and finances of Messiah Church . . . I need for you to level with me. I have asked before. I have received only temporizing replies. At this juncture, I need some positive action to accommodate my personal state of mind and to restore some semblance of family life to my home."

With nothing resolved, Dan made his way from the Bishop's office to go home and relate this exchange to Mary, who felt that she was at last making herself heard. She stopped the conversation to remind Dan that he had been planning to attend a basketball game of Forest Middle School at 4:30 p.m.

Years later when Dan asked himself why he did not pursue his intent to make a change from Messiah Church, the only response which he could give to himself was not a satisfying answer by any measure. He *had* come to an agreement with Mary that he should actively seek a transfer to another parish. He *had* stated his case to the Bishop, threatening to leave the ministry for secular employment, if that was his only way out of his present situation. He had so earnestly stated his case to the Bishop that at one point he had, to the Bishop's surprise and even more to his own momentary embarrassment, addressed the Bishop as "George."

It was quite true that the Bishop did nothing. In moments of remembrance and exasperation, Dan would say to himself, and two or three times to Mary, "The Bishop doesn't keep his word!" "George Gossert lied to me!" "A leader of our church cannot be trusted!"

Once Dan did make an appointment with the Bishop, who opened their conversation with the words, "Dan, I have been looking for the right opportunity for you. I regard you as a richly gifted servant of the Lord, and I would be remiss in my responsibility if I did not see you in a work which exploited your talents to the fullest for the Kingdom."

He did not have time to discuss those "talents" because he received a call saying that the cab was waiting to take him and Ada to the airport. He urged Dan to make another appointment so they might continue their discussion as soon as possible.

In his honest moments, Dan admitted to himself that he had not followed up with the Bishop. He had not changed his mind about his desire to move somewhere, anywhere . . . to do something else, anything else. His relationship with Mary was civil . . . and polite for the childrens' sake. So, why didn't he, Dan Clark, do something? The only answer he could manage was that he was *BUSY.*

BUSY. There were STAFF needs.

Mr. Benson and Mr. Padgett were supposed to be working only part-time; they – together with Dan – were swamped with the names and addresses of families on whom calls should be made. A secretary was engaged full-time to assist. The work load called for another two men working part-time, or an Assistant working full-time. They were looking for such assistance.

Carol had submitted a draft of her dissertation. She would shortly be leaving.

A Director of Christian Education was needed. Dan's hopes bounded one Sunday when Kathryn Mac and her husband were in the congregation, but she said they were only visiting. In their conversation, she told Dan that she had read in a church publication of a couple whom she had known in school; they had gone to Indonesia as missionaries. Almost the same time she received a letter from the lady – Ellen Gregory – saying that her husband had become ill and died only a few months after they had taken up their work abroad. Ellen had now returned to the States, where her daughter was in college. She said that she was looking for a job. Kathryn gave Dan an address and a telephone number for Ellen, and Dan called her the next morning. Ellen was in the church over the following weekend; when she left on Tuesday, Ellen Gregory was the new Director of Christian Education, beginning as soon as she could get moved.

BUSY. Plans should be made for Lent and Easter.

There had been two Easter Sunday services, and people had been turned away last Easter. This year they would have *three* Easter services in the sanctuary; perhaps they should also have services at the same hours in the Chapel. Music for Holy Week and Easter required a running series of conferences with Mr. Hoffmeyer.

Mr. Benson and Mr. Padgett wanted to make Lent a time for evangelism with broad participation by lay people in making calls. They would have classes at a variety of hours to prepare persons for Christian discipleship. They had good reason to believe that the number of people uniting with the church would surpass any imagined figure.

Who are the people who are not participating in some part of the life and witness of Messiah Church? There should be a special effort to see that no one is allowed to be forgotten. Did their evangelism effort bring people into the church to be forgotten? If the church could not take care of the members it had, then it should not seek the addition of more people.

BUSY. The Schuster Center.

Political leaders, civic personalities, the media all had quickly accepted The Schuster Center as a living and useful – and therefore necessary, institution in the city. There was no question but that Dave's leadership had made the difference. After preliminary experimentation with programs, they were more confident with what they were doing, and could do, and should do. Dave had been able to enlist an almost unbelievable wealth of volunteer help. (Mary was in charge of a Day Nursery one morning a week.) Lou Street was becoming a city-wide youth leader of significant influence. Looking at a financial report, Dan had said, "May I be permitted a touch of envy?"

The Board of Directors met in the luxury atmosphere of the Music Room. Dan looked across the room in one meeting at the immaculate figure of one who was now known as "Thomas J. Davis." Dave said of him, "Tom wrote the book on public relations."

The filling station was now "DAVIS OLDSMOBILE & CHEVROLET," selling new and used cars. He was the only member of a class in "English and Speech" taught by one Rose Davis. Dan learned of this when in exasperation Rose said to him, "I have told Tom over and over, 'You should call him Dr. Clark or Dr. Dan. That is what everyone else calls him.' Do you know what he said to me? 'I'll try to put a "g" on "goin"'and say "are not" instead of "ain't," but it just wouldn't be right to call him anything but *Revner Dan*. That's who he is for me.'"

BUSY. Tom Davis.

Thomas J. Davis. For all of his physical bulk – "It's a little difficult to conceal Tom Davis in a choir loft" – he was a most sensitive spirit. Dan never ceased to marvel at Tom's ability to read him and his moods. If he stopped at Tom's service station for gas, there were times when Tom would smile and wave, and then there were other times when he would tell a story which went on and on, always a good story that made Dan forget himself. There were occasions when Tom would get into Dan's car and sit with him for a while, saying nothing. Yet again, he would speak rapturously about the goodness of God or the loving forgiveness of his Saviour. Relating these personal encounters to Dave one time, Dan said, "After being with him, I feel as though I have been anointed with the balm of Gilead."

Dan was in Dave's office at The Center when an excited Tom Davis entered, bursting with news.

"Revner Dan. Mr. Schuster. Look here." A legal-looking paper. was in his hand. "That's an option. That's what it is. An option. Rose has said ever since we moved here that she wanted a better place. There. There it is."

Dave took the paper and glanced up from his reading of it?"

"Where is this located?"

"Purcell Avenue. Rose says it is what she always wanted. And there it is. An option." He turned to Dan. "You know, Revner Dan, you used to say to me in Pawley, 'Tom, you ought to have your own place.' The Lord is good. I have my own place, and now Rose and me . . . Rose and I will have a house like Rose always talked about. Bedrooms for the boys. We're going to put in a new kitchen for Rose."

Tom paused for their approbation. Dan said, "Purcell Avenue. That's on the east side, isn't it?"

Tom nodded.

Dave folded the option and laid the paper on the desk. Tom was frowning at their obvious non-encouragement.

"Tom, why are you moving from this area?"

"Revner Dan, you know Mister Stockwell won't do anything to that house, and it looks worse and worse. He just wants rent money."

"But, Tom, why do you move away? Your business is here. Your church is *here*. I live *here*. Dave lives *here*."

"Well, Rose and I want a nice house in a nice neighborhood. We want a nice place for our boys. *I can afford* a nice house."

Dave picked up the option and handed it back to Tom. "Tom, I have been in Sam Stockwell's house many, many times. It's a fine house. No one could want anything better."

Tom was shaking his head. "It isn't very nice now. It needs lots of work."

Dave's words had a sharpness quite unlike Dave. "Then why don't *you* do that work? Two weeks ago I bought the house directly across the street from you. I'm going to restore it. That's where I lived as a boy."

BUSY.

Mary had become engrossed in activities relating to Stone School. She tried to keep reminding herself that she had a son who was in Eighth Grade in Forest Middle School, but she was wholly supportive of Stone School for what she saw the school doing for her daughter. She was First Vice President of a Mother's Auxiliary. This year they would be raising money for the purchase of computers for classrooms. She was so pleased with Debbie's development as a gifted young lady. Her conversations no longer included the subject of Dan's transfer to another parish. She was so busy coming and going that she seemed to ignore their place of residence. One morning the children had already left for school when Dan came downstairs.

Mary placed a cup of coffee before him and poured milk on a dish of cereal.

"I was sorry to waken you this morning when I got up to get the children off to school. We both seem to be so very busy these days that we do need to get some rest. I think that I should put the twin beds back in the master bedroom."

Dan held her in a searching look and turned away to his coffee and the morning paper. "Yes."

BUSY. John Phillips.

John invited Dan to have lunch to tell him that he had put together a group of clubhouse cronies to form a real estate investment program. John's friends said that you could count on two things in any conversation with him; first, he would say something about what Jesus Christ had done in his life; second, he would extend an invitation to attend Messiah Church "next Sunday."

Many who accepted his invitation noted the decline of the general area about Messiah Church. One thing led to another; there were casual conversations; one or more of them checked on prices of properties in the area being offered for sale. John suggested that some money might be made if they would band together and put up a few dollars. They formed a corporation and contracted for a feasibility study. John now confided to Dan – who he said had been included as an equal partner – some features of their initial plan.

1. There were several blocks of large single houses and mansions. They would promote the sale of these places to individuals who would restore them and live in them. They would provide – at minimal cost – the service of architects, designers and contractors capable of doing restoration work.

2. There were a few blocks of row houses. These would be restored. With brick streets, brick sidewalks and gas street lights, they would seek to recapture a desirable atmosphere for living.

3. There was a five-story industrial plant building which had been thrust into the area, but its operation had been short-lived, with the building abandoned. The solid structure would lend itself for adaptation as a condominium. There was sufficient land area about for trees and grass and planting to give the building a green setting.

BUSY. Diane Marshall.

There was person after person with personal problems who came to Dan for help. Dan could lose self-confidence if he thought of 150 Church Street. He would say to himself, 'Physician, heal thyself'; however, the continuing press of individuals seeking assistance did not allow him the luxury of self pity.

Dan came into the office one afternoon to find Carol talking with a young woman whom she introduced as "My friend, Diane Marshall." Dan sat down in the office to hear Diane tell Carol and himself that she had graduated from high school two years before, and that she had recently come to Indianapolis, where she was living with her father and brother and attending a commercial school. Carol said she had met Diane in a coffee shop where she ate once in a while, and where Diane was working to support herself.

Diane volunteered, "I guess I'm black, but I can pretty much pass for a white girl whenever I choose to do so."

Carol said that Diane liked to sing, and they were waiting for

Mr. Hoffmeyer so that Diane could sing for him.

Mr. Hoffmeyer called Dan late in the evening. "Dr. Clark, it is late, but I must tell you the excitement it is to hear Miss Marshall. When Miss King called me, I think this is another volunteer soprano who thinks she belongs in opera. Ach! How many times I have to hear that and remain a gentleman! But this girl, Dr. Clark! This Miss Marshall! Just a few notes, and you know! Her voice is an experience!"

Mr. Hoffmeyer was not finished. "With a voice like this, I lose all sense of time. It was late and so I take Miss King and Miss Marshall for dinner. I know everyone in the dining room ask how an old music teacher can have not one, but *two young* and *beautiful* dinner companions."

Mary wondered who could possibly have been at the other end of a conversation that would make Dan say, "If I hear any gossip, I'll savor it for a while before I pass it on to you . . . and everybody else I see."

"I should pay to work with her voice." Mr. Hoffmeyer was ecstatic. With her first solo he said, "This morning, the voice was there. Yes. But it lacked the quality that makes for a spiritual experience."

Following Diane's first appearance at choir rehearsal, Tom said to Rose, "I know Diane's father and brother. Maybe it would be good if you took a special interest in her."

BUSY. Larry Gossert.

Larry Gossert reported periodically on his progress in his studies at the theological seminary. He would be taking two courses at the university in the summer term. He planned an extra course load in the fall in order to finish the following May. He had told his parents of his plans and course of action, but neither of them had made any comment. He and Carol had found one another.

BUSY. Dan and his "job."

Of course, there were the regular weekly and daily responsibilities which fell upon Dan as Pastor of Messiah Church.

1. Dan was the administrator of Messiah Church. The Staff reported to him. He was Chairman of the Official Board.

2. He was the preacher whose messages from the Word of God were central to the life and growth and influence of the church. Daytime hours were so occupied that he spent many, many night hours in study and research, in writing and rewriting.

3. He had a major responsibility in calling upon people who were in hospitals. Mr. Padgett had tried to carry out this ministry. He reported to Dan with a wry smile, "They all said they appreciated my visit, but before I left each one of them said, 'When is the Pastor coming to see me?'"

4. Dan felt that he should show his leadership by making calls on new people to invite them to take their place in Messiah Church.

5. However much Dan tried to restrict his activities outside Messiah Church, he had a schedule of civic and church committees and programs that occupied most of his luncheon hours every week. "For the sake of Messiah Church and its witness in the city . . ." was the premise by which Miss Hazel frowningly filled his appointment book week after week.

6. There were the hours daily and weekly for reading the Scriptures, for meditation, for prayer. If he was to be a spiritual leader, it was necessary to renew his own spirit in the things of God.

TOO BUSY FOR SUCH AS THIS. Sam Stockwell.

In the thick of his Lenten schedule, Dan answered the telephone one day to hear a cheery voice, "Hello, Dan. How are you?" Dan thought he should know the voice. "Dan, this is Sam." Of course. Sam Stockwell.

"Yes, Sam." Dan was trying to think how long it had been since Sam had been in a church service.

"Say, Dan, I just wanted to call you for old times' sake." Dan couldn't think of any old times with Sam that would warrant special remembrance. "I thought I'd call to tell you that the wife and I are moving to Florida."

"Thank you for calling, Sam."

Sam wanted to talk. "Yes, we managed to sell my old drug store building. I dealt with a man named John Phillips, who said he comes to church now. Mr. Phillips said that they are putting a real estate office downstairs, and some architects are to be on the second floor, as I understand. He said he knows you and that he goes to Messiah. You know what? He invited me to come to church! I told him that I've been a member of Messiah Church since he was a little boy."

"Thank you, Sam. I'm glad . . ."

"Wait. There's more. We managed to sell our house here, and got a better price for it than I thought we would. Sold it to a colored fellow that you knew down in Pawley. I thought I'd call and ask you to have lunch with me, as a kind of commission for your help in getting out from under my property."

Dan's disgust in turning down the invitation didn't get through to an ebullient Sam.

"Soon as we clean up a few things here, we are taking off . . . the wife and I . . . Remember, if you and your wife ever get down South, that lunch offer still stands . . . Oh, say. I see where Rev. Frenell is now Assistant Bishop. I always said that that fellow was a good one . . . Well, look us up if you ever get down south."

Tom said nothing about the house after that day in Dave's office. When Dan asked him about it, all Tom would say was, "Rose and I prayed about it."

Central Church in Grand Rapids, Michigan was seeking a pastor. The Bishop had been asked if he had a person to recommend. Daniel Witt Clark? Obviously, he would be just the man for that pulpit. But then, who would fill Dan's big shoes at Messiah Church? According to the latest word – he had talked casually with Miss Hazel on the telephone – the church membership was something more than 2700, and the attendance was increasing almost weekly. There was a new and growing – that was the word, "growing" – number of strong leaders in the church. They were young, and they had money, and they would work. The Bishop could think of two or three names to suggest to Grand Rapids; but he couldn't come up with a single person to replace Dan Clark, whose name and reputation, whose influence in the Cause of Christ, had grown significantly in city-wide renown.

∝　　∝　　∝　　∝

May 12

Dear Mother and Daddy

I am sorry that you (Mother) are not feeling up to par. Please keep me informed, or I shall just worry about you. I think it is much in order for you to have a complete check. Of course, I hope that you will not need to have surgery but if that is necessary then I want to help in any way that I can. We could get away here shortly after June 1, and I know that Dan would want me to do what I can.

We are planning to be in Glen Rock again for the month of July. If necessary, Dan could take the children with him, and I could stay on with you. Don't you worry about anything. I haven't had a chance to talk with Dan since you telephoned, but I would be willing to work it out to be there and run the house and take care of you for a period of eight to ten weeks. I would do anything for you to help you renew your health and strength.

Debbie is doing very well in school, and I am so thankful. She is already enrolled for the fall. She was in a play which was staged by her English class. It was beautifully done. Dan said he was very proud of her performance. She enjoys having "Luncheon" at the school; she has had diner there on some special occasions. She is very conscious of table manners. She tells Mark that he should not put his elbows on the table, and that he should take smaller bites. That doesn't help in getting Mark interested in going to Stone

School.

It seems to me that Mark is getting rougher. Dan says it is my imagination, or my subconscious trying to find reasons for sending Mark to Stone School. Next year he will be in Ninth Grade, his _final_ year at Forest Middle School. He fully expects to be the quarterback on the football team, and he thinks he will be a starting guard on the basketball team. I keep saying that he must be more academic minded, but I can't complain about the grades he is making. And this fall he will be starting with Latin. So maybe I should just be thankful.

Dan is out and gone so very much. I told him last night that I could go away and it would be two or three weeks before he noticed I was missing. Mr. Benson is leaving, and this is a serious problem for Dan and the church. He has been most, most helpful in recruiting new members for the church. His wife has been wanting him to retire _again_ for them to move to Florida.

He will take the services in July. Dan is really concerned. He says that Mr. Benson has been instrumental in turning the church around. Dan says that Mr. Benson is of "a different generation of ministers," and his kind are not about any more, and yet Mr. Benson, or someone very like him, is precisely what the church needs.

Dan no longer talks about the Bishop doing something to place him in another parish. I met Mrs. Gossert in a store downtown last week, and she was asking me some questions. So I thought it was my turn to speak up, and I really told her how I felt about it all. Dan was furious with me when I repeated what I had said. But I told him that Mrs. Gossert agrees with me.

It will be good to see you both again and to try to be of help for you. Mark says he wants to _work_. He wants to become stronger. I am amazed that he is _my_ boy. Just wait. You won't recognize him when you see him.

Please keep me informed on your medical reports, and the plans which your doctors recommend. I am praying for you.

With all my love,

Mary

∝   ∝   ∝   ∝

Mary had barely posted her letter when she received a telephone call from her father, telling her that her mother was in the hospital for major surgery. She came into the Study to say, "I must go . . . now. Mother and Daddy need me."

With that word she left to work furiously throughout the day. All of the children's dirty clothing was washed. The house was dusted and vacuumed. A quick trip to the market prompted her to call Dan and ask what he thought about her car. Dan took it for a check; and the service manager called to say that it needed front end alignment, a new set of tires, new lining for the brakes . . . and the master cylinder of the braking system should be replaced. Dan gave the order to complete this work, and the manager said they would wash the car and vacuum the interior at no charge . . .

Mary wrote furiously to complete a sheet of notes for Debbie, with another sheet for Mark. A paper on the breakfast table suggested menus for the next two weeks, with the items on hand encircled. She called a woman to come and clean the whole house, and wash all of the windows she could reach. She had two bags packed and standing in the hall outside the master bedroom. Dan suggested they all go out for dinner, where the conversation was dominated by a rehearsing of their daily schedules. Dan would have to drive to Stone School twice a week – morning and afternoon. Mark would take the school bus in the morning and come home in the afternoons on the city bus. Dan and the children interposed this recital periodically with, "Yes, Mary," or, "Yes, Mother."

Dan showered and waited for Mary. He knew she had called her father to talk for a long, long time. Dan thought ruefully, 'She will be seeing him tomorrow morning.' It was not one of Dan's better times. He admitted to himself that he was probably feeling sorry for himself, but he felt very much alone. For several years now, he had labored body, mind and spirit, for uncounted hours day and night; he was deeply aware of the seeming personal insignificance of one man against the onslaught of urban change. Probably more than anything else, he had had to struggle to maintain his sense of personal importance, over against tremendous forces which seemed to overwhelm him as nothing and nobody. And now, he went to sleep admitting to himself that he was little more than a sideline figure within his own family group. In an abbreviated whirl of activity in the morning, Mary was gone – after getting back out of her car to give Dan a peck on the cheek.

Two weeks later, Dan drove to Rockford to take the children. Her mother was still in the hospital for therapy following the surgery. Dan found Mary living in her mother's medical world. When he and the children had emptied his car of their things, the only thing for him seemed to be to get back in the car to drive home. He stopped for a sandwich at a McDonald's on the outskirts of Rockford.

The month of June was to be interesting. Dan was invited to meet with the Bishop's Ad Hoc Committee on the Urban Church. The notice came from the Assistant to the Bishop, who would chair the committee. At the appointed hour, Dan presented himself at the Bishop's office, accompanied by four laymen from Messiah Church: Thomas J. Davis, Alfred Hirter, John Phillips and David Schuster. They were ushered into the Conference Room where they met a nonplused Philip and four other committee members.

The Chairman said, "We thought you were coming alone. We did not anticipate that you would bring a committee."

Al Hirter moved forward a half step. "Philip, we understood from your correspondence that this meeting was to have some special reference to Messiah Church. The Official Board believes that the lay people of the church have a right and an obligation to *know everything* which in any way might relate to their church. The Official Board elected the four of us laymen to come to this hearing and to report at the next meeting of the Board on the purpose of this meeting and the issues which are raised."

Philip looked helplessly at the other committee members, who nodded their assent. There was activity and commotion as chairs were moved about to put the committee on one side of the long table and the Messiah people on the other side facing them. Somehow the meeting never got off the ground; as questions were posed, the Messiah Men generally took turns making response. It was twenty-three minutes by Dan's watch, when Professor Maynard observed that he thought they had received "from the Messiah people most everything which this committee needs from them."

By agreement, the Messiah committee left the Bishop's office and met at the church to compare notes. It was obvious that the appearance of the laymen had upset the committee's plans. Dan did not want to miss a chance to explore a new opportunity for the church.

"I want to try out a possibility with you. I would ask for your confidence for now. After you have had time to think and pray about this idea to your satisfaction, we might get together again and work up a presentation. I shall pursue this only *if every one of you* thinks that this idea has merit for Messiah Church."

They all encouraged Dan to continue.

"I know we are all grateful for the way the church is going at present. We know well that the city is an arena for change. My suggestion is something for the future. Physically, Messiah Church will become even more a Christian symbol and witness at the center of the city. I would hope that Messiah Church might take a place of leadership for Christ in this city. My proposal is that we put our Sunday eleven o'clock service *on television*. The sanctuary offers an ideal setting for this kind of outreach. We might call the program something like, 'The Church Speaks.' With this new public medium, we might reach out to claim the role of a first-line witness to the whole city, to the entire area. People such as we saw earlier this afternoon might well object to our claim to speak for the Church, because they view themselves as church leaders. On the basis of what you saw this afternoon, I would ask you to imagine what they – individually and / or collectively – would offer as the Word of the Lord for this city in our time."

Dan paused and realized they were waiting for him to continue. "Obviously, we are talking about a lot of money. We would have to buy equipment. It would cost for air time. I think we would start in faith . . . faith that it would pay for itself by way of larger congregations, additional contributions and a substantial growth of membership . . . Well, there it is. I would only ask now how much time you want to think and pray about it."

"Goodness, Dan, this catches me without a ready answer." Dave chuckled and shook his head. "When we left the Bishop's office earlier, I thought that this was to be a wasted afternoon. You have just made the time worthwhile. I could give an immediate reaction, but I agree that there are ramifications which we would need to explore."

Tom was sober. "Revner Dan, I think the lady and the four gentlemen that we saw earlier this afternoon are not going to like this idea."

Al Hirter agreed. "Tom's right. In their set of mind, I daresay they might feel themselves – and certainly their eminence – threatened somehow."

John Phillips was brief. "I have come to a conclusion. Let's not think about it, let's do it."

Dan, together with Al, Tom, John and Dave, worked up a presentation of a Messiah television ministry, and presented it to the Official Board. Various ideas were discussed, including:
1. They would need cameras and other equipment in the church.
2. The choir would need new robes to have a color more suitable for this new medium.
3. The ushering would need to appear more professional. (Someone suggested that ushers be dressed in cutaway coats and striped trousers.)
4. A special "production" committee should be named and trained.
5. There should be a special post office box for this ministry of the church.
6. A separate budget should be established for the television ministry.

7. There was the matter of money to finance the extra expense.

It was summer, but the idea had galvanized the entire Board as nothing in recent memory. Without question, the Board picked up the idea to run with it. They agreed that this significant public program addition should be cleared with the Bishop. They would vote in the regular August meeting – "if the way be clear" – to proceed with a television ministry beginning the second Sunday of October.

So long as Messiah Church was not seeking any financial assistance, the Bishop's office did not voice any objection.

Dan would leave at the end of the month to be the preacher for the month of July in the chapel at Glen Rock.

YEAR SEVEN
AT
MESSIAH CHURCH

Mary brought Mark and Debbie for a few days at Glen Rock. When she would leave to return to Rockford, Mark said that he had decided that he would stay with his father. Mary was nonplused, "But we didn't bring your clothes . . . and Daddy is expecting you . . ."

Mark waited to speak with her privately. "I have my swimming trunks and my football. I can get some new shorts and shirts. And besides, Mother, I think Dad needs someone here with him."

At the end of July, Dan and Mark returned home to continue their "bachelor" establishment. For a proper start, Dan took Mark to the school for the first football practice. As Mark was opening the door, the coach walked by. Dan got out of the car to shake hands and exchange a few words with the coach, who remembered Dan's playing years at the university. The conversation came around to some hesitating words from the coach.

"Sir, we don't get enough money for an adequate coaching staff . . . I know that you're awfully busy . . . But I really need some help coaching our defense. Do you suppose . . . ?"

Dan agreed to spend some time with the defense in the early practice days. While it was true that he didn't receive any compensation, a local sportswriter recognized him and wrote a story about him with pictures – one of Dan in his playing days at the University, and another taken on the practice field without Dan's knowledge. Before Dan saw or even knew about the story in the *Sunday Edition*, he was puzzled after the 8:30 service at the people who wanted to shake "the hand that threw the football to bring the University its first conference title."

The story was not lost on Mark, who borrowed two copies of the

"Sports" section of the paper to send the article to his two Grand-fathers. He put his own copy in a scrapbook which he had started.

When Mary returned for Debbie to begin the Seventh Grade, she had to make a conscious adjustment from an atmosphere of illness, human weakness and dependency, to a world of physical strength, activity and driving vigor.

The Labor Day weekend had a feature story in a continuing series entitled: "Another Success Story." The subtitle read:

"Thomas J. Davis." The writer noted that "Tom" Davis was demonstrating that it could still be done. From an old service station to a new service station; to a garage, with the addition of a used car lot: and now with a new car franchise. There were pictures of the Davis home on Fourth Street – "Before" and "After." Mr. Davis and his wife, Rose, were the incoming presidents of the P.T.A. at Lincoln School, Member of the Official Board – and the choir – of Messiah Church and a Director of The Schuster Center. He also served on a list of significant business and civic committees. Even Dan found himself surprised with the testimonials for Tom which the paper had secured. The writer had not missed the reach of personal influence exercised by Tom and Rose, who maintained personal and prayer relationships with a surprisingly large number of persons.

One of the individuals in whom they were interested was Diane Marshall. They encouraged (and helped pay for) her private voice study with Mr. Hoffmeyer. She was frequently in their home. It was not in the paper that they were presently concerned because Diane seemed so restless.

Rose said, "Maybe it's her home."

Tom grunted with disgust. "I hired her brother, and he only lasted a half a day."

Rose went to Dan to talk about Diane, and the following week Diane began working at Messiah Church as the Church Secretary.

"Just to keep the peace," Dan and two Board members waited on the Bishop to talk with him about the proposed television ministry. The Bishop and his Assistant – upon hearing the proposed title for the televised ministry – questioned seriously whether Messiah Church could, or should, arrogate itself into the position of "presuming to speak for the church." After all, within their polity it was the Bishop who possessed the authority to speak authoritatively. Dan said he would "not presume" to speak for the Bishop, or his office, or the whole church. Dan said it was their intent to speak on the authority of the Holy Scriptures, under the guidance and in the power of the Holy Spirit.

Dan left with the suggestion that they meet again for further discussion and a decision. No one followed up on this.

On Dan's part, there might have been an excuse in that he had other quandaries to claim his attention. For example there was the matter of "room vs. rooms." Mary had returned the first week of September to find all of Dan's things in the guest room. She said nothing until the first morning the children were off to school.

"Dan, why have you moved into the guest room? Debbie was hinting at this before she left for school . . ."

"That is where I have been all summer. I prefer that bed to a twin bed."

The room had only the sound of the newspaper as Dan turned the pages, while drinking a cup of coffee.

"It doesn't look right to the children. Each of them has spoken with me to ask if something is wrong."

"What did you say to them?"

"I told them that you are out so late on so many nights, and that you need your rest."

"Yes, that's what you said to me."

Dan had not looked up from reading the morning paper.

"Well, I think you should move back into the master bedroom now that we are all here."

"Why?" Dan looked up from the editorial page.

"You are not making this discussion very easy for me."

"Mary, at one point you moved the twin beds into our room as a kind of punishment of me for something or another. You switched them back for no reason that was apparent to me. Then concern for my sleeping moved the twin beds back. I don't like the twin bed. But more than that, you well know that we have been living as separate individuals for a long while now, and I will not be party to a show of untruth."

"But, Dan, you never said anything . . ."

"No, Mary. I do not beg well. I work and I work hard and I work long hours. Times without number I have come home really needing to be wanted, but you are gone – you are angry about something and want to argue – you are asleep or at least you don't want to be bothered. I have ceased to expect any support in love in my home. I find my renewal and my strength in the awareness that I have done my job for the Lord and done it to the best of my ability. I am not great, and I am not very good. But, doggone it! I will not mask a lie."

"What do you want me to do about it?"

"Mary, if you have to ask that question, maybe you should go back to Rockford, and be your parents' little girl."

Dan arose to go to a meeting with representatives of a local television station to further the preparations for beginning the telecast on the second Sunday of October.

∝ ∝ ∝ ∝

September 20

Dearest Mother and Daddy,

I am thankful for the good news that you (Mother) are feeling much more like yourself. I was happy to be able to be with you and to do all that I could after your surgery. You have been through a great deal, and you must do your part to keep what you have gained back, and to make more progress to renewed strength.

We have just finished the Fall Festival at Stone School. I have been terribly busy as a member of the General Committee. We made lots and lots of money, and we are to meet with the Head- master to decide what is to be done with our profits.

Debbie is so very happy and she has so many good friends. Nothing is said, but she does not invite any of her friends to her home. She was invited for dinner at the home of a girl whom she mentions frequently, and the family insisted on driving her home instead of us calling for her. Debbie was terribly upset, and I kept her home the next day.

Mark, of course, is playing football. He is the starting quarterback for Forest Middle School.; there is a Middle School League here in the city. He comes home with terrible looking bruises all over him. Dan says he is really doing very well, and Forest has won all of its games so far. Mark was absolutely thrilled to see his name in a story about the team on the Sports page. I was glad for time with him this summer. For all of the roughness of the school, and now of football, he _is_ more of a gentleman. Dan and I go to their games. Sometimes they play on a field that doesn't even have any bleachers, and we have to stand for the entire game. Dan and I see the game differently. He looks for plays that are executed well, and particularly for occasions when Mark has excelled. At the end of almost every play, I see a stack of bodies on the field, with Mark usually at the very bottom.

As you know, I have tried to talk with Dan about taking another church, or another anything. Since coming back, I spoke with Dan about this. Something has changed. He says that he is no longer interested in moving to another church. He says he is committed to working for Messiah Church to be greater than it has ever been. He has a fixation on this, and he is out and gone day after day.

Incidentally, the other evening Dan and Mark were standing and talking about something, and I was shocked to notice that Mark is nearly as tall as Dan.

The really BIG thing in the church now is television. The plan now is to begin televising the 11:00 o'clock service every Sunday. Dan says that no one anticipated the myriad of details – and the amount of money – that would be involved in this. But they are committed, and there is great excitement about it.

I'll mail this on my way to a committee meeting for the Mother-Daughter Luncheon and Fashion Show. Debbie and I are to be the Hostesses at one table.

I love you very much,

Mary

P.S. I might as well add what I really started to write, but I have not wanted to write it. Something has happened, and something is happening, to Dan and me. I have known this for some time, and I have been afraid to admit it. But now it is in the open, and Dan and I have talked frankly. I can't say that we have solved anything so far, and we do have an awkward situation here. For the children's sake, I hope that we can work out something better for our home. M

∝   ∝   ∝   ∝

The television ministry was launched on the second Sunday of October with great publicity. The biggest problem of the day was the crowds in attendance. Many who had attended the early service decided to stay in their seats for the 11:00 o'clock service. The narthex and the aisles were crowded with people standing for the entire hour; it had been difficult to get the choir through in time for the processional. Although he said it didn't feel right, George and Ada Gossert stayed home to watch the hour on television.

David Schuster seized Nan by the hand to find and to greet some visitors *he* had seen *in the balcony,* Fred and Marge Hudson. The ushers had practiced and practiced to make their appearances a model of perfection. The choir, in new robes, established a watermark of musical excellence; Mr. Hoffmeyer told Dan later that his problem was to find places for all who had volunteered to sing solos.

And then there was Dan . . .

Throughout the church there were discussions of Dan and his preaching. The people of the church were prompted to become objective about Dan. They asked themselves what it was, how it was, why it was that they had found, and were finding their lives touched in significant ways by this person. There was a consensus that Dan was as effective on the television screen as he was in person. The television reproduction didn't add anything, nor did it take anything away from Dan as a witness to his Lord.

For very personal reasons, Nan Schuster had come to the worship that day with a new sense of the divine. On Friday, she had been cleaning and straightening their living room, and she had accidentally knocked Dave's Bible off the coffee table. As she picked it up, her thumb was pressing on a page where she noticed a marginal note. In curiosity, she kept the place as she now opened the book in proper fashion to what proved to be the Gospel According to St. John. Beside John 14:14 in Dave's printing was one word: "NAN." There was a date as well, which she recognized as a day in the week after Dave's conversion. She read the verse, and reread it, and returned the book to its place. She dropped to her knees on the floor which became for her for that moment a "Holy of Holies."

When Dave stopped by later in the morning, he looked at her closely, and went to her. "My dearest Nan. Is something wrong?"

"No. No, no. Quite the contrary; everything is so right. Please put your arms around me and hold me tight for a moment."

It was the time for the Official Board to establish a budget for the coming year. A first order of business would be for the Official Board to name a Budget and Finance Committee.

There was the dullness of the late hour in Dan's mood as he sat down in a chair in "Mary's room."

"Guess who is Finance Chairman."

"I haven't the slightest idea."

"Art Brehmer."

"I don't think I know him."

Frustration aroused Dan. "Art Brehmer! *Art*! Of all people who ought *not* to be in charge of a financial program . . ."

"Who is he, that you go on like that?" Mary was now wide awake and sitting up in bed.

"Oh, Art is a long-time member of Messiah Church who has

stayed on, and I suppose that one must give him credit for that. The reason you don't know Art is that that is the kind of impression he makes. We have all been so totally involved with getting the television ministry started, that nobody noticed it when the Secretary put Art's name down to chair Budget and Finance. If you just stop to think, you wouldn't ask Art to do this job."

"Oh, maybe he will surprise everyone. It could be that he has needed an opportunity to show what he can really do."

Dan stood up to take off his coat. "I don't know what kind of salary Art receives – probably not too much. The thing is that he is totally incapable of thinking about money in terms beyond what he himself makes . . . After he was named tonight, he made some statements which had the rest of us looking at one another in despair. With Art as Budget and Finance Chairman, about all we can do is to pray for a surprise."

"You can't help by fretting now. Take a shower, and get a good night's rest. Things will look better in the morning."

Dan walked to the bed, to bend down and kiss Mary.

"Thank you. I certainly hope so."

When Dan came from the shower, he pulled a robe from his closet and stepped to the door of Mary's darkened room. He waited for a moment and then went down to the den to read.

There was sheer dismay when the Official Board met again to review the finances for the coming year. Nobody used the word in the meeting, that it would be "an understatement" to say that Art Brehmer was a little confused. After struggling with some figures of questionable origin and veracity, Art reported that the income of Messiah Church would be about $25,000.00 less than the proposed budget. This was unexpected, because attendance in all aspects of the parish program was significantly higher. Church membership had increased substantially. The entire program and the church leadership were proving to be much more effective than anyone had a right to hope.

Admittedly, the budget was to be pushed with new demands:

1. Rev. Willard Benson and Rev. Charles Padgett would be retiring the end of March. They should be replaced by full-time

Associates. The response to the television ministry might require the addition of a fourth minister to the staff.

2. Ellen Gregory was asking for a full-time Youth Director to replace Larry Gossert. Larry would finish at the seminary in May, and presumably he would be going to a parish of his own. The Christian Education Committee wanted to begin a Christian Day School with classes for Age Four and Age Five.

3. The television ministry would require financial support, and no one could predict a figure for this.

4. Carol King Gossert had started a Christian Psychological Counseling service – both in the church and in The Center.

5. Mr. Hoffmeyer was approaching retirement, but his work load had increased with multiple services and the additional responsibilities occasioned by the television ministry.

Someone spoke for the entire group when he said, "Dr. Clark, the Number One item on any list of proposed budget changes is, and must be, a salary increase for the Pastor. And I make that as a motion."

The Secretary looked around and felt the approval and said, "I'll enter that as having been approved by acclamation. For my part, I'd say that we give the Pastor a blank check and let him fill in the amount."

The Secretary was abashed that his statement brought spontaneous applause.

To return to the budget, the question was raised, "Is there any place that we can save some money? Just to get things started, I suggest – or I will put it in the form of a motion – that we delete The Bishop's Fund from the new budget."

Once again the meeting went out of control as voices rose from around the room.

"We've given too much already . . ."

"This program has financed what would have been the destruction of Messiah Church – would have been apart from the Lord and Dr. Dan and Willard and Charlie."

"Within the last two months we have lost one hundred and twenty-five members to colonize another church. The Bishop can't take away our people and expect money at the same time."

"We have already contributed money, people, leadership to such an extent that *I* say, *drop* the whole thing."

When they had removed or reduced as much as seemed possible, the budget still appeared to be out of balance.

Art Brehmer volunteered, "Even if we didn't raise Dr. Dan's salary, he would still be making more than a lot of us in the church."

Even Art got the point of the unfeigned disgust which wordlessly rolled over him.

Mark had bought some extra copies of an issue of the daily *JOURNAL*. The Sports section carried a story about the football season of the Middle School League. Forest had been undefeated as the outstanding team of the year, the first time that any team had gone undefeated since the league was formed. A City-Wide First Team had been selected, and Mark was the Quarterback; there was an individual picture of each player chosen for the first team. Mark sent a copy of the paper to Rockford and to Belvoir. Then, too, he told and retold about the football coach from Northside High School seeking him to talk with him and to say that he looked forward to having Mark on his squad next year.

The Secretary of the Official Board read a letter in the December meeting of the Board:

> *The Official Board*
> *Messiah Church*
> *Indianapolis, Indiana*
>
> *Ladies and Gentlemen:*
> *We want to express our deep regret and distress that the Official Board of Messiah Church has taken action to remove The Bishop's Fund from its budget for the coming year.*
> *The needs of the Church have made such great demands upon*

this Fund that we strongly urge the Official Board to reconsider this decision. This Fund supports the greater outreach of the Church in its mission in our time. We believe that a Church is blessed in its own work as it gives to the program of the larger Church.

We offer the resources of this office to meet with you in a possible review of your participation in The Bishop's Fund in the coming year.

Very Sincerely,

Philip Frenell

Assistant to the Bishop

∝   ∝   ∝   ∝

Messiah Church

Columbia Avenue and Church Street

Indianapolis, Indiana

Pastor

Dr. Daniel Witt Clark

Dear Mother and Dad,

I think it is wonderful that you have finally decided to go on a cruise. For about as long as I can remember, Dad, you have talked of doing this. It all sounds great! As I understand it, you will board ship in San Diego, go through the Panama canal, and then cruise the Caribbean for ten days. And then a month in Florida! I am glad for you. I envy you.

We shall miss being with you at Christmas, but we shall get

together at the earliest opportunity after your return. We are
counting on you taking lots of pictures to share all of your
experiences with us.

With my devotion to you,

Dan

∝   ∝   ∝   ∝

December 6

Dearest Mother and Daddy,

I have time for only a note.

We are so very sorry, Mother, that you do not feel up to a trip
to spend Christmas with us here. I shall plan to come with Debbie
and Mark on the day after Christmas. We can stay only a few
days. Plan now to hear all about football at Forest Middle School
and Northside High. Save another ear to hear about a formal
dance from someone who didn't have enough places on her card to
accommodate all the boys who asked (begged!) for just one dance.

I love you,

Mary

∝   ∝   ∝   ∝

Dan and Mary wanted to display brightness and color for
Christmas, so they put the Christmas tree on the porch. Debbie
and Mark worked to decorate it. The second night of its presence in
glory on the porch, all of the bulbs were stolen.

When Mary returned from taking Debbie to school, she came
into the den to sit on the sofa.

"Dan, I'm afraid." She shuddered. "The thought of prowlers *on
our porch* . . . stealing the lights . . . I'm afraid."

Dan went over to sit beside her and put his arm around her. They talked quietly until Mary's courage was renewed, and Dan had to leave for an appointment.

Christmas was still a week away. Mary and Debbie and Mark and Dan were all in the dining room. On this first day of Christmas vacation in the schools, they had gone shopping and had dinner in a French restaurant suggested by Debbie – where Mark pronounced and translated the various items on the menu. Now they were home to wrap gifts and tie bows.

There was a crash of shattering glass and a heavy thud!!!

Dan led the rush to the living room. Glass fragments from the front window were scattered on the floor and furniture. A winter wind was rushing a chill through the broken window. Mark picked up a brick from the rug and stood holding it; for a moment Dan thought that Mark would throw it back out through the window. Mary closed the doors leading to the dining room, and Dan closed the door of the den. Mary and Debbie put on coats to begin picking up pieces of glass and cleaning the carpet and furniture. Dan asked Mark to put down the brick and go with him. They found a piece of plywood in the garage, which they cut and fastened to the window frame. In the morning, Mark and Debbie took the decorations off the tree, and Mark dragged the tree to the alley for the trash men to haul away.

The window was replaced. Art Brehmer stopped by to check the installation. He told Mary not to worry because the cost was covered by insurance.

David Schuster looked up from his desk, and in recognition went to the door, reaching out his hand to John Phillips.

"John! It's been so long! Take off your coat. Sit down. Tell me about yourself. Would you like a cup of coffee?"

When he was seated with his coat removed, John made reply.

"Dave, I am trying to catch up after being away so long. You know, of course, that Lib and I finally took the cruise that we have always dreamed about. We have been gone for several months, and returned just in time to have Christmas at home with our children . . ."

"We are glad we went, but it is horrible what can happen to a business when you are not on top of it . . . I walked over to see Dan, but he was out as usual. I want to do something for the Lord . . . Tell me, do you have any suggestions? That's why I stopped."

When John paused, Dave leaned forward.

"I'm not one to decline such an offer, but you might be particularly helpful in the church right now."

"Can you tell me, or shall I talk with Dan?"

Dave shrugged his shoulders. "It doesn't take a theological degree to say 'money.'" Dave continued, telling John about Art Brehmer and the financial mess he had produced. John said that he didn't know Art. Dave continued, "As Dan says, Art can stand watching a hole filling up with water, and he can't shout 'Help.' The budget and financing of the church for next year need to be reworked in some special effort.

"You and I understand each other, Dave. We must say, 'Anything' to the Lord."

Dave looked at his watch. "Art Brehmer works an early shift; he ought to be home now." He looked in the directory and dialed. "Hello, Art. Dave Schuster . . . Fine. And how is your family? Good, good. Say, Art, I have been thinking about the financial situation at the church . . . Right. I agree that *we* have done everything *we* can . . . I have a suggestion . . . What would you think of asking the Official Board to set up a special committee to see what might be done? . . . That's right, Art, there are a lot of us who are already giving *more* than we can really afford . . . Think about it and let me know what . . . That's important! But first, the idea should come from you to the Board . . . If you say so, I'll try to think of a couple of names."

Dave hung up. "All right, John. You're chairman – unofficially, of course, for the present."

Dave and Nan Schuster spoke with Al and Betty Hirter following the 9:30 service on Sunday. Dave stopped by to see Al on Monday.

Al started their conversation. "Betty and I think that Dan is better than ever." Dave listened and waited. "Betty and I just attended the morning service at Cedar Knoll; they have people and money enough now, and there wasn't anything for *us* to do. We weren't getting much out of the services . . . So we came back to Messiah."

Dave told Al that there *was* something to be done . . . And John Phillips had a committee member.

Thomas J. Davis stopped by The Center. Dave closed the door of his office.

"Now then, Tom, you and I both know that you have been saying a lot about black people having places of greater responsibility and leadership in Messiah Church . . ."

That would be the committee: John as chairman, with Al and Tom. Dave called Dan to tell him what he had done.

Art Brehmer was on the telephone to say to Dave, "Mr. Schuster, I've been thinking about the money problem down at the church. I think it would be a good idea if we asked the Board to set up a special committee to go over the budget and financing for next year."

"Art, that seems like a workable suggestion. Do you have any persons in mind for this committee?"

"Not right off hand. Can you think of anyone? I thought of you, of course."

"Art, give me a couple of days. I'll see if I can offer a couple of names for your consideration."

Two relieved men hung up their telephones.

John Phillips and Al Hirter and Tom Davis went to work. In the February meeting of the Official Board, there would be a revised financial report by Art Brehmer – with John and Tom and Al sitting around him to keep the figures accurate. Dan's salary was raised. The Bishop's Fund was still omitted. The Official Board commended a happy Art for his encouraging report.

Dan wakened early on New Year's Day so that he was in Rockford before noon. He knew immediately that it was a mistake to have come. If Mary had told him, he had forgotten. He arrived to find Mary working in the kitchen, as this was the day for an annual family reunion, and the rotation brought it this year to the Carters. Mary's mother was unable to do very much, but her brother and his wife, as well as her father's two widowed sisters, together with another couple who were "cousins" – all were coming for dinner at three o'clock. Mary said that everything was "under control" in response to his offer to help.

Debbie had cornered her grandfather. Dan joined an obviously bored Mark to listen.

"But there was this one girl – her name is Ruth Ann. Well, we were good friends until this boy that she likes to call her boyfriend, but he really isn't and most of the girls don't think he cares one thing for Ruth Ann, anyway, this boy sat beside me at the Christmas program at school, and Ruth Ann was so mad that she said she wasn't ever going to speak to me again. And I said I couldn't help it if this boy came and sat down beside me and I can't help it if there are no reserved seats, but she said that they had been planning to sit together, and he asked me if he might sit beside me for the performance and he gave me a program, and when I said something about Ruth Ann, he said to me, 'Who?' He is really a nice boy, and after the program he said he had enjoyed sitting with me, and then Ruth Ann came up and said that our teacher wanted him for something . . . she looked so smart as she walked away with him, but I don't think the teacher . . ."

Dan felt that he understood the troubled world scene a little better . . . 'If *one* Eighth Grade boy could manage to create so much upheaval, what might be the potential of a room full of congressmen?' He returned to the kitchen, but Mary was too busy to talk. He found Blair Carter in the office which he maintained in his home, and learned about the business outlook for Rockford for the coming year. He returned to help put the food on the table and pour coffee. With Uncle Walter at the table, Dan would have preferred that someone else be asked to pray.

Mary's mother went to bed as soon as the guests left. Mark and Debbie helped to clear the table. Dan and Father Carter removed the extension leaves from the dining room table and stowed them in the closet, to the accompaniment of a sigh of relief from Mr. Carter.

"I'm glad that one's over . . ."

Dan ran the vacuum, hoping that there would be lots of crumbs around Uncle Walter's place at the table. He joined Mary in the kitchen to help empty the dishwasher and carry Mother Carter's "good china" to a cabinet in the dining room. He went to talk briefly and pray with Debbie and Mark. With his coat over his arm, he loosened his tie as he approached the room which Mary referred to as "my room." The room was dark. Mary was lying quietly in bed, apparently asleep. Dan stopped and waited for a time.

Dan spoke to the room. "I'd better get back. I have a lot of work to do."

As he started his car, he realized that he had never taken his bag into the house. He stopped at the first motel.

Blair Carter walked into the kitchen in the morning.

"Where's Dan?"

"He left last night. He said he had a lot of work to do."

"He could at least have stayed overnight. Didn't you try to stop him?"

"No. Daddy, I didn't. I was too tired."

"I don't like this, Mary . . . I don't like this one bit."

Later in the morning, Mary called Dan at the church, but Miss Hazel said he was on the line with the Bishop's office.

Philip Frenell called Dan to say that they had received no reply to his letter about The Bishop's Fund. (Dan thought he needed to pray about Philip particularly, because Philip always seemed to bring out the worst in him.) He told Philip that no reply was Messiah's answer to his request for more money from Messiah Church for The Bishop's Fund. Philip was being 'Philip' for Dan when he persisted in the matter. Dan held the receiver away from his ear as Philip rambled on and on. Dan seized a break in Philip's discourse.

"Philip, I will tell you once more, and you may quote me to Bishop Gossert. The answer is 'No.' I must go now."

Dan returned Mary's call.

"Dan, I called to say that we are all sorry that you left so abruptly last night."

He should have waited. He should have gone to the chapel for a time of prayer. After talking with Philip he was not in a conciliating mood.

"I should not have gone in the first place . . ."

"Goodness, Dan, I don't know why not . . ."

"Don't interrupt me, please. I should not have gone in the first place, and now that you have called, let me say this: I don't need a cook. If you want to cook, you can go and cook for your Uncle Walter. I don't need a housekeeper. If you want to be minding a house, then you might as well stay in Rockford, to look after your parents and their house . . . I want a *wife*. I love you, and I need you. But, unless you are prepared to come back to live with me as my *wife*, then perhaps you should consider staying in Rockford, in *your room*, to look after your mother . . . and your father."

"Dan . . . Dan . . . I don't know what to say . . . You never talked like this . . . ."

"Mary, you don't need to say anything. Just make up your mind. If you decide not to return, I'll understand . . . So, I'll leave it with you. Excuse me, but I must go now."

"Dan, I'm sorry, but I don't know how to answer . . ."

"Mary, I'll have to leave this one with you. Bye, now. I have a call on another line."

The children were downtown with their grandfather. Mary sat at the kitchen table and cried. She was stirred from her sense of hurt and loneliness by the sound from the telephone which she had not replaced in its cradle. She washed her face and went to find her mother, who was reading the morning paper in the sun room. She told her *exactly* what Dan had said.

"Oh, Mary. I'm sorry. I am especially sorry because much of this is *my* fault. I should have canceled the dinner, or we should have taken everybody out, or something. *I know* how Walter irritates Dan. The responsibility is mine. I shall write to Dan, or call him. I have put you in a difficult position with Dan and that's not right."

"No, Mother, please leave the whole thing to me. It's my marriage and Dan is my husband."

The telephone call was from Dave Schuster, who wanted to come and see Dan. They seated themselves in the Study in an atmosphere of mutual respect and friendship.

"Dan, I want to talk with you about The Center and about Messiah Church. What I have may be old hat to you; if so, I am sorry to have taken your time. On the other hand, we have some information which I think is significant for the program and future of The Center – and I dare to think – important for the future of Messiah Church."

He stopped.

Dan waved his hand. "By all means, carry on."

"In looking over our program and our statistics, we find that the neighborhood is changing in substantial fashion. We have directed our program on the assumption that this area of the city was peopled by substantial *groups* of people, people who are in transit. These peoples could be described in terms of economics, national origin, color, and the like. We have tried to meet their needs in terms of language, employment, housing, culture adaptation, and the like. And I think that we have served a purpose."

Dan nodded and waited.

"The statistics would indicate that such groups are not coming to live in this district to the extent that they were coming only two years ago. Some of the housing restoration projects have brought a greater degree of stability to the population of this general area. While these efforts may seem insignificant, they have reduced transiency and welfare housing wherever they have been carried out. This has been done to enough of an extent that we know the effects of such efforts upon the population which The Center program has been designed to serve. I am telling you this because we both know what the population shifts did to Messiah Church. I guess that I think the program of the church should take into account the present changes which we have marked, and, even more, the changes which are coming. I came upon this in a talk with John Phillips, who is one of the movers and shakers in the city – this district in particular. I have come to tell you of the demographic changes which we have marked. I want to suggest that you talk with John. Maybe the church can be doing something to be in the forefront of change, rather than to be everlastingly playing catchup."

The next day Dan walked across the street to meet with John Phillips, who was more than ready to show Dan what they were planning and hoped to accomplish. He took Dan to the second floor and into a room dominated by sectional maps of the city, enlarged and mounted for ready reading. "First of all, Dan, our experiments in some restoration projects have been accepted beyond our most optimistic predictions."

"Secondly, we envision an expansion of commercial and governmental building to cover this area. (He moved his finger over the map.) Please note, Dan, that this expansion of the city's core will reach out to here. (He pointed.) That means that Messiah Church will have a substantially different position in the city as a whole. It will *not* be a regional church in any sense of the word; it will be a center-of-the-city church, situated as though to speak authoritatively to the entire city. If we carry through with this development – and that is about as certain as anything in this business can be – I think that Messiah Church will be in a new strategic situation. To follow your interest, I don't know what this will mean to the program of the church; I daresay we must look for the guidance of the spirit in this."

"Thirdly, our one small venture into condominium living has indicated that this type of housing is viable. We are, and have been, actively buying up properties to amass land sites. We are currently working on multiple exterior designs to give character to the district as a whole. We think of recreating housing close enough to the work place that people can walk to work rather than to spend hours every day on jammed traffic arteries. For Messiah Church, I must take back part of what I said. If this is accomplished, there will be a population within walking distance of Messiah Church which is many times over the size of the population when Messiah Church was at its presumed zenith."

∝   ∝   ∝   ∝

January 15

Dear Mother and Father Clark,

I hope that by now you have received "Thank You" notes from Mark and Debbie.

We are all very anxious to hear about your cruise. If you cannot come here, then Dan says we shall drive over to hear about it and see your pictures. We should particularly like to come and see you now you are in Florida.

The children are back in school and very busy. Mark is playing on the Forest basketball team. He had to start late because of football, but he says he will be one of the starting guards in another week or so. He is most impatient if the weather interferes with his practice out in the alley. He has a line marked for foul shots.

I do not need to tell you that Dan is very busy. The television ministry has added so much to his work load. He says that he is not trying to put on a television "show"; he sees it as a means to enlarge the sanctuary many times over. Then too, Mr. Benson and Mr. Padgett are leaving. Replacing them is almost impossible. The church is looking for two full-time Associates, and maybe even a third one.

As though this were not enough, the church is starting a Christian Day School, to be called "Messiah School." The hunt is on for personnel to start two pre-school classes in the Fall. The Church has even started buying property adjacent to the church for a school building eventually.

My mother is not well. She seems to have a bit of everything. They could not come for Christmas, and I took the children to be with Mother and Daddy for a few days after Christmas. Mother called this morning to say that they certainly miss having Mark and Debbie in the house. Much, much quieter.

With our love for now,

Mary

∝   ∝   ∝   ∝

There was one thing to be said about serving as the Minister of a church such as Messiah Church . . . life and work could never slip into a dull routine. Dan received almost daily reminders that he was not allowed to take anything for granted. As a way of life, Dan was forced to "practice what he preached"; he must go in a day-by-day, step-by-step reliance upon God. But all of this was so easy to forget. For example, everything about Messiah Church was heartening. Nobody said, 'Messiah Church is the way it used to be.' It was a new and different church. It was going and growing. It was exciting; no one could venture to predict what it would be.

And then one day, Dan received first a letter and then a telephone call . . . from the Bishop. Dan was asked to call for an appointment with the Bishop at his earliest convenience.

The next morning Dan was in the office of the Bishop, who opened the conversation. "Dan, we feel that the church as a whole must take a hard look at the parishes within the city. I am pleased with the broad support I have received in naming the committee to study the character and problems and opportunities of the urban church – with special consideration of Messiah Church"

"I do not understand the special reference to Messiah Church. Several of the lay leaders sat down with this committee some time ago. They were there to speak to any point which the committee might want to raise."

"Yes, of course, and the committee was much impressed by the character and quality of lay leadership which Messiah Church possesses. And I just heard that Al and Betty Hirter are back at Messiah; they can make a significant difference."

"What more, sir, does the committee want?"

"The committee would have liked more input from you. There are some personal nuances in the Messiah Church situation which remain unexplored to the committee's satisfaction. The Ad Hoc Committee is asking for a meeting with you, personally."

"What do they, and you, mean by that?"

"As you know, Dan, I have a unique sort of continuing personal interest and relationship with Messiah Church in the decisions and actions of my son. He was divorced, and then he was caught up in his relationship with Messiah Church. I know some of the problems in his home, and I know he has more than fulfilled his financial obligations to his daughters and his former wife. But then he resigned from a responsible position, and something possessed him at his age with his status in the business world to go off to theological school . . . And as you well know, he has married the Church Secretary. I only met her the evening of their wedding. She did go to see Ada, and Ada likes her very much. But I understand she is going to be involved in some sort of personal counseling . . ."

Dan couldn't believe he was hearing what he was hearing. He broke into the Bishop's recitation without apology.

"I don't believe this . . . Carol is a Christian. I know her well from her working in Messiah Church for several years. She has her Ph.D. in Psychology from the university; she has established a private practice as a *professional*. To question her character, her motives, her abilities . . . this, sir, is a *slur* which *I will not* permit to go unchallenged. If *any* suggestion of this ever surfaces, you will do two people – both Carol *and* Larry – irreparable injustice and harm. Sir, this is not worthy of you. Where did something like this come from?"

Dan paused. The room had been listening. 'Maybe I should apologize . . . NO! . . . . NEVER! . . . The Bishop owes an apology . . . !'

The Bishop was chastened by Dan's blunt rejoinder.

"I'm sorry, Dan. Perhaps I have spoken ill-advisedly."

Dan sat back unappeased. His voice was cold. "If this is any indication of what I am to encounter with this special committee, you have my word now that I will *not* come."

"No, Dan. Just this week, the committee expressed their desire to . . ."

Dan broke in without apology.

"Bishop Gossert, this is all to some purpose. Your words are suggestive to me that I have become *persona non grata* in the church."

The Bishop spoke quickly. "Of course not, Dan. I have nothing but the highest personal regard for you and your work. And we anticipate that the Ad Hoc Committee will come forward with some positive and practical suggestions for city parishes . . ."

Two days later Dan was surprised with a word from Miss Hazel that Fred Hudson was in the outer office and wanted to see Dan.

Dan's voice was genuine. "Fred, it's *good* to see you."

Fred held onto his hand. "I hope I am wrong, but I had to see you."

"Please, sit down. I hope we don't need some special reason to get together . . . ever."

"Dan, this is, or it may be, special. Only this morning I heard that you are to meet next week with a special committee of some kind."

"I didn't know the word got around that fast, but you are right. Next Monday morning at 10:00 o'clock."

"That's why I am here. From the person who told me, I was getting strong and negative vibrations. So much so, Dan, that I have come now to say that *you should not go alone*. Take some one with you . . . If there is no one else, I'll go . . . But that would only create problems . . ."

When Dan walked into the Bishop's Conference Room, the committee had already been in session prior to his arrival. Dan introduced the members of the committee to Jerry Whitman and Mr. Whitman's personal secretary, Mrs. Anne Forster.

"Mr. Whitman is a member of the Board of Messiah Church; professionally he is an attorney. Mrs. Forster will make a recording of my interview with you."

Philip Frenell stated, "It was our purpose and our understanding that this was to be a conference with *you* personally."

Professor Maynard added, "I have never pictured you as needing anything or anyone."

Claudia Stevenson noted, "Having a recording device running makes me nervous. Is that necessary?"

Dan broke into the uncertainty. "I will talk with this committee only with Mr. Whitman beside me and with a complete recording of what transpires here. I assume that we are Christians who are not ashamed of what we do and say."

Dan and his friends were asked to leave the room for the committee to discuss these terms. He and Jerry and Anne were shortly called back into the room.

Philip opened a folder and began. "Dr. Clark, the Bishop's Ad Hoc Committee on the Urban Church previously met with several of the lay leaders of the church. It has familiarized itself with the statistical and financial record of Messiah Church. As Bishop Gossert indicated to you, there are some personal factors which enter into the Messiah situation which this committee has felt it should enquire . . ."

With this introduction, Philip began to enumerate a series of what the committee had termed "personal elements" in the Messiah situation:

1. There was a swing to the right theologically; the preaching and teaching were reminiscent of a fundamentalism of other times.

2. The church had hired Rev. Willard Benson and Rev. Charles Padgett without clearing these individuals through proper channels.

3. There had been an extremism of sorts in that the church conducted a weekly "healing service" so-called, in which the work of modern medical science was discounted.

4. For some years the church had used materials for its educational program which came from other than denominational sources.

5. The church had separated itself by refusing to include The Bishop's Fund in its annual budget.

6. The church conducted what was called an "evangelistic service" which was not in keeping with the traditions of the denomination.

7. The Minister had been antagonistic and combative toward his fellow clergymen – this in public.

8. The church would not accept persons as members on the basis of Letters of Transfer from other churches of the denomination. They required a special class of instruction to be a member of *Messiah Church*.

9. Messiah Church began and continued to televise a morning Worship Service under the title: 'The Church Speaks." This public activity and its title were undertaken without prior approval by the church, i.e., the Bishop.

10. There was a spirit or possession abroad in the church such as to persuade a man to resign a high level administrative position and enroll in theological school.

11. Messiah Church had rejected and thwarted a studied course of action in keeping with the Bishop's strategy for the city.

12. There is reason to question personal relationships . . . (Philip: "No, strike that.")

Philip paused, "Perhaps Dr. Clark might begin this discussion by addressing any one of these items which he might select."

Dan looked at Jerry quizzically. Time hung heavy as he looked from one to another of the faces of the committee members.

"Philip, what I say to you, I say to each of these members of this committee . . . All of this has nothing to do with a denominational strategy to take this city for Christ. This, even at its best, is a witch hunt. If you all approved of this procedure, then being in the same room with you makes me feel unclean. I will have nothing to do with this presumed agenda; indeed, I will have nothing to do with you . . . Come, Anne . . . Jerry. I need some fresh air."

Dan heard nothing from the committee, and he eventually prayed the remembrance of this meeting out of his mind. He thought that he had put it behind him when the Secretary of the Official Board personally delivered a notice of a special Board meeting on the coming Tuesday night. The notice said that it was "imperative" that he be present. The members – all thirty-six of them – were absolutely uncommunicative.

A mystified Dan arrived at the Board Room to find *every* Board member present. Also present were: Bishop Gossert and all the members of the Bishop's Ad Hoc Committee. Dan was told that the President of the Congregation would occupy the chair for this special meeting, which he opened with prayer. Dan felt like an observer, not a participant, for one reason; that is how it was that night.

The President called on Jerry Whitman, who went to the door, returning with Anne Forster. Without a word, she placed a tape recorder on the desk, and with a nod from the President she turned it on. Not a pin was dropped through the hearing of the recorded transcript of the meeting. Anne Forster picked up the recorder and left the ominously silent room.

The President's voice shocked the quiet: "Mr. Secretary, will you please read the motion."

"The Official Board of Messiah Church demands that this file and everything associated with it be destroyed immediately. The Official Board demands that any and all harassment of Rev. Daniel Witt Clark cease immediately. The Official Board of Messiah Church demands that there be a formal and full apology from the office of the Bishop, and from the members of this special committee of the Bishop.

"If any and all of these demands are not met, the Official Board authorizes and commissions Jerry Whitman to institute such legal action as to make Messiah Church an independent church of the Lord Jesus Christ – recognized as such by common law and canon law."

The President said, "That is the motion. Do I hear a second?"

There was a chorus of voices. "SECOND."

The Bishop and the committee sat dumbfounded. The Bishop found his voice and wanted to speak, but the President would not give him the floor.

The President said, "The motion is seconded. The Secretary will read the motion again."

After the Secretary read the motion, the President said, "And now we shall vote. The Secretary will call the role, and each member will give voice to his vote."

From the first name through the thirty-sixth name, the Bishop and his committee heard the response: "AYE! And so say we all!"

The President asked the Secretary for the count.

"Thirty-six votes for the motion. None against."

"The motion is passed."

The Bishop again asked for the floor. He tried to speak some placating words, but found himself confronted by a steel wall with no dents nor fissures.

The President called upon Thomas J. Davis to close the meeting with prayer. When Tom finished, no one would ever again question what it means to "love one another with a pure heart fervently."

In Messiah Church change seemed to be a way of life. Dan walked into the church office one afternoon. He had worked on sermon preparation in the morning, and left directly for a luncheon meeting. He stopped to see Messiah people in two hospitals before returning.

Diane jumped from her seat to run to meet him.

"Dr. Clark, thank heaven you are back. Another day would have been too much. Please go and see Miss Hazel."

He found a disconsolate Miss Hazel with red, swollen eyes, who upon seeing him blurted out, "Dr. Clark, I am leaving."

"Come, Miss Hazel. Supposing we go into the Study, and you tell me all about it."

"You know, Dr. Clark, my sister, Helen Curtis, passed away twelve months ago. Mr. Curtis has been calling on me. Last night he said to me, 'A year has passed, and since there is no woman in the world like a Croft woman . . .'

"And he asked me to marry him . . . Dr. Clark, you will think me a giddy fool, but I said I would marry him . . . And Dr. Clark, Mr. Curtis is a very positive man. He thinks that once a person has made up his mind, he gets on with it."

Dan nodded and waited for Miss Hazel to get her breath.

"Mr. Curtis says that whatever I want is fine with him, and I want you to marry us here in Messiah Church . . . Next week, Dr. Clark. And I'd like Carol – Mrs. Gossert – to stand up with me."

On Sunday Dan invited the congregation to come. It was short notice, but they put it together. People of the church displayed their deep affection for Miss Hazel and filled the sanctuary. Diane sang. David Schuster gave the bride away. Mr. Hoffmeyer kissed the bride. Betty Hirter and Marge Hudson were responsible for the reception. Everyone said it would be difficult to think of "Miss Hazel" as "Mrs. Curtis." Frank Curtis stated flatly to all and sundry that "Mrs. Curtis doesn't have to work for a living." Everyone agreed that the bride looked "beautiful."

The day after the wedding, Dan remembered to call the Employment Advisor at The Schuster Center. (Dave thanked him ". . . for remembering us *this* time.")

In early afternoon Diane came to Dan. "There is a lady in the waiting room to see you. She says that The Schuster Center sent her over."

Dan went out to meet an immaculate, lovely Vietnamese lady. She came in to introduce herself as a widow with four children; her husband had fallen overboard in a rough sea in their escape from Viet Nam. She was the personification of Oriental graciousness. Her English was impeccable. Dan noted happily that she did not even split her infinitives. She said she needed to work to support herself and her children. Her face lightened as she declared simply, "Sir, I am a Christian."

Dan said she was hired and offered a word of prayer for her and her family. He spent the rest of the afternoon explaining her responsibilities and showing her about the office area, and particularly her work center.

"Please, sir. When do I begin?"

"Right now!"

The church bulletin for the following Sunday would include in "THE STAFF":

Pastor's Secretary · · · · · · · Mrs. Kuo Tsingh

And of course there was Diane. She was allegedly the Church Secretary, and she was splendid for this role – that is, when she wanted to be. There were days when she did not show up for work: no call, no explanation, no apology, no nothing. Dan talked with her. Rose talked with her. It had reached the point where Dan told Rose that he didn't want to do it, but it was very likely that he would need to get someone else for this position.

Fred Hudson called and invited Dan to have lunch with him; he said that he might invite someone else if that would be all right.

When Dan arrived at a corner table in a hotel dining room, he discovered that Fred had invited another person – his wife, Marge. The table talk quickly and naturally centered on Messiah Church. Marge had enjoyed doing the reception for Miss Hazel; Fred had received a complete report on the special Board meeting. His summary was: "I wish I *had* been there to vote."

∝   ∝   ∝   ∝

March 5

Dear Mother and Father Clark,

Debbie and Mark have Spring vacation coming the week after Easter. I have thought that I might try to bring the children to Belvoir, for a few days of that week – if this would be acceptable to you. They keep repeating that they want to see your pictures.

Mark and Debbie are not children any longer, but I would prefer that they do not have time here when they are not busy in school. As you know, Dan thinks that I have done too much to make our house into a fortress. Be that as it may, the children talk of you and brightened happily when I suggested that we might visit you during Spring vacation.

Messiah Church is doing very well indeed. Dan and Mr. Benson and Mr. Padgett have worked untold hours in visitation; in addition, one hundred and fifty couples (or teams) – only yesterday I heard the number was two hundred – have been doing visitation. On Maundy Thursday, there will be a reception of new members – the largest group in the history of the church.

But there is a problem. Isn't that how it always seems to be? Mr. Benson and Mr. Padgett are leaving. Neither of them wants to quit, but their wives want them to have some retirement years together. Bensons are moving to Florida, and Padgetts are going to Arizona.

Please let me know if a visit at this time will work out for you.

With love,

From ALL of us,

Mary

∝   ∝   ∝   ∝

April would be a special month in Messiah Church.

The first Sunday of April was Easter. There were services at 8:00, 9:30 and 11:00 in both the sanctuary and the chapel. In each service Dan asked the congregation to welcome the persons who had been received as new members on Maundy Thursday; to identify these individuals he asked them to stand. Following each service, the comment was heard: "I grew up in a church that never had that many members."

Dan asked each congregation to think about the possibilities and the problems if *next year* Messiah Church would have a *single* outdoor Easter service . . . maybe in the ball park.

The reaction was not what he wanted. The single observation repeated most frequently was, "Thank the good Lord, Dan Clark is planning to be with us next year!"

The second Sunday of April was the day for Rev. Willard Benson to preach. Even his wife did not know how he would get through it. It was difficult to tell who was the sorrier that Rev. Mr. Benson was leaving: the congregation and the officers, or Mr. Benson himself. He *was* unhappy. He *looked* unhappy. He *said* he was unhappy. His only look of brightness came on the day he brought a friend to meet Dan: Rev. Ralph Booker.

He said to the congregation in his sermon:

". . . Goodness knows I've said it often enough, but all of the years of what we call my 'active ministry' I served small churches in small towns or rural communities. The people in those churches were wonderful, believing, faithful Christians – and I choose to use that word. They put up with me, largely I think, because they knew that I was about as good as a church like theirs would ever get.

"I worked, and I sought the face of God, and I hoped that my life would be useful to my Lord Who had claimed me with His own blood. I spent what I thought was my working life doing just that. The church from which I retired after a lifetime of service was smaller in number than the first church to which I went as a seminary graduate. I tell you now, shamefully I admit, that I worked on with many periods of discouragement, a sense of defeat, and a feeling that somehow I was a failure for my Lord. I mean no disparagement of all those good people. I see them now as agents of the high God.

"It took all the courage I could muster to speak to Dr. Dan. And then these months and years with all of you have brought me to see that through many long, long years, God was teaching me and preparing me for a work in this city in Messiah Church.

"Listen to me, please. Perhaps my life in God suggests an answer for you now. Whoever you are. Whatever you are doing. Give your life to the keeping of our Lord Jesus Christ. Trust Him . . . even when you walk through the valley of the shadow of death . . . trust Him. If you can trust my experience, He will bring you through in glory. For what it's worth, I feel *younger* than I did the first day I came to this sanctuary.

"One more word. A line from a hymn I love:
'When we all get to heaven,
What a day of rejoicing *that* will be!'"

The third Sunday of April would be the time for Rev. Charles Padgett to preach.

He said to the congregation in his sermon:

" . . . I want to take this opportunity to repeat what some of you may have heard me say a time or two already. What I think and what I say is not what is important. The Word of Almighty God is what is of absolute importance and relevance to our human existence. And this Word is to be found in the inspired pages of Holy Scripture, the Old Testament and the New Testament. May I say once more: I believe that the Scriptures are the Word of God, the only infallible rule of faith and practice.

"When I was twelve years old, the church which my family attended conducted a 'Catechism Class' for boys and girls. It was two hours, every Saturday, for two years. We learned the Heidelberg Catechism, and we memorized – let me repeat that – we memorized Bible verses and passages by the yard. I will repeat what most of you have heard me say many, many times. One of the most moving experiences of my life was when my mother's Bible was given to me after she passed away. It was in tatters! She had actually read it to pieces! I gave it to a bookbinder and asked him to do the best he could to put it back together. Here it is. (He held up a black leather volume.)

"God spoke, and the universe came to be. God said, 'My word shall not return unto me void.' From my first day in theological school, I have read the Word for daily devotion. I have made every effort to be a scholar in my continuing study of the Bible. I know that congregations which I served at times thought me to be hopelessly mired in an historical age long since gone. I have made a conscious effort all of my life to stay close to what God has revealed to mankind for life and eternal salvation.

"I join with you in giving thanks for seeing the Word of the living God proclaimed in Messiah Church, and I join with you in rejoicing in God's approval evidenced by the wondrous blessing of renewal of which we are all a part, and which no man can deny. Glory to God!"

The fourth Sunday in April was to be the final Sunday and the official farewell to the Bensons and the Padgetts. Bishop Gossert was invited to preach. The President of the congregation gave an engraved scroll of appreciation to both Mr. Benson and Mr. Padgett. He said in part:

" . . . I remember a meeting when we talked about the need of building the church in membership and attendance. Dr. Clark said that he thought we should have to do it 'the old-fashioned way. We shall have to get out and ring doorbells, and call on people, and tell them about Jesus Christ, and give them a personal word of invitation to accept Christ as their Saviour and to come to the worship services of the church.' Rev. Mr. Benson and Rev. Mr. Padgett, you have joined wholeheartedly with Dr. Clark to take the leadership in this old-fashioned way. I think I speak for every person here this morning when I say that you have assisted mightily in the demonstration that this is the modern way, and we believe that it is God's way of doing business in the salvation of human beings."

The President invited Mrs. Benson and Mrs. Padgett to come to stand beside their husbands before the congregation.

"One thing more, Mr. Benson and Mr. Padgett. I have bad news and I have good news. The bad news is, when you leave the church today, you will find your automobile is missing. The good news is that in this envelope (He gave each of them an envelope.) are the keys for a new car which is parked where you left your old car. If you don't like the make, and model, and color of the car, you will please speak to your wives, because they personally made the selections . . . For all of us, may you go to share in the richest blessings of Almighty God! . . . . Bishop Gossert, we shall ask you to offer prayer in behalf of these great and good servants of the Lord."

Mary was in Rockford with the children on the Second Sunday after Easter when Larry and Carol Gossert were visitors in the congregation. Dan saw them before the service, and he asked them to wait until the congregation had left, and then go to dinner with him.

At the dinner table, Larry said he was completing his seminary requirements. He was in the process of taking standard denominational tests required of those seeking ordination. He said to Dan that he was asking for Messiah Church to support officially his request for ordination. In addition, he asked Dan for his personal help in finding a parish in which he might begin his new life and work as a minister of Jesus Christ and His Church. He had the full support of the faculty and administration of the seminary where he had achieved a straight "A" average. He hoped his status as a divorced and remarried man would not be an insurmountable barrier.

Carol spoke up. "You might as well know, Dr. Dan, that I am

pregnant. Larry entertained questions. I told him that I want to be a mother. The Lord willing, we shall have this one child, at least."

Dan told them he would see what he could do. In another special meeting (!), the Official Board welcomed the privilege of supporting Larry's application for ordination. The Board – on Dan's recommendation – enthusiastically voted to call Larry as Associate Pastor of Messiah Church.

Dan approached the office of the Bishop with some uncertainty. Since "the" meeting of the Official Board, the lines of communication between the Bishop's office and Messiah Church had been severely formal. Dan was promptly ushered into the private office of the Bishop, who greeted Dan with a single word and waited for Dan to state his business.

It had come to the attention of Messiah Church – Dan stated – that one Lawrence Gossert was now completing his theological education. He added that Messiah Church would support Lawrence Gossert's application for ordination to the Christian ministry. The Bishop nodded. In addition, Messiah Church was formally inviting Lawrence (presumably Rev. Lawrence) Gossert to become Associate Pastor of Messiah Church. The Bishop was obviously caught unprepared for this request. He was in great trouble at home when he told of this request and his uncertainty on what to say or do.

However, the Bishop did hesitantly agree to the ordination of one "Lawrence Gossert" upon his satisfactory completion of required examinations and personal interviews. And, "if the way be clear," on the second Sunday of June he would be ordained to the Christian ministry and installed as the Associate Pastor of Messiah Church.

It had been a long day. George Gossert and his wife Ada were glad to get home. They had come from a dinner which had been arranged for the clergymen and their families, who had shared in the service of ordination and installation of Rev. Lawrence Gossert. Ada seated herself on the sofa with a glass of iced tea and a plate of wafers on the coffee table. The Bishop was holding his glass of tea as he stood looking out a window.

"George, it has been a big day and a most satisfying day. Just to think that our son is now an ordained minister and the Associate in Messiah Church."

The Bishop mumbled something.

"And when Larry stood up to preach. I declare, George, that I could hardly recognize my own son."

The Bishop acknowledged her experience.

"And as he was preaching, I swear I had to keep persuading myself that it was all real. He was *good*. I don't know why I was surprised by my own son, but I had no idea whatsoever that he would be, or *could be, that good*. I am ashamed to admit this to myself."

"I had talked with a couple seminary people and they had told me that they were very high on Larry."

"You never told me! You *should* have! But to see him there in your old pulpit . . . I could have died happily on the spot!"

"I confess it was something I never thought I'd live to see . . ."

He walked away from the window as though the topic of conversation was finished.

Ada watched him closely for several minutes when neither spoke. She broke the silence.

"George, I know you. Why is it that I am getting negative vibrations from across the room from you?"

"Oh, I'm not negative . . ."

"George, it's *me* . . . *Ada*. Don't try to put me off. What is it?"

"Oh, I don't know. It seemed awkward somehow for Larry as a divorced man to be there for ordination, with a very pregnant new wife looking on . . ."

"Oh, no! I think we should both get down on our knees every night to thank God that Carol has come into our son's life. She is almost too good to be real. She has her doctorate. She has built up a practice as a counselor. I can see, and I know you must see, all sorts of subtle changes in Larry since he and Carol have been married. I just say to myself . . . 'Why couldn't Larry have had a wife like Carol to start with?' I don't know what part she had in Larry's decision to enter the ministry, but she is in it somewhere. I know how *much* she wants to have this child . . ."

"More than that. I guess that if Larry is going to serve in a parish, I would prefer that it be a place other than Messiah Church."

"Of all churches, I would have thought . . ."

"Ada, there are many things you don't know. Messiah Church under Dan Clark has become increasingly a kind of maverick."

"What on earth do you mean by that?"

"I have talked with Dan several times about his move toward a fundamentalism. Unfortunately, I am hearing that same beat in Larry's message today."

"I don't know what you mean, but I thought it was a good sermon."

"And there has been a disposition on Dan's part to go his own way. He didn't ask me about Larry, *he told me* that they wanted Larry as an Associate. He didn't ask me about the television ministry; *he told me*. Just this morning *he told me* that Messiah Church wants a Ralph Booker as an Associate . . . And too, there is bad blood between Dan and Philip. Only a few days ago, Philip told me that Dan holds him in contempt, and that it is useless for him to contact Dan on behalf of our office . . . for any matter."

"But George, Dan can't be all wrong. Look at this church bulletin from this morning. (She proffered the bulletin to her husband, who waved it away.) Just look at this schedule. They have *two* morning services in the sanctuary. I heard that they are going to *three morning services* in September. There is a Sunday evening "Evangelistic Service" in the chapel, and someone told me that they will probably have to put this in the sanctuary in the fall. There are Communion Services *every* Wednesday in the chapel at 7:30, morning and evening. They have a Healing Service on Friday. There are study classes, service programs, a whole spread of youth activities. The membership must be something; there were several *hundred* who joined the church on Maundy Thursday. The eleven o'clock service is now on television; a columnist says that it is the most popular religious program in this area."

"Yes, I know, and that's what I was just saying. Dan came in and said they wanted our concurrence in this television ministry. He told me that it was to be entitled: 'The Church Speaks.' I thought it was presumptuous of Dan and the people *now* at Messiah to say in effect that Messiah Church speaks for the whole church . . . And I told Dan as much."

"George, you ought to be ashamed of yourself. It is a marvelous idea. Mr. Hoffmeyer was going to retire, but he is staying on. They have added a couple of stops to the organ which Mr. Hoffmeyer has said for years are needed. This morning the choir had a magnificent sound, and I am startled at how few people I know in the choir now. I think you and your office should face the east first thing every Monday, and thank God for Messiah Church and Dan Clark . . . . Thank God! Now they have claimed *my son* for Jesus Christ!"

Ralph Booker had come back on appointment to talk with Dan. He had grown up in a small county seat town, where Rev. Willard Benson was the Minister of the church his family attended. While Mr. Benson was their Pastor, Ralph had been led to commit himself to become a Christian Minister. Mr. Benson was his friend and counselor when no one understood. He was the only boy from the church – indeed, from the whole town – who ever had decided to become a Minister. He was a country boy who loved the Lord, who believed that God wanted him serving in the church . . . who knew how to work.

There was a small community on a bay of Lake Michigan which had a church that was open three months a year. The church owned a furnished house which was made available as a residence for each of the three clergymen who served a month each in the summer. (The house was rented during the other nine months as a source of income for the church.) Park Shores had invited Dan several times, and this year he decided that a change in scenery and situation from Glen Rock would be good for all of them. They would be there in July. Mary and the children would go to Belvoir for the last two weeks of June, and spend the first two weeks of August in Rockford.

∝   ∝   ∝   ∝

Dear Mother and Father Clark,

I want to thank you for everything you did to make the two weeks with you in Belvoir such a wonderful time for all of us. I am reasonably certain that you both are luxuriating in the peace and quiet, following the tempest that two young people can generate. I have no answer to your question: "Where do they get all that energy?" If I knew, I should get some for myself.

Getting some of that energy channeled into writing thank-you notes is something else. But whatever Debbie and Mark have written has come from their hearts.

Park Shores is a delightful and picturesque community. The church is an architectural gem. It was built by a missionary to the Indians, and it was an Indian church for many, many years — until the white man moved in. We are told that most of this area was an Indian reservation until twelve or fifteen years ago.

There is no question that Messiah Church has turned a corner and is, as they say, "going and growing." Father Clark, I am glad you had a chance to talk with Dan alone. Dan has changed. He is, of course, terribly busy. Much of the time he is preoccupied. There is no question whatsoever about our leaving the city at this point. Dan is committed to Messiah Church, and I don't know anything that would sway his dedication there.

I hope that Dan can relax here. I hope that there will be nothing to interrupt our vacation. I trust that we shall have time and opportunity to look at our family life and our goals from a different perspective.

Thank you again, with Love,

Mary

∝   ∝   ∝   ∝

Dearest Mother and Daddy,

Here we are at Park Shores. It is delightful, and a totally
different situation than Glen Rock. (I have no maid.) I'll tell you
all about it when I see you, and when I can have pictures to show
to you.

Mark will be in the Tenth Grade at Northside High School.
He is very unassuming around the house, and I confess that I look
with unbelief at this young man with all the big muscles in
swimming trunks. The coaches wanted him to stay in athletics, so
he was on the track team as a "weight man." He says that the
Northside quarterback graduated this year, and that the position
is open to the best performer. There are some upper class players,
but Mark says he is going to win the job as a sophomore.

And Debbie. Stone School has been right for her. She, of
course, will be in the Eighth Grade. The School has several
functions at the end of the school year. I saw her as one of the
leaders in a school convocation. It struck me forcefully that she is
a young lady. I almost said "woman." She has developed quite a
figure, as you will see for yourselves. I was really proud in saying
to myself: "That beautiful young lady is your daughter."

The city about us changes almost week by week. The church
has been growing, and Dan sees it moving forward to a new and
more powerful Christian witness in the city. There are two new
Associate Ministers. Dan has a new secretary, a Vietnamese lady.
The Staff and the program are to be significantly enlarged in the
fall.

This means that we are at Messiah Church and in the city indefinitely. Dan admits pushing as never before, and he needs time away from his work desperately. We look forward to being with you in a few weeks. If it made you (Daddy) feel old last year to see Mark as "your grandson," perhaps you should plan this year to introduce him as your "Associate" or "Partner."

With all my love,

Mary

YEAR EIGHT
AT
MESSIAH CHURCH

When Mary returned the 15th of August, Dan said he had much to report and discuss with her. The second night she was home, they sat in the living room to talk.

"Mary, the first two weeks of this month have been as busy and brought more decisions than I would have thought possible in months. I hardly know where to begin . . .

"It started with the need to provide some housing for Larry and Carol, and for Ralph and Elaine Booker. There was some thought to giving them a housing allowance, but John Phillips said that there were still three or four places available in the Waterford section; you know, the section that has been restored with brick streets and gas lights and all. While we were away, Larry and Carol and the Bookers had looked at them, and they loved them. These old homes are completely and beautifully restored; they have three bedrooms and two baths, with a half bath on the first floor. There are two rooms on a third floor, and either of them will make a delightful study. Larry and Carol picked one on the end of the row, which has a small side yard in addition to the back. Anyway, the Board voted to buy them, and Larry and Carol have moved some things in. The Bookers will be moving next week."

"That is good. I still have difficulty thinking of Larry and Carol being married, and of him as a Minister."

"We have called Craig Hartwell to serve the television ministry. He will be here by the end of the month. He will handle all the correspondence and follow up with all the people who have indicated some need, and with those to whom we should go for a personal decision and possible membership in the church. Craig and his wife want to get their own home, and he will receive a housing allowance."

"We have been anchored to this place for seven years, and all at once the church has money for housing its ministers . . ."

"I'm coming to that. The need for visitation must be met and we are going to do something different. The Mellons and the Kramers are going to become full-time lay visitors. They are leaving their current employment to work for the church. Everyone agrees that we must maintain personal contact with our people, and we have thought to try this instead of hiring more clergy . . . Ellen Gregory has a whole staff of part-time and some full-time people for education. The Youth Director needs space for what has become a seven-day-a-week operation . . .

"The Senior Citizen Center has need for some identifiable space and place . . . In short, the Board is looking at *this* house for some of these needs . . . And that brings me to what I am supposed to discuss with you . . .

"John Phillips and his group, are building a high-rise condominium over by River Drive. John and the committee are talking about a three-bedroom unit for us. It is being built and they say they can work out a small room that I could use for a study. They want us to see their model units, and if we like what we see, they want us to sit down with the architects and work out anything we might want to include – such as another room for a study."

"How is it that the church can be purchasing all of this real estate, and hiring all of these people?"

"Well, Mary, the amount of money in the offerings has increased tremendously week by week. The Official Board has accumulated a balance that even I don't believe. Two things in particular are responsible for this spending activity. For one reason or another, the offerings on Easter Sunday were unbelievable. The Board had to see the bank deposit slip to accept what they were being told. And the church is receiving more and more from the television viewers. We have been paying television expenses out of our budget, and the money which people have been sending was put into a special account in the bank . . . But they have been waiting anxiously for you to get back and see the condo model units . . ."

"Dan, this is certainly a new and a different beat than we have known. I daresay that I shall be the one discordant note in all of this. But you see, Dan . . . I don't want to move to another place here . . . . *I want to get out of the city completely* . . . I have had it all *up to here.* I am an alien in an alien land. I think that you . . . that we have done our part for the church in the city. And, Dan, I want out . . . all the way out."

After a seeming unending silence, Dan spoke, "I really don't know where that leaves us. I think my commitment to the Cause of Christ is here in Messiah Church."

∝   ∝   ∝   ∝

August 26

Dearest Mother and Daddy

I want to thank you again for the happy days we had with you earlier this month. I appreciate your speaking to me in such a complimentary fashion concerning Debbie and Mark. In spite of many misgivings about raising them here in the city, they have – so far, at least – become wonderful young people.

Debbie has gone to the school to talk with the class counselor. Debbie is to be an officer in her class, and a member of the Student Council. She is thrilled to be signed up for Driver Training.

Daddy if Mark had time I know he would be writing to tell you that as of now – at least – he is the starting quarterback for the Northside High School football team. He is very conscious of Northside's outstanding athletic tradition; they are always state champions in one thing or another.

BUT . . . . I guess nothing is perfect. There has been some trouble. Just down the street from the high school is a place called "Freddy's." In years past, it was sort of a hangout for students at Northside. However, in recent years it has become a place for older, gang-type boys and girls to gather. They are high school dropouts who can't get jobs, or who can't keep jobs they do get. They are both black and white, but I think predominantly black. Tom Davis says that the city keeps looking for reasons to close up the place. Somehow (????) these persons manage to have cars and money for gasoline and cigarettes and alcohol. They delight in bullying boys and girls going and coming from the school.

It was with some of this crowd that Mark became involved in a fracas the first week of practice. Mark was walking from the bus stop to the school. Some of the crowd were calling him names. One of them stepped in front of Mark and when Mark tried to walk around him, the fellow pushed Mark. And Mark says, "So I knocked him down." Fortunately a police car was going by at that moment, and the officers stopped the whole thing.

I guess I ought to be glad that Mark can take care of himself, but I tell Dan that I don't think our son should have to fight his way to school to get an education.

Do take care. Be well.

With all my love,
Mary

∝　　∝　　∝　　∝

Mark took great satisfaction that he had earned the position of starting quarterback for the Northside High School football team. Northside had handily won its first four games, with Mark receiving his share of the credit for the victories. The first Friday of October, they would meet Eastside, their traditional rival. It was a school holiday, so the game time would be 1:00 P.M. Dan told Mark that he had to attend a district meeting, but that he would come as soon as possible.

"Debbie, I sure would like to have you see me and my team play Eastside."

"Oh, I've been wanting to see you play on a high school team. May I go, Mother?"

"Debbie, I don't think you should be going alone."

"Oh, *Mother*! I'll ask Francie to go with me. She has seen Mark's picture in the paper, and she has said several times that she would like to meet him."

Mary agreed to drop Debbie and Francie off at the school. She said she would come back for them to pick them up at the same place, the main entrance of Northside High.

The district meeting ran overtime. Dan stopped at a phone booth as he neared the city limits to call the church. Recognizing his voice, Diane said immediately, "Dr. Clark, you should come home at once."

As he came down Columbia, he could see Church Street was filled with cars. There were three or four police cars with their blue lights flashing. Before he could park and get out of the car, he saw two men unknown to him come from the house. Dan ran to push his way through the front door to find Mary and Debbie and Mark sitting on the sofa in the living room.

'Thank the Lord. They're all right.'

A policeman – with a cap on – was talking on the telephone in the den. Dan recognized Principal Emmons, who was talking to a policeman – with a cap on – in the dining room. A man unknown to Dan, wearing a topcoat and hat, came out of the den; he paused to look Dan over very carefully. The house was chilled with the front door standing open. The atmosphere was charged. News people with cameramen arrived and tried to take over. The policeman left the telephone in the den and began writing furiously on a clipboard.

From one and then another, Dan put together the story. The game ended with a lopsided Northside victory. Because the game ended sooner than expected and because Mary encountered heavier than usual afternoon traffic, Mary was not at the door to pick up Debbie and Francie. Debbie started down the street looking for her mother's car. There was the usual crowd at Freddy's, who called out to Debbie and Francie. Debbie thought she should go to the school. She said she was frightened when two of the fellows came up to walk on either side of her. They said they would help her and had taken hold of her. She said she tried to run, but they held her. Then she heard a car start up. They said she was too cute to walk alone and they would drive her home. She couldn't get free. She didn't know where Francie was. They began to half-drag and half-carry her to a car at the curb. She began to scream for help when they tried to force her into the car.

Then she heard Mark's voice: "LET GO OF MY SISTER!"

Mark pulled one boy away from her and then knocked him down. A fellow got out of the car – she thought – and jumped on Mark, who had his arm around the neck of the other guy to pull him away from Debbie. Boys and girls poured from the school. More were coming from Freddy's – which was now *across* the street. When Mary did arrive she couldn't get close to the school. The melee had spilled out into the streets, into the school yard . . . Teachers came from the school . . . Men were stopping cars to get out – to try to do something. Finally, there were police cars everywhere. The police herded the whole crowd into the school yard. There were several ambulances to treat some who were wounded. The fellow that Mark had knocked down and stepped on to get to Debbie had struck his head on the sidewalk; he had been taken in a semi-comatose condition to the hospital. The whole affair had turned into a big street fight with Debbie and Mark at the center of the whole messy business.

In the noise of the commotion in the house, Mary's voice snapped, "Tell your father what else happened, Debbie."

Debbie hesitated as she looked at all of the strange people in her house.

"Well, Daddy . . . this one fellow had his arm around me, holding me. His hand . . ."

"Tell him!!"

"His hand was here . . ."

She put a hand on her right breast."

"Go on. *Tell him,* Your father *must* know!"

"Well, Daddy . . . he kept talking in my ear . . . and he put his right hand inside . . ."

Mary's voice crackled. "TELL HIM! Debbie!"

"Well . . ."

Again she scanned the faces in the room. "Under my skirt . . ."

The house was in total disorder, with people coming and going through doors standing open.

When he could, Tom Davis spoke only to Mary. "Mrs. Clark . . .

I'm sorry . . . We're sorry."

Dave Schuster. Then Larry Gossert. Then Ralph Booker. Everyone seemed to stay and stay as though waiting for something more to happen. Rose came and went directly to the kitchen and began making coffee and sandwiches. A man and woman from the Juvenile Department of the police came; they went into the dining room with Mary and Debbie and Mark and closed the doors. The whole story had to be repeated in detail with a secretary recording their words. The Bishop and his wife came. Ada went to Mary and put her arms around her for a moment; then she did the same with Debbie, who felt and looked ill at ease.

Finally, they were all gone – after some question over whether charges would be filed against Mark for assaulting the fellow who was now in the hospital. Dan had never known Mary as he now found her. She was not angry. She was not excited. She did not cry. She did not ask questions. She did not seek to persuade. She was cold, deliberate, decisive. When Mark and Debbie had gone to bed, she came to Dan.

"Tomorrow morning, I am taking Debbie and Mark, and we are going to Rockford."

"Yes, I think that might be good."

She moved to be squarely in front of Dan. "You don't understand. We are going to Rockford to live."

"To live!!! You're leaving?!!"

"That is precisely what I mean. Tomorrow morning. Mother is not well, and Daddy needs help."

Mary spun about to start picking up and straightening the living room.

"Mary, this has been a rough experience . . . But we should not be precipitate."

Mary stopped her chores to come back to Dan.

"Dan Clark, this is no snap decision and you know it. For *months and months and months* I have been saying that I want to raise my children in a better atmosphere. I have felt guilty for *years* for the kind of growing up to which they have been subjected. I talk, I ask. I beg. You always say that you're going to do something, but we never have any action or decision. The Official Board is always going to consider a new home for the minister. The Official

Board buys new homes for an Associate and Assistant . . . but we continue to live *HERE*."

I'm sorry, Mary. It's my fault . . . I have neglected . . ."

Mary would brush aside all responses. "Dan, you feel you were called to serve here. God knows – work is needed in this area, and maybe you are the one to do it. All *I* know is that *my* children are *not* going to pay the price for *that* service."

"I don't intend that they should . . ."

"*Dan!* There *is no more discussion,* no more delay. I've taken all I can take. Mark and Debbie *will not* live here any longer. We are going to Rockford. We are going to Rockford tomorrow morning. You can say that Mother and Daddy need help, if you need something to save face for your precious church."

Dan sat down in resignation. "I am certain that the Official Board will want to do something now."

"What does it take to get them to move? Oh, well . . . It makes no difference any more. The children and I are leaving in the morning."

Mary was up most of the night packing her car. Mark and Debbie were confused by her decision. She was not to be swayed. She was sharply taken aback when Mark said, "I'm sorry, Mother, but I'm not going now. If you say so, I'll come after the football season.. But I'm not going to be a quitter. I have worked too long and too hard to be the quarterback. The other fellows on the team are counting on me. The coaches are counting on me. I'll stay here with Dad for the rest of the season, or the end of the semester."

Mary looked at her son keenly, as though seeing and hearing him for the first time. She said nothing, but went to her car to remove a bag and a box containing Mark's things. She walked firmly past Dan returning to her car. Dan could not remember later whether she had said good-by.

At Mark's request, Dan took him to school for a study of films of the game. Returning home, Dan walked through the house and felt as though he had come back to a cemetery.

Dan went into the den and collapsed into a chair.

'What to do? . . . If I move away, then I am in the same category as a lot of others for whom I have had no respect. How many times have I castigated people who have regarded this area as good enough to provide them with money, but not good enough to provide them a place to live . . . who take money out, but put nothing personal back into the community. How many times have I – me, Dan Clark – questioned the courage of people who at first sign of difficulty pack up and run. I have privately and publicly declared for Christian courage in this day to capture the center city for our Lord. If I move, I join in a cowardly retreat.'

The following week, Dan was beset with phone calls. Reporters wanted quotes for follow-up stories. He didn't tell them about Mary. He said to Mrs. Tsingh, "I have tried again and again to make my witness for the Lord, and most of the time it seems that my word doesn't get beyond the sound of my voice . . . Then something like this . . ."

Mrs. Tsingh said she wished she could help. She did not yet know that Mary had left.

Larry Gossert came in. Ralph Booker came in. There was really nothing for them to do, but Dan appreciated their caring.

Larry had said, "That was a dreadful business, Dan."

"Thank you, Larry. We will survive, thanks to the Lord."

"Yes, but Debbie!" Larry seemed to shudder a bit. "Have you heard from Dad . . . I guess I should say, 'from the Bishop'?"

"They came that night, but there were so many people, as you could see. I haven't talked with him since."

"Dan, *I* have, and I asked him what *he* is going to do or say."

Dan tried to picture Larry confronting his father.

"That wasn't necessary, Larry."

"Maybe not, but it was necessary for me, Dan."

Mrs. Tsingh opened the door to ask a question, and get an answer.

"Dad said he regretted it, and that he is naming a committee to consider the matter. But Dan, who can wait on a committee – at least an *ecclesiastical* committee? What about Debbie? What about Mary? . . . while members of the committee are adjusting their linens around a conference table?"

Dan's voice was in the quiet of confidence. "Larry, you will hear it sooner or later. Mary has taken Debbie and gone to Rockford to live for the present."

"Oh, no!"

"Don't worry. We'll get something worked out."

"Why should you be alone in this? When Dad told me about this committee thing, I told him he was pussyfooting. I said that I would be back if they didn't get out of executive session fast."

Dan was shaking his head. "I don't know whether I shall want to see your father or not . . ."

"Oh, don't worry about Dad. To tell the truth, Dan, I don't think dad could decide whether to be angry with me, or glad to see me with some courage to stand up and make myself heard." Larry suddenly laughed at himself. "I can hardly believe that I really did talk like that to Dad."

The newspaper in a story on the incident, quoted Bishop Gossert:

"The Church regrets incidents of civic and racial tension, and is particularly regretful if such events involve the clergy and their families in any way at all. We are naming a special committee in order to keep close to the situation. We have named as chairman of that committee our Assistant, the Rev. Philip Frenell."

Dan did not hear from the special committee. The same week he *did* receive a large manila envelope which indicated that it had been hand-delivered from the office of the Bishop. He was planning to telephone Mary later in the evening. There might be some good news here with which he could encourage her; their telephone conversations since she left had been pretty grim. Mary said that she had come none too soon because her mother was a very sick woman, and she was distressed to see her mother in this condition. She said only that Debbie was "fine" and returned to talking about what the doctor had said concerning her mother's condition, and maybe she would need to be hospitalized, and she had never seen her father so distraught.

Dan was aware of an unaccountable feeling of optimism. He would have welcomed some light, some hope for his personal life from any quarter. He acknowledged to himself later that it was an indication of his desperation that he should have expected something helpful in this communication from the office of the Bishop. He sliced open the flap of the envelope to reach inside for the con-

279
Messiah Man

tents. letting the envelop sail to the floor. He found pages of text with tables of statistics, maps and charts. There was a cover letter on top, and he turned on a light to read:

Rev. Daniel Witt Clark, D.D.

Messiah Church

Indianapolis, Indiana

Dear Dr. Clark:

The Bishop's Ad Hoc Committee on the Urban Church wants to acknowledge your helpfulness in the study which has been made at the special request of Bishop George Gossert. The entire committee found your presentation to be informative and stimulating, and the questions which you posed to be relevant and searching.

The Bishop's Ad Hoc Committee on the Urban Church has taken cognizance of the changing patterns in American life as we move from a rural to an urban society. It is the belief of this special committee that the Church must exercise a concern for the whole of life. That is to say, we should seek solutions which reflect the broad spectrum of the totality of human existence.

The Bishop's Ad Hoc Committee on the Urban Church finds the issues committed to it for study to be of greater scope and consequence than the time and resources available to the Committee. Therefore, The Bishop's Ad Hoc Committee on the Urban Church is recommending to the Annual Assembly that consideration be given to the establishment of a commission of representative persons to study the impact of urbanization of American life upon the Church and her ministry. The Bishop's Ad Hoc Committee on the Urban Church would request that it be dismissed in deference to the larger work of a commission repre-

senting the entire Church.

The Bishop's Ad Hoc Committee on the Urban Church expresses its appreciation for the insight of Professor Maynard: Change in and of itself is a descriptive factor; it is the kind of change, as well as what we do in and with that change, that are of importance. The Bishop's Ad Hoc Committee on the Urban Church is grateful for the counsel of Dr. Lawler: In a time when the old barriers are being broken down, the Church must be structured to lay claim upon every potential good.

The Bishop's Ad Hoc Committee on the Urban Church has noted with satisfaction the fine work which you have done, and which you are currently doing in Messiah Church. The Bishop's Ad Hoc Committee on the Urban Church wants to commend you for your devotion to duty and the service which you are rendering in the name of the Church and her Lord.

We wish for you the peace and blessing of God.

> Respectfully
> Rev. Philip Frenell
> Chairman, The Bishop's
> Ad Hoc Committee on the
> Urban Church

cc: Bishop George Gossert
     Committee Members
     FILE

Dan did not mention the communication to Mary, who would not have been interested anyway. She wanted to talk with Mark to check on his class work in school and the maintenance of his personal habits. Mark's part in the conversation consisted of a repetition of, "Yes, Mother."

Dan gave the communication from The Bishop's etc., to the Secretary of the Official Board. Over Dan's objections, the Secretary read the letter to the Board. In spite of Dan's genuine protestations, the Board passed the following motion:

"The letter from the Chairman of The Bishop's Ad Hoc Committee on the Urban Church was read, noted and filed."

Dan found himself totally occupied with the fall program of the church. There seemed to be countless details involved in the schedule change to *three* morning services in the sanctuary *each* Sunday. There was the instruction and initial supervision of two new Associates and the two couples who were doing visitation; an additional secretary was hired. There were almost daily conferences with Craig Hartwell concerning the burgeoning television ministry; for the present he would need two corresponding secretaries and a financial secretary. Requests for Dan's appearance and/or participation in community occasions multiplied until he told Mrs. Tsingh, "Please say 'No' to all first requests, and then let us see who, if any, call back."

The overarching question in Dan's mind, and admittedly in the minds of the lay leadership of Messiah Church was, "What will be the reaction of people to the school melee, and to Mary's departure to take up her life in her parental home?"

As the experience of time developed, Dan said to himself, 'I should have trusted Christian people more.' In general, there seemed to be understanding and compassion. People were saying – not to Dan, "If Debbie were my daughter, I don't know what I'd do . . . probably something such as Mary has done . . . or more."

Again and again, Dan noticed that people seemed to want to hold his hand a little longer as he spoke with them at the door of the sanctuary following the services. One after another would say, "Dr. Dan, I'm praying for you and Mary . . . and Debbie."

Dan and Mark would have done nothing but eat from early morning to nightfall, seven days a week, if they had accepted all of the dining invitations which came to them. As it was, each week day Dan would pick up Mark at the school, and they would have dinner somewhere on their way home. Foot-long hot dogs still appeared frequently on their dinner menu. Dan would leave Mark at home and he would go on to a meeting or out for a round of visitation. They would have some kind of "man talk" every night before retiring. On Saturday nights, they would place a call for both of them to speak with Mary and Debbie.

There was much to encourage. Ralph Booker had learned his lessons well from his boyhood pastor. He was a full-time working, youthful embodiment of Rev. Mr. Benson. He said to Dan, "I love Jesus, and I love people . . . for Jesus' sake. I tell Elaine and I thank the Lord every day for the joys in serving my Lord. I never expected to be so happy this side of heaven."

The Mellons and the Kramers had come into their own. Dan could scarcely believe the numbers of personal contacts which they were accomplishing, and the results which they were achieving in their witness and invitations for decision.

Larry Gossert matured and blossomed in his new life work. Former working associates at the power company would come to hear Larry preach and go away shaking their heads. "We can't believe this is the Larry we worked with for all those years. How could he have been hiding these gifts?"

Larry said nothing to anyone, including Dan. He had taken the personal goal of winning for Christ the entire Board of Directors and the managerial staff, up to and including the President of the power company.

Bishop Gossert could not hide his obvious pleasure in being asked to preach in a televised service, which was not just any service. He was participating in the service especially to christen "George Gossert II." Tears ran unashamedly down his cheeks as he and Ada walked up and down the aisles with now one carrying their grandson, and now the other. One television cameraman picked up Larry and Carol and Larry's two daughters standing at the chancel, watching a "George Gossert that many had never seen before." Many in the television audience wrote to ask how they might contribute to a college fund for "little George."

∞   ∞   ∞   ∞

November 4

Dear Dan,

Thank you for sending the extra check. I have already spent a good bit of it on clothes. I found a couple pairs of shoes, but I am still looking for a dress. Miss Debbie's "needs" are determined by fads and a clothes consciousness.

As I told you, I have started house cleaning on a schedule of a room per week.

(Dan stopped reading to tote up mentally how many weeks this schedule would require.)

I probably won't be able to achieve that goal. I'm afraid that the women Mother has had to do her cleaning have been skimming over the top and missing the corners.

Debbie is getting along well in school; in many ways she is in advance of her class. She was very readily "accepted" and is well adjusted. There was an "Open House" at the school last week, and I went to talk with some of her teachers. They are all delighted to have her.

Daddy is able to get out more now that I am here.

('I have to get out more and more day and night, regardless of where you are, but I'd like awfully much to be able to come home to someone who loves me.')

Debbie and Mother and Daddy join me in our love to you and Mark.

Mary

∞   ∞   ∞   ∞

The following Saturday evening Mary called. Mark answered the telephone and spoke at length with his mother.

"Dad, Mother wants to talk with you."

Dan picked up the phone to hear a recital of medical tests, comments by several doctors, as well as Mary's personal opinions on her mother's medical problems. She described Debbie's daily activities in great detail. The conversation was punctuated regularly by quotes from her father.

"Dan, are you there?"

Dan assured her that he was there; he didn't say that he was waiting for something new. Then Mary introduced the "new."

"Dan, I went into Debbie's room the other night and she had been crying. I asked why, and she said that she misses her brother. And *I* miss Mark *terribly.* I have been thinking that the children ought to be kept together as long as possible; goodness knows that they will soon enough go their separate ways. I was talking with Mark just now, and I said to him that I want him to come and be with us when the football season is over. I wanted to know what you would think of that."

Dan felt that his response did not help his preparation to preach the next morning about "the Christian Spirit."

"Mary, you have been talking for some time now. I am aware that not once in this conversation – indeed, not once since you left here have you ever said that *I* am missed. And Mary, I have reluctantly come to the conclusion that I figure in at about zero in our marriage as *you* see it . . . Enough! I have work to do. I'll put Mark back on and whatever the two of you decide is acceptable to me . . . Mark!! . . ."

Northside High football team played its final game to conclude an undefeated season. There were pictures and praises for everyone involved in the record of a team which sportswriters voted the Number One team in the state. The extravagant praise for Mark's leadership of Northside's offense led Dan to caution Mark repeatedly not to believe everything he read on the Sports pages. "Save that kind of belief for your reading of the Scriptures." Then too, Mark never hinted to his father how many times he had sauntered by "Freddy's" just to bait the regulars about the place to challenge him.

There *were* genuine problems in that Mark had agreed to go to Rockford to be with his mother and his sister . . . and to continue in school there. A sorrowful Mark spoke to his father, "Dad, *I don't want to go*. But I promised Mother."

"Mark, you know that I shall miss you more than I can say; however, the important thing is that you keep your word."

The telephone rang. Dan and Mark were at home following the Wednesday evening service. Tomorrow would be Thanksgiving Day. There had been some talk of going to Rockford, but nothing had come of it. Rev. Mr. Booker had welcomed the opportunity to preach for the service on Thanksgiving Day.

Mark answered. "Hello. Yes, sir. I'll call him . . . Dad, it's for you. I don't know who it is."

"This is Dan Clark. What can I do for you?"

"Dan, this is Sheriff James Dodd of Forest County . . . You remember? . . . Jim Dodd? We went to school together."

"Of course, I remember you, Jim . . ."

"Dan, I'd rather someone else had to call you, but it's my job . . . I have bad news for you."

The news was that there had been an automobile accident, and Dan's father had been killed and his mother was in Intensive Care and not expected to live . . . They were returning home when their car was struck by a semi-trailer which ran through a red light.

"Dan, I doubt that your father ever knew what hit him, or for that matter, what happened. I doubt your mother knew either. She is comatose. They are doing everything they can for her in the Emergency Room right now . . . Dan, I'm terribly sorry, and I feel awful having to call you with this news."

"Jim, let me make a couple of phone calls and I shall be on my way within the hour."

"I can't tell you what to do, but I hate to see you on the highway at night . . . tonight. There's nothing for you to do now. Try to get some sleep and come first thing in the morning."

"Thank you, Jim. I'll have to work some things out here before I can leave."

Dan called Larry; Dan forgot that Larry was already scheduled to preach in the Sunday morning services. He called Kuo, who was all Christian compassion; she said she would do *anything* to help. Dan said he would leave the office to her, and he would call her as soon as he knew anything definite. He called Mary to say that he and Mark would be leaving for Belvoir very early in the morning. He sent Mark to bed and went into the den and closed the door, to get down on his knees and seek for himself the consolation of his Lord and Saviour.

There was a memorial service in their home church to "celebrate the Resurrection in the name of Amos Clark." Mary and Debbie drove down for the service and left early the next morning to return to Rockford. Dan's mother had not regained consciousness; the physicians said that there was nothing more for them to do.

"You will understand, Dan, that we have had to place her in the hands of Almighty God."

Two days after his father's service, Dan's mother died. The head of the medical team that had worked on her said to Dan, "Her permanent injuries were such that you would not have wanted her to survive."

There was a memorial service "to celebrate the Resurrection" for Mrs. Amos Carter. At the last hour, Mary had called to say that she could not come because of another crisis with *her* mother in Rockford. Dan had to stay on for nearly a week to handle a myriad of details; he closed down the house and locked it until he could come back and deal with it in some way.

Mark Amos Clark had come to Belvoir as a high school boy; he left Belvoir greatly matured.

Dan returned to a Messiah Church which was the center of great activity in preparation for the celebration of Christmas. The church had been stirred to its reaches by the tragedy in its Pastor's personal life. Everyone tried to be helpful. More than anything else, there was great interest and concern about what this disastrous real life drama might have done to Dan and to his personal faith. People flocked to Messiah Church on Sunday morning till there was no standing room. Thousands turned to the television program "The Church Speaks" to find out what "the Church" might have to say in this situation.

Dan mounted the pulpit. He opened his Bible. He bowed his head.

"In the Name of the Father, and the Son, and the Holy Spirit. Amen.

"We are led of the Holy Spirit this day to turn to Philippians Chapter Four and Verse Thirteen. Hear now the Word of God: 'I can do all things through Christ who strengthens me.'" . . . .

"In conclusion, this is what we have and what we offer in and through our Lord Jesus Christ . . . the grace and strength to live joyously and triumphantly.

"It is no secret. None of us needs to be reminded that our human life can be, and too frequently is, a burden . . . a problem . . . a challenge . . . and all too often, a tragedy. We do not deny and would not diminish any of the experiences in life which reduce us to a feeling of helplessness and total defeat. It is the glorious good news from God that in Jesus Christ there is the grace, and peace, and power to meet the demands of such experiences. It is more than the ability simply to meet and to endure. It is a light and grace and power that enables us to come away victoriously with a song in our hearts . . . Hear the word again: 'I can do all things through Christ who strengthens me.' Amen."

Dan descended from the pulpit, and with the sudden inspiration of the moment, he strode to the center of the chancel.

"Please, my friends, I am led of God to do something different in *this* service . . . We shall not sing the final hymn. I am constrained of the Spirit to make an offer. Here it is. If you do not know the power and the joy of God which is in Jesus Christ, I invite you here and now to accept Him as your Saviour and the Lord of your life. Somehow, to make it definite in your own mind and spirit, I am asking that you put your acceptance into definitive action. Step out from the place where you are and come here to the chancel *right now* as your way of saying, 'I accept Jesus Christ as the Saviour and Lord of my life. I ask for his grace and power to live joyously and triumphantly.'"

"Mr. Hoffmeyer, may I ask (People were already rising and starting forward.) that the choir sing a couple of verses of the hymn 'Just As I Am.'"

It was a "different" kind of service; everyone lost all sense of time. Mr. Gossert, Mr. Booker, Official Board members came to speak personally with each one in the crowd that thronged the front of the sanctuary.

Many said: "It looked as though the whole congregation surged forward."

There was a word of promise to call upon and speak with each one personally. There was one common experience. Those in the sanctuary – as well as those watching on television – said that they were made much aware of a sense of "The Presence" in that hour on that day.

This was Dan's response in the 8:00 o'clock service to all questions concerning what this personal tragedy might have done to him. And this was the reaction to his word of personal testimony. His same words had grown in depth and power for the 9:30 service. Without any personal awareness of what was happening, for the 11:00 o'clock televised service, Dan now spoke with words weighted as though he were indeed a prophet of the Most High God. Responses to his word at each of the hours left Dan himself almost mystified at what was happening.

Monday morning, Dan was with Rev. Mr. Gossert and Rev. Mr. Booker in the Official Board room of the church. They were trying to go through the names and addresses of individuals who had come to the chancel in the service on Sunday. Mrs. Tsingh came into the room to ask Dan if he would see a couple who were in the Study.

Dan came into the room to find Fred and Marge Hudson. Fred spoke up as soon as they were seated.

"Dan, Marge and I were in the 11:00 o'clock service yesterday. I don't know whether you know it or not, but we have been coming to one of the services every Sunday for some time now. We found ourselves in the aisle walking to the chancel yesterday, and we have come today to say that we want to come back to Messiah Church – if *you* will have us. We should never have left; I know that, and I am ashamed of myself for doing so. Marge and I have been talking and praying about it, and here we are – *if* you will have us . . ."

Tears in the eyes of all three stated the request and shouted the answer. As they rose to leave, Marge impulsively threw her arms around Dan, and Fred stepped up to put his arms about the two of them.

Mrs. Tsingh said to Dan, "What happy people!"

The Bishop told his secretary that he personally wanted to see the statistical report of Messiah Church for the year. When it did come, he asked his secretary to call the church office to double check the figures. That many new members? At this rate, the church would soon be double the size it was when he had left it!

The Assistant to the Bishop spoke aloud to himself; " All that money, and they won't contribute a dollar to The Bishop's Fund."

The morning after Christmas, Dan and Mark left to drive to Rockford. Mark had selected the things he wanted to take with him. As they were ready to go, Mark paused to speak to his father. "Dad, I don't want to go. Please understand that. I *am* going for two reasons: One, to keep my word. Two, to bring Debbie and Mother back."

Debbie was ecstatic at seeing her brother and her father again, and she made no attempt to conceal her feelings. Blair and Estelle Carter appeared happy and vigorous. Dan thought they were effusive in talking with Mark and Debbie. He wanted to talk with Mary, but she bustled about doing things which Dan thought were pointless. No one seemed to think the situation was anomalous at best to have Dan's wife and children living in Rockford, with him living and working in Indianapolis.

At one point Dan followed Mary into the kitchen, and they were alone. "Mary, I miss you. I miss Debbie. I want to talk about getting all of us back together."

Mary would not look at him. "Oh, Dan, I don't want to talk about that *now*."

"Mary, if not now, when do you want to talk about it?"

"I don't want to talk about it now, because I don't want to talk about it at all . . . (She finally faced him.) . . . not at all."

"I'm sorry, Mary but we *are* going to talk about it. We are going to talk about it *now*. Do we do it here . . . or in the living room with your parents and the children as spectators?"

Mary said, "Come." She led the way upstairs to her room and closed the door.

"Well . . ."

"Mary, for many obvious reasons I think we cannot continue this way."

"What's wrong with it? You are where you want to be, and so am I."

"Mary. You are my wife. We should be living together."

"Dan, I have given you my judgment in simple language. I will not live in the city. I will *not* live where my daughter's person is violated. I will not live where my son is turned into a street brawler. If that is where you insist on working and living, then we shall *not* be there with you. It's that simple. Goodness knows I have stated my position dozens and dozens of times."

"Mary, you have known from the beginning that I believe I am called to serve the Lord Jesus Christ. For me that means that I serve where I believe He places me. And as of now, that is Messiah Church."

"Very well, if you think the Lord called you there, then that's where you should be. I don't have any sense that *I* am called *there*, and I must regard myself as free to choose my own living situation."

"No, Mary. There is more. We are supposed to be *one*, not two individuals. And yet that's what we are, two separate individuals.

We sleep in different bedrooms. We have not been together in love, sexually, for months and months, even years. This is not marriage; it is only a living and sleeping arrangement."

"I was frightened half out of my wits that I would have a baby there in the slums."

"Mary, you have gone away for weeks and months at a time, with no sense of absence from me . . . When you *are* there . . . I have worked long hours at difficult tasks only to come up with bitter disappointments, and I have come home wanting – needing to be cherished . . . loved . . . held in your arms for a little while. But I have felt increasingly alone in my own house . . . And now this sense of separation is very real with our living apart."

"I never wanted to go to Messiah Church and the city in the first place. I have tolerated being there for these years, but I have now come to the end. I will not take the children back there. *I will not go back there to live . . . ever!* And that is final."

"And Mary, I have every reason to stay and continue in the work which I believe God is doing there . . . As of now, I am *committed* to Messiah Church as never before."

Neither of them spoke for what seemed an age. Dan said, "So then, Mary, where does this leave us?"

Mary shrugged her shoulders.

"What do we do?" Where do we go from here?"

Mary shook her head.

"Very well, Mary. Then I shall say it out loud . . . I think we have come to a parting of the ways. I see no future for our marriage. I suppose that we may as well say it out loud and admit it to each other."

"I . . . will . . . *not* . . . go . . . nor . . . take . . . the . . . children . . . back . . . to . . . the . . . city. That is *final*."

"I think that our present situation is unacceptable . . . no, it is intolerable. We should do something about it, but I shall leave that with you. And I have no idea whatsoever what this will do to me as a minister in the Christian Church . . . I shall go now . . . Good-by."

Dan stood looking at Mary for a time, but she did not move nor raise her head. He walked from the room and down the stairs, going into the family room to speak a word to both Mr. and Mrs. Carter. He hugged and kissed Debbie. He spoke briefly to Mark who followed him to the car.

"I'm counting on you to look after your sister and your mother."

Mark stood up straight when he was released from a bear hug. "Has it happened, Dad?"

"Yes, Mark. It has happened."

Mary did not mention Dan when she came down the stairs.

Diane was no longer studying with Mr. Hoffmeyer; he said she was not practicing enough to make the lessons useful. On their way home from choir rehearsal, Tom made note of Diane's absence that evening. Rose pursued the subject.

"Tom, do you know something you aren't telling me?"

"Oh, there is some talk going around about Diane."

"What kind of talk?"

"There is talk that she is being seen here and there with a white man – a white man lots older than Diane . . . I checked on him. He's married and has three children."

The next day Rose came to the church office and asked Diane to have lunch with her. She opened the conversation as soon as they were seated.

"Diane, we haven't seen much of you lately."

"Yes, Rosie."

"We missed you at choir rehearsal last night."

"I'm pretty busy these days."

"I have tried several times to find you at home."

Glancing at the clock. "Pa told me."

"Honey, is something wrong?"

"Oh, no, Rosie. Everything's fine."

"Diane, Tom and I love you like our own. Tom says he has heard some talk about you."

"People talk too much."

"Diane." Rose tried to sound stern. "Tom says you're seeing a white man."

Diane flared. "What's wrong with a white man?"

Rose looked around to see if others could hear their voices. "Nothing . . . unless he already has a wife and three kids."

"I know what I'm doing."

Rose found the door shut. "Please, Diane. Won't you talk with Tom, or Mr. Booker, or Ellen?"

"I already know what they'll say."

"Then talk with Dr. Dan . . . please, honey."

"Rosie. I *know* what I'm doing."

A week later Diane was not in the choir on Sunday. Tom and Rose stopped at her house on the way home from the church service, but no one answered the door. Diane did not report for work on Monday.

Her father told Tom, "She's been gone before."

Tom put the word out that he wanted to see her, but Diane was gone. Dan told Tom that he would have to replace her, and Rose begged Dan to let her work until they could find Diane. A week later Rose spoke to Dan as he entered the office.

"Diane called us last night. She didn't say, but we assume she is back home."

"That's a great place for her! Her father and brother will be a big help!"

Again and again throughout the day, Dan thought about Diane. 'So much depends on someone getting to her now.'

As he was putting his car away that night, he had not yet heard from Diane herself. On an impulse, he walked some six to eight blocks to her house. He went up on the porch and pushed the bell. He pushed it again. 'Like everything else in this place, the bell probably doesn't work.' Dan knocked. He knocked again. The door opened slightly, and Dan spoke to an unidentifiable grunt that came from the unlighted interior.

"Is Diane here?"

"Why?"

"I heard she had come back home, and I want to see her." (Dan never knew why it did not occur to him that he should have identified himself.)

"Pa, it's that white man."

Dan was fuzzy about what happened after that. He didn't know how, with what, or by whom, but a blow on the side of the head sent him reeling. Before he could recover his balance, he was pushed and stumbled down the steps. He only remembered falling. His head struck the sidewalk.

The police received a call that someone was lying in the gutter – probably a drunk . . .

Dan regained consciousness in the Emergency Room. Dave and Nan were there and they had taken charge. When the physicians said that Dan should be kept for observation, Dave's instant reply was, "Absolutely!"

They were waiting for an orderly to take Dan up to a room. Nan was standing beside the cart holding Dan's hand. Dave was standing by as though to defend Dan from another attack.

Dan mustered up the resolution to say, "*Mary must not know.*"

"But Dan, she's your wife! And you're hurt!"

"It would only make things worse." Dave did not seem to be convinced.

"Now *listen to me*! I know what I am saying."

Early, very early the next morning, Tom was there.

"Revner Dan, who do this?"

Dan thought Tom's sheer bulk was ominous.

"Forget it, Tom."

Tom was not to be put off. Dan tried to explain. "Tom, they thought they were doing something *for* Diane. If I were in their place, I'd probably do a whole lot more."

"But Revner Dan, they shouldn't *touch you.*"

Dan was diagnosed as having a concussion. Dave called the physician, who then told Dan that he would have to remain in the hospital for a few days.

Everyone agreed with the decision to keep Dan in the hospital. "He has been looking terrible."

"Some rest right now is what he needs, and he won't get it any other way."

"He has lost weight recently."

"Yes, he probably isn't eating properly."

"Keep him there – by force if necessary."

Two figures appeared at the door of Dan's room.

"We come to say we sorry." Dan glimpsed a Tom-sized figure just outside the door – close enough to monitor a proper apology.

After more than a week in the hospital, Dan was sitting up in bed to look out the window. He spoke to the visitor in the room. "It is a beautiful day, and I haven't felt so good in a long while. I wish the course was open now . . ."

There had been no story in the newspaper, but the word went around. Larry stopped one evening to see his parents. He sat on the edge of a chair.

"Dad, have you heard about Dan?"

Larry's mother asked if he had had dinner. And could she fix something?

"Thank you, Mother, I have just come from dinner . . . Well, Dad, what are you and the rest going to do?"

His father did not miss the accusatory tone. "What do you expect me to do? Go and engage in a street brawl?"

"Oh, come off it, Dad. You know what I mean. For starters, did you or your Assistant or anyone in your name call on Dan in the hospital? He has been there for ten days now."

"No."

"Did you send him a card or a note?" His father did not speak and Larry rushed on.

"Dad . . . did you even *pray* for him?"

Bishop Gossert stirred. "Larry, that's below the belt."

Mrs. Gossert spoke up, "Now, now, Larry. Aren't you being hard on your father?"

He turned his head to speak. "Mother, the whole church is involved in Messiah . . . not just Dan. The program of the church literally wiped out several times over the leadership of Messiah Church in starting up new suburban churches, and nobody . . . (He stared at his father.) . . . *nobody* ever thought to put anything back into Messiah. Dan Clark was thrown into a meat grinder, but by he grace of God the church under his ministry has turned around to prosper gloriously. Dan Clark is a great one . . . And I know, and you know, that Dan is treated with suspicion, petty criticism, and mean badgering. And now he is denied the concern, and prayer, and care of those who are supposed to be his brothers in Christ."

Larry's father came to him and put his hands on Larry's shoulders to say, "It is very obvious, Larry, that you are very fond of

Dan."

His father's sudden tenderness softened Larry. "Why shouldn't I be? He brought me to Jesus Christ. He has helped me to stand on my own two feet before God. He has given me a chance at a ministry which is more than life for me. To forsake Dan is, in my judgment, a disservice to the Cause of Christ." He could speak no more.

Dropping his hands from his son's shoulders, "Maybe you ought to be the Bishop."

"I wish I were . . . . for just this one instance."

Larry excused himself. His parents waited for each other to say something. Finally, Ada spoke in a small voice.

"George. Larry is right."

"I know, Ada."

"What are you going to do about it?"

"I shall go tomorrow morning to see Dan and pray with him. Ada, it is a satisfying experience to discover that you have a son who is smarter than you are."

The Bishop was in his office by eleven o'clock. The Assistant to the Bishop was waiting to report on several items; included in his rundown was someone's observation on Sunday television from Messiah Church.

The Bishop stopped him in mid-sentence. "I just came from seeing Dan Clark who is hospitalized with injuries suffered in a physical assault on his person while he was engaged in his work as a pastor. Mr. Frenell, the Bishop is not and will not be pleased with any slighting references to the Rev. Dr. Daniel Clark. This is not an observation but a statement of policy."

Diane came to the open door of the Study. "When you have some time, I would like to talk with you."

Dan was reading, and he laid his book on his desk to make reply. "How about right now?"

"Just a minute. Let me ask Mrs. Tsingh to cover the phone for me."

Dan rose from his desk to go to a group of comfortable chairs in the office, as Diane returned and closed the door behind her. She started speaking before she had taken her seat.

"Dr. Dan, I want to apologize for all of the hurt and trouble you have suffered because of me . . ."

Dan waved his hand as though to dismiss the subject . . .

"No. You gave me a chance with this job. It is an important job and I appreciate that you trusted me. If you had known more about me, you probably wouldn't have let me inside the door. I have been happy here, and I have been proud of the place I have in Messiah Church."

"Diane, you have done a superb job. That's why you are still the Church Secretary. I may have had something to do with giving you a chance, but you have earned your right to stay in it . . . I'm sorry to interrupt. Please go on."

"Thank you. I don't know what got into me. Tom and Rose say it was the Devil. But I just took off. The thing that I couldn't get out of my mind was that 'Dr. Dan will be disappointed in me.' Then, when my father and brother assaulted you, I could have died. That's what I want to talk about . . ."

"Diane, that is all in the past now . . ."

"Dr. Dan, I couldn't forgive myself. Then, one day when you were still in the hospital, Mrs. Schuster came into the church. She does that quite often you know. She goes into the sanctuary; sometimes she is there for only a few minutes, and at other times she may be there for a couple of hours. Anyway, this one day when you were in the hospital, Mrs. Schuster came out of the sanctuary and was going out, but she stopped to speak to me. Well, one thing led to another. Then she asked me to go into the sanctuary with her, and I did. She was so easy to talk to that before I knew what I was doing I had told her the whole story of my life. I told her I felt responsible for you being hurt, and being in the hospital. Do you know what? She began to talk to me about Jesus, and how he died for us to be forgiven . . . And then she asked me if I would accept Jesus as *my* Saviour for all he has done for me . . . Dr. Dan . . . and *I did.* I want you to know that, and I want you to know that I feel so different somehow. I feel as though I have a new pair of glasses, and that I am seeing myself and my life . . . my work here . . . just everything, straightly and clearly. That's what I wanted to say to you and ask for *your* forgiveness."

"Diane, there is an old rule: Whom Christ forgives, we must forgive. The only thing I want to say is to thank God here and now . . . We thank Thee, Almighty God, for the forgiveness and new life that Diane has found in our Lord Jesus Christ. We ask that Thou wilt use her to Thy glory. Amen."

Diane wiped her eyes and rose to leave. She turned back to Dan.

"One other question . . . There is a fellow who sings bass in the choir; his name is Gunnar Kaseman. He has asked me over and over to go out with him. Would it be all right? . . . He's a white boy, you know."

"Certainly. I know Gunnar. Ask Mr. Hoffmeyer to arrange a duet for the two of you."

In the afternoon Dan walked over to The Schuster Center. He would find something to talk over with Dave, if he was there. The person Dan really wanted to see was Nan. And she was at home. So Dan told her of the conversation with Diane.

"I must have said it to you a dozen times, but Kurt and Peggy – especially Peggy – used to say that there was *something* about Dave. And she was right. It's true! There is an undefinable quality about Dave . . . I don't know what I wanted or what I expected when I came back here . . . There were times when I would think it would be easier if he would only threaten me, or beat me, or something! . . . but that doesn't make sense either . . ."

Nan stopped, hoping that Dan would pick up their conversation. Dan waited.

"We have never talked about this. At the beginning, Dave said said he was so thankful to have me back that he was satisfied. He said he wanted to respect how I felt . . . you know, about Lee. And he said that I should come to him – you know what I mean – only when I felt I was not betraying my own inner self . . . Dan, you know that Dave is so doggone lovable. When I thought I knew myself well enough to say to Dave, 'Now,' by then I knew him so much better that he seemed like a veritable saint. I felt like one of those people who were supposed to tempt a saint to make him sin . . . there was somebody like that, wasn't there?"

"Yes, Chrysostom."

"Who?"

"John the golden-mouthed."

"Anyway, best of all is the new level of existence which I have come to know and to enjoy. This garage apartment (She waved her hand to point about the room.) is a long way from corporation headquarters in New York. There is peace and joyous contentment here such as I never knew was possible. It's because of Jesus, and Dave and I are careful to give credit where credit is due . . . But Dave says we must pass it on . . ."

"And you have . . . to Diane . . . to all of the primary department children. And you should know that the Word is showing up in the homes of many of the children . . . and *now* particularly in Diane."

It was raining in Rockford. The downpour cut the afternoon schedule for Blair Carter. Mark and Debbie were not yet home from school. With his wife resting in the bedroom, he found Mary working in her room, and he entered to seat himself on the chaise.

"Mary, I have been wanting a word with you."

He paused to listen for movement in the house. "You don't know how good it is to have you here, but . . . you have a husband and your place is with him."

Mary dried her hands with a towel, poured out some lotion and rubbed it into her hands.

"We've gone over this before, Daddy. I have told you, as I have told Dan, that I will not take Mark and Debbie back into that jungle. And Daddy. *That's how it is.* If there is neither need nor place for us here, or if I am a source of embarrassment to you, then I shall take the children and move elsewhere . . . But I will *not* take them back to live on Church Street."

Her father studied her. "While I was bringing Mark home yesterday from track practice, he said he hadn't seen his Dad for a long time. That came out of nowhere."

"Oh, I'm sure that Dan is very busy."

"Mary, maybe I have missed something. Have you heard from

Dan, or talked with him, since Christmas?"

"He sends a check twice a month. As you know, I have opened an account at First National. Dan knows where we are."

Blair Carter shook his head. "Mary, I know your mother. Don't have an ache if you can make a pain out of it. If she could, she would keep you here indefinitely for all of the attention she gets from you – not to mention breakfast in bed. Why don't you go down and be with Dan for a couple of weeks over Easter? We'll manage. Your mother my even rediscover that she can boil an egg."

Mary's voice was unsteady. "There is so much to do. The children are involved in some Easter programs . . ."

"Ordinarily, I try not to stick my nose into your affairs, but I am going to do just that, because I am a concerned father who doesn't like the way things are drifting. When you came, I thought you might be here until Christmas . . . Mary, this could very easily stretch out into a broken home. I think you know that as well as I do, and it doesn't seem like you."

"Daddy, you might as well know how it is. I suppose I have been waiting for something to happen . . . When Dan brought Mark after Christmas, we had a talk. We had to admit the truth that we live in different worlds, that we see our children in different light . . . Daddy, we simply recognized that our marriage has been over since we moved to the city, and it was time to say as much."

"Oh, no, Mary."

"Dan left it with me, and I have delayed going to an attorney on the chance that something might change. I don't know why I think that anything is going to change, and I really should make an appointment with Mr. Jones and get it over."

Dan's Lenten schedule was too full, as usual. He had occasion to call at the office of the Bishop. The receptionist was unexpectedly gracious. As he walked past the door of Philip's office, Philip jumped to his feet to come to the door smiling to offer his hand in greeting.

And the Bishop. "Dan, how are you today? Have you fully regained your strength after that unfortunate experience? Sit down . . . sit down . . . Dan, you must be more careful. We just can't have anything like that happening to you again."

When Dan could get to the reason for coming, he told the Bishop, "We are talking of the need for adding another clergyman to the staff of Messiah Church. We would ask that you keep this in mind. Bishop Gossert, we require a man who loves the Lord Jesus, and who loves people. *And* he must be willing to *work* to bring them together. You may assume that we would insist that the individual have an evangelical personal faith."

That night the Bishop happily told his wife that "Dan Clark came in today, *asking us* to help find a minister to be added to the staff of Messiah Church"

Dan had another concern. He needed an old friend. He was in the private office of Fred Hudson. "Fred, this must be in absolute confidence. I need to talk with a friend in Christ that I can trust . . ."

Fred nodded and waited with no idea of what was to come.

"Fred, as you may or may not know, Mary packed up and left some five months ago. She has not called. She has not written. She is at her parents home in Rockford, and for now she uses the excuse of her mother's illness as her justification for being there. I drove over at Christmas, and we talked. She has absolutely refused to come back with the children to live here. I have not heard from her since. I send money to her, and also to each of the children. But that is how it is. That is how I live . . ."

"Now then, Fred, would you understand it if I said that I have had it with Mary? Every day I leave an empty house, and every night I return to an empty house. Maybe I am feeling sorry for myself. I hope not, because I don't play well the role of a martyr . . . But frankly, Fred, if I could I would get out of my marriage with Mary. Don't misunderstand. I am not messing around, and I have no other woman waiting in the wings. I firmly believe that only God could make Messiah Church move as it has, and as it is moving. The Official Board has voted to add yet another Minister to the staff, and we have the money for this position. For now, I am here for you to check my thinking. If I were to file for divorce on the grounds of desertion, I think that there are lots and lots of people who would understand. Or, to put it another way, if I filed for divorce, I think I might very well endanger the whole movement for Christ which is presently running in a full stream . . . . Am I correct in my thinking at this point? I know that I am throwing this at you from left field, but I have to talk with someone . . . My problem is twofold, as I see it. First of all, I think I know what the answer is, and must be. And secondly, I don't know how I can continue indefinitely with things as they are. I find my personal faith and strength so frequently drained to meet my own personal needs, that at times I feel I have nothing left over to offer to anyone . . ."

Fred was quiet with his head down.

Dan spoke again. "That's all right. Please think about it and maybe we can talk another time. I'm sorry to bother you with my problem. I am sure that I ought to be able to handle whatever comes to me, or there is a real question whether I deserve the role of a leader and teacher of Christian Faith."

Dan reached the place where he was mumbling to himself. "Me and my big ideas! When will I learn to keep my mouth shut? Holy Week and Easter are busy enough without this . . ."

"This" would be what was being called "The Easter Experiment." Instead of the multiple services in sanctuary and chapel, Messiah Church would offer one Easter service . . . outdoors . . . in the ball park . . . a spectacle of sorts! Dan had a checkoff list of things to get done, all quite apart from the preparation of his message which was presumably the most important contribution he would make to the celebration of the Resurrection of Jesus.

1. Ushers: Recruiting, Training.
2. Parking.
3. Design and build a worship center to be at home plate, or at pitcher's mound.
4. Preparation of the order of worship.
5. Text for service bulletins.
6. How best to get names and addresses of first-time visitors in a Messiah service.

7. Mr. Hoffmeyer and music.
   How to get the congregation to sing.
8. Tape recording to be edited and televised the following Sunday.

In the first few minutes of a conference with the television people, they had given up the possibility of a live television presentation of the service. But they still had the Sunday morning hour for which they had contracted and for which they would necessarily pay. They agreed to prerecord material for this hour; it would include:

1. Much music, choral and organ.
2. Spoken words by the three Ministers.
3. Some words of personal witness by church people of all ages. They would invite viewers to come and visit the services and activities of the church.

The taping would need to begin as soon as possible in order for professional editing to the time limits.

The Messiah Easter Service was big news, big religious news. The service itself and the attention given to it served to establish Messiah Church in the public mind as the preeminent Christian leader in the area. Dan remembered to invite the Bishop to have a part in the service. Dave and Tom assumed responsibility for inviting civic and political leaders to occupy reserved seats. Police estimated the attendance at 10,000 persons as a minimum, but more likely close to 12,000. A summary of the event was: "It was a great day for the Lord."

Dan struggled for words to describe the irony of his personal situation. The week following Easter he received a telephone call from Rockford, and a letter from Mary.

∝   ∝   ∝   ∝

Saturday Afternoon

Dear Dan –

It is now six months since the children and I came to Rock-

ford. I think I am being reasonable to expect that something would have happened to offer a solution to our situation. After three months we talked. And now after another three months we are exactly where we were — and where we have been for much too long now.

I cannot continue indefinitely the living arrangement with my parents. Mother and Daddy need more quietness in their home at this stage of their lives. Then, too, it is not good for the children. It is not that they are not welcome because Daddy spoils the children terribly.

After our talk at Christmas and our subsequent talk on the telephone, I decided that I should take some kind of action. So I went for an interview with the Superintendent of Schools, and with his encouragement I made application for a teaching post. I was called two weeks later about an opening for a high school Social Studies teacher; following an interview I was told that I might have this job if I wanted it. I have now signed a contract to start in the fall.

I am writing this letter to let you know personally that you will be receiving a communication from an Attorney here in Rockford. I have filed for divorce. The Attorney is Ralph Jones of Smith, Jones and Carson.

This course of action is not what I would choose. Never in my wildest imaginations did I think that my marriage would end in a divorce court. I feel you have left me no other choice. I think you have never appreciated my concern and my desires for Debbie and Mark. I reached the breaking point when my daughter was mis-used and my son became involved in a street brawl and was charged with assault. You do not seem to understand. If you did, you would have made some basic change in our living situation. So, if we have arrived at the place where our marriage must come to an end for the good of Mark and Debbie, then that is how it *will have to be.*

Daddy owns a house on Third Street which has just become vacant, and he has very reluctantly said that I may live there. He is much opposed to what I am doing, but I said I would rent another place if he chooses not to let me have that house. He has agreed to have the house painted inside and out and have all the appliances and utilities renewed, or replaced as necessary. He says that this property would have been mine in their will, and he will give it to me now if I want it.

Mr. Jones said I should not write nor talk with you. I felt that our marriage deserved this much at least. Mr. Jones said he will be in touch with you about the divorce.

I am sorry that our marriage has come to this. But as I have said repeatedly it is not of my choosing.

Mary

∝   ∝   ∝   ∝

Mary's letter did not come as a surprise, inasmuch as Dan had already received a telephone call from the attorney. When Dan said he thought he should talk with Mary, the attorney interrupted to say that "Mrs. Clark" had specifically commissioned him to sustain all discussions and negotiations. Having made that clear, he went on to say that "Mrs. Clark" would be asking for the following provisions in this action:

1. Sole custody of the children:
   Mark Amos Clark
   Deborah Estelle Clark

2. Provision for the college education of the two children:
   Mark Amos Clark
   Deborah Estelle Clark

3. Some of the household furnishings which she would select for her new home.

4. Clear title to the new Buick automobile.

5. Attorney's fees and all costs relating to this action.

He said that Dan would be receiving a letter with this information spelled out, but he thought he would call to see if there would be any problems to work out.

It was Wednesday before Larry and Mr. Booker and their secretary had finished sorting through the names of people who had registered their attendance as "Visitors."

They were working in the Official Board Room as Dan went to them.

"I want to help in the follow-up with these people. Please now, let me have some to visit today."

They had arranged the cards in a geographical order for convenience. Dan made two or three calls in the group given to him. The next card read as follows:

Mrs. Roger Wilkins
Riverton Arms, Apt. 907

Riverton Arms was a new apartment building, the first such structure in the redevelopment program of John Phillips & Associates. There had been many stories – with pictures – about the building, its singular exterior lines, the new technology involved in its construction and operation. John had showed Dan some initial sketches one time when he spoke with Dan about joining the firm as an engineer. As he approached Riverton Arms, there were landscaping crews at work, and Dan stopped to watch them for a few moments.

For some reason it occurred to him, 'I may yet have to renew my acquaintance with bulldozers.'

Dan entered the lobby – marble floors, high ceiling and large crystal chandeliers. There was a receptionist behind a desk. He gave her his card and asked for "Mrs. Roger Wilkins."

The young lady dialed a number, spoke briefly, and looked up to Dan. "You may go right up. The elevator is on the right."

Dan noted the decor of the lobby. John had said that they were going to do this place with "class."

The Mozart music in the elevator brought Dan to the ninth floor all too quickly. Dan walked down the corridor following the numbers. A door opened ahead, and a slim figure stepped out. Dan heard, "Hello, Dan."

He nearly stumbled in confusion and surprise.

"SALLY!"

Dan closed the door of 907 behind him and followed Sally Garner Wilkins into the living room where she motioned him to a seat and sat across from him.

There were questions and questions, and answers and answers. How long since they had been at the University? Only half an answer would prompt another question, which would elicit the remembrance of a name, a place, an occasion . . . Repeatedly they found themselves talking at the same time, and they would break off laughing.

"How are your parents? How are you and what are you doing in Indianapolis? How is Roger? Where did you meet him? Do I know him from somewhere?"

"My parents are well, and Dad is the perennial 'Old Grad' who continues to go back to football games and talk about the great teams in the old days . . . I am fine . . . After the University I went to New York and took a graduate degree in Interior Design." (Dan glanced about and readily identified the professional touch.) She had met Roger while in New York, and they had gone to live in Columbus, where his father owned a newspaper . . . She and Roger were divorced five years ago. "I was home with my parents for two or three years for some healing of my spirits and a recovery of my self-confidence. I have been moving from here to there, working and looking for a place to settle down and establish myself. Then I heard on the grapevine that John Phillips & Associates were looking for a designer, and I came here to see them and they hired me on the second day of our talks. I was really tired of wandering, and this seemed as good as, or better than, any other alternative – for now."

"But tell me. How did you get to Messiah Church? I mean, how on earth did you get out to the ball park?"

"I wanted to go to church on Easter Sunday, so I looked at the church pages in the Saturday paper, and all over the paper were the stories about the Easter Service at the ball park. It was certainly different, and I decided to go out of sheer curiosity . . . But Dan, I nearly fell out of my seat when I opened the bulletin and saw your name! . . ."

"We have been calling it our 'Easter Experiment.'"

"Oh my, Dan, it was a wonderful service. The music was magnificent. And if I may say so, I thought you were simply wonderful."

"I am probably more at home on an athletic field . . ."

The conversation rushed from question to question, and answer to answer.

"How are you? How is Mary? Do you have a family? And your parents? How long have you been here in Indianapolis? . . ."

"Mary is fine. We have two children: Mark, who is in Tenth Grade; and Debbie, who is in Eighth Grade. I have been here about eight years. And my parents . . . they were both killed in an automobile accident the day before last Thanksgiving."

Friends from days at the University . . . Stories . . . Remembrances . . . Individuals and events.

"Dan, have you seen any of these people lately?"

"No, I have lost touch, although I did see Al Parrish at Glen Rock a couple summers ago. Do you have contact with anyone that I might recall?"

"No, I have lost touch completely. It is strange that of all the friends I had and the people I knew at the University, you – Dan – should be the first one I should encounter in years."

Dan had forgotten the "Visitor" cards in his pocket – all of those calls he had planned to make that afternoon.

"Oh, Dan, I am a terrible hostess. Would you have a cup of coffee, or something cold to drink?"

"A cup of coffee would be good."

(He would drink the coffee to be courteous and then he would be on his way to make at least some of the calls which now burned a hole in his pocket.)

"Dan, if you are fending for yourself, I'd like to invite you for dinner some evening. Then I'll know that you have had at least one decent meal."

They agreed that Dan would come for dinner on Friday evening.

To see Sally again was cheering, but after her apartment which seemed to be waiting for a photographer, Dan was dismayed with the appearance of his home.

'Heavens! This place needs dusting, straightening out and the proper touch. I ought to do something. Maybe Kuo or Diane can help me get someone. But I doubt anyone would want to take this confusion in hand . . . For now, I'll go out to dinner and make a few calls.'

Seated in the restaurant, Dan took out the cards with the names of persons and families on whom he was to call. As he went through them, he came again to the one with Sally's handwriting.

'Goodness, I should have recognized that slanted script.'

The street and the house were dark when Dan returned home later that night. For no particular reason he walked from room to room, upstairs and downstairs. He stopped to look in a full-length mirror, only to confess to himself that he was hardly the epitome of the athlete.

'Well, we have come through a hard fight, a life-or-death struggle for Messiah Church and its witness in the city. By the grace of God, we are winning at the moment . . . How can it be thought? . . . Winning seems to be more demanding and strength-consuming than losing.'

Even so, it had been wonderful seeing Sally again. It was almost too much that after all of these years she had come to be on the staff of John Phillips & Associates . . . *across the street from Messiah Church*!!!

Dan arrived on Friday evening with a rose for his hostess, who said that dinner was ready. The dining area glistened with reflections of candlelight on the china, silver and linen. Out of the window they could see the night sky and some of the lights of the city. Sally asked Dan to pray. The dinner was simple: steak, salad, biscuits and coffee. When they had finished, Sally suggested that Dan go into the living room while she straightened up a bit and put things away.

"I'll bring the dessert and coffee to the living room."

Dan seated himself on the sofa and promptly fell asleep. He wakened to find himself propped up with pillows, and with Sally watching him from a chair which she had pulled up. Dan wakened with a start to look at his watch, not believing the time to be 1:30 a.m. He apologized over and over for being such a poor guest. To Sally's obvious amusement, he mumbled something about what people might think and left to drive home in a sleepy haze.

He telephoned Sally at her office the next morning to thank her for the dinner and to apologize again.

In the same mail, Dan received invitations to be a summer preacher from both Glen Rock and Park Shores. It seemed to be a reason for calling Mary that evening.

"Mary, I have received invitations from both Glen Rock and Park Shores. And, as you know, I have also received some communications from Ralph Jones . . . I am calling to ask whether you might be able to come down for a day or two for us to talk at length."

"Have you heard anything from the Bishop, or the Council about a new parish assignment?"

"Nothing, Mary. They have said that everything is going so well at Messiah Church that they don't want to make a change."

"Don't they have any consideration for family?"

"Mary, why don't you come for a few days so that we can talk with each other?"

"Dan, that isn't possible. Mother has been having more trouble. Mark is playing baseball, and Debbie is in a school operetta. Is there any possibility of a transfer for you?"

Dan's irritation showed in his voice. "Mary, I am doing all I can for the Cause of Christ where I was called and to which I am committed. What can I say? The Lord is blessing our word and work here in ways and to an extent that amazes all who come close. I cannot walk away from that without good reason . . ."

"Dan, there is good reason. You are not listening to me. Things here are very discouraging to me. To see Mother suffering . . . And Daddy spoils Debbie and Mark, so that I am having to speak to them more than ever."

"The Northside football coach called and said he hopes that Mark will be coming back . . ."

"Dan, I *will not* bring Debbie and Mark back to Church Street . . . or to any place in the city. I have taken them away from there for good. I never wanted to take them there in the first place. So far as I am concerned, any discussion about our future *must begin* with moving out of the city."

"Very well, Mary. We seem always to come back to the same point. I shall turn down both invitations for the summer."

"Since bringing the children to Rockford, I have had a chance to look over our life and marriage. That is how I see it, and for me that is how it *must be*."

"Mary, you are sounding hard and harsh . . ."

"*Someone* must face up to things. Apparently it is up to me to see that the children have a chance at decency . . . Until the Bishop offers another parish . . ."

"Mary, I now want you to listen well. Before we ever had a date, I had committed myself to serve the Lord Jesus Christ and His Kingdom. No one knows better than you that I have tried to do what I believe the Lord wanted me to do . . . Are you listening? . . . (No response.) . . . I was persuaded that it was God who called me to serve Messiah Church . . . In times of defeat and discouragement and despair, I have often been left with no reason to go on but that I believed God had a work for me to do here . . . By the grace of God, the situation in Messiah Church has been turned around one hundred and eighty degrees . . . We are now seeing the richness of the blessing of God in many ways . . . I cannot and will not leave my responsibility here until God gives me some clear sign that my work is done. God put me here. God is using me for His glory. I will move when God – not Bishop Gossert – tells me to do so. I will *not* move because I merely want to do something else, or because you think that I should. I will *not* move for Mark and Debbie. This is the Cause of Christ. Do I make myself clear?"

"Yes, Dan. What you say is not new. You can sacrifice yourself, if you will. *I will not* sacrifice my children . . . I think Ralph Jones should go ahead. I shall call him tomorrow and tell him to get on with it as soon as possible . . ."

A few days later, Ralph Jones called to say that Mary's petition for divorce was scheduled in two days. Did Dan want to have legal representation in court? And Dan said he wouldn't bother. Mr. Jones asked when Mary could secure the household items she would be awarded in the settlement. Dan wanted him off the phone.

"Whatever Mary wants, and whenever Mary decides."

It was time to face up to the profound change in his life. Without telling Mrs. Tsingh where he was going, he went to look for Fred Hudson.

Fortunately Fred was free, and Dan launched into his story.

"Fred, I want to tell you that I don't have the option of trying to decide about the effects of a divorce before the fact. I have come from a telephone call with Mary's attorney, who said that her petition will come up in two or three days. As of now, it is all over with my marriage."

"I am truly sorry, Dan. I can appreciate that this cannot be easily handled in your case. However, this may be the best way out. But I do want to make one point . . . Don't you do anything foolish yourself. I say that because I know you, and it is just like you to say that this has compromised your ministry to such an extent that you must simply resign for the good of the Church."

Dan offered no reply.

"I repeat. This may be the best thing. Let me suggest two things. First, go and lay it out before George. And second, take the Board into your confidence and get their counsel – at least before you resign and go riding off into the sunset on us."

The Bishop was in his office and Dan went in to tell the Bishop of his marital situation.

"Oh, Dan, I am so sorry. I had no idea . . ."

"Bishop Gossert, I have apprised you of my family situation repeatedly. I know I have told you that my marriage is in tatters by reason of Mary's opposition to our living in the city. But that is past history. Where am I now? Does the Church expect me to resign and give up my ordained status? If so, I shall address such a communication to you."

"Now, now, Dan. There was a time when divorce was fatal to a clergyman's status in the church, but times have changed . . . Let me think . . . Here is what I suggest you do. Call a special meeting of the Official Board of Messiah Church. Tell them what has happened and is happening, and see what they say. If the Board feels that your ministry is destroyed with this, then they should say so. And if the answer is for you to continue . . . Well, we shall be guided by the judgment of the Official Board."

Dan called a special meeting – another one! – of the Official Board of Messiah Church. "Ladies and gentlemen. We have a crisis to confront. Mary, my wife, took our children and went to live in Rockford the day after the melee at Northside. As you may or may not know, she did not want me to accept the pastorate of Messiah Church, and she has never been happy here in the city. Six months after leaving here on October 1, she filed for divorce. In my most recent conversation with her, she stated that her one absolute demand for the continuation of our marriage was that I leave the pastorate of Messiah Church and assume a pastorate or some other kind of employment outside the metropolitan area. When I refused, she ordered her attorney to proceed. As of two days ago, I am a divorced man."

"I have talked with the Bishop who asked that I seek your counsel on what to do. He will be influenced by your decision tonight. The question stated too simply, would be this: Does my divorce destroy my usefulness as a Christian minister, and more particularly, destroy my usefulness as the Pastor of Messiah Church? To bring the whole matter to point, I am submitting my resignation as Pastor of Messiah Church, effective as of this date. I ask the President of the congregation to moderate the meeting at this juncture. I shall leave the room. Please give this your best Christian judgment. I only remind you that the issue here is not 'Dan Clark,' but 'Messiah Church' and its usefulness for Christ. Please be good to one another, and let the meeting from this point on be conducted in strictest confidence."

Two and one-half hours later, Dan was called back into the room to hear the President say, "Everyone has been given opportunity to express his or her opinion. There has been no effort to persuade. We have voted by secret ballot on the proposal to accept your resignation. The Secretary will give you the result."

The secretary said, "Thirty-three voted 'Nay.' There were two abstentions."

A moving van was parked on Church Street at 8:00 a.m. Mary arrived a short time later, with both Mark and Debbie in the car. It would not be easy at best, but when Mary started to walk away with the driver, Dan stopped her with the request that he speak with Mark and Debbie.

"Don't keep them too long. I want to be sure that the things they want are loaded."

Dan took Mark and Debbie into the den and closed the door. They sat together on the sofa and were painfully ill at ease. In such a short time they seemed to have changed so much. Obviously, 'the sooner we end this, the better,' was the key.

"Mark . . . and Debbie. I am very, very sorry that we have come to where we are today. If there is ever *anything* that I can do for you, you need only to call . . . And you always must know that I love you with all my heart. Now I think you had better go and see what you can do to help your mother."

They rose and started for the door, when Debbie broke and rushed to throw her arms about he father's neck. She sobbed broken-heartedly.

"Oh, Daddy! I miss you just awfully!"

Dan kissed her and hugged her and tried to keep himself under control. "Then you know how I miss you, Debbie my dear."

Debbie wiped her eyes. Now they would go. But Mark reached out to throw his arms around his father, crying unashamedly. "Dad,

I don't think I can make it without you!"

Dan held him tightly and then let go suddenly. "Go help your mother for now. We'll work something out."

Dan went immediately to the church, leaving the house to Mary and the movers. He worked in the Study until it was time to go for a luncheon appointment. The van was still there. He made some calls after lunch and thought he would go by the church. The van was gone. Dan put his car in the garage to enter the house.

The kitchen was empty with cupboard doors standing open. The dining room was empty; Dan thought, 'The *memorial* furniture is gone!' The living room was bare. He went upstairs. The door to the linen closet was standing open. Debbie's room and Mark's room looked as though they had never been inhabited. There was nothing in the master bedroom, with closet doors standing open to emphasize the point. The guest bedroom was still furnished, although the lamps from the bedside tables were gone and there was no rug on the floor. With some hesitation Dan went downstairs to open the closed door leading to the den; everything seemed to be there . . . Then he noticed that his typewriter was gone.

Dan spoke aloud to the empty house. "Well, I said Mary could take anything and everything she wanted."

There was no note. They were gone. The house rattled with emptiness . . . He would go out for dinner, and maybe he could stop somewhere and get some paper plates, a pan, and a coffeemaker of some kind. He would get a folding table and chair from the church for the time being. It occurred to him that he would be spending August in Belvoir, in his parent's home, and perhaps he could bring back a few things that he needed.

Dan had been particularly anxious, but so far as he could determine, the church was going along without missing a step. He checked with Fred, who said he had taken care to see what effect the knowledge of Dan's divorce might have had on anything and everything in the church.

"The congregations continue to grow. No one has left the

church. More and more people keep uniting with the church. The offerings increase from week to week. The television ratings are better than ever. There has not been a ripple to the best of my knowledge. Of course, Dan, let's face it, and I don't mean to be unkind. Mary did not carry much, if any, responsibility in the work and life of the church."

Dan met with the Bishop to tell him of the Board meeting and he suggested that the Bishop invite some of the lay leaders of the church to come and give him their evaluation of the situation in the church. The Bishop suggested that Dan "go back to work with our blessing and prayers." He did not say that he had already spoken privately with several persons whose knowledge and judgment he trusted.

Sally continued to attend the services of Messiah Church. Some Sundays Dan saw her to speak with her after the service, and there were other times when there would have been a crowd in the narthex or when she left by another door. Several times when he had missed speaking with her, he had telephoned her to say that he appreciated that she had been in a service. John Phillips was talking with Dan about a committee role in the church which he sustained; when they had finished their business, they talked briefly in the friendship which they shared. Before he left, John said, "By the way, Dan, we have a very capable lady on our staff who says she knew you in college days. Her name is Sally Wilkins."

"Yes, we were good friends."

"She is making a fine contribution to our program. But more than that. Two or three times when she and I have finished the business at hand, we have taken the opportunity to talk about the Lord."

Dan telephoned Sally that evening to say that John had spoken of how pleased they were with her part in their projects. Sally mentioned that her parents had recently been with her for ten days or so. She said that she had brought them to church for two Sundays, and they had been overwhelmed in being there. Her father had said before they left, "Your mother and I are going to consider selling our house and moving here. There are three reasons: your mother wants an apartment like yours, and I can do without mowing the yard; two, we would be near you; and three, it would be a privilege to go to Dan's church every week."

"They are much too generous. It was good seeing them again. And please remember me to them when you write or speak with them."

"They are wondering happily what is happening to me, especially when I told them that I go every week to the Bible class which John Phillips teaches."

It was raining. Dan – together with Mr. Booker and Larry and everyone else they could command or enlist – was trying to keep up the personal visitation on everyone who signed a visitor card in the services. Even though he was told not to let himself be involved, Dan was continually being asked for his suggestions on the current building program: Messiah Church had been buying properties about the church site as they had gone on the market. They were now buying such additional land as was needed for the construction – which had already begun – on the first unit of the Messiah Christian School building. Classes were to begin for Four-year-olds and Five-year-olds in September. Classes were to be limited to forty students each, and Ellen Gregory had said in a Staff meeting weeks before that their rolls were filled almost immediately.

Dan stopped to telephone the church, and Mrs. Tsingh told him that a committee meeting scheduled for that night had been canceled. Dan replaced the phone with a sudden awareness that he was weary. He started home, but the dreary prospect of fixing something to eat prompted him to stop at the first fast food place he saw to get a hamburger and a cup of coffee. Then he drove home.

A rainy night seemed to be a good time to catch up on his reading. There was a pile of journals he had been saving. Before too long, Dan realized he was only turning pages; he couldn't remember a single thing he had read, and he had to look at the cover again and again to remind himself what magazine he was reading.

With a sudden unthought decision he picked up the telephone to dial. He recognized the voice that answered. After some formalities he said, "Are you busy this evening? . . . Would it be all right if I stopped by later?"

The cheery response was an invitation.

Apparently the young man at the receptionist's desk was expecting him, for he merely nodded as Dan walked by him to the elevators. The door to 907 swung open to his knock for Sally's greeting. Dan noticed that her dress was plain but cut to her figure; her only jewelry was a string of pearls. Dan closed the door to follow her into the living room where they seated themselves as they had on Dan's first visit.

Dan asked about her parents. The discussion turned to Messiah Church, and Dan told her of what the church had been, of the changing city and their almost hopeless struggle to survive, and their desperate search for answers. He described The Schuster Center and said he wanted her to meet Nan and Dave.

On her part, Sally said she had been driven through this section of the city, and then briefed on the plans and hopes of John Phillips and his people. As a first duty when she was hired, she had taken it upon herself to go up one street and down another. She had obviously seen Messiah Church, but for some reason she had not noticed Dan's name on the bulletin boards in front.

"I'm not surprised. That's the kind of impression I make on people."

The conversation led to other topics, and Dan heard himself say even though he had not intended to speak of it, "Mary left me several months ago and she has taken the children, because she refuses to live in the city."

He told her of the "incident" – the melee or brawl, whatever term one might want to use. Dan said that after six months away, Mary had filed for divorce, which now had been granted, and Mary and the children were living in Rockford. He couldn't remember that he had ever spoken so freely about his personal situation.

Sally was attentive. "Dan, I can understand that it would be very difficult to raise children properly in this urban atmosphere. Let's talk some more about it, but for now let's have a cup of coffee."

Sally called Dan to the table with apologies. "These 'store-bought' cookies are the best I can manage on short notice."

After more talk at the table, Dan looked at his watch and said he must be going. Leaving the dining area, Dan was much aware of her being close. "Sally, it has been a wonderful evening. Thanks for listening to me ramble on and on . . . And please remember me to your parents."

"Do you have to go? It's not so late."

They were at the door and Dan reached out to put his arm about Sally. As though waiting for the signal, Sally reached up to put her arms about his neck and pull herself close against him. Dan kissed her . . . and he kissed her again, longingly and lovingly. Dan held her tightly. He said nothing because he knew what he wanted to say . . . and *he didn't dare*! Still holding her closely, he kissed her again. With obvious great reluctance, he released her and stepped back. And when he found his voice he muttered, "Sally, I *really* must go . . . I must go before I say what a gentleman shouldn't say to a lady."

"Go ahead and say it. Maybe I'm not a lady tonight."

Dan struggled with himself. "No. No, Sally."

He put his hand on the doorknob. "I must go, but before I leave, may I say, Sally, that I love you."

Somehow – Dan never did know how – he got out of the door to walk to the elevator. In the elevator, he took a handkerchief from his pocket to wipe his lips, and was almost destroyed seeing the handkerchief smeared with lipstick. He found a clean place on the handkerchief to rub his lips again. Passing the young man at the receptionist desk he said, "Good night" looking away lest there still be some red on his lips or face or shirt.

Dan unlocked his car and got into the driver's seat. He put the key in the ignition but was stopped by the thought, 'Sally wanted me! Oh, my Lord! Forgive me, but I wanted her desperately. Help me, my Lord! I have not been wanted in love for months and years!'

Dan forced himself to start the car and drive homeward. he confessed to himself later that it was a miracle that he did not have an accident while driving with little or no attention to traffic, lights or signs. Arriving at the alley on Church Street where he would turn in for his garage, he took control of the car with firm purpose and drove back as fast as he could manage to the parking lot of Riverton Arms. But he could not get out of the car. After too long a time, Dan felt that he had managed to regain his common sense, and he drove home to put the car in the garage.

Before Dan went into the house, he remembered his handkerchief. He looked about to find a metal bowl on the work bench; he dumped out some screws to put the handkerchief in the bowl, set the bowl on the cement floor and poured charcoal lighter fluid on the handkerchief. It was only when he had touched the handkerchief with a lighted match to see the flame that he came to himself and said aloud, "You idiot! You could set the whole place on fire!"

The next evening he dialed Sally's number. He spoke very somberly to apologize for his behavior. He thanked her for being a good listener, but insisted that that was no way for him to express his gratitude. His solemn, penitential mood was unprepared for her cheery response, "Why are you apologizing? I thought it was wonderful. And so long as I have you on the phone, let me say that I love you . . . And last night. I knew that you were telling me that you really do love me . . . I confess that I don't know where I go, or we go, from here, but I find myself so happy in being able to say to you plainly and with all my heart that I love you."

They agreed on Dan's insistence that for now they would talk with one another only over the phone.

The telephone was ringing as Dan came into the house one evening. It was nearly 11:00 o'clock as Dan picked up the receiver to hear Mary's voice.

"Dan, I have been calling for two or three hours. And I have kept Mark up because I want you to talk with him. The Bradbury boy has a car, and I have told Mark again and again that he is not to ride with that boy, because I have seen some of that boy's driving . . . Today . . . Mark didn't come home from work at the usual time. Debbie said she hadn't seen him. He didn't come and didn't come . . . Well, it seems some of the boys were standing around, and this Bradbury boy offered to bring Mark home. I have told Mark repeatedly that he is not to get in that Bradbury boy's car. But today he did, and they started out for some place or another . . . some place other than home. I don't know and I don't care. And the car broke down. They couldn't fix it themselves, and they had no money for repairs."

She paused for breath and Dan waited without saying a word. "*Finally,* they called Mr. Bradbury and he told some man at a nearby service station to get the car running and he would stop by tomorrow and pay the bill . . . So then, about *eight* o'clock Mr. Mark *finally* arrived home. I was nearly out of my mind. I asked him why he got into the car in the first place and why he did not call to let me know where he was – I would have gone to get him. But I'm not getting any straight answers, and I said that he would have to talk with his father *tonight.* I am going to put him on . . . *Here, Mark.* It's your father. Take the phone . . ."

"Hello, Mark. What's this all about?"

"Hello, Dad. I'm sorry. I *am* sorry to bother you with this, because it's not all that much. Something happened to the distributor and we couldn't fix it. The man at the service station wanted his money up front, and we didn't have enough. I'm sorry, but I didn't think it was all that much. I'm especially sorry that Mother has called you about this."

"O.K., Mark. If your mother doesn't want you in the Bradbury boy's car, then it would be better if you stayed away from it. There is nothing to be gained by creating problems. Now let me have your mother back on the line."

Following a time when Dan could hear talking in the background, Mary said, "Mark said you wanted to speak with me."

"Yes, Mary. I shall be brief. You must realize, Mary, that you have taken the children away from me. I can only assume that you have taken charge over them. Now I want *you* to understand that they are *your* responsibility so far as I am concerned. For the sake of everyone involved, I hope that everything works out well for each of the children and you; however, Mary, I will not be dragged in as the 'heavy' to administer scolding language and punishment from long range."

"Well! I certainly thought you would be interested in your own children!"

"Mary, I am so interested in my own children that I want them to be living *with me* during these years of their lives . . . But don't expect me to enter significantly into their lives as a voice over the telephone long distance. And if *you* can't handle them, then send them back to me and I shall be ready and happy to assume responsibility for them. Just tell me when they are coming. And I might as well take this time to remind you that they are to be with me for two weeks at least in August in Belvoir. Now, if you will excuse me, I have had a long day, and I am very tired. Good night."

The next morning Dan called Mary's residence in Rockford. Mary answered the telephone.

"Mary, I am afraid I was not understanding nor helpful last night. I'm sorry. I do care. I care tremendously. Please have Mark call me tonight after ten o'clock. I hope you have a better day today. Remember me to your parents."

Dan decided to spend his vacation in Belvoir. He would stay in his parents' home as he prepared to dispose of furnishings and to place the house on the market. Mark and Debbie would be with him the first part of the month "to help." Larry would be the preacher for the Sundays of August and the first Sunday of September in Messiah Church.

Several of the churches in Belvoir wanted Dan to preach, but he declined all of the invitations for one simple reason which he was almost ashamed to admit: he was tired. He would also have admitted that he had taken a psychological bashing in the breakdown of his marriage and subsequent divorce. The continuing growth of Messiah Church on all fronts could not remove his sense of the loss of Mark and Debbie.

And so, the first two weeks at Belvoir were of crucial importance. A high school friend of Dan's now owned and lived on a large farm where he raised and trained quarter horses. They would accept his invitation to go riding. They would swim and sail at some nearby lakes. Debbie had taken golf lessons in physical education and now she would test her skills with her father and brother. Since Dan was breaking up his parental home, each of the grandchildren was to select what he or she might want as keepsakes from their grandparents' home. Debbie wanted the sterling silver coffee and tea service, sterling bowls and flatware. Mark was very positive; he would like to have his grandfather's antique oak roll-top desk with a matching high-backed oak swivel chair. Dan rented a truck to take them and their treasures back to Rockford. Dan had thought to select some items to furnish his house more adequately, but the work involved negated this idea. Dan gathered up jewelry and personal items – one old-fashioned suitcase contained the lot. Everything else was sold at public auction, and Dan listed the house for sale with a realtor whom he had known as the center on the high school football team. Dan now took up residence in a local hotel for the balance of the vacation time. He slept, he read, he prayed, he played some golf. He was beginning to feel as though he was indeed alive and ready to work again.

After Debbie and Mark had returned to Rockford, Dan and Sally talked almost nightly on the telephone. Sally delighted in any opportunity to tell Dan that she had always loved him. Dan found a personal warmth in speaking to Sally of his love. There was, however, a problem in their conversations because Sally would always quickly change the subject or the drift of their conversation if they seemed to be approaching the possibility of their marriage. It was obvious and Dan was disturbed by this, but this was not something that was to be resolved over long distance lines.

YEAR NINE
AT
MESSIAH CHURCH

Dan returned to a full schedule of activities, problems, and opportunities.

The MESSIAH CHRISTIAN SCHOOL was opening with publicity and a round of ceremonies. Ellen Gregory came into a staff meeting with a handful of letters and some pages of statistics – all of them asking for the school to be expanded *IMMEDIATELY* to include all grades through high school. They had planned to add one year to the school in each year of its existence, and they had agonized over the completion of the building to house the initial effort. Before committing themselves further, Dan thought they should try to learn from the Roman Catholic experience with the parochial school; they would schedule appointments with Roman Catholic officials.

The Bishop had really come through with a winner. Beginning the first Sunday of September, a fourth Minister had come on the staff of Messiah Church. Dan told the Bishop, "We need another Willard Benson or Charles Padgett."

The Rev. Karl Meyer was a sixty-year-old reincarnation of the men Dan had set up as the model. He exuded the love of God for individual human beings; like the Apostle Paul, his first sentence in a conversation would find him identifying himself with his Lord, Jesus Christ. But if one really wanted to know the man – or his wife – the secret was to ask him to pray. Dan found himself humbled by Rev. Mr. Meyer. The word quickly was abroad that here was a man who "knew the Lord first hand."

The Easter television program which they had prepared brought a host of requests for copies. Rev. Mr. Hartwell wanted to put edited copies of this service on a cassette and offer them as an additional means of ministry. There were many complications, but eventually they had been made available. They had underestimated the demand and were now awaiting a second lot to fill the requests.

Mr. Hartwell was asking if this suggested an additional means of ministry which they should explore and exploit for the Lord if it had possibilities. Enlarging the television ministry brought again the question about adding several new stations to widen the scope of the ministry of Messiah Church. He and his committee were compiling data on stations, coverages and costs. Mr. Hartwell was ready to talk of a nation-wide telecast to any and all who would listen.

Dan had been back on the job three weeks. He counted the weeks by the newspaper accounts of Rockford High School football games. He also read stories of the Northside Coach experimenting with different quarterbacks in an effort to put together a winning combination. He called Mrs. Tsingh from the hospital to give her a message. She responded, "Mrs. Sally Wilkins has come to see you. Will you be returning to the church this afternoon, or do you want me to make an appointment?"

Dan asked Mrs. Tsingh to have Mrs. Wilkins wait in the Study.

Dan closed the door. He would have gone to her to kiss her, but when he turned about she was already in a chair, sitting straight and prim. Dan took the cue and seated himself.

"Doggone! It's good to *see* you, Sally. I was trying last night to reach you."

Sally was the business professional. "Please, Dan. Let me say what I have come to say . . . (Dan nodded and settled back. 'Golly she is beautiful.') . . . One time some years ago, I made a big mistake when I wrote you a letter in haste and misunderstanding. Over the years, I have lost count of the times I have regretted writing that letter to you."

She thought she should make another start.

"You never knew Roger. He was good fun, and in his way a good man . . . We tried. I honestly think we tried to have a good marriage . . . But we were never able to find what was lacking, but both of us knew almost from the start that our marriage was not right. That is why we never had children . . . It was not easy, but we finally came to admit the obvious and inevitable . . . So the years have passed and all I have to show for them is a bit of money . . . and loneliness . . . a loneliness that eats away inside . . ."

She stopped to look in her purse for a handkerchief.

"Seeing you again, I realized at once what had been wrong." . . . (She looked at Dan as if to ask if he wanted to know what had been wrong.) . . . "Seeing you again has made me realize that I have always loved you, Dan. And that's what I think was wrong with my marriage. I really loved you and Roger was not you . . . And when you said that Mary had left, I found myself asking what might have been, or . . . Dan . . . what could be."

She paused to collect her thoughts. Dan had learned long since *to listen* and *to be patient*.

"And then, Dan, I almost made an even greater mistake. I am afraid that it was pretty obvious on one rainy night that I wanted you to make love to me. I gave no thought to where it might lead. *I wanted you.* Thank God, you were the good and strong person that you are . . . You see, Dan, I have been coming to the services, and I have learned very quickly that you are someone *very special* for God. John Phillips has helped me. Your name came up in a conversation, and he lost all sense of time to tell me about the new life he found in Jesus Christ, and he says that God used *you* to show him the way . . . John is truly a great person, and he takes every opportunity to give Jesus Christ the credit for what he is and what he has been able to do . . . . I have attended the services and listened most carefully, because I wanted to find for myself what John has. I have come today to tell you that last Sunday the way opened for me, and I gave myself to Christ. Dan, I simply had to come and tell you that I have found something of what John has, and what you have and offer so wonderfully and well."

"Sally . . ."

"Please, let me finish. I have come particularly because I almost made an even greater life mistake. I feel as though in my thoughtless desire for you, that I would have done you irreparable harm. As I see it, I would have broken something very precious to God and to all of the people for whom you are a channel of the grace of God. I ask your forgiveness."

"Please, Sally, don't ask such a question. I am sorry for anything I might have done which was in any way less than what the Lord would approve."

Sally closed her purse. "If you ever can . . . and want to come again, Dan, there will be nothing to embarrass. Nothing that your Lord *and mine* would not approve."

"Good. I happen to be free tonight . . ."

"Dan, I love you. And I have been thrilled to hear you say that you love me. In several telephone conversations, you know that we have approached the subject of marriage . . . but I have backed away."

"Yes, I was much aware of that."

"Oh dear. Was it so evident? You see, Dan, I knew that I had to share in the same spiritual world that you and John live in. That is what I found and where I am . . . after last Sunday. I pray I won't drive you away now, but Dan . . . if you ever again ask me to marry you, I won't say 'Yes.' I'll say, 'How soon?'"

"If you will be home this evening about eight o'clock, supposing we put your resolve to the test."

Mrs. Tsingh and Diane might not have picked up the spring in Sally's walk. But they did see the clothes, the figure, the hair, and shook their heads to think but not to say: 'Some women have everything!'

The first Sunday of October would be the celebration of World-Wide Communion. Among the names of the persons who were received into the membership of Messiah Church was:

Wilkins, Sally G.   Riverton Arms, # 907

The National Assembly of the church in this current year would be held in Seattle. Bishop Gossert had been pleased to suggest to the inner councils of the church who planned the events of the annual meeting, that there might be lessons for the whole church from the persons involved with one of the fastest growing parishes in the church. With the denomination as a whole declining in membership, Bishop Gossert was commissioned to arrange the program in an effort to confront this most critical situation in the church. Dr. Daniel Witt Clark would address the total assembly. Workshops were set up in various aspects of parish life, to be led almost entirely by staff members of Messiah Church. One of the much-publicized working seminars would deal with "Parish Visitation." The two persons invited to lead this group were Rev. Willard Benson and Rev. Charles Padgett. For about a week, Messiah Church was served by volunteers. For example, Mrs. Tsingh and Diane were to lead a working session on "The Church Secretary."

The Advent season was at hand. This seemed especially a time for Dan to speak the word of the Lord to the needs of individuals. The people whom he had been seeing lately were so burdened in one way or another by events, illness, and fateful circumstances that would not go away. The problems of many individuals and families in the city were staggering. Dan's own family difficulty had served only to make him more sensitive to family stresses. He had been shaken badly with the realization that he could be such a problem to himself. The expanding outreach of the ministry of Messiah Church demanded the addition of some new program experiments to meet human need . . . So . . . What to say on the first Sunday of Advent? What would be the word of the Lord for the people of Messiah Church on this Sunday?

The human situation is complicated because man himself is complicated. There is not an easy answer. There cannot be *one* grand solution. 'One thing is for sure,' Dan said to himself in reading and reflection. 'It is only in the spirit and within an atmosphere of love – the divine love in Jesus Christ – that there is any hope of an answer for the tragic dilemma that is man.'

This, or something very like it, would be the message for the first Sunday of Advent.

The experiences of the previous Sunday brought crowds back to the sanctuary and before their television sets on the first Sunday of Advent. It was the 11:00 o'clock service, the third service of the morning in the sanctuary. Mr. Hoffmeyer would have only the Sundays through Christmas at the console of his beloved organ. His inspired accompaniment led the congregation to sing with glorious enthusiasm.

Dan moved to the Lectern.

"The New Testament lesson today is to be found in the Fourth Chapter of the Epistle of First John, verses seven through twenty-one. Now hear the word of the Lord."

"Beloved, let us love one another, for love is of God; and every one that loveth is born of God, and knoweth God.

He that loveth not knoweth not God; for God is love.

In this was manifested the love of God toward us, because that God sent His only begotten Son into the world, that we might live through Him.

Herein is love, not that we loved God, but that He loved us, and sent His Son to be the propitiation for our sins.

Beloved, if God so loved us, we ought also to love one another.

No man hath seen God at any time. If we love one another, God dwelleth in us, and his love is perfected in us.

Hereby, know we that we dwell in him, and he in us, because he hath given us of his Spirit.

And we have seen and do testify that the Father sent the Son to be Saviour of the world.

Whosoever shall confess that Jesus is the Son of God, God dwelleth in him, and he in God.

And we have known and believe the love that God hath to us. God is love; and he that dwelleth in love dwelleth in God, and God in him.

Herein is our love made perfect, that we may have boldness in the day of judgment; because as He is, so are we in this world.

There is no fear in love; but perfect love casteth out fear: because fear hath torment. He that feareth is not made perfect in love.

We love Him, because He first loved us.

If a man say, 'I love God,' and hateth his brother, he is a liar: for he that loveth not his brother whom he hath seen, how can he love God whom he hath not seen?

And this commandment have we from him, That he who loveth God love his brother also."

There was only a whisper of sound as Dan slumped to the floor. No one grasped immediately what had happened until the sanctuary was rent by an anguished cry: "REVNER DAN!!!"

Tom Davis charged from the choir loft to the crumpled figure behind the Lectern.

The congregation sat unmoving in stunned silence. In the appalling stillness, two or three individuals broke for the doors leading to the office – and its telephones. Two of the ushers at the main entrance burst through the front doors to wave down an ambulance that "just happened" to be passing by on Columbia Avenue. No one else had moved, and the congregation – and the television camera – stared fixedly at the scene of the paramedics rushing in and up the chancel steps, lifting Dan up onto their stretcher and placing an oxygen mask over his face, to cover him – pulpit robe and all – with a blanket, fasten the straps, and rush him out of the Church Street entrance – with Tom Davis accompanying them.

The death-like hush was broken by a sob, which led to a crescendo of audible weeping. The television cameras remained focused as they had been; the cameramen could not see their screens. No one wanted to move, nor could move.

The Rev. Lawrence Gossert stepped to a microphone and began to sing to the tune of a simple chorus line:

"Hallelujah, Hallelujah,
Hallelujah, Hallelujah,

Hallelujah, Hallelujah,
Hallelujah, Hallelujah."

He finished the chorus still singing alone. He started again, and Mr. Hoffmeyer began to play an accompaniment. Here and there a voice joined, and then a few more, and still more until most of the congregation was singing. They came to the end of the tune and Larry led out with a new line to the same tune:

"He is my Saviour . . ."

Everyone waited in shock in their immediate confrontation by the basic issue of human life. People from all over the metropolitan area who had been watching the service confessed that they were transfixed by the very real life-and-death scene going on before them.

Larry Gossert found his speaking voice. "I am going to ask that we all join hands with the persons nearest to us."

No one would forget the sight or the experience of a people united in a simple prayer to commit "Dr. Dan" to God.

No one wanted to leave. Maybe Dr. Dan has 'only fainted.' They would all wait for some word . . . They waited . . . They prayed. The television period ended with a station announcer saying that they would break into scheduled programming with the first word which they received from the hospital.

Dave had to run to his car to drive crazily in pursuit of the ambulance. "It must have been the Lord who took over to keep me from having an accident."

The congregation waited. They sang the chorus again. Then Mrs. Tsingh came from the office to hand a note to Larry. He looked at it and moved to a chancel microphone – not the one at the Lectern where Dan had been reading.

"We have a first word from the hospital. Dr. Clark has had a heart attack. He is in critical condition in the Emergency Room of General Hospital. The physicians will make no statement on his prognosis. They assure us that they *are* doing, and that they *will be* doing *everything possible* for him. The physician in charge says that the best thing we can do for Dr. Dan is to pray for him.

Now Larry took charge.

"My dear friends, Dr. Dan would want us to remember that we are Christians. Let us now in quietness and confidence pray for him, and entrust him to the hands of Almighty God."

Larry confessed to Carol, and to his parents, that he found himself strengthened to lead the congregation in prayer, committing Dan to God and praying that their manner of living through this crisis would demonstrate the peace which passes all understanding.

Larry urged the people to continue in prayer. They were, of course, free to go. He said the sanctuary would be open twenty-four hours a day for all who wanted to come there to pray for Dr. Dan.

No one at General Hospital on that first Sunday of Advent would forget two people: The brooding figure that hovered tirelessly in a corridor leading to the Emergency Room. Tom's eyes absorbed every detail of every movement about him. His lips moved continuously, and the only words which anyone heard well enough to recall were, ". . . no better friend 'cept Jesus . . . no better friend 'cept Jesus . . . . no better friend 'cept Jesus .; . . no better friend 'cept Jesus . . ." and, the beautiful woman magnificently dressed whose personal life line seemed to reach out to touch only the figure in the Emergency Room.

The whole city was caught up in the human drama which made life and death so very real. It was a front page story in the Monday *JOURNAL*. Radio and television programs were interrupted with the latest bulletin, which declared what the previous bulletins had announced:

"Rev. Dr. Daniel Witt Clark, Pastor of Messiah Church, continues in critical condition at General Hospital after suffering a massive heart attack while conducting a morning worship service which was being seen on television throughout the metropolitan area. We shall break into our regular programming if there is any change in Dr. Clark's condition."

The newspaper carried a communication from the Roman Catholic Archbishop in which he had requested that every local parish include a prayer for Dr. Daniel Clark in all of its services. The account said that the Archbishop himself had gone to General Hospital to offer prayers in the hospital chapel for Dr. Clark.

Bishop Gossert expressed his admiration and his love and present concern for Dr. Clark. The Bishop, whose son was Associate Pastor of Messiah Church, would preach in the church on the following Sunday.

The lead editorial on Tuesday was devoted to the Pastor of Messiah Church. The Editor cited the long decline in the fortunes of Messiah Church, and marked how the church had made a dramatic turn to assume a place of moral and spiritual leadership in the city. He noted the church's support in the establishment of many churches in the new residential suburbs of the city. The Editor concluded by saying that "the city might well give back to Dr. Daniel Clark what he has so freely given to and for the city . . . prayer. More than anything else, this city needs men like Dr. Dan Clark praying for it."

There was a brief release of tension when a bulletin from the cardiology team at General Hospital announced:

"The condition of Rev. Dr. Daniel Clark appears to have stabilized somewhat in the last few hours. He remains, however, in critical condition."

Each day in the news there would be some story about Dan, which would make people respond in astonishment, "And I thought I knew Dan Clark."

One feature story about Dan centered on a businessman in the city who had noted, "I never saw Dan Clark wearing a pair of shoes that did not have to be resoled. It reached the point where I would not talk with him standing up. I wanted him to sit down so that I could check out his shoes. And sure enough! There would be a hole in the bottom of one or both of his shoes."

A sportswriter wrote in part:
"Last year as the Northside High School team began to build its undefeated record, I thought I should see them play. I confess that the Quarterback of the Northside team intrigued me. I said to myself, 'The unconscious moves . . . the obvious command of the offense . . . something about his release in passing.' Then I looked at the program for the name of the Quarterback, and I knew: Dan Clark's son, of course."

The latest bulletin from General Hospital read:
"It is the judgment of the medical team of General Hospital that Rev. Dr. Daniel Clark's condition has stabilized over the last twelve hours."

The caller did not identify himself, but he told Mrs. Mary Clark that Dr. Dan had suffered a heart attack and was still in Intensive Care at General Hospital. Mary thanked the caller, but she made no plans to drive to the city to see Dan. Mark and Debbie were much exercised with the news, and Blair Carter spoke to Mary offering to take the children to the city to visit Dan. Arriving at the hospital, they discovered that they could see their father for only a few minutes at an appointed hour; after being in their father's room briefly, they learned that they could not go in again for two hours. With their grandfather, they talked with Rev. Mr. Booker and decided they would leave shortly if they were to get back to Rockford before dark.

Debbie was riding in the front seat with her grandfather, and Mark was in the back. In a small voice Debbie asked her grandfather, "Is Daddy going to die?"

Mark leaned forward to hear every word of his grandfather's reply.

"Debbie . . . Mark . . . your father is a very sick man. I spoke with Mr. Schuster who introduced me to one of the doctors, and I asked the doctor that very question. The doctor said that your father is a very sick man; they have hopes that he will recover, but they don't know. The doctor said, 'he has the prayers of the whole city, including mine, in his favor.'"

"Gramps, do you think this would have happened to Daddy if we hadn't left him?"

"Now, Debbie, you are not to blame yourself in any way. Your father would not want that."

At the first opportunity, Mr. Carter pulled the car to the side of the road to stop and put his arms about Debbie. Mark reached forward to give Debbie a brotherly pat.

Reaching home, Debbie went directly to her room and closed the door.

Mary spoke to Mark. "You will have to be the one to tell me about your father. Neither Debbie nor my Daddy will say anything to me."

"Mother, we only got into the room once for a few minutes, and I couldn't really see Dad. There was so much equipment around the bed, with tubes and wires running everywhere. I tried to look down through all that stuff, but I honestly couldn't even see Dad. And I'm sorry. I wish I could at least have seen him."

The next morning Mark spoke to his mother. "I hope I'm not responsible for what has happened to Dad . . . I don't think I have been nice to him, and I feel awful about that."

That night when he could speak with his mother privately, Mark said to her, "Mother, maybe we made a big mistake in leaving Dad."

For days Diane and Mrs. Tsingh did nothing but sit at the telephone to respond to queries about Dan's condition. They would conclude every conversation with a request to the caller to pray for Dan.

There always seemed to be a contingent of Dan's friends in the waiting room for Intensive Care at General Hospital. They did not go in and see Dan. They did not hold prayer meetings in the room. They would speak briefly with one another, perhaps to review the latest bulletin on Dan's condition. If pressed, they probably could not have given a specific reason why they were there, but all would have admitted that they felt they had to come and that they hoped somehow to be of help to Dan. In particular, they wanted to be on hand for the first suggestion of good news.

There was a three-day story and spread about The Schuster Center and its program to improve the quality of living in the city. The persons interviewed would give credit to Dan for his initial vision and for his continuing support and wisdom in the operation of The Center.

At last – with universal agreement that it seemed "an age" – there was word that Dan's vital signs had shown a measure of improvement. The atmosphere about Messiah Church changed markedly. Then, too, there was something new.

The third Sunday of Advent the preacher for the morning was the Associate Pastor, Rev. Lawrence Gossert. He seemed to have grown overnight in stature, in spiritual maturity, in ability. His mother had been in the congregation and reported to her husband, "George, I swear I didn't recognize my own son. Something almost dramatic has happened to him. There were big shoes to fill this morning, and I believe that Larry has been transformed by the grace of God to fill the void at Messiah Church."

In a follow-up story to accompany a medical bulletin on Dan, the newspapers had sent reporters to talk to people in the streets and to knock on doors to speak about "Dr. Dan."

The editors summarized the story by confessing that they did not know how one person could have met so many people in such a short time – he was now in his ninth year – and have touched these people for good in such a multitude of ways, by their own confession.

Dan *was* improving. Barring some severe setback, he would live. Some lines into the future were becoming clear. It was now certain that if indeed Dan did survive, he was through as the Pastor of Messiah Church. Dave Schuster, Tom Davis, Fred Hudson and John Phillips heard the head of the cardiology unit say that it would be "suicidal" for Dan to resume the responsibility and workload entailed with being the Pastor of Messiah Church. They said nothing to Dan, and there was no word to the congregation. They did go to sit down in confidence with Bishop Gossert.

Dan was out of Intensive Care and now in the Critical care unit when Blair Carter came again to bring Mark and Debbie to see their father. Blair Carter did not come into the room, but Mark and Debbie entered to find a person sitting up whom they scarcely recognized by sight. He was so thin! His voice was so weak! They could only stay a few minutes, and they left. Mark didn't want his father to see the tears in his eyes. Debbie gave a very wordy report to her mother.

Time passed and Dan was improving slowly. With great trepidation, some of the individuals close to Dan went in with the physician to tell Dan that he would not be able to return to the pastorate of Messiah Church. Dan smiled to see anxious faces and told them that he had already discussed this topic with the physicians.

"I have one request. Do give Larry fair consideration."

There were problems. A successor for Dan at Messiah Church was not one of them. Larry stepped from Dan's shadow to reveal himself as a first rank Christian preacher, teacher and leader. "As for preaching ability, he is the son of his father who has grown taller, but the Biblical message is the one he learned from and through Dan."

If someone would observe that "Larry isn't Dan Clark," the unanswerable question given in response was, "Who is?" And then there was Carol. She had become an outstanding leader in the understanding and utilization of Christian resources for becoming and being a whole person. Any contact with Larry and Carol together reduced to insignificance the fact that Larry had been divorced. Larry was schooled in administrative leadership, a role of first order in a parish of 4,000 communicants. Rev. Lawrence Gossert would become Pastor of Messiah Church. His mother described this development as "heaven in Messiah Church for me."

One of the topics in the waiting room was Dan's financial situation. Presumably he would go on a church medical pension, at least if the Bishop had anything to do with it. He had said to his Assistant, "Dan Clark will not be able to work and he is to receive a medical pension. I am going to see him in ten days. I want you to clear all the paper work and see that I have a first check to take to Dan at that time."

The Bishop's Assistant demurred and called attention to the necessary forms to be completed and the series of decisions involved in this matter. He was stopped in mid-recital of the process by the Bishop.

"Philip, the Bishop is *familiar* with procedures. The Bishop will take the first pension check to Dan Clark ten days from today. If the Bishop's Assistant is unable to have this check on the Bishop's desk ten days from now, the Bishop will require the person and services of a new Assistant as of eleven days from now."

Dan's "financial consultants" had knowledge to agree that Dan had no money; his assets consisted of some books and a junker – Al Hirter and Tom Davis agreed on this – of a car. Oh, he did have some furniture for one bedroom, but the folding table and folding chair in the breakfast nook had "Messiah Church" stenciled on the underside. The money he had received from the sale of his parents' home and possessions had been set up in two trust funds for the college education of Mark and Debbie.

Something should be done in recognition of the situation as Larry Gossert had described it:

"Dan Clark has given to Messiah Church and the Cause of Christ in this city: eight and one-half years of hard work, the finest of his talents, his family, and now almost his life."

The word went out that they were establishing a trust fund for Dan; they would accept monies from people of Messiah Church and also from people of the city who were not members of Messiah Church. Fred Hudson's name was at the head of the committee creating this fund. With one announcement, the money poured in with gifts from $1.00 to amounts which Fred never disclosed. If anyone asked Fred to suggest an amount to contribute, Fred's stock answer was, "How much is a Messiah Church worth to this city?"

There was an immediate, personal problem. Dan was reaching

the place where he could be discharged from the hospital. Where could he go? He would need attention and care for a convalescent period of time. The "obvious" answer was for him to go to some kind of an extended care institution. John Phillips and Mrs. Sally Wilkins happened to be among the group in a waiting room discussion when this was the problem of the day. The talk went from one to another with one suggestion after another being posed only to be knocked down. Sally was startled to hear her voice come aloud in the room.

"He can come to my place. I have a guest room. *I'll* look after him."

There was an awkward silence and then the demurring of uncertain voices.

"That's very thoughtful of you, but it seems sort of . . ."

"Yes, but for a Christian minister . . ."

"Oh, that shouldn't be your personal responsibility . . ."

Sally made no rejoinder and when the conversation turned to another topic, she rose and walked from the room.

John Phillips noted her departure and said, "We shouldn't have been so negative. I don't know whether you all are aware of it, but Dan and Mrs. Wilkins have known each other from college days. She told me once that they were engaged when they were Seniors at the university. She works with me and my people; that is how I know her. I have been thankful to the Lord to have seen her grow as a Christian. I am sure that she meant well."

The conversation had rolled over another subject or two when Sally re-entered the room. She walked up and waited for their attention.

"Gentlemen. How would it be with you if I took *my husband* home to care for him . . . Or, do you have a *better* suggestion?"

She told the group that she and Dan had been engaged at one time when they were in the university. They were both now divorced. She said, "Just now, I went into Dan's room, and I said to him, 'Dan Clark, will you marry me?' He gulped two or three times, and his monitor did a couple of loops, but he said, 'Yes.'"

The Bishop was asked to perform the ceremony. In the hospital chapel with the cardiology team of physicians and nurses present, the Bishop married Rev. Dr. Daniel Witt Clark and Sally Garner Wilkins. The "waiting room crowd" with their wives and/or husbands were the attendants.

Same few days later, Mrs. Sally Clark took her husband home.

EPILOGUE: PARK SHORES

Park Shores in July is a bustling place. A half block from Lake Michigan, Dan and Sally stood on the sidewalk watching a car pull away, and then waved as the car turned the corner.

"It was great seeing Dave and Nan again."

Sally started to walk up the wall to a stone bungalow with a porch which stretched across the front of the house.

"Two such people can make any day brighter."

There were three steps to the screened-in porch. Sally seated herself in a low rocker, and Dan went to a swing which hung from the ceiling of the porch by two chains. He wanted to talk about Dave.

"Look what he did to create The Center, Sally. I can remember worrying what might happen if Dave should ever give up the leadership of The Center, and all the while he was training Lou Street. So when Dave resigned to make a run for the seat in Congress, there was Lou – ready to take over. Dave says that under Lou, The Center has grown and altered its program to match strides with the changes in the district. While they have kept all of the service programs for which there is still any need, the program emphasis has been shifted to make The Center undoubtedly the leading cultural agency and influence in the city."

"I think that Nan is the best friend I have ever had. She says she misses Messiah Church when they are in Washington. You know better than I that she and Dave say they owe everything to the Lord Jesus, and both of them came to Christ in Messiah Church. When I said that we would be married, almost the first question in the minds of some people was whether it would compromise the witness to Christ if the two of us as divorced people were to marry each other. Nan heard someone voice this concern, and she said, 'Which one of us is not in need of Christ's forgiveness for one reason or another? Let her throw the first stone.' She said conversation in the room stopped and everyone looked at her, but the subject never came up again – so far as she knows."

Dan patted the cushion in the swing. "Please."

When Sally had moved to sit next to him, he continued, "No one ever said a word to me . . ."

"There was no reason to do so. Of course, John Phillips wanted to talk with me, and I told him that I was as surprised as anyone else in the room when I heard myself say that . . . But I also told him that second thoughts, and third thoughts, would have found me doing the same thing . . . I don't know if anyone ever told you, but *just before* that, some of the ladies of the church had gone in to clean and set your house in order. And they were shocked – so was everyone else, including me – to find the living conditions which you called 'home.'"

"I guess I never paid much attention to that . . ."

"For lots and lots of people, it gave substance to something Larry had said about you. He said that you had given everything for Christ and Messiah Church. He ticked off on his fingers that you had given your 'talents, time, strength, professional opportunities . . . your health, your family, your home, and now almost your life for Christ and His Church.'"

"That's a little strong. Honestly, Sally, that's more than I deserve because I never felt nor thought anything other than that I had a job to do for our Lord."

"As it turned out, I heard repeatedly that no one could see you recovering in the barrenness of that place. In those almost daily discussions in the waiting room, someone said very early that he would see you in an extended care place only by court order . . . Do you know that three or four people called Mary? And then there were at least two dozen families who would have gladly opened their homes to you, but for most of them it was simply not realistic . . . Anyway, there came a day and an opportunity, and *I* put in *my* claim . . . And *I* got you!"

Sally leaned over to kiss Dan's cheek.

"And I'm *glad*. It was a long way back . . . longer than I ever would have imagined. I honestly think that I never would have made it without you and the Lord. I *am* grateful and I don't know how I can ever repay you."

"Knowing Christ and living with you have given to me a joy in living such as I never would have thought possible. And when I think of all that I have missed in my life because of my stupidity, I think I can never forgive myself. I hoped and I thought I might deny the years and recapture something of what I lost if I could have your child . . . I had to accept what that doctor told me after my miscarriage, and to admit that it was not meant to be . . . Well, even so, it has been wonderful to have Mark with us for the summer and Debbie for a month . . . All of which reminds me that Mark will be coming home from work before too long, and I must get some things out for dinner."

A driver passing by tapped his horn; Dan and Sally waved.

"Sally, Rob Leyden is really an unusual Christian gentleman. Of course, there were lots of remarkable people in Messiah Church. With Dave in the Congress, the Lord has at least one witness in Washington. And Tom Davis on the City Commission. It's good to think that the Lord has His people everywhere."

"But for now, I think it would be good for you to lie down for a while. With Dave and Nan here, you have been going more than usual, and I don't like those little lines at your eyes. They probably don't mean a thing, but I would prefer that you get back on schedule."

There had been a great sadness with Dan's resignation, but Dan had always maintained that a good leader prepares someone to succeed. Dave had done so with Lou Street. In Messiah Church, the preparation of a leader had been going on, although none of the participants were aware of it at the time. When Dan was stricken and resigned of necessity, Larry Gossert was there. When Messiah Church needed a new Senior Pastor, Larry Gossert had grown so in presence, in gifts, in stature, in powers, that there was never any question about who would be the Pastor; he would be the Rev. Lawrence Gossert.

The Bishop came for a special service in Messiah Church. He would preach the sermon. He would install his son as Pastor. AND

. . . He would christen his second grandson. Larry's two daughters were part of the family group.

Messiah Church had not missed a step. The experience of Dan's heart attack and subsequent resignation seemed only to lengthen the stride and give purpose to the will of the church. In the growing congregation, the new Governor and his family, together with attendants, now filled two pews in the 11:00 o'clock service every Sunday when he was in the city.

Carol Gossert had shaken the city's self-styled intellectually elite. She had offered a premarital counseling service at The Schuster Center, which was proving useful – with statistics to support it. As a part of the Messiah Church program, she worked at a course for couples in the first year of their marriage. For high school age young people in Messiah Church, she had incorporated sex education into a larger framework of study in preparation for marriage and responsible adulthood. This had received much favorable publicity, and she was invited to offer this course of study in one of the high schools. There had been discussions and interviews, and now Carol was to appear before the Board of Education regarding this new dimension of study.

Carol was sitting at a small table confronted by the members of the Board who were seated behind the imposing, curved bench on a raised platform. There had been questions and answers, some discussion; then the President addressed Carol. "It must be a stipulation of this Board that this course will have no religious orientation nor religious references."

Carol raised her head to face the President. "Is that your personal provision, or does that express the opinion of the Board of Education?"

The President looked from one to another of the Board members, and they responded by nodding their heads.

Without hesitation, Carol Gossert, Ph.D. said, "If that is your stipulation, my answer is, 'No.' If this Board thinks that non-Christian, or even non-religious existence is a possibility for humankind, then I suggest that the members of this Board need basic education in human existence and human values."

The newspaper account included two pictures:
1. Carol pushing her papers into her briefcase.
2. Carol walking from a shocked room.
The reporter described the room as one that "offered no sound to compete with the clicking of her heels."

Mark came from his room prepared to go out on a date. Dan and Sally were in the living room after clearing the dining room and kitchen following dinner.

Dan counseled, "Be careful in driving. You know there are too many cars for our streets at this time of year."

Mark nodded and went to Sally to kiss her on the cheek. "And I'll remember to be a Christian gentleman, Mom."

"Did you hear Dave telling about Tom Davis?"
"No, I don't think so."

There had been weeks when there was a "No Visitors" sign on the door of Dan's room in the hospital. When he could speak, Dan had muttered two words to the physician.

"Sally . . . Tom."

The doctor hesitated and then nodded.

The hospital staff looked forward each day for the sight of the perfectly groomed, beautiful lady who was admitted to Dan's room. The word was that upon entering the room she went to the patient's bed to touch him and to say one word: "Dan."

Then she would sit unmoving, and after an hour would let herself quietly out of the room.

Tom Davis would come into the room without making a sound and he, too, would simply be there. With the doctor's permission, he would speak to Dan.

"You gotta do it, Revner Dan."

And Tom would always pray. How he prayed! After the physician's first experience with Tom in Dan's room, he said to anyone who was listening, "That man is better than anything I am prescribing."

Dave had said of Tom, "He succeeded me, you know, on the City Commission. Now Tom is admittedly the conscience of the City Commission, and of city government. He is acutely aware of right and wrong in issues which come before the Commission. If the other commissioners, or anyone from city administration, looks over and sees Tom frowning, he backs away from whatever he was proposing. Whether others like it or not, there is general recognition that Tom has put morality into government, into city politics."

Dan and Sally were still living in Riverton Arms when Dan received a second invitation to the pastorate of University Church. He had recovered sufficiently that he was thinking at times of going back to work. He was disappointed that Sally did not share his enthusiasm about this opportunity.

"Dan, my dearest. I am so thankful to have you looking and acting more like yourself. I don't want anything that would interfere with your progress. Without any judgment on this invitation, please do one thing for me."

"Name it."

"Please go and speak with the doctor before you pursue this any further."

At her insistence, Dan made an appointment for an evaluation of his progress. More difficult than the experience of his initial attack was the acceptance now that his physical condition did not at this time warrant his assumption of a major work load.

Dan received an invitation from Rob Leyden to be the preacher for the month of August in Park Shores. In a subsequent conversation, Rob had said that they were hoping to change from being a summer preaching post to becoming a year-round church. Thinking about this, Dan told Sally he felt led to pursue the matter.

Park Shores was a resort community on a small bay of Lake Michigan. There was a tool and die plant, a shop where two men handcrafted sailboats, and a new company which produced flags. The town's chief industry was caring for the summer visitors. When Labor Day passed, the summer homes and cottages were closed. The hotel and one or two motels were shuttered. Shops on

Bay Street put signs in their windows: "Open May 15." The town of Park Shores would nestle down for a winter's hibernation.

There was a small group which attended the old mission church during the winter months for a service which would be read by one of the lay readers. Beginning the weekend of Memorial Day and continuing through Labor Day weekend, the summer residences, streets, parking lots, the beach, the markets and specialty stores were all full, and open from early morning till late at night.

After correspondence, telephone conversations, prayer . . . Dan and Sally came to believe that the Lord would have them move to Park Shores for Dan to be the Minister there. No living person could recall when the only church in the community had a Pastor to serve the year around. The first summer they were there, the Park Shores Community Church was forced to begin having *two* Sunday morning services. The next year they had moved the services from the church to the Community Auditorium. This year, they were turning people away from both services every Sunday, and Dan suggested that next year they might consider having *three* services each Sunday. This idea only lasted long enough for Sally to say "NO."

The previous year, Mark and Debbie had come together to spend a week with Dan and Sally. At the airport, Dan and Sally met two very uncertain young people who did not quite know how to accept Sally; for that matter, Dan and Sally did not want to cause any greater distance between themselves and Dan's children. They left at the end of the week, Debbie to become a high school Senior and Mark to be a sophomore and the quarterback of the university football team. BUT . . . The barriers had come down in that week. Debbie cried for both of them at the airport where they were to board their plane.

This year, they would come as soon as school was out. Debbie would stay for a month – she added another week; Mark would stay the summer – with a job locally – until he had to return for football practice.

Debbie and Sally started off the visit as pals. They went to the nearest city to shop for Debbie's college wardrobe. And they talked. They were in the kitchen with Debbie wanting to show her ability to make a cake. And they talked. They would go to the beach together. And they talked. They worked together to teach a Sunday School class. And they talked. Debbie needed an additional week to talk some more. She clung to Sally at the airport, and she promised everyone that "next summer I'll stay the whole summer – if I'm invited, of course."

Sally kissed her and said, "You're invited."

"Dan, I'm sure I'm not breaking any confidence if I relate some of my conversations with Debbie. From things she said again and again, it was obvious that she wanted you to know."

They were in the swing on the porch – a favorite place. Dan had returned from a walk through the business district where he had spoken with most of the shop owners.

"The first subject was sex. She is going off to college and she doesn't know ABC. She has been dating some, and she has had problems. There was a dance where one boy kept pulling her tight against him . She told him she didn't like that and he wouldn't dance with her again. Another time she had a date with a fellow who asked her flat out if she would go to bed with him. Dan, I talked with Debbie very plainly about sex, and we understand that sex is something within the marriage bond *only*. In addition, if she has difficulty with a boy who doesn't want to accept that, we arrived at a way for her to handle such a situation. She will tell any boy at the University who wants her to permit his advances that he is to speak personally with her brother and first get permission from him."

"Do you mean "Muscles Mark?""

Sally laughed. "The very same, if you can picture *that* scene . . . She says her mother is very unhappy. Since Mr. Carter died a couple of years ago, her grandmother seems to have experienced a miraculous recovery. She is up and out and going; she went to Florida over the winter and now plans to spend six months of every year in Florida because she says, 'There is so much going on there for senior citizens.' Debbie said that Mary has a 'gentleman friend.' He is the Deputy Sheriff in the county. He comes for dinner once in a while; Debbie said she didn't know if they ever went to a movie or out for dinner. Mary doesn't go to church at all. She seems to stay

349
Messiah Man

home alone most of the time when she is not working at the school. Dan, it's really very sad to hear Debbie say that she 'feels sorry for her mother.'"

"I'm very sorry for Debbie, Sally. What can I do to help? It's obvious that she's very proud of Mark, and he's most protective of her. She has done well in chemistry and math in high school; she thinks she wants to study something in the medical field. I told her that the money is there for her to pursue whatever course she wants."

"Dan, we talked a lot about Debbie and Mark in the long period of time when we didn't see them, but you should know that Debbie thinks *you* are simply wonderful. I told her that I agreed with her. At one point she told me that she and Mark had been talking, and they wanted to know if it would be all right if they called me 'Mom.' I said I would be pleased and honored if she and Mark want to address me in that way. I'm sure you noticed . . . As you know, she asked if she could come next year for the entire summer, and I told her that she and Mark are always welcome . . . Any time and for as long as they can and want to stay."

"Thank you, my dearest . . . Almost every day I seem to find some new reason to thank God that you're mine."

"I think I've talked enough for one time."

"Then let me tell you what I heard today . . . Some big entertainment company is negotiating for a big, big area of land, acreage to include at least a couple of the hills. There is talk of developing a winter sports resort which would make Park Shores a twelve-month resort community."

"*But what does that do to us?* The present calendar has worked so well for you. By September, you are always so very weary. Any more could be too much. Besides that, I can now look forward to having you pretty much to myself in the off season, and I like it that way."

"*That's* what I *really* like to hear."

Ada Gossert was deceased, and now Bishop Gossert had decided to retire. There was always much speculation with the election of a new bishop. The name of Rev. Dr. Daniel Witt Clark had been placed in nomination. The name of Rev. Philip Frenell also had been put forward. The observation of Larry Gossert raced from one end of the jurisdiction to the other and back again overnight.

"To have Philip Frenell as Bishop would at least require that everyone pray unceasingly for the Church."

The Special Committee for the Election of a Bishop reported the results of the first ballot:

Daniel Clark	176
Philip Frenell	4

In response to this vote, Dan wrote to the Chairman of the Special Committee (in part):

"I am highly honored by the balloting for me to become Bishop of Central Jurisdiction. I will accept pending the approval of my physician at University Hospital . . ."

The following week, Dan and Sally were coming back to Park Shores following medical tests and a consultation with the Chief of Cardiology at the University Hospital, which now had Dan's medical records. Sally was driving.

"I told the committee that I needed the approval of my physician. And now today, Dr. Walters says that my physical condition does not warrant my assuming a greater workload. So . . ."

Dan didn't know how to go on.

"Dan, he said you are making progress. You have come along well in the last four years, and it makes sense for him to say he wants you to continue just what you have been doing."

"Well. I went to him for his opinion . . . and I got it."

"My dearest, when I think how critical you were, I thank God every day that you are still here . . . and that *I have you*."

"How about those doctors!" Dan chuckled. "He almost apologized for language that he thought sounded too religious when he said, 'Excuse me, but you should realize that you are alive by the grace of Almighty God.'"

"Why shouldn't he say it? It's the truth!"

"Sally, I have been thinking. I have a unique opportunity in Park Shores. As people come from all over to spend some time here, we are given the privilege of ministry to see the lives of individuals touched by the Spirit of God. And they go back with a new life in Jesus Christ to effect changes in the churches and the communities where they live. God can use us here in a unique way."

They were nearing Park Shores. Sally exclaimed, "Look, Dan! This is one of my favorite views. See how the church spire stands out against the blue of the lake."

"It *is* a lovely place. And the Scriptures say: 'I must work the works of Him that sent me, while it is day.'"

MESSIAH MAN

would make an ideal gift. Birthday . . .
anniversary . . . Christmas. Also, a perfect gift
for the serious Bible student.

To order, fill in the appropriate space and send check or money
order. We accept VISA and MASTERCARD orders.
(404) 518-1890

NAME: ⎯⎯⎯⎯⎯⎯⎯⎯⎯⎯⎯⎯⎯⎯⎯

ADDRESS: ⎯⎯⎯⎯⎯⎯⎯⎯⎯⎯⎯⎯⎯⎯

⎯⎯⎯⎯⎯⎯⎯⎯⎯⎯⎯⎯⎯⎯

I would like to purchase ⎯⎯⎯⎯⎯ copies of *MESSIAH*

MAN. Enclosed is my payment of ⎯⎯⎯⎯⎯.

OLD RUGGED CROSS PRESS
1160 Alpharetta Street
Suite H
Roswell, GA 30075
(404) 518-1890
We accept VISA or MASTERCARD

OTHER BOOKS BY OLD RUGGED CROSS PRESS

☐ SOLDIER-PRIEST

    John J. Morrett / Paperback / $12.95 / 332 Pages / 22 Photos.

    SOLDIER-PRIEST is a moving testimony to the power of faith in a young soldier's darkest hours.

    Captured by the Japanese during the Battle of Bataan, it was his faith in God that sustained him, giving him the strength and courage to help his fellow prisoners-of-war.

☐ FAR JOURNEY: A Psychiatrist's Chronicle

    Dr. Yitzhak Hanu / Hardcover / $21.95 / 298 Pages.

    FAR JOURNEY is the story of therapy, of mythic symbol . . . of the psychic dance between patient and healer . . . and healer to his soul. *FAR JOURNEY* begins and ends at the interface between psychiatry and religion, disolving the boundary which has for too long separated the two.

☐ HE CALLED HIMSELF THE SON OF MAN

    NORMAN L. MACLEOD, JR. / Paperback / $12.95 / 338 Pages.

    HE CALLED HIMSELF THE SON OF MAN will shatter any complacency you may have about being a Christian. Compelling . . . honest . . . provocative. A book that should be read by serious Bible students. Whether you agree with his point of view or not, *HE CALLED HIMSELF THE SON OF MAN* will provoke you into re-examining your views on the Trinity.

☐ EYES THAT SEE

    Bertha Ives Petersen / Paperback / $5.95 / 122 Pages.

    EYES THAT SEE focuses on the great prophet, Isaiah. Ms. Petersen breathes life into Isaiah, allowing the reader to understand both the man and the society in which he lived. EYES THAT SEE is a remarkable book.

These books may be purchased by sending check or money order to:

OLD RUGGED CROSS PRESS
1160 Alpharetta Street, Suite H
Roswell, GA 30075
(404) 518-1890
We Accept VISA and MASTERCARD

OTHER BOOKS BY OLD RUGGED CROSS PRESS

☐ SAY YOU'RE NOT LEAVING, DADDY
  Will Lester / Paperback / $4.95 / 136 Pages.
  A young father is contemplating divorce. The breakup of his family seems inevitable. Only his young son is willing to fight to save his family. *SAY YOU'RE NOT LEAVING, DADDY* is a book about the power of prayer that you will remember long after you've read the last page.

☐ THE GOSPEL OF MARK IN VERSE
  Paul Buchheit / Paperback / $5.95 / 81 Pages.
  THE GOSPEL OF MARK IN VERSE is one of the most creative books about the Book of Mark published in years. Mr. Buchheit writes with great passion. His book will prove helpful to people who have yet to experience the healing power of God's love.

☐ A BANGED UP ANGEL
  Joyce Price / Paperback / $6.95 / 192 Pages.
  "We will not give the child up," the young woman exclaimed.
  "Tracy, you're not being practical," the old man replied in a stern voice.
  Tracy reached down and picked the five-year-old boy up. As she gazed into Ted's angelic face, another small boy's face flashed before her, the same face she had seen so many times in her nightmares. "I'll never let you take Ted from me," she screamed. "Never!"

These books may be purchased by sending check or money order to:

OLD RUGGED CROSS PRESS
1160 Alpharetta Street, Suite H
Roswell, GA 30075
(404) 518-1890
We Accept VISA and MASTERCARD